WIDE ONLY VERSION

Original Ebook/Print Cover: 100covers.com
Alt Covers: Pretty in Ink Creations
Editing , backgrounds, & Formatting: Little Tailfeather Publishing
Cassandra's logos: Pretty in Ink Creations/Artlogo
Goosebusters Alpha team: Kat Silver, Becky Ross, Erica Taryn
Arc / Street Teams: Cassandra's claws
Sensitivity Readers: Brit Mason, Gail Jericho
Legal Services: Joshua Farley, esq.
Representation: Laura Pink at SBR Media
Images/Fonts: Creative Fabrica, Depositphotos, Shutterstock, & Photoshop
Map: Cassandra Featherstone

No GenAI was used within this book. All errors and greatness are by an adhd muppet.

❀ Created with Vellum

SIGNATURE PAGE

CASSANDRA FEATHERSTONE

Rejected In The HOLLOW

M.P.P.

CONTENT INFORMATION

This is a *paranormal whychoose romance with poly elements*—our FMC, Jolene, will not have to choose between love interests.

There are many situations included that are intended for <u>mature audiences (18+).</u>

In this book, there may be instances/references (be they small or lengthy) that could trigger some individuals such as:

- liberal use of appropriate consent
- the fucking Fae
- group scenes
- MMF, MM, MFM, MF, MFMMM, and more
- poison
- assassination attempts
- alphahole/possessive MMCs
- cinnamon roll MMCs
- bargains made by asshole Fae
- slightly unhinged chaotic MMC
- unhealthy coping mechanisms
- spoiled, selfish gods, goddesses, and royalty
- extremely aggressive boundaries
- age gap (from 10 yrs to immeasurable)
- weird Fae drugs and tricks

- BDSM
- raw sex
- shifted sex
- traumatic childhood
- Alcohol use and abuse
- threats of bodily harm
- death
- body modifications
- fancy genitalia
- mate knots/barbs
- the goddamn Fates meddling
- bullying (in person and on social media)
- PTSD
- blood
- emotional abuse from outside poly group
- body dysmorphia
- adult language
- pop culture references
- literary references
- emotional manipulation
- power play
- adorable nicknames
- physical intimidation
- emotionally abusive/manipulative parents (MMCs)
- voyeurism
- rough sex
- wings/tails/horns/magic in sex
- masturbation play
- markings/tattoos
- Easter egg character cameos from other series in the universe
- lawyers (ugh, but Jackson is a doll)
- family dysfunction
- super awesome BFF and her poly group
- animal companions
- absolute disrespect for shitty parents
- brief mentions of non-body positive dieting culture
- brief mentions of parental death
- very liberal re-imagining of history
- ancient secret society who only cares about bigger picture
- official corruption

- name calling
- occasional misogyny
- exhibitionism
- hand necklaces
- adult bullying
- magical kinks
- impact play
- elitism
- bribery
- corpses
- fat shaming (not by MCs)
- drama
- physical threats to FMC and others
- species-ism

No sexual practices in this book should be taken as safe or appropriate for real life application.

Content information is important and I don't ever want to harm a reader with inaccurate information.

Stalk Cassandra Featherstone in the Dark Corners of the Web

Join my Facebook group and follow me everywhere!

Want More?

Sign up for my bi-weekly manifesto for a free series sampler:

Join my Ream as a FREE follower or exclusive subscriber to get access to cover reveals, WIPs, Serial Stories, and personal chats from me!

CASSANDRA FEATHERSTONE

Notes for Readers

To understand this book, you must read Road to the Hollow and Return to the Hollow first.

The world in which our characters live is set up in those books and you will be very confused if you do not read them. This is technically book **two** in the series, not counting the prequel.

The series is planned to have five **whole** books and several **bonuses and gap novels**. I always recommend reading those because they often contain info you'll want later on.

This is a multi-book series, so *everything will not be revealed at once.* Some plot lines will continue through series in a larger arc and not get resolved in the first or even the third book.

I write lengthy books with intricate world building, strong character development, and *lots* of tiny threads that stretch throughout a series that may not always seem important at first glance. However, I promise nothing I put to paper and leave in the book is unimportant; it may simply become *more* important later on. There is no 'throwaway' detail in my worlds, so every scene will mean something eventually.

I promise it will all get tied up and have a HEA; don't worry!

Rejected in the Hollow is a why choose/poly romance, which means our FMC will not have to choose.

I would consider it a medium burn, slow build family group. It will continue to get spicier in the following books. If you're looking for porn with little to no plot, no judgment, but this isn't the series for you. It's also not closed door or FTB, so I believe the spice will be worth the wait. I realize spice scales are subjective and everyone has different opinions on it, so forgive me if mine and yours aren't totally aligned.

There are some characters and creatures that speak in other languages. I made the *translations clickable end of chapter notes* to help.

There are some words that are slang, jargon, or foreign that may seem to be spelled wrong—*please email the author or find her on social media rather than report to Amazon* if you find a typo. This has been proofed and edited *several* times, so the error could be a stylistic or dialect choice. Every effort is made to find these pre-publication and since the publishing industry standard is below two percent of word count (and my books are almost always over 100K), I promise what you find is not out of the accepted range for the editors and teams who have reviewed it.

Please do not email critical feedback that is not a simple typo or formatting issue—this book is written and released. It will not be changed after publication to suit personal preferences.

If you see this book *anywhere besides major retailers or my website in ebook format,* please reach out to me via social media or email. Pirating kills my ability to write full time and I am so grateful for your help.

Contact my team for typos or to report piracy: teamcassandrafeatherstone@cassandrafeatherstone.com

Author Ramblings

Readers, I know I've said it before, but I damn near killed myself finishing this book after *Bloodthirsty*. For real, my brain is destroyed, y'all.

But I couldn't disappoint the people who have been patiently waiting for our girl Jolene to get her justice.

As usual, there are Easter eggs for those of you who are inclined to read the heavier PNR/SFF series *Codename* or the contemporary book *Bloodthirsty*, but if you don't, those references won't leave you behind the curve.

Jolene is slowly finding her way in the world of the Hollow and as you learned in *Roused in the Hollow,* her friends and men are trying like hell to keep her safe until she emerges. There will be of the info you crave about everyone and more about the hidden secrets of Jolene's past. She's going to start seeing things she didn't before, but that doesn't mean we are near the end of her tale.

As usual, I've done a lot of research and added quite bit of mythology, depth, and information to my rich world. RIP my Google algorithm and the ads I see—you have *no idea* what it shows me now.

Thank you to everyone who has read and recommended on Facebook, Instagram, TikTok, on Goodreads, and on Amazon. Your recs in groups and continued support help me get closer to my indie muppet dream of going full time.

I am so thankful for all of your support and kindness as I've navigated the start of series and worlds that I know will become some of your favorites. It's been a *very* rough year for me, both personally and professionally, but when they knock me down, I come up swinging, just like my FMCs.

You will find that the women in the *MPP, Faetal Attraction, Codename, Villains & Vixens*, and *Triangles and Tribulations* are no wilting flowers and they will make you laugh, scream, shiver, cry, and gasp as we progress through their tales towards something *much* bigger.

Enjoy the world of the genteel South where the women—like me—are filled with *sugar, spice, and steel.*

Blood and guts,

Cass

A Note To My Loving Family Members and Their Friends...

THANK YOU FOR SUPPORTING ME BY BUYING THIS BOOK!

I KEEP TELLING YOU I DON'T WANT YOU TO LET ME KNOW WHEN YOU READ MY STUFF, AND I'M NOT JOKING.

TO THE PEOPLE WHO DID SO AND REACHED OUT IN SHOCK, WHAT ABOUT ME SAID I WAS KIDDING ABOUT THE BONDAGE AND KINKY SHIT?

THE HOLIDAYS ARE GOING TO BE A NIGHTMARE; I JUST KNOW. THAT'S WHAT I GET FOR GOING TO A SHOWER THIS SUMMER.

CAVEAT: IN CASE YOU MISSED THIS STATEMENT—IF YOU CHOOSE TO KEEP READING, KNOW THAT AT NO TIME WILL I EXPLAIN TERMS, POSITIONS, THEMES, TROPES, OR ANY OTHER PART OF THIS NOVEL AT FAMILY EVENTS, IN GROUP CHATS, OR ON SOCIAL MEDIA.

THAT MEANS STOP ASKING ME, LADIES.

Rejected in the Hollow Playlist

CHAPTER TITLE SONGS

Rejected in the Hollow Chapter Playlist

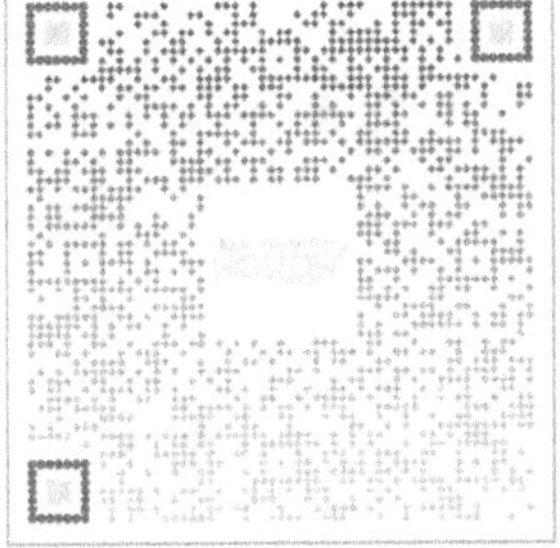

BONUS PLAYLIST

The Hollow European Travel Playlist

WAIT!

A FINAL REMINDER BEFORE YOU READ...

My series typically have prequels, gap novellas/novels, and bonus material that are integral to your having a satisfying reading experience.

If you have not read the other pieces in this series, you may feel as though you have missed critical details, developments, plot points, and other information. This will cause the book to appear to have continuity gaps that it does not have.

If you have not read the bonus material for this series, it is available online here, in audio versions (if applicable), and in print special editions (if applicable).

I highly recommend consulting the bonus page prior to reading this new title so you're up to speed on all the things going on in this world.

Happy reading!

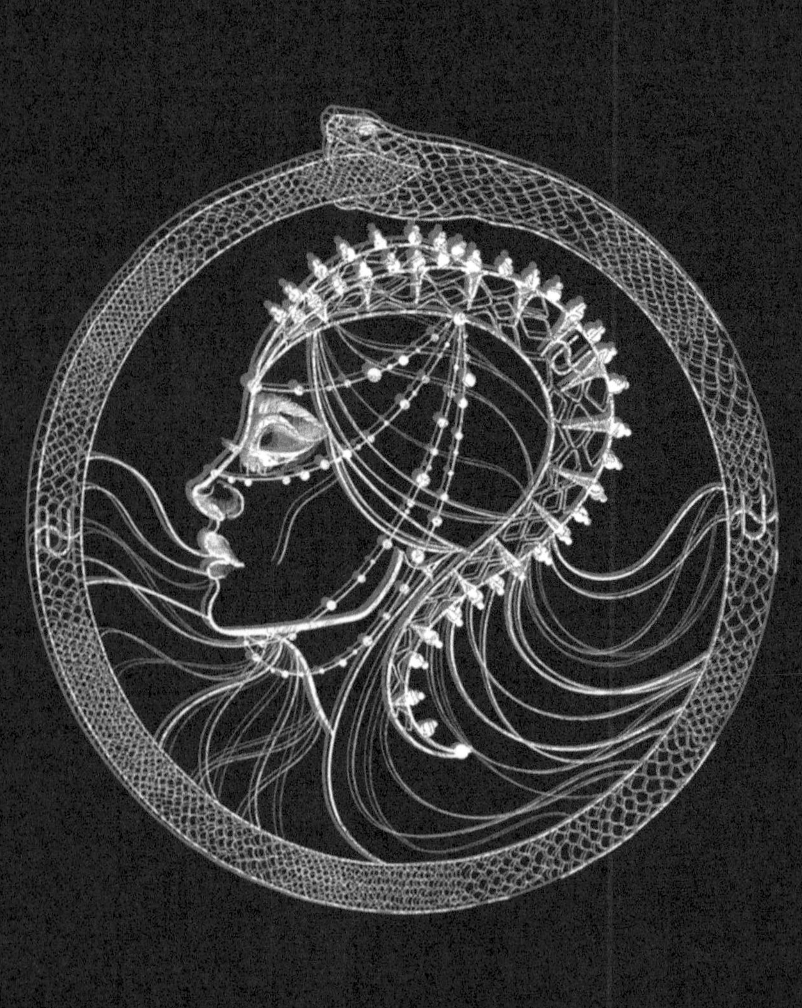

Prologue

Julia

"I don't agree. She may have warmed up to me, but I don't think mine is the first face she should see. We don't have that kind of connection," I argue as my girlfriend's entire cadre of men glare at me.

"That's *exactly* why it should be you, Jules," my former charge says softly. "If she remembers when she wakes up, she's going to be angry with all of us for not telling her the truth. She has no such expectation with you."

Tharin rumbles low, giving me an imperceptible nod. "The fairy is correct. Her mind will scramble for connections and if she can attach her emergence to the feelings of betrayal, it will make everything harder."

I roll my eyes, but I can see the wisdom in his words. Newly emerged supes with knowledge of our world can struggle with the change. A lost one of this age who has lived a lie amongst people she cares about is going to be very difficult to manage. I fear Saoirse is not sufficiently ready for this undertaking—and nor are her mates.

"Have you considered what we will do if the unknown spell has not completely lost its grasp on her mind? Has anyone asked the Society what we may do?"

The silence tells me they hadn't even considered the possibility. They all want so badly to share their lives fully with their friend or mate that it's clouding their judgment. I peer over at my cunning merman, hoping he has a suggestion that might benefit the situation.

Zasha strokes his chin, looking pensive as he leans against the hospital wall. "I believe that even if she remembers some of tonight, she will not make the connections on her own. This woman seems to possess multiple sides, and you admitted that this could be the one that has previously presented."

"Her hound fully shifted, but in the morning, she was clueless about the previous night," Boone says as he runs his fingers through his hair.

Tapping my fingers against my lips, I consider the options again. Whether Jolene remembers what happens or not isn't the only concern; what powers she's unleashed and what's coming are important variables that tie directly to the secret of her heritage. If she awakens with a partially broken spell but no memory, she will gain access to at least one shifter side and all the abilities that come along with it—with zero knowledge that it exists or how to control herself.

That's a recipe for disaster.

"Okay. We need several plans. They need to account for the most predictable possibilities and the results are correct. Seer, you need to contact the Society and give a brief verbal report of the incident. Get their take on what we're permitted to reveal to your charge based on what she remembers when she wakes up." Zasha tilts his head at her and I nod, agreeing that he can go with her to help her remain diplomatic.

The winged doctor squints at me. "I'm expected to examine her fully as soon as possible, so whatever plans we make must consider procedures for newly emerged lost ones. I can hold off as long as I can, but there will only be so much leeway I can give you to help her understand."

"As hard as it would be to continue the charade, it might be easier if she *didn't* remember," Wolfgang says softly. "Until Sugarplum has everything come out, we'll keep her under constant watch and that will really piss her off."

Boone snorts. "Fuck yes, it will. Tilly is barely accustomed to having us all around, much less *following her.*"

Frowning, I glance at Tharin. A decade ago, they sent our team to help a Guardian named St. James track down her errant lost one. We spent months sniffing trails across the country, both online and live. If a charge is both smart and angry enough to decide to disappear, they can. We never found St. James' lost one, but it seems the missing supe came back to find *her* recently.

Seer and these idiots would lose the fucking plot if Jolene went walkabout for a week, much less an entire decade. I have to handle her carefully or I'm going to ruin all of their lives.

I'm not known for coddling people, so this is going to be interesting.

"Boone, I need you to consult with the Mayor. If our fearless leaders put the kibosh on telling Jolene before she's gone through the entire emergence, she'll need to issue a Council decree with provisions for possible 'accidents' so you don't go through another one of those ridiculous trials." I pause for a moment, considering what else we will need. "Haggerty, if you could visit Hazel and MacAuley to see if you can charm *anything* out of them, it would be extremely helpful."

They both seem irritated, but their big dick energy will *not* help the situation. In fact, they probably should be the last two people to see their girl, so she's calm by the time they come in. Tharin tilts his head at Foster, waiting for me to decide how someone with his particular issues can be of help.

"Benjy? I'm putting you in charge of the companions for the moment. Take them out for a stretch every once in a while, but keep your phone on so we can call you back if Jolene wants them close by. We weren't able to pry the python loose, and that may end up benefiting us. Seer says it's like an emotional support blanket; hopefully, she's right."

"Jules? What should I do?"

I glance over at my former charge with a warm smile. It doesn't surprise me that Wolfgang has found a family; he's the most lovable hybrid I've ever met. The trauma of his childhood, paired with the nightmare that is his birth mother, created a perfect storm of caring and needing to be cared for that makes him irresistible. "Wolfie, I want you to stay here. I'm not the… friendliest person when I get frustrated, and if it goes downhill, I think you will be the most soothing presence I can offer."

He beams. "I'll do my best."

"Does anyone know where Bane got off to?" I ask. "I'd like her to brief me on Jolene's file from school. The way it's written leaves much to the imagination and I suspect there were things she didn't want to put in formal reports." The others appear shocked, and I shrug. "Guardians are sworn to protect their charges and to be loyal to the Society. Sometimes, the two things are in direct conflict. We need to… finagle… our reports and documentation to prevent people from making rash decisions."

Sometimes we hide our knowledge or suspicions about our supes to make certain some power hungry jackhole doesn't come after them in secret.

Tharin lumbers over to me, looking down at me with a concerned expression. "Are you sure you can handle this? It has been many years since the incident, but we do not know what secrets this girl is hiding. If she should lose control, it may force you to choose."

I sigh and rub my temples. "I was much younger, Tharin. A baby, really. It hasn't been necessary to calcify a hybrid or lost one since before humans came to this shore. You've always been a worrywart."

Grinning toothily, he shrugs. "That is my job now. Zasha smooths things over, I worry and bulldoze things, you strategize, and our Saoirse will keep us light-hearted. It is a good fit, I think."

It really is, and this backwards town and its irritating residents are to thank for it. How humiliating.

"Tharin, I need you to go with the doc for a few. He needs to bring me all the research his girl's been doing since she got home. While we wait for Sleeping Beauty to wake up, I want us all to get on the same page. We can't protect or help her if we don't know what the hell she's mixed up in."

Presley nods, dangling his keys at my grumpy dragon. "C'mon, Chuckles. With you along, this shouldn't take long."

Watching as they all head off to their assignments, I drop into an armchair next to Wolfgang. "Do you think she'll be able to forgive all of you for lying to her? That part of it is much easier when they're young like you were. Adults hold grudges."

He stares at the closed door to her room, setting his face in his hand. "I don't know, Jules, but I hope so. Everyone in this room cares about her in different ways and for different reasons. The rest of this place only wants to tear her down—except for the fucker stalking our place. If she sends us all away, the weight of dangerous enemies will fall on her shoulders while she's relearning reality. That seems like it would be scary and lonely."

Not to mention what will happen if she's completed any mate bonds—she'll be lucky if that doesn't kill her.

But I don't tell him that. Worrying about fated mate bonds is *much* further down the 'what if' list at the moment.

First, we have to see if the girl that's captured the attention of an entire town ever wakes up.

I Knew You Were Trouble

Jolene

The silver-haired woman walks in slowly, her brow arched as she notes my raised fists. I don't look very threatening in a hospital gown and connected to tubes and wires, but cornered animals are the most dangerous.

"I'm not a threat. Not to you or your friendship with my girl," Julia says softly. She continues moving closer, making certain I can see her hands.

I'll be damned if she gets to see how terrified I am about this situation.

I snort, raising my chin. "Tell me something I don't know."

"You will not get the answers you want yet. It's going to piss you off and you'll have to make peace with it. We all know that."

Blinking, I gape at her. She's as blunt as I am and in this situation, I appreciate it. No wonder they sent her instead of Seer or one of the guys—Julia has no intention of coddling me. I drop my dukes in my lap and jerk my head at the chair next to the bed. "Fine. Have a seat and tell me why I'm going to be angry."

To my surprise, she complies without an argument. Propping her elbows on her knees, she looks at me with a serious expression. "Jolene, there's so much you don't know and much of it, I cannot share with you. Your men and our girl are similarly bound by rules and obligations so deeply woven into our beings that you cannot comprehend them."

"Oh, please. If this is some Southern Skull & Bones shit, I'm not buying it. Whatever happened at the ball put me in a fucking hospital and I'm not even sure which one or how much time has passed. I don't have 'clearance' will not cut it."

Not to mention my heart is splintering into pieces as we talk. I haven't let *anyone* besides Seer in since Trevor until I came home and now look where I am. Everyone I care about is lying to me and I'm hashing it out with someone I've only met a few times. I'm so numb that all I can access is the fury inside of me, burning like a righteous sword held by an angel.

"Whoa!" Julia holds her hand out in a 'stop,' gesture. "Whatever you were just thinking, you need to *calm down.*"

Who the hell does she think she is telling me how to feel?!!

My joints ache, and my heartbeat speeds up, blood thumping in my veins like fire. I've felt like this before, but it's part of yet another memory I can't access. A primal scream rips from my throat as I bury my hands in my hair and yank, unable to bear all the emotions assaulting me at once.

"Jolene, control your anger. Feel the waves and soothe them. Picture the fury as a red ball and gather it up, then cup it in your hands. When you're holding it, the colors will fade…"

The soothing voice penetrates the haze in my mind and I follow the instructions, forcing myself to get a grip on the feelings that seem to engulf me. I breathe slowly, closing my eyes as Seer's girlfriend continues murmuring to me, and after a few minutes, my brain reactivates. I've never felt anything like this and no doctor or shrink has ever pulled me back from a blackout.

She's a fucking wizard, that's what.

"How… how did you do that?" I ask shakily. My eyes open and I look at Julia in shock. "No one has ever kept me from going into the blackness—not even Andromeda."

Raking a hand through her rainbow highlights, she shrugs. "I've had a lot of training. Hard cases are a specialty of mine."

I frown, lying back against the pillows. My body feels beaten and bruised, but I don't see any visible marks. The ache is bone deep, though, and it's why I haven't tried to get out of the bed and leave. "Where am I, Julia? How did I get here? You have to be able to tell me that much."

She nods, settling back once she realizes I'm calm. "You're at State U Medical Center in a private wing. When you… blacked out… after Antigone showed up, you got transported here. The entire group followed, and we've been here ever since."

"Jesus. How long was I out this time?" The room doesn't have windows and I can't get a read on the passage of time. Julia looks rumpled, but she's not in her costume.

"Five days," she murmurs. "Zasha and Tharin went out to get supplies for us after the first night. Clothes, toiletries… all that shit. I couldn't get any of your men or Saoirse to leave the waiting area. Your sweet vet had to be sent to pee; he was that inconsolable."

My chest tightens at the mention of Wolfie, and I have to turn my head and bite my lip. If I keep thinking about their betrayal, I'm going to cry and I do *not* cry in front of people. But the pain is slicing through my soul like a hot knife through butter and my eyes sting with unshed tears.

I trusted them instinctively, and I was wrong.

"Jolene, they all care deeply about you. I daresay they love you, even if some of them haven't realized it yet." I don't turn around, nor do I answer, so Julia continues. "Everyone has secrets. We all have things we aren't ready or able to share, even with loved ones. The reason your family hasn't told you everything is because people have died for breaking this vow."

The rage bubbles up again, competing with the sorrow for domination. Her excuses aren't helping and I still know next to nothing about what happened to me. Whirling around, I glare at her.

"Julia, I don't give a flying pig's balls about anyone's vow. You *all* have information I do not and it's about *me*. I don't know if it explains why I black out or what's wrong with me, but I'm never going to be okay with being lied to."

She steeples her fingers and nods, looking pensive. "That's fair. It would frustrate anyone in your place. I won't justify their actions, but I *can* tell that you won't be able to resist hearing them out."

This woman has lost her goddamn mind.

"I have no interest in hearing lies. I hope you have a lot of room for houseguests. Stock up on groceries," I mutter. "My house is a no-fly zone from now on."

She sighs. "I can't tell you why that's an incredibly poor decision, but if need be, I'll accept the burden."

"Why? Why is it bad? You admit my best friend and the men I… they're *all* lying to me! They have no plans to stop, according to you, until some mythical moment when everything will become clear. What about that makes my decision to hold them accountable wrong?"

"Shit. Dancing in the fire," Julia says as she rolls to her feet and paces across the room. "It is not wrong to want those who have behaved poorly to make amends for their actions. However, it is very difficult to maintain that distance, regardless of what your mind wants."

Arching a brow, I cross my arms over my chest. "I'm pretty sure I can live without jumping anyone's bones, especially when they refuse to admit they're hurting me."

Her eyes widen as she stares at me. "Hades' bells, Jolene! They *know* it hurts you; every single one of them is beating their own ass over it. Taking responsibility isn't the issue here."

Is she kidding me? They know and I'm supposed to forgive them?

"I don't… I don't even know how to respond to that."

Stalking over to the wall, Julia puts her hand on it and leans in. "I think they need to talk to you themselves. Whether they wanted or meant to hurt you, Seer and your men need to make their amends for their errors. You won't be able to see this clearly until they apologize for betraying your trust."

"No shit, Sherlock." I huff the sarcasm at her with bite, but inside, I know she's right. If I'm ever going to get past this, I need them all to admit they were assholes and apologize. I can't even comprehend forgiveness until they admit what they did was wrong.

When she turns back to me, the silver-haired woman gives me a sheepish grin. "That's the spirit. No one said having a good reason for behaving badly prevents you from being angry. You have every right to feel hurt and betrayed."

"Thanks for giving me permission," I grunt. "But it doesn't change the fact that you've clarified that the lying won't stop. How am I supposed to look at my friends or… lovers… when I know they aren't being honest? How can I trust them with anything else?"

"I can't answer that for you, Jolene. I can only tell you that your family would tell you if it didn't put them or you in imminent danger. And I don't mean 'get fired' danger—I mean death and disfigurement."

How is that even possible?

I close my eyes, trying to sort through all the emotions coursing through me. After Trevor, I swore I would never allow anyone to abuse my trust in that way again. I was young and naïve, too starry-eyed, to pay attention to all the giant red flags waving around him. Until the ball, I didn't know the woman he cheated with was Antigone. I was too mired in self-pity after he broke up with me to even ask who he'd left me for.

I don't know if I can let these people lie to me every day and not relive that trauma.

"Did the 'special guest' leave after I…" I open my eyes and look at her, pushing the revulsion down.

Her laugh echoes off the walls. "Oh, she definitely left. I don't know if she'll stay gone or if you have a new enemy to contend with when you get home. I have sequestered us far from that mess while we waited for you to awaken."

"Where do I go from here? Am I even able to leave? Have the doctors cleared me?"

"Well, *your* doctors haven't, but the staff here have. No one was allowed in until we checked you from head to toe. I have clothes for you and your animals are waiting outside, just as anxious as your men."

Why the hell didn't she start with that?

"Bring me the clothes and let the animals in—and *only* the animals. I want out of here."

"Aye, aye, Captain," she mutters.

This is going to be a fun ride home, I can tell.

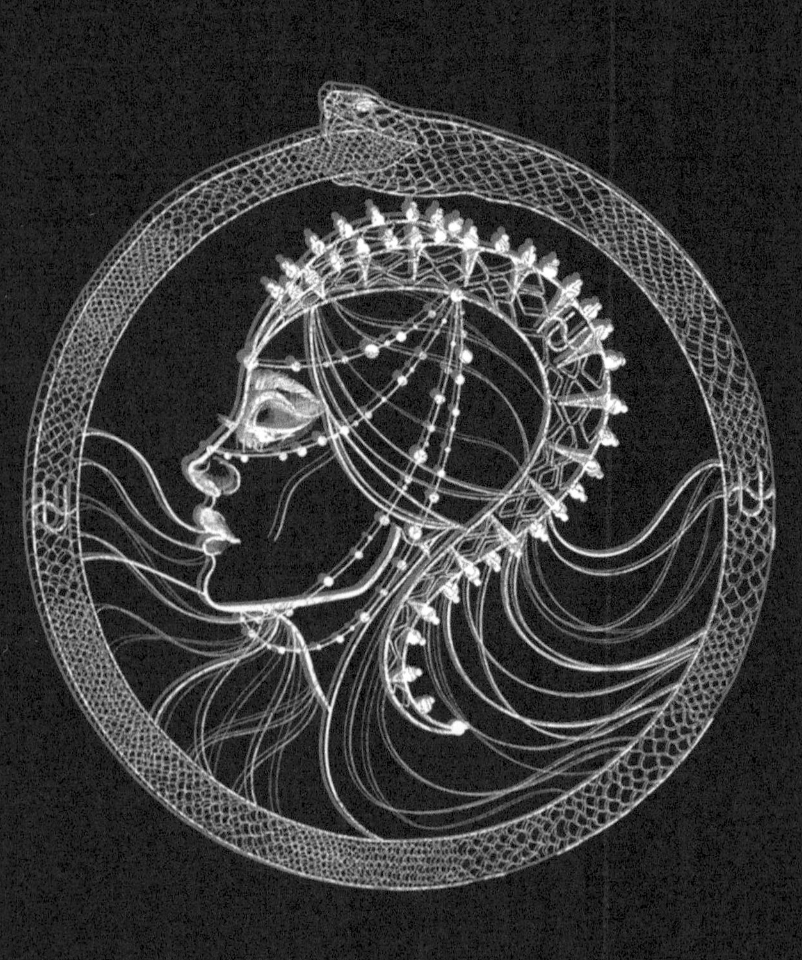

Don't Give Up On Me

Edgar

My *drugar*[1] is not speaking to any of us and she rode home with the pixie's tribe and her animals. Before our girl came out of the room, Julia warned us that the truth did not sway her. Our idea of sending her to smooth the waters didn't work as well as we'd hoped.

The hound is howling inside and I feel like tearing something to pieces.

"She knows we don't have a choice, right?" Wolfie whispers from the back seat.

The pup is wrapped in the doc's arms, looking about as fragile as I've ever seen him. It makes the beast inside of me growl louder and I slam my palm on the steering wheel in frustration. Benjy tilts his head at me from his seat at shotgun, his eyes knowing. My old friend recognizes when I'm struggling with one of my sides, but I've never felt it this keenly before.

My other sides are eerily silent and I don't know what that means, but it's not good.

"Lucy, she just needs some time. It will be okay," Prez murmurs as he strokes his hair.

Doyle is quiet for once, but he sighs and nods. "Aye. Knowing you're the only person who's on the outside and you can't come in is hard on the psyche."

"It's going to take longer than any of you think," Saoirse whispers. She's crunched between Prez and Doyle, looking about as miserable as a person can. "Because of Trevor, yeah? That right arsehole tore her to pieces and this will reawaken that dragon."

"Dragon? That guy from the dance? No way," Benjy mutters. "He smelled human."

Saoirse snorts and shakes her head. "You're right—sort of. Of course, Peanut had no idea, but once she told me about her days at State U, I did my diligence. He's a low level mage from a moderately wealthy family in another state."

"Our girl deserves better than a tool like that," I growl. "He couldn't even look her in the eye *before* she shifted."

Presley grins at me in the rearview mirror. "If only she could remember it, we'd be golden. It was majestic—a perfect shift for such a newly emerged supe."

I nod, feeling the fire within spark as I recall. "The way she pinned that witch that betrayed her in high school was hotter than shit. Almost hotter than doing it myself."

"Antigone is the one who stole Trevor at SU," Seer says. "Jolene might have let go of the high school bullshit and made peace with her if not for the targeted campaign to steal her fiancé. Those queen bees from high school packed their bullshit up with their dorm supplies."

I was too busy drinking and fucking my way through sorority row to notice what Sherilynn and her cronies were up to.

"Don't beat yourself up, Edgar. It wasn't your job to monitor those harpies."

"That's true," Wolfie finally speaks again. "None of us can change what happened in the past. If we want to fix this, we have to go to Sugarplum by ourselves and own up to our mistakes. It's not her responsibility to come to us; we fucked up by not starting this conversation sooner."

Doyle sighs dramatically and thumps his head on the seat. "Can't we just fuck it out of each other? Hate sex is not only cathartic but calorie burning."

The sound of multiple fists hitting skin followed by a yelp makes me grin a little. "As appealing as rough, angry group activities sound, I don't think that will get us out of the doghouse. No pun intended."

"Who's going first?" Seer asks as she leans forward. "We'll be on our own, regardless, because Peanut will not let anyone make excuses for anyone else. She's got boundaries for days after that quack in London hypnotized her."

"I'm sorry... what?"

The tiny woman looks guilty for a moment when she realizes she's accidentally betrayed a confidence. "We were visiting one of her mates from 6 and she had a big episode. She was out for two weeks that time and when she woke up, she went to see this 'hypnotist to the stars' that one of our clients recommended at an embassy party. Her reasoning was if doctors couldn't fix her, maybe voodoo woohoo—her words, not mine—could."

"There are so many questions; I don't even know where to start," Prez grumbles. "Was this guy for real? Did you go with her? Was there any change? What was his name? Did you report it to the Society?"

Seer shakes her head, looking even more rueful. "I figured *she* was a fraud, so I didn't write it up. You know celebrities—always trying some hoaxster garbage and it was this hot rock star who told her so... I noticed nothing worth mentioning. She didn't have another fit, but they come and go. Her blackouts were unpredictable until she came here. Now they seem triggered by stress."

"Jaysus, woman! Didn't it occur to you this might be important? What if this chit was an empath or a witch or some version of a mind-bender? I can think of a dozen beings that would take joy in spreading chaos by fucking with an unemerged supe's head!"

Doyle's right. As much as I hate to admit it, it's entirely possible that part of why her emergence is blocked is because of this mystery hypnotist.

"Seer, do you have any idea who this woman was? Her name, or maybe who recommended her? It seems extremely coincidental that Tilly has a block created by some major magic no one recognizes and she had a private visit with some con artist a couple years ago." I frown, considering the possibilities Doyle tossed out a moment ago.

The Guardian scratches her head, pondering for a second. "Dionysus, help me. We were partying so much with so many feckin' celebs back then... I might have to pull out some photo albums from storage and try to jog my memories. I know it was an embassy party because we wore the naked swoosh dresses that night."

"The... what?" Benjy almost chokes, and I have to cover a laugh.

"They did it up like fashion as an art—a Met gala rip-off theme. I designed these bloody *hot* dresses that—with a wee bit of magical help—were basically metallic swirls that crawled over the important bits, and not much else. Being as my girl is curvaceous and not a stick like me, she drew a *lot* of attention, hence the rock star."

The growl escapes before I can stop it, and everyone laughs. I know it was years ago and I have no right, but my imagination is running wild. Jolene running around encased in some mystical metal goddess garb is sexy as fuck. "I have a feeling poking through your albums is going to make all of us crazy."

She snorts, shaking the wild braids around her head. "You have *no* idea, doggy. Peanut's secrets aren't as world shattering as ours, but she spent five years as part of the glitterati in ways none of you are ready for. It's how she healed after that fuckwit destroyed every ounce of confidence she had left after you and your friends stomped her in high school."

"Then it sounds like we need to make a trip to your place to find these albums before we go home," Doyle says. "To the dragon's den, doggy!"

I suck in a calming breath, trying not to let my temper get the best of me. The question has to be asked, though I'm fairly certain I know the answer— and I *hate* it. "Where are we going after we pick them up? I assume we're not welcome in our current abode."

"Definitely not. She won't even look at us, much less allow us to live there right now," Wolfie murmurs sadly.

Prez finally loses his cool. "I *knew* we should have talked about this sooner. Our place is being renovated for the new offices already."

Grimacing, I nod. "Same. Repairs and upgrades for the sale. Fucking elf-infested at the moment."

"Christ on a cracker, you're all pathetic. Since the pixie has a place to go, you eejits can come to mine. I'm not happy about it, though."

I'll be damned. The prickly asshole didn't even give us hell.

"Then it's settled. We get Saoirse's old books and take them to whatever this nut job calls a home. Maybe if we can understand what happened between the Catastrophe and now, we can figure out how to fix the mess we made."

None of us expected this—it's fucking surreal.

We stopped at Saoirse's house to pick up ten boxes of shit she swears may have insight into their time in Europe first. Then we headed for Doyle's house with an eerie quiet falling over us. I'm not sure if it's because of the weight of what's happened hit or because we don't have the slightest inkling of how to fix the mess without making it worse. That all changed when we pulled up to a normal-looking Southern house just outside the end of town, opposite from where everyone else lives.

Doyle rolled out of the car and whistled, calling the spooky Raven he calls Odie, and turned to us as if he was going to say something. Instead, he grinned and muttered, "Fuck it."

It seemed like his subsequent departure was our cue to move, so we did.

I almost ran into the idiot as he stood in front of his door, looking at it but not touching the knob. He ignored my grumbling protests until the rest of the crew followed, and then waved his hand in an intricate pattern in the air.

That's when a goddamned portal opened instead of a door.

When we stepped through it, we were in the middle of a Classical Greek temple style entryway full of columns and marble. His bird took off to sit on an ornate golden perch above the arch in front of us, squawking like it was auditioning for a fucking Poe poem. No one knew what to say—every single mouth was dangling open.

Finally, I grabbed the dipshit by the shirt and let the hound out a little. "*What. The Fuck. Is. This?*"

"It's my home, you furry arsehole. I'll thank you for not assaulting me since I'm being so kindly by letting you stay here."

Words escape me, but luckily, the Irish lass untangles her tongue. "You feckin' bastard! This... You live in a Bloody Mary Poppins portal!"

Doyle smirks. "Aye."

"What's a Mary Poppins portal?" Wolfie steps around Prez, gravitating to my side, and I immediately feel the calm rush over us both.

"It's not real. It's some sort of glamor. These don't exist," Prez mutters. "I mean, not unless..."

The red-headed jackass rolls his eyes, waiting for us to get on the same page.

"Unless he's a son of a whoring *deity!*" Seer shouts as she stomps over to him. She pokes him in the chest with her finger, a ripple of energy filling the air as armor and scales cover her body. It riled both of her sides, and she's ready to pull the sword from the scabbard at her waist when I finally put the pieces together.

"Stop." Jolene's best friend whirls on me, glaring at me with the slitted eyes and golden glow of her people. "He's not a deity."

"Explain the bloody temple then, Edgar!"

I ruffle Wolfie's hair when he presses closer and then shrugs. "At least, not fully. He's a dirty hybrid, like most of us. Prez excluded, of course."

Doyle claps, his eyes full of merriment. "Very good, Judge! Although, much like young Wolfgang, I don't have a clue who dear old dad is. My mum is disinterested in me on a good day and despises me on others. Withholding the info seems to be a thing for powerful mythical women, I suppose."

Wolfie flushes bright red and curls his head at the mention of his mother. I don't know much about the situation, but Prez looks murderous at the mere mention, so she must be worse than mine.

That's saying something.

Before any of us can blink, Seer puts her blade to Doyle's throat and hisses. *"Which. One?"*

I'll give him credit; he doesn't even blink. But I suppose being immortal makes threats a bit blasé. Lifting one hand, he pushed the blade away with a sigh and shakes his head. "I can't tell you—or anyone. Even Nelia doesn't know. My mission here wasn't ordered by my mother and the letter of law unfortunately states I can't reveal my heritage unless you find out on your own. Hence, bringing you here started a dialogue."

"Games. All you ever do is play games," I growl.

"That's my nature, doggy. Some say it comes from my father, but fuck if I would know. I only know it's not from within our own house, so to speak, or I wouldn't be the big secret that I am."

Interesting. He's clearly partially Greek—and ancient as hell probably—but whomever his mother did the deed with isn't from their pantheon.

"You're telling us a Greek goddess played slap and tickle with another being that she shouldn't have, and you ended up a hybrid?" Presley frowns and pushes his glasses up, but I can tell he's intrigued.

"Aye. You lot thought the only abandoned lost ones were shifters, fairy, and the like?" Doyle snorts and then laughs. "Fuck, no. My kind—of all them, not just the olive lovers—mess about like fools, too. Many of them broke ancient accords in doing so and I'm likely not the only mixed breed demi out there. But it's not like there's a club or handshake, so don't ask if I know any of them."

"It makes sense that any high level being caught coloring outside of the lines before the Society came about would cast the proof out. I'm sure that's what my mother and father did, though obviously more recently," Wolfie says softly.

Aw, fuck. I can feel the sadness radiating from him.

Leaning down, I press a kiss to the top of his head and wrap an arm around him. Prez smirks at me and I blink, unsure of why I felt I had to comfort him that way. It must be the mating thing—that's a whole other ball of wax we haven't had time to deal with properly. I glare at him before looking at the demigod in front of us.

"You know, this is going to be the hardest part for her."

His laugh is mocking. "No, she'll have others who will be more difficult to grasp; I promise."

"Right now, we need to figure out how to apologize and make her understand the limitations we have, not speculate on potential mates," Saoirse snaps. Sheathing her sword, she backs away from the idiot and her shift disappears like shimmering water. "Let's get to work, you eejits."

She's got a point. I don't plan on staying in this weird ass marble mausoleum for very long.

---

1. Mate

I Hate Boys

"What the *fuck* were they all thinking?!"

I've been pacing a hole in the floor of my living room, tossing meatballs to the cats and dogs while Isis tries in vain to squeeze my panic into submission. The animals can sense my mood—none of them have misbehaved even a whit. Eury took off to hunt the minute we hit the driveway, and I stumbled into my house without a backward glance at Julia and her merry men. I simply *cannot* wrap my head around the fact that every single person I trusted—even Seer—has been lying to me from the beginning.

I had one fucking friend after Trevor—one.

Tears of both rage and pain leak from my eyes as I stomp around, yelling to the gods about the course of my life like a lunatic. I don't understand why I let any of them in when I *knew* caring about people *always* leads to heartbreak.

Seeing Trevor didn't hurt me like I thought it would—no, he and Antigone betrayed me long ago. The damage their betrayal did, however, *that* is ripping my chest apart. Antigone caused one of the worst traumas in my life —the Catastrophe—and for her encore, she destroyed what little I'd done at State U to rebuild myself. The most grating part of the situation is she *enjoyed* decimating my self-esteem and making me spiral out of control.

I don't know what I did to her in high school besides being her friend, but clearly, she wasn't the person I thought she was.

But her coup de grâce at college was pure evil, and I've never figured out if it was her own plan or if Sherilynn put her up to it. The allure of popularity and wealth certainly charmed my geeky friend; I don't know if it corrupted her entirely. That doesn't matter, though. Whatever goodness she offered died when she systematically pursued, fucked, and stole my fiancé for sport.

Now she's back with that wet napkin in tow, gloating like a true mean girl on her throne.

Adding her to the original group of snarky witches would have been bad enough. But I'm alone again—drifting on a sea of betrayal and lies from the people I was falling for and my best friend. I don't have a support system in place and I have no idea how I'm going to go to work tomorrow, much less walk around town.

How can I face all the people lurking in the background waiting for me to fail?

"What am I going to do, guys?"

Kali and Hecate put their heads on their paws, letting out mournful doggy noises. I turn to Jekyll and Hyde, who sit up tall, their carriage haughty as they '*mow*' in response.

"Strut in like I own the place and ignore the women trying to bring me down?"

The affirmative sound from my cats tells me I understood.

Now I just have to figure out how to do that.

Walking into the school the next day is one of the hardest things I've had to do in a long time. I feel the eyes on me as I stride to the animal enclosure and even more on me as I push the front doors open with my head held high. I considered dressing up to bolster my confidence, but I nixed that idea fairly quickly.

I am who I have always been and I don't need to do anything to impress these closed minded assholes.

A warm tug inside of me tells me Teddy is nearby, but I keep moving towards my classroom without meeting any of the gazes of lookie-loos. They won't get me to break down or lash out today; I am prepared to weather whatever storms appear with grace and firm boundaries. No student or staff member is going to get the satisfaction of seeing the emotions roiling inside of me. None of them deserve it.

I'm almost to my studio when something flashes in front of my eyes. Stopping to put my hand on the wall, I steady myself enough to walk the ten feet I have left and slip inside. Closing the door quickly, I lean back against it as another wave of fire runs through me. It feels like it's seeking something and when I refuse to move, the flashes of memory spark behind my closed lids.

The smell of the night and ash. Bright moonlight and burning fire. Heat and cool breezes. Branches and brush touching me.

Muscles flexing as I run and run until I pause to let out a long, low sound that echoes off the hills. I hear birds screech and answering howls. Furry companions rub against me.

Every sense feels sharper and the smells… I can smell everything. *There are several enticing scents I want so badly to follow until I find them, but my mind and my instinct are at war.*

Frustration and anger flood me, making the fires burn hotter and higher around me.

Am I at a campfire? Is this a memory from my childhood?

It can't be. Nothing about how the world looks or feels is familiar—it's all so focused. Nothing has ever looked like this, especially at night.

The angry ball in the pit of my stomach loses patience and I take off into the darkness, heading for the forest. My soul is aching and part of me is fighting against my brain, trying to push me toward the scents that call to me, but I don't care.

Howling into the starry sky, I focus on the satisfaction of running free and being one with nature.

Suddenly, I snap out of it, gasping for breath as I look around the room. There's only an empty art studio and a soft knocking behind me. Putting my hand on my chest, I whirl around, sniffing the air as if I can smell what's coming. Of course, I can't, and I shake my head to clear it. I've never had waking dreams like that before now and it scares the living *shit* out of me.

Goddamn it, this shit has to happen when I have no one *to talk to or lean on.*

"Jolene? Jolene, are you in there? Is everything okay?"

Blinking, I have to stop and place the voice before I realize that it's Hugo. He has an odd habit of showing up at exactly the right moment and I don't know how he does it. "Uh, yeah. I was… uh, hold on. I'll open the door."

I scrub my shaking hands over my face, trying to gather myself, and when I feel like I can look somewhat normal, I open the door with a forced smile.

He tilts his head at me, studying my expression for a moment. "You don't seem okay. In fact, you look like you've seen a ghost. This place isn't haunted, to my knowledge, so what made you look so stricken?"

How do I answer that?

"I saw a mouse," I blurt out. "It scared me."

His brows furrow and his face goes from concerned to suspicious in a blink. "A mouse? Doesn't your bird eat stuff like that? You don't seem like the type to be worried about creepy crawlies."

Glaring at him briefly, I turn on my heel and head to my desk to organize my papers for the day. "It caught me off guard. Why were you creeping around my classroom? Come to ask about my humiliation in person rather than stare at me all day?"

"No," he says as he shuts the door behind him. "I actually came to see how you are. I know you were in the hospital for quite a while and now that you're back, I wanted to check on you."

Okay, that's a little sweet, especially coming from someone who looks so serious all the time.

"I'm coping." I shrug and look out the window. "That incident brought back some rather ugly wounds from the past that I thought I had healed. And it also shined a light on things that were unacceptable in my life recently, so it's a lot to process. Thank you for checking on me, though. No one else has."

Admitting that is actually the hardest part. I sent my friend and the guys away, but not even Niecy has been by the house to see how I'm doing.

He gives me a tiny smile. "That might have been Mayor Nelia's doing. After your entourage left for the hospital with you, she got up on stage and read the entire room the riot act. She said she wouldn't stand for this type of rude, childish behavior and we will not tolerate it at events in her town. Then she sent Antigone, the guy, and all the Harleys packing. There was also a mention of not bum rushing your house when you returned home because you would need space to process such a flagrant violation of decorum and boundaries."

My hand flies to my mouth, and I choke back a gasp. I assumed people were doing the old 'shun the embarrassment' thing from my youth, but Nelia has warned off even the people who might have supported me so I'd have time to sort myself out. I'm not sure if I'm grateful or aggravated that she didn't think I could handle the confrontation—but I know she meant well. Outside of the weird dreams that are now coming when I'm awake, space to breathe has been good for me.

"Oh. I suppose I can't be mad at the people who didn't come to check, then." I give him a sheepish look. "But you're in violation of her decree right now, aren't you?"

"I am. But I have a sixth sense for when I might be needed, and Mayor Nelia will understand." His eyes sweep over the projects in various stages of completion. "You have your students doing an impressionist unit?"

Beaming, I nod. "Monet is a personal favorite, though Dégas is a close second. When I'd visit Paris, I'd spend hours sketching at the *Musee D'orsay* or in his garden at Giverny. Pastels and watercolors, of course, but I love the emotion in them. And I can relate to things that look beautiful from far away and are a big mess up close."

Hugo laughs and the sound warms the ice in my chest a bit. His eyes twinkle as he looks at the canvasses again, studying them closely until he approaches one in the corner. "This. You did this one as an example."

"Good eye, Mr. MacAuley." I say as I join him in front of my large waterlily. "The Waterlilies are my favorites, though I'm surprised you picked it versus a couple of other students' versions."

"Your energy radiates from it." He steps closer and touches the edge of the canvas carefully. "There's sadness and loss, but also this infinite joy and yearning to be seen. It comes across in how you paint."

I arch a brow. "Uh, huh. You get all of that from a flower?"

Of course, I'm testing him. Good art always grabs you by the ovaries and tugs; I would accept no less from myself. But I want to hear more from him.

"I do. The brushstrokes, the colors, and the vibrancy... they all speak to the emotions you were feeling when you were creating it. It may be a flower on the canvas, but it's your heart in my senses," he replies as he turns to look at me.

His face is so earnest and guileless that my heart leaps and I *almost* breach the distance between us to kiss him. But before I do, a voice in my head whispers to me—it says I have other issues to clear up before I make decisions like this again. It would be unfair to cast them out for their mistakes and start something with Hugo, especially because I don't know he if he *also* knows this big stupid secret. So I back away, giving him a sad smile before I go back to my desk. "Thank you. I'm always appreciative when people compliment my art in such a lovely manner."

"Anytime, Jolene. If you need me, all you have to do is call." Hugo waves and heads for the door without another word. Disappointment is evident on his face, but I don't address it.

I've got enough men frowning at me at the moment; one more might send me off the deep end.

Numb

We've been stuck at Doyle's ostentatious abode for days and it feels like the only thing we've learned from going through Seer's boxes is that our girl was wild as fuck in Europe. Photos of the two of them at movie festivals, raves, galas, state dinners, and even a few in castles show a progression from an unsure graduate to a confident, take-no-prisoners type of woman. Seer really helped her heal and grow into the person she wanted to be, but along the way, they definitely made the most of Jolene's connections.

The judge looked like he was going to burst from his loungewear every time we hit snaps of them with guys; unfortunately, there were a *lot*. Girls, too, but that seemed to set him off less. Typical Southern jock upbringing has him frothing about random dudes when I'd bet the ranch Jolene was far more attached to women. But to his credit, the grumpy oaf is trying because Wolfie has snuggled him out of a fit every time. Hell, he even let me flank the other side of him and that's definitely progress. I'm actually amused as hell as I wait for him to figure out he's falling like a stone for my darling boy. The mating should have told him, but sweet Athena, he's dim with emotions.

What we *haven't found* are the pictures Seer mentioned of the rockstar Jolene cavorted around Italy with for a bit. That's the person who recommended the hypnotist and we need that link to figure out if it ties to the strength of her emergence spell. Clearly, the debacle at the ball shows she can shift into a hellhound form—whether she got that from Edgar or her true parents, we don't know. Since she still doesn't have a damned clue about our world, her spell is weakening, but not gone. She must have other sides like Wolfie and Edgar, but Seer says even her handlers don't know where Jolene appeared from.

That's suspicious, right? Usually, intakes at the enclaves have some information on species or parentage. They have ways of trying to find it out, don't they?

"Prez, pass me that album from Germany 2018," Edgar mutters as he sips his bourbon. "I'm finished with Spain 2017."

Seer grins broadly. "That's the year we ran with the bloody bulls. There were these triplets who—"

The glare Boone gives her forces me to smother a chuckle. Perhaps I spoke too soon about his irrational jealousy of the past. "You were so close to the enclave when you were in Tokyo in 2016. Did you find time off on your own to visit? My mentor still lives in the area despite being retired."

"No. Peanut and I were there for a fashion show and some big gaming thing she wanted to see. It was only a couple months after we met and she was still making a name for herself as a corporate consultant. We partied a lot, but we also took a fuck ton of meetings. Drove me batty because I don't speak Japanese, nor do I have the patience for sitting there and looking all *waifu* and agreeable."

Wolfie sits up, waving his album before I can reply. "I found pictures at a knighting ceremony. Sugarplum is standing with some guys who look like rock stars—or criminals, I can't decide which."

All four of us crowd around the book, looking at the pages as Wolfie points at the people. I tilt my head as I look, sighing. "I'm useless. I don't follow the big names, but I assume at least some of these people are famous because they're at a bloody royal family event."

"You think, Hamilton?" Doyle rolls his eyes. "This idiot offed himself two years ago. If it was him, we're shit out of luck. However, the other eight people are still kicking. Some of them are even still touring because this was pretty early in their careers." We all stare at him and he shrugs. "I like modern music. Much better than half the shit I've seen over the centuries in terms of being accessible."

"Okay. So Doyle may be a Swiftie and we think we have eight dudes to look into. We're going to have to put faces to these names, you know," Wolfie says as he leans back against Edgar's side.

"I know who they are!" Doyle stands and runs his hands through his hair. "All of you need to take me more seriously. I know I play about and enjoy the products of chaos, but I'm a good bit older than half of this town put together."

Seer rolls to her feet and sets the albums we finished aside. "Look, that might be the picture, but we need to meet again tomorrow night to finish the rest of these. We met over eight rock stars in the four years we flitted around the globe. There might be another handful of morons to look into before we're done. Since none of you have approached our girl yet, that means we have plenty of time to work on this."

My eyes narrow and I look at the valkyrie as she issues commands. "Would you like to tell us what happened when you spoke to her?"

"Oh, fine. I haven't, either. What the feck am I supposed to say? 'Sorry I lied about our totally *not* random meeting in Europe because they assigned me to you' and follow it up with why I can't explain about being assigned?" She digs her hands into her wildly streaked hair and groans. "I have *no idea* what to tell her, so I've avoided anywhere I think she'll show."

Edgar sighs and sits his glass down, leaning his forearms on his knees as he looks at all of us. "It's time for us to discuss our secrets, folks. The leprechaun over there might not give specifics, but we need to get used to admitting things we've kept secret for whatever reason before we approach my *drugar*. If we can't do that, we'll never be able to tell her the things we can actually share, much less what we can't."

I hate when that asshole is right.

"I'll start. Obviously, as the town physician, I'm a caladrius. My people are secretive and tight-knit because otherwise we become the targets of bounty hunters. When the Society places us in enclaves like the Hollow, we are safe because of the amount of supes in town who can help protect us. The entire population of caladrii live in a hidden village that no outsiders may know about or visit. Parents send their children to schools and mentors recommended by the snakes until they go to medical school. For our own protection, we are a pipeline for enclave doctors and nothing else."

Even my darling boy blinks at me when I finish. Clearly, no one talks about how unsafe it is to be my species and that we don't have options outside of being healers under the protection of bigger supes. Our innate healing and therapeutic abilities make us far too appealing to trophy hunters and those who would want to lock us up for their own gain.

"Your people don't do *anything* else? Like they go to school, grow up, become doctors, heal, and retire without going anywhere but home and their assigned enclaves?" Seer asks, her brow furrowing.

"Correct." I shrug. "We're made for this, truthfully, and being able to take care of those who need us is fulfilling. But usually, we are required to come home to… propagate the species rather than have actual relationships. It's mostly arranged by our parents. Luckily, mine have passed on, so I'm not under pressure yet."

Wolfie lets out an indignant gasp, climbing onto Edgar's lap so he can settle into both of us. "Fuck that. It's not happening."

I open my mouth to speak, but feel the hound next to me wind his other arm around my waist as he growls darkly, "It's not an option, pup. The doc is ours, and no bullshit tradition will force him to act like a breeding stud."

Well, I'll be a son of a beer swilling frat boy. There's hope for the judge yet.

"If anyone cares, despite my heritage, I'm not okay with that shit, either. There are plenty of ways to keep your species going without forcing people to take part. Fucking hell, Doc, it's 2022 and your people are all medical personnel!" Doyle runs his hands through his hair in aggravation and he glares. "This is shit that makes it impossible to get all the supes to come together—rare groups like yours are clinging to ancient bullshit that the rest of us can't abide."

"On a lighter note, I don't know any of my people," Seer interjects. "Valkyries and veela are both fairly solitary, but I've also grown up with adoptive parents who are high in the Society. I never questioned being adopted, nor was any of their lifestyle hidden from me. So I didn't feel the need to look for others or my bio donors. We are prone to bad tempers, though. I've always had one."

Doyle arches his brow. "That could just be *you*, little rich supe. Though, the valkyries I've met over time have been pretty aggressive. Every single one is a badass, metal undies wearing Domme—at least the ones I knew."

"Can we focus?" Edgar leans his forehead against the top of Wolfie's head as he sucks in a slow breath. "You all know about the hound. That was the first side that appeared when I was about eight or nine. Once I was a preteen, the lust fog started and Bane deduced the incubus. Dual sides aren't uncommon anymore, but when I didn't emerge after that, we waited. The Quetzalcoatl appeared after a severe loss my freshman year of high school. Luckily, it was on the way home and I was riding with two older teammates, not on the bus. Their parents summarily shipped them off to some boarding school, but I suspect Andromeda bribed them to do so. No one but her has ever known about my third side—not even my parents."

Tilting my head, I pull back and give him a serious look. "How did you hide such a rare and temperamental side? You had to have struggled."

"I still struggle. Part of my risk-taking shit has always been about giving as much serotonin and adrenaline to my three sides as possible to keep them satisfied." He sighs and runs his other hand through Wolfie's hair. "The bird came out first with Tilly. It's always liked her. I'm just lucky it was in private."

"Hecate in a handcart, we've all got enough hidden shit to float Charon's boat," Doyle mutters. "You know I can't say more than I have until you figure it out for yourselves. Real mother unnamed on high and father likely as high, but also unnamed. Older than anything in most of this country. Not Irish. I simply like this persona."

Seer rolls her eyes. "Helpful as always."

"I'm probably dark Fae. My adoptive mother is in the hospital and has been since my dad died. My actual mother is awful and the only one of her kind. She won't tell me who my dad is, but it's obvious that's where the Fae comes from," Wolfie says softly.

"His mother is an absolute bitch," I add. "She's known for her frigid demeanor, but she treats him like a chess piece."

"Yes," the vet murmurs. "I found her when I was young and I've regretted it ever since."

Edgar looks at each of us. "Is this everything we can share? Because if so, then our next step is to each figure out how we're going to talk to my *drugar*. We also need to get more information on the last lead we had in her parents' death—that's one of her biggest stumbling blocks and if we can help her solve her mysteries, she'll have less to worry about. All we can do until she forgives us is try to ease her burdens from afar."

"What about MacAuley and Benjy?" I ask. "Should we talk to them as well? Haggerty thinks they're joining the boy band, eventually."

"I'll talk to Benjy. You find MacAuley at lunchtime tomorrow, Prez. Doyle, find time to visit Hazel. She always knows more than she's letting on."

"What about me?" Seer rises to her feet and stretches, giving Boone a curious look. "What's my assignment, Coach?"

His lips curve up as he replies, "You get to handle the Society angle. Talk to Bane, your handlers, Julia… anyone you can find to track this deputy crap down. We all have to work during the day and you don't."

"I'm on it." She turns to head for the door, glancing back at us to add. "Be good, boys."

I roll my eyes and stand, offering a hand to Wolfie. "If we must."

"You must," Edgar mutters.

Yes, sir.

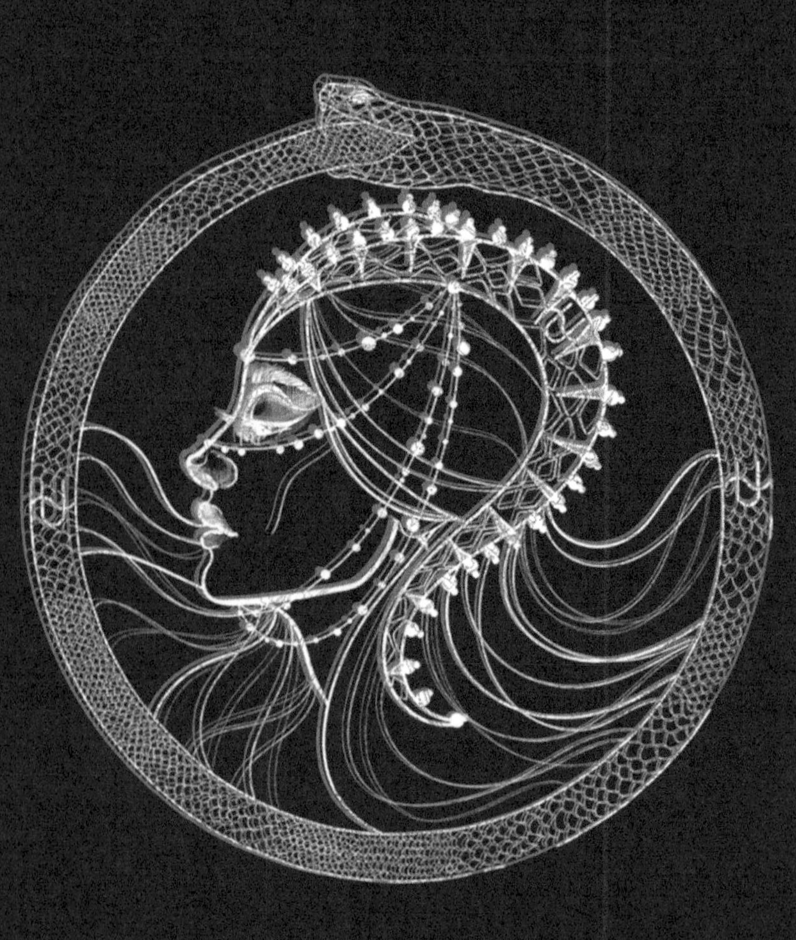

Fight Song

E very day for the rest of the week, I have to endure the stares every time I come into town. It doesn't matter if it's at work or after lessons… people watch me like they think I will break down right in front of them. I'm sure some are rooting for it since I dared to fight back against the cruel prank the Mean Moms of Whistler's Hollow set up, but I refuse to give them the satisfaction. I make sure I'm groomed, caffeinated, put together, and flanked by threatening animals no matter where I am.

In a small town, any chink in your armor is a weakness to exploit, even something as small as a messy ponytail at the store.

To their credit, the students haven't misbehaved any more than normal. The jocks stuck in the low level art class for humanities are still painting flicking dipshits and the AP students are working like Trojans to get portfolios done to submit to shows in the city. My private students are quiet or as standoffish as normal—a fact that I'm grateful for. When I was their age, so many of the adults talked freely in front of their kids that every conflict made its way to the schools. That's how the Nip/Tucks ended up pulling the Catastrophe stunt that led to my big public humiliation.

I honestly don't have the spoons to dance around those kinds of topics with kids without losing my temper. Sherilynn and her friends brought Antigone back because I got them in trouble after the newspaper incident. It was a petty revenge enacted by petty women who have nothing better to do than tear other people down. Unfortunately, it's not only a 'small town boredom' reaction. When I taught in the inner city and even when I was a fixture in boardrooms, I watched bullies look for targets and systematically destroy them for the fun of it.

Niecy used to tell me that 'People who play in filth, stay in filth.'

It took a lot of therapy and years for me to realize she meant some people enjoy being nasty because it makes them happy. Whether it's making themselves feel better or because they're broken is inconsequential. Their joy comes from other people's pain and they won't stop until they've completely obliterated the person they're focused on. They surround themselves with toadies and 'yes men' who adore everything about them while ignoring the red flags. That's why there's always a pack… they have to have an audience.

We're all too old for this shit, and I will not be part of the abuse cycle.

That's why I'm pulling to the parking lot of Atwater's getting groceries rather than having them delivered. It's been over two weeks since that damned Halloween party and I'm tired of hiding. My phone rings as I slide out of the Impala and I click the button on my Airpods to answer. "What?"

"Oooh, touchy, Jo-Jo."

I roll my eyes and sigh as the cats jump out of the car first. "Jackson, how many times do I have to tell you—"

"I know; I know. Don't call you Jo-Jo. But I *love* getting under your skin, so it's never going to stop."

"Did you call me for a reason or just to annoy me? I'm unloading pets so I can go to the store," I growl in response.

My old friend laughs and I can hear a faint echo of another chuckle. "Eli and I have been working on the leads your men sent us. It surprised me to hear from Boone because the word is, you gave them all the heave-ho."

Jesus Christ in a tweed suit. The gossip about my sex life made it to another fucking city??!!

"Jackson, I refuse to discuss my sex life with you while I'm standing in Atwater's parking lot. Get to the point."

Kali and Hecate bark loudly and the cats make a low *'mrowr'* sound that catches my attention. I look over and see Zelda Grant gaping at me next to her car. I'm about to tell her what she can stick in her giant piehole when Eury swoops out of the sky and grabs at her hair. The harpy eagle makes a sharp turn upwards and when I look back at the nasty woman who called me a whore on my first week in town, she's wearing a wig cap over gray hair.

Holy fuck, my bird just snatched the wig right off of her head.

This will not end well.

"Monster! Thief! *Unruly hooligans!*" Zelda shrieks as she tries to wave her hands and cover her head at the same time.

I cover my mouth with my hand before my laughter tumbles out of my mouth. If Eury had swiped something that she wore for any reason besides vanity, I'd be chagrined, but it's obvious old Z just didn't want anyone to know she'd gone gray. The dogs and cats are jumping around, clearly hoping Eury will allow them to play too, and I don't even know how to handle this without making it worse.

"Jo-Jo? Where'd you go? What's that yelling?"

I have to close my eyes for a minute so I can gather myself to respond as Jackson keeps babbling in my ear. When I catch my breath, I take my hand off my lips and gasp, "Zelda. Wig. My eagle. Have to call you back."

He's still yelling when I click the phone off. Eury notices me paying attention again and decides that's her cue to ascend higher into the air to fly away from the store—with the wig still clutched in her claws. Zelda continues squawking and pointing at me, but I don't know what to do. The bird has taken off and I can't very well do some weird *Game of Thrones* raven thing to get her back.

Looking down at Kali and Jekyll, I mutter, "Guess she'll have to stay here and look like a fool. Nothing we can do, right?" My answer is a resounding set of barks and *mows*, so I pull my reusable totes out of the trunk and give Zelda a wave as I head for the door.

Man, karma is a straight up bitch when she wants to be.

Jekyll and Hyde bound into the store first, with Kali and Hecate behind me. Since I left the hospital, the animals have formed a circle of protection around me everywhere we go. Eury takes the air and Isis now curls around my torso and left leg in a familiar pattern at all times unless we're at home. It's odd that Teddy's dogs refuse to go see him, but since he's a stubborn asshole who hasn't stopped watching since I got to town, I'm not surprised his pets are just as fucking bullheaded. Luckily, the dogs didn't lie to me, so I'm happy to let them snuggle up in his spot at night.

"Jolene! It's so good to *see* you!"

Ten. Fucking. Seconds.

Craning my neck, I look to see who is foolish enough to be calling me from across the grocery store before I even get completely inside. The waving woman is Mina Cantwell and I'll be *damned* if the woman looks a day above forty. I walk over towards where she's molesting oranges as she selects them, trying not to look like a moron. Mina is Jamie and Fidelia's mother… she can't be a day under sixty and yet she looks fresh as a daisy. When I used to ride at the farm as a kid, she always brought out flowery herbal tea and deliciously citrusy biscuits that made my entire body tingle with happiness.

It was a bit like magic, how she used to brighten even the stormiest day with her presence.

"Hello, Mina. It's been a dog's age," I say with a smile. The animals study her warily and I shake my head at them. Mina isn't a danger; she's as threatening as a Kleenex.

Before I know it, I'm engulfed in a warm hug and my body stiffens. I've never been big on people touching me without warning, and after the newest disaster, I'm even more withdrawn. Isis wiggles her head out from under my shirt, letting out a hiss until Mina pulls away. Her lips split and she lets out a tinkling laugh that floats through air like sleigh bells.

"Oh, what an interesting accessory you're sporting, dear. You seem to have a mini army of protectors. I don't blame you after that shameful display at fall event." Her expression changes to one of sympathy when I flinch. "Don't worry, honey. Poor breeding *always* shows itself when given the chance. I fear the harvest from those your age was a bad crop altogether for this town. So many weeds in the garden and no one ever bothered to trim them— that's what I told your father."

My brow furrows and I pick up a few oranges of my own for the house. "Mina, I didn't know you were friends with my father."

"Not friends, really. But Jamie took an interest in you and you remember how rigid his father was back then. We had little get togethers with him and your mother every once in a while after you started coming around so often. I think Anderson was afraid Jamie would get sweet on you and since there's a four-year gap in your ages…"

What.

"Mina, are you telling me you and my parents met to make sure Jamie and I weren't dating?" I rub my temples, trying not to lose my temper at the woman who was kind when others were not. I was never interested in Jamie that way, but who the hell were any of them to monitor us like the mares on the farm?

"Oh, no, dear. Your mother and Anderson were quite the schemers. They thought they could push you together. Jamie's heritage and name with your wildcard possibilities seemed like *such* a good recipe for the future. You were so good with the horses and so smart. When you left for State U, we were sure you'd come back for your destiny. Your parents promised."

The bag of oranges I'm holding drops to the floor and my vision goes fuzzy for a second as I try to process that. Snippets of an old memory echo in my head, making me freeze in place.

"Jolene, you can't just flit off wherever you want when you graduate. You have responsibilities!"

"Eloise, she's an adult. We can't force her to come back because we made a promise."

"No one asked for your opinion, Andrew! Do you know what this will cost me? It will set back my ascension to the Council by years!"

With a soft gasp, I snap out of it, looking at Jamie's mom in shock. One thing my brain wiped out was about this weird arranged marriage our parents had in their heads. All I can think of to say is, "Did Jamie know?"

The petite blonde woman shakes her head. "Definitely not, honey. We were all committed to allowing you two to find the right path on your own. We didn't tell either of you on purpose."

Oh, how sweet of you all—not.

"It was nice chatting with you, Mina, but I need to get moving along. I'll call on you for tea sometime?"

She doesn't need to know I have absolutely no intention of doing that. I'm being as genteel as people would expect because I can't afford to make more enemies at the moment. Every time I think I've got my hands around the bullshit going on here, someone throws a curveball at me and I'm getting pretty tired of it. Mina finally nods and I bend to pick up my oranges, collecting them before I go back to the front of the store to get a cart.

It takes everything in me to roll that fucker to a corner near the restrooms in the back where people can't see me, so I can freak out in private.

Not only were my parents distant and disconnected, they were planning to fob me off as some kind of political power move?

And what did she mean by Jamie's heritage and my wildcard possibilities?

Why the hell *is everything in this town a goddamned riddle?*

I lean back against the wall near the ladies' room door, sliding down until I'm sitting on the floor with my forehead on my knees. It's too much, all at once, and I don't know how I'm going to handle it by myself.

I need to get out of here and feel something real.

Rolling to my feet, I ditch the bag of oranges on a shelf, leading my animals out the door without a single purchase. I know where I'm going before I even get in the car—I'm going to the farm to work all of this out of the system as I fly over the bluegrass on the back of one of the most beautiful horses I've ever seen.

It's time to fly.

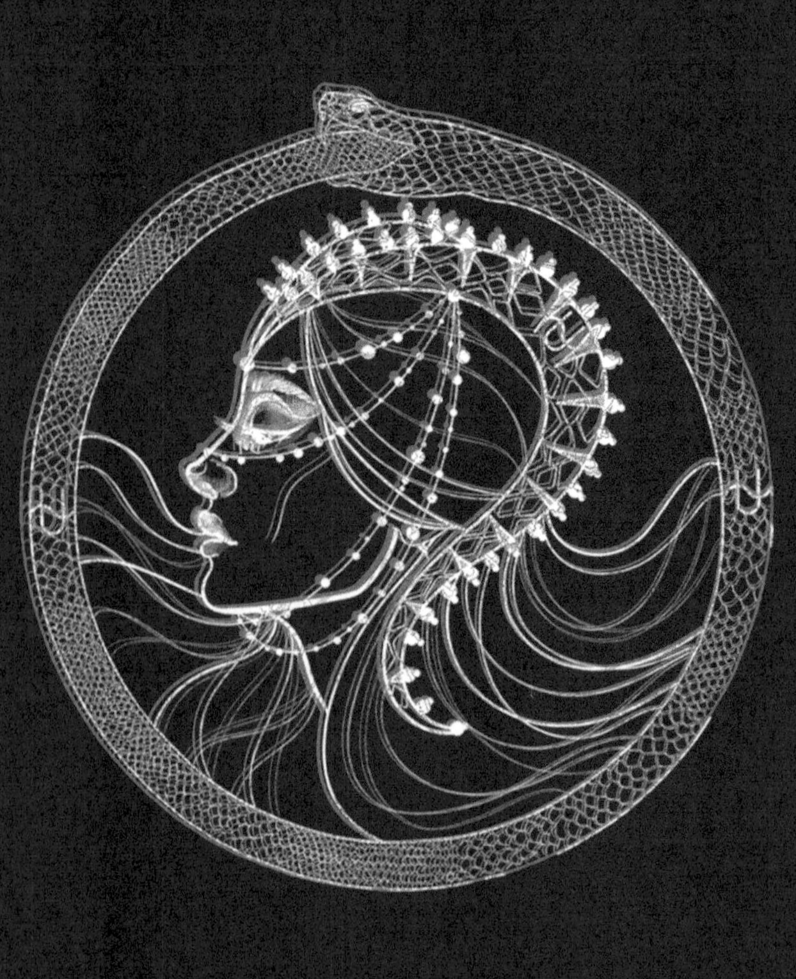

Let It Out

DHAMEER

The energy in the air changes abruptly, and I stop talking to Eliot about the pause in Medhi's training.

"She's here," I murmur as my eyes close. Everything around us has become charged; there's such *power* filling the atmosphere that I sense it even though she's far from the main building. Confused looks greet me when I open my eyes. Isra shifts, her hand instinctively reaching for whichever concealed weapon she's chosen, but I shake my head. An excited smile graces my lips as I turn to Fazal. "Go outside and bring her to me."

His speedy exit makes my Southern business partner scratch his head. "Amiri, don't leave me hanging like a lost ball in the high weeds. Who's here, and why did you send Fazal after her?"

"The lost one from the city—I did not find out her name until I researched the trainer I wanted for Medhi. Your people's need to gossip is both useful and perturbing, though you know that. Miss Whitley has arrived, and I am eager to speak with her about her plan." Settling back in my chair, I steeple my fingers as I contemplate the visions in smoke when I had her on stage.

Cantwell pales and looks nervous. "She might not be in the best of mindsets to discuss that right now. As I mentioned, there was a problem a couple of weeks ago, and she's been recovering after a stay in the hospital."

Before I can dismiss his concerns, Fazal slips into the room with a look of shame on his face. "I apologize, Your Highness. She… refused to accompany me to visit."

I frown, noting his intense discomfort. "What did she say *exactly*, Fazal?"

My lifelong valet pales and shakes his head. "I do not think—"

Isra pushes off the wall, approaching him like a ninja in her all black suit and flashing silver blade. "The sheik did not ask for your opinion, Fazal. Know your place."

Waving my hand, I gesture for Isra to back off. She knows better than to throw my family's titles around to demand people bend to my will. I can make them bend to my will on my own and without making a spectacle. "Fazal, repeat what she said. I am unconcerned that it is not to your liking."

Though I sense it will be amusing…

"Miss Whitley said 'if that rich asshole wants to speak to me, he can get off his ass, mount up, and find me. I have a horse to exercise.' Then she headed for the stable as if on a mission."

"Sweet baby Jesus, Jolene," Eliot mutters. His hand scrubs over his face and he looks at me apologetically. "My apologies, Amiri. She's had a rough go of it lately."

Biting back a laugh, I shake my head at him. "No need, Cantwell. My *muharibi aleaziz*[1] would not be herself if she wasn't fighting the world."

"Your…" He frowns and looks at me curiously. "I didn't think you'd met."

"Ah, but we have. I was graciously allowed to perform at *Howl* when I first arrived in the country and she was present in the audience with her Guardians." His eyes widen and I shrug, as if it is of no consequence. "I called her on stage to receive the gifts of my people. I feel like I know her very well, though she does not know it."

"Shit. What were they *thinking?* Taking her to *Howl?*" Once he processes that, Eliot turns back to me with a serious expression. "There are things you should know about her before you decide to chase her."

Arching a brow, I wait.

"It's clear you know she's unemerged, but rumor has it she has mates— several and the possibility of more to come. I've known her since we were kids and our parents were close at one point. She's had a lot of emotional trauma in the past. Some of that recently came back, so if you're simply looking for an interesting notch on your bedpost, look elsewhere."

Alqaraf almuqadas.[2] *That was a brave statement.*

"I admire your honesty and your defense of your friend, Eliot. But I assure you, I do not have ill intentions. What I see in the smoke is quite accurate, and I know that the threads of our fate are intertwined. I will not hurt her; that I guarantee." I give him a sharp nod as I stand, looking over at Fazal. "Fetch my riding clothes and I will change. It seems I have a runaway woman to locate."

"Why do I think this is a bad idea?"

"Because his Majesty should *not* be chasing after some common woman like a lovesick teenager?"

Whipping around, I lose control of my anger for a moment as my guard forgets to mind her tongue. Tendrils of dark magic spiral out from my palm as I hold my hand up for her to stop and they wrap around her neck like ropes. Her face reddens almost immediately and the lights flicker above us. My temper is well known in my home, but rarely do I allow people in the new world to witness this.

But Isra will learn to respect the woman who is meant for me or she will suffer the consequences.

The lower *djinn* dangles as I raise my arm, lifting her towards the ceiling while she sputters and gasps for air. "Disrespect will not be tolerated, Isra. Practice what you preach."

She struggles, phasing in and out of her humanoid form for a moment as the impact of my powers on her causes her to weaken. After a few long moments, she ceases to fight me and I lower her to the ground. Her voice is raspy as she dips her head and says, "My deepest regrets, *sahib alsumui.*[3] It will not happen again."

The rage filling me subsides as she submits and my magic releases the grip on her neck. "Do not forget again, Isra."

Fazal is the peacemaker because he clears his throat and gestures for the door. "This way, Amiri. We will make use of the same room we did on our previous trip here. I will ask the staff to prepare your other horse while you dress for the ride."

"Excellent." I look over at Cantwell with a narrowed expression. "Non-disclosure, my friend. I do not allow most people to witness the extent of my powers and though this is certainly not the limit, I'd prefer you never to speak of this."

I don't wait for his answer as I stride out of the room, following Fazal eagerly.

Regardless of her mood, I am quite excited to see Jolene again. It feels fortuitous that she stormed in when she did, and I do not question the whims of the universe when they present themselves.

MALIK THUNDERS ACROSS THE FIELD, TAKING HIS HEAD AS I USE MY MAGIC to follow the trail of my errant prey. I'd be lying if I said I'm not enjoying my hunt—I may not be one of the animalistic species of supe, but predatory instincts come easily to my people. Eons of searching the deserts for those who have desires they cannot fulfill to feed our power runs through my veins. The *djinn* may not have the population density of more common species like wolves or witches, but those who remain keep our ancient traditions intact.

It would amaze both humans and supernatural beings alike to find out how many successes and failures in history have been at the hands of wishes we've granted.

Our own ethos demands we keep living records of what we have granted so as not to cross another's source. Since we draw power from the beings who request our services until they meet their end, it is imperative none of us shift the balance by contaminating the reality created by each individual wish. It's extremely complex and takes an enormous amount of communication—arguments about what qualifies as upsetting balance can only be solved by viewing other realities together. For ancient *djinn* like me, this is not a painful process, but the younger ones like Isra struggle with it mightily.

However, I did not have to alter reality when I delved into my *muharibi aleaziz*[4]'s mind. Her destiny has been written in the stars for much longer than she was a twinkle in the eye of her parents. I only helped by removing the mental restraints she'd put on herself during her unhappy past. The family she coveted so strenuously was a foregone conclusion if she simply allowed it to form. Unfortunately, some devious little brats in this town have thrown a knot in the threads of Fate, and I am honor bound to help her untangle them.

For her own good and that of the world in the future.

When I reach the crest of a higher hill, I tilt my head to look into the waning light. It is dusk and finding her in the dark will be more of a challenge, but I can do it. The more pertinent question is how skilled she is at riding in the dark. That is unknown and given the value of the horse she's mounted on, I need to pick up my pace. *"Asrae ya milaki[5]!"*

The wind blows my hair out of the loose ponytail I had it in as Malik gallops over the terrain. There's an old swing in a tree at the edge of the horizon, and I feel a wave of sorrowful energy radiating from it. Jolene is hiding in that far corner with Medhi picking at grass along the fence line. The gold from my mare's coat picks up the light when we get closer, and I tug the reins to slow our progress. Crashing in like an invading horde will not endear me to the woman I hope to soothe.

She doesn't look up as we approach, though I suspect she can hear the beat of Malik's hooves. I can't tell if she's surprised that I accepted her challenge or if she's irritated that I'm intruding on her private moment. Regardless, I slide out of the saddle in a practiced motion, even though my horse hasn't stopped yet. I land on my feet gracefully and prowl over to where she's hunched over. The sound of soft sobs stops me for a moment, but only briefly.

She needs me.

"Jolene…" I wait for her to acknowledge me, but she continues sniffling into her palms silently. "I am certain you meant for your challenge to be ignored when you instructed Fazal to tell me. You will find that I am not one to back down so easily."

Her head lifts, and she squints at me with tear-reddened eyes. "You… *You* are the prince who owns Medhi? *You?*"

Ah, so she recognizes me without all the stage glamor.

"Indeed, little one. I did not know when I met you at *Howl* that you were the new trainer Eliot bragged about—that I can assure you. But I will admit to researching you afterward; it was purely a business decision at first."

Her eyes close, and she tips her head up to the sky. "At first. Hera, help me if this is another one. I don't have the spoons for this!"

I can't help but laugh at her cry to the heavens. As if our capacity to cope with the whims of the Universe means anything to the women who weave the threads; it's adorable that she's been raised so completely ignorant of our world. It feels blissfully naïve, but I know it's a lack of comprehension about the true nature of life.

"I don't believe any of us can convince the gods of our preferences by yelling at the clouds. Though it may be therapeutic, I'm sure." I give her a small smile, walking a little closer. "You may continue if you wish. I will send the horses afield so they do not get spooked."

"Really? You don't mind?" she asks in a tiny voice. "It might be loud."

"Really," I reply. Winking at her, I stride over to Malik and Medhi, murmuring low in my native language. They toss their manes and trot away from us at a relaxed pace. "See? Let loose, *muharibi aleaziz*. Do what you must and unburden yourself."

Jolene rises from the swing, looking up to the slowly setting sun and shakes her fists. "*I do not. Have. Enough. Strength. To take all of this. At once!*"

Crossing my arms over my chest, I watch her quietly. I disagree with her assessment, but she does not need me to correct her, only to allow her to vent the riotous emotions inside of her. The human part of her is so over-whelmed with the events transpiring that it's impossible to see a road forward. I would love to help her see there are other paths, but I've found that simply allowing people to realize on their own is more empowering.

So I stay silent.

"*It took me years… years! I had to hit the bottom and be scraped out by Jackson before I could start the healing process. Afterwards, I was alone for almost a decade before I allowed a friend in. And look what it got me!*"

Her rage and sadness are heavy in the air as she drops to her knees on the ground and starts sobbing again. My heart aches for the woman I believe is meant for me. Though she may not have had a life that everyone would consider difficult, the doubt and shame created in her childhood impacted her indelibly. Trust is a thing to fear and every time someone breaches it, the voices in her head remind her they were right.

I have known many who are damaged like this; it is not an easy belief to overcome.

"And the guys…" Those words are followed by a crack in her voice and another shivering sob. "I let it happen so quickly. It felt right, and I allowed them to become integral to my life. Why did I do that? *I know better!*"

Approaching slowly, I offer my hand to her. She looks up at me suspiciously and I try to convey my sympathy with my gaze. It is not time for words yet, but I can sense what she needs. When she finally takes it and rises, I envelop her in my arms. She struggles a little at first, but I don't let go. I'm not a small being and I've been told many times that my embrace creates a feeling of warm safety.

"I barely know you," Jolene murmurs. "I don't know why you're being so nice. And it worries me because I barely knew most of *them*. That hasn't worked out so far."

I look down at her, waiting until she tips her head to meet my eyes. "You are hurting right now—rightfully so—but I believe your assessment is not accurate. It is too raw for you to see clearly what the addition of your friend and men have heralded positive changes."

She snorts. "A house full of shit that isn't mine and people who are hiding things from me like I'm a child. That's not positive."

Tapping her nose, I shake my head. "Try again and hold the rancor, *muharibi aleaziz*. What good things have come into your life along with them?"

"Well…" She sighs and closes her eyes as if thinking about is causing her pain. "Seer and I had such amazing adventures in Europe. I'd never had someone who was so close to me before. She's like a sister."

"Mmmm. What else?"

"When Wolfie asked me out, it was the first time I felt… this spark. Like I knew he was more than the casual flings from my time overseas. I felt it with Teddy the first night and Prez when he showed up for Eury's arrival. Something about them made me feel complete." Her eyes open and she frowns. "Why am I telling you this? Are you a sorcerer?"

I throw my head back and laugh at her suspicious question. She has no idea how close she is, but that is not why she is opening up to me. I'm not using my power on her; she's reacting to the bond connection I feel. Jolene doesn't know it yet, but that's part of what she's describing from when she met the others.

"No, I am not. Many have complimented my listening skills, though. It comes with age, I believe."

She squints at me. "You're not *that* much older than me."

If only you knew…

But I grin instead. "I don't know how old you are and my mother would take a cane to me if I asked a lady how old she was. I cannot answer that in good faith."

Rolling her eyes, she snorts. "Age is a man-made construct used to make women feel a need to propagate the species. I'm thirty-four and I don't give a shit who asks."

How delightful she is when she's fighting me. I like it.

"Then I shall reply that, alas, I have a few years on you. I am thirty-nine."

That's shaving off a thousand years, but who's counting?

"See?" Jolene smacks my chest. "You don't get to pull the sage wisdom act when you only have five years on me. I won't allow it."

"Your wish is my command," I reply. The irony of that phrase isn't lost on me, but the change in her demeanor is so enchanting that I can't help but tease back. Her eyes have dried and some of the hopelessness is gone from her face. That's what I wanted.

"Ugh. No, thank you. I never want someone to give in to me just to win my favor. Fight me if you want; I prefer it."

No shit.

"You are not ready for my version of fighting, Jolene. But you will be and when you are, we will dance together." I lean down and place a gentle kiss on her lips. "For now, you have other bridges to cross and mend. I am happy to be your sounding board anytime."

She's quiet and I think perhaps I've offended her, but she finally nods. "You're right. I need to make peace with the mistakes I made and the ones those I care about made. At least enough to come to decisions that aren't rooted in my past trauma."

"Ah. Therapy, I assume?"

"Oh, so many hours. Enough to know when I'm self-sabotaging and that's definitely now."

I smile and jerk my head at the swing. "Perhaps we can avoid that by chatting? I'll push and you can answer whatever you feel comfortable with. It will be an excellent distraction."

Pulling back, she tucks her hair behind her ears and nods. "I'd like that."

"Excellent." I walk over and wait for her to settle before I give the old rope swing a shove. "It is wise to remember that sometimes, in order to be mended correctly, things have to be re-broken. Your doctor would agree."

"Stalker," she grumbles. "That info isn't online for research."

"I may have had Isra do a little checking around. Call it precautionary. I *am* a prince. People seek to take advantage of that."

"Whatever you say, Your Highness."

Now, when she *says it, I like it. Who knew?*

---

1. Darling warrior
2. holy shit
3. your highness
4. Darling warrior
5. Faster, my king

Blow

The time I spent with Dhameer left me feeling more at peace than I have since the Halloween disaster. His gentle yet firm way of addressing the problem could have felt condescending, but… I felt like he was trying to take care of me. He's right—I need to sort out my mess before I do anything else. That's the same thought I had with the enigmatic Hugo earlier.

Looking over at my cats sitting shotgun, I sigh. "Am I wearing some sort of pheromone? I'm no blushing virgin, but why in the name of Aphrodite are so many hot dudes rushing to my aid lately? I feel like I'm wearing a 'princess in distress' placard."

"*Mow!*" Jekyll replies. Hyde adds nothing, but the dog in the back let out a low mournful sound.

Worried about whether I'll give their Master an Irish goodbye, I suppose.

"I'm not saying I'm abandoning Teddy or Wolfie or any of them, guys. I have shit to work out, sure, but there's this weird draw to Hugo and Benjy… and now the sheik. Does the universe want me to stock my own bunny mansion? As if the women in this town don't hate me enough…"

I can't seem to wrap my head around the whole situation, so I turn up my playlist, singing along as we speed towards Main Street. There's no hope of me cooking anything now. I'll have to pick up some pies at Derby Pies. I'd go to the diner, but something tells me old Hazel would see right through me and I don't know if I'm ready for that much wisdom in one day.

Pulling into an open spot down at the end of the block, I note how busy the restaurant and Speakeasy are. There's many people going in and out, which means I need to be careful with my animals. I open the door and they jump out, flanking me as usual. A screech in the air tells me Eury is circling, so I know I have another ally in this snake pit, but I can't allow any of them to get us in trouble.

"You guys need to stay outside. *Do not* get involved if anything goes wrong. There are too many people around and we all know some citizens here are looking to have you locked up. Isis is with me and I can handle getting some pizza for us. Got it?"

The dogs bark first, looking angrier than my servals. Teddy definitely ordered them to protect me—the tension in their bodies speaks volumes about their dislike of my command. Hyde steps in front of the others, taking point as they follow behind me. She's the first to jump onto an empty bench close to the doors to the restaurant. I pause, waiting for Jekyll, Kali, and Hecate to join her. Once they do, I blow them a kiss and walk the final few steps to the crowded entryway.

"What are *you* doing here?"

For the love of Jimmy Choos… of course, *Sherilynn is here instead of Benjy.*

Ignoring the screech, I walk up to the counter and smile at the teen working. "One extra large Animal Kingdom Meat Lovers, a dozen meatballs, two garlic cheesy breads, and a small vanilla Coke to go."

The girl's eyes dart back and forth, then she sighs as if she's in pain. "Are you sure you don't want to try… our new Pineapple Under the Sea special?"

I snort so hard it actually hurts for a second. "Uh… no. First, pineapple doesn't belong on pizza and second, that sounds like it's some weird combo of pineapple and tuna which… is beyond unappealing. I'll stick with my relatively sane order, thanks."

Her lips quirk for a moment and I realize the employees must be required to suggest this rancid sounding new menu item. And if they're being forced to do something so stupid, the creator of this ridiculous hodgepodge of pop culture reference and cringe, it's probably Sherilynn's brain child. I flash her a sympathetic look—I can't be the first person to tell her I wouldn't feed that garbage to a hog.

"It'll be about ten minutes, ma'am. We're pretty busy tonight. The 'Cats are playing."

Nodding, I point at a corner near the door. "I'll wait over there."

"What name should I call when it's ready?"

"You could write *loser* on it and she'll come running," Sherilynn cuts in as she walks up. "Make it snappy so the trash doesn't stink up my restaurant, Beth."

I close my eyes, counting in my head to keep my cool. No matter how many times I let the bullshit go, this chick just keeps coming. Even after the debacle at the Ball and the mayor's supposed decree, she still won't leave me alone. I don't know if it's stupidity or what, but I cannot continue to allow this woman and her groupies to abuse me in public. They can call me bitchy or crazy or whatever they want, but this fuckery ends tonight.

"Sherilynn, I have to confess something."

"We know you're a washed up tramp, Whitley. It's unfortunate that so many fine gentlemen have rolled around in the mud with a low-class pig, but men aren't known for being discerning when they want to fuck."

The room goes quiet as heads turn our way and I have to suck in a slow, deep breath again. I cannot lose my shit like I did a few weeks ago. What-ever happened, I ended up in a hospital for a week, and Sherilynn isn't worth my mental or physical health.

"Sherilynn Foster," I say, emphasizing her maiden name because of the divorce. It's petty, but the look on her face says my bar hit. I need her to shut up long enough for me to say my piece. "I confess to being confounded. After the mess in high school, I left with no intention of coming back. In fact, before I arrived home, I hadn't thought of you in *years*. I was out in the real world, creating my success and living my life to the fullest."

"Clearly, *that* didn't work out for you. You came crawling back."

"When I returned, I had no intention of dredging up childish bullshit. But there you were, still here and being followed around by a mindless bunch of twats who believe every ounce of tripe that escapes your mouth. Still, I didn't engage with you until you sought me out."

She starts to reply, but I shake my head, holding up a hand. "It begs the question, Sherilynn… How unhappy and pathetic is your life that you only derive pleasure from tearing others down? I want nothing to do with you, your minions, or your inferiority complex. I'm tired of you running around spreading gossip, lies, and hateful shit about me and anyone else who sees you for who you really are. You may present a pretty picture to the masses, but you're rotten to the core."

"Oh, Jolene. Do you really think the *Catastrophe* can order me around? My parents are part of the founding families! I'll have you blackballed in every social arena before you get home tonight. You'll be ruined." The bottle blond runs a hand over the carefully coiffed updo she's sporting and sniffs at me imperiously.

Seriously? She thinks I'm afraid of her?

Fuck. This.

"Go ahead. Tell everyone far and wide all the nasty things you think about me, Sherilynn. You can call me a pig in public and say I'm a talentless loser. Knock yourself out." I walk closer to her, my gaze narrowed as I look into her eyes. "But know this: if you want to make me the villain in your story, be prepared for me to wrap that shit around me like a warm winter coat. When I was younger, I let you get away with your abuse, but I won't now. I will dig up every skeleton, every body, every single speck of dirt you've buried and make sure it goes so viral that you won't be able to step into a Waffle House without the whole joint pointing and whispering. Do you really want me to expose all the backstabbing nastiness you're capable of?"

"You've got nothing, Whitley. I have hard evidence that you're trash and my name means something—you're a failed loser living in your parents' house." Her sneer is ugly, but it matches the narcissism in her words.

"I'm giving you one last chance. Back off, leave me alone, and keep your toxic bullshit away from me and mine. If you don't, I won't be kind and I won't back down. Actions have consequences and if anyone is going to be held to account, it's you. Think carefully about the things you've said and done in the past. How many of your *fans* will stick around when they find out who you really are?"

Her brow furrows, and I smile slowly. I have her now. She doesn't know what I'm referring to and she can't ask without revealing whatever evil shit she's done. I'll make certain Jackson and Eli do a deep dive into her social media and phone records. I have a feeling there's some socially unacceptable things she's said lurking within easy reach of my hacker friends.

"Um… your pizza… is ready," the girl at the counter squeaks as she tries not to draw Sherilynn's attention.

I walk over and take my food, feeling Isis squeezing me under my clothes. That's the best compliment I could receive, and it makes me glad I kept the other animals outside. They would not have dealt well with Queen Bratwurst's outburst. "I'm going to take my food home now. I suggest you seek some therapy for your issues, Sherilynn. I know you're still smarting because your Oxford scholar sister makes you look dumber than a kumquat, but the rest of the world doesn't have to suffer because your daddy loved her more."

Turning on my heel, I stride out of the silent room with a smug smile on my lips. I know I played dirty, but I've been the bigger person since we were teens. She wasn't going to stop coming at me and though I've never understood why I live rent free in her head, I'm tired of her and her flying monkeys. I have bigger concerns than her self-centered sociopathy and I'm not wasting anymore of my energy fighting a battle of wits with an unarmed amputee.

Jekyll wanders up to me as I exit, letting out a questioning, *"Mrrp?"*

"Don't worry about it, buddy. I had to show an emotional terrorist how we deal with their kind." I pause for a moment and grumble under my breath, "And I didn't do it with a weapon, so everyone should be proud of me."

Once I got home, I got all the food ready and spread out my research in the living room.

I'm stretched out on the giant beanbag on the floor, looking at files and the various emails Jackson has sent since our talk. Eury is perched on my mother's buffet table—which would *horrify* her—and the dogs and cats are lounging on various furniture. I have the Firebird suite on the wireless speakers Prez set up and though remembering the hijinks of four men trying to outdo one another while they installed all of this high-tech equipment all over the house.

All I have to do is call for one of the robot women and my house will practically live my life for me.

Frowning, I rub my chest as an ache starts up. Since I left the hospital, I've had a lot of random aches and pains, ranging from dull throbs to odd pain in my joints when I wake up. I probably should contact a doctor, but in this town, that means Prez and I'm not ready for that yet. One drawback of living in a small town like this is that you can't avoid anyone for very long; there's simply too much crossover in day-to-day lives. Sighing in annoyance, I wiggle my way over to the TV stand where I left the ibuprofen yesterday.

I swallow them dry and scoot back to my research. While I was driving home, there was a niggling sensation in my head that I missed something that was said. I don't know if it was when I talked with Dhameer or Hugo or even someone random. There's just a bit I'm missing, and it ties to the stuff in my files. I've read the reports and supplemental information about the mysterious disappearing cop over and over, but I can't figure out why it bothers me so much.

It's so strange that someone with those means would get hired for something completely out of their skill set and be able to move with no issues.

Based on my experience, moving to Europe was a process that I had to endure for the entire last semester I taught in the city. Passports, visas, selling extraneous items, long-term storage for others, canceling leases and services… It was a nightmare of red tape and paperwork. How could this dude manage it within a month for an entire family? He had to have majorly powerful help to get all of this pushed through so quickly. There's virtually no trail left after he skedaddled overseas.

I can't run around asking people about this guy without raising eyebrows if there's some sort of conspiracy going on. The only way I'll find out any *actual* information is to get it from the horse's mouth. I have to go to Istanbul and pump this dude for information myself. It's the only way I'll be able to put this line of inquiry to rest.

Honestly, time away from all this bullshit would be good for me.

WHFS takes the month of December off for the winter holidays, so I'll have time to really dig deep. I can't leave the country with some dipshit stalking me and no one to watch my back, though. I have to take the animals and *that* will require a great deal of favors unless…

Jackson.

Grinning to myself, I text my old friend about my plans. His family owns several private jets and arriving on a plane owned by the Thorns will provide me with almost no security or customs issues, even with two cats, a bird, a snake, and two dogs. The ultra-rich are allowed to do *so* many things normal people would gasp in shock over. Luckily, I have a valid passport and a folder full of vet records Wolfie provided me when he examined all of my menagerie. All I need to do is guilt my old friend into allowing me to whisk myself away to a foreign country on one of his jets for a month long clue hunt.

Shouldn't be hard, right?

I wait for his answer, tapping the pen cap against my teeth. No, it won't be hard to convince Jackson. What will be hard is what happens when the guys figure out I took off for parts unknown, telling no one.

That feels like it'll earn me a punishment someday.

Oh, well.

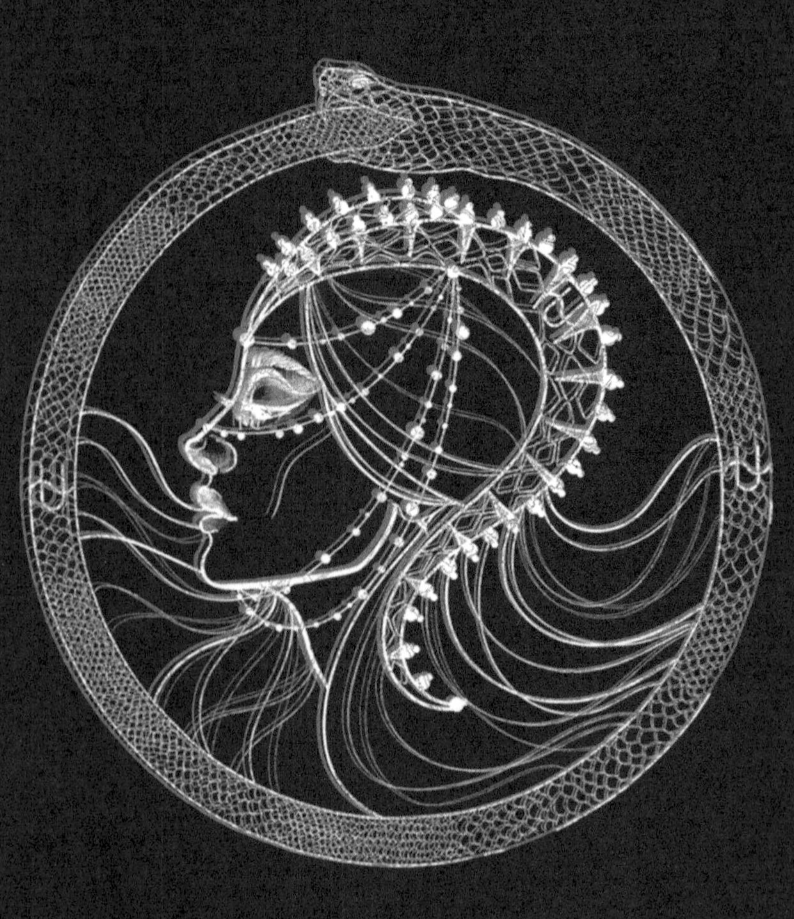

The Monster

The sound of Eminem blasting at full volume jerks me out of sleep like a tornado alarm. Blinking blearily, I look around the room for the source of the sound. My eyes finally land on the smartphone vibrating on the dresser. I'm not fully awake, but the case appears to be shiny and black, so it's definitely Teddy's. Of course, unless the Irishman got ahold of either my or Prez's phones, it'd have to be his because neither of us even keeps our ringtones on, for fuck's sake.

It's the minor differences that remind of the age gaps in our family.

I scoot out from under the heavy arm holding me to the judge's warm body. Prez's spot is still warm, but he's obviously left for the office already. Late November is a busy season because of colds and flu, so his schedule is full just about every day. I know that's helping him not to focus on our separation from Jolene, but I miss waking up with him just the same.

My feet hit the floor and I marvel again at the crazy power it has to require for Doyle to keep this place the way he does. He shrugs it off. But having a marble temple decorated and furnished to the nines that stays both warm and cool at the same time is beyond my comprehension most days. I pick up the phone and scurry back to the nest of blankets, poking Teddy's side as I hold the phone up.

"It's for you," I say softly when his eyes open.

"Hell, baby, you could have answered it. It can't be anything *that* important early on Saturday morning," he mumbles as he takes it. "That's not a work tone, anyway."

Ducking my head at his casual use of 'baby', I settle behind him as he flicks the screen open to answer. I'm still getting used to having a man like Edgar Boone claiming me as his. Presley is so easygoing and fluid; being topped by my laid-back doctor is like a warm, comfy blanket. A sexy one, mind you, but it's so different from the vibe with Teddy. Everything from his broad, tall, muscled quarterback body to his alpha male demeanor is a direct contrast to Prez's style. Teddy engulfs me from head to toe and while he's still figuring out how to navigate how he feels about me, I know without a doubt he'd rip someone's throat out for upsetting me.

It's hot as fuck and I have no idea how to handle him without getting ridiculously deep in sub space.

But he likes it and Prez enjoys playing the softer Dom in opposition. Thinking about the two of them together makes my dick throb, and I close my eyes. A low chuckle rumbles out of Teddy's chest, and he looks over his shoulder at me with a smirk. Apparently, I've been so lost in my thoughts that I missed whoever he's having a conversation with.

He pushes the speaker button and I hear Jackson Thorn talking about reserving a private jet. Before I can suss out what this has to do with us, Teddy hits the mute button. His eyes are ringed with fire as he ignores the babbling lawyer to roll over. His big hand reaches for my cock, running his fingers over the rungs of my ladder slowly. He knows that drives me crazy and I whimper.

"Teddy…"

"Mmmm, I don't think so. We're in the bedroom," he chides as his fingers squeeze the head of my cock gently.

"Fuck."

"If you're a good boy, yes. Now try again." His hand cups my balls, rolling them in a way that makes my hips arch up.

"Y-yes…. Daddy," I pant. I lift my hand to touch him, but he shakes his head. "Please."

"Oh, I love when you beg and we have time. Thorn will talk until he passes out if I let him." His hand releases me and he picks up the phone, placing it on the pillow. Then he pushes me onto my back, leaning in to nip at the mark he left on the juncture of my neck and shoulder. His teeth make me cry out, but I know the rules, so I don't arch up to press against him.

I have to get permission first.

"*Such* a good boy this morning, my little Wolfie." He rolls back over, reaching into the drawer in the nightstand. "Let's see how long that lasts."

When he pulls out the vibrating cock ring, my eyes widen. Presley has been giving him tips for sure. He knows how much that particular toy affects me. "Shit."

His grin widens, and he grabs the lube before using it to help slide the silicone down my shaft until the vibrating piece is resting against my balls. I suck in a breath and his mouth covers mine to kiss me hungrily. When he pulls back, he puts his fingers to his lips and unmutes the call. "I'm glad you called me to tell us, Thorn."

Jackson starts talking again—something about a trip to Istanbul—but I'm not paying attention because Teddy goes back to the drawer. He comes back with a set of nipple clamps and it takes everything in me to keep still, like I'm supposed to. Applying them one at a time, his eyes darken as he watches me fight not to squirm or make a noise. I bite my lip hard enough to draw blood and he dips his head to lick the droplets away. A low growl echoes through the room, and I give him a satisfied smirk.

I know how to push his buttons, too.

"Someone's asking for it," he growls. Teddy reaches up and grabs the phone, barking into it. "Thorn, I'll call you back about the arrangement later. I have something pressing to attend to."

That said, he flings the phone across the room and I can feel the hound beneath his skin pushing to break free. Teddy's sides are stronger than mine or Prez's; when even one of them is close to the surface, you can feel the energy crawling all over you. He slides down my body, hands gliding over my skin until his face is hovering over the head of my dick. Sharp pains at my hips make me gasp and he looks up with a feral grin.

"Holy fuck, daddy… are you… that's…"

"Mmmm, yep." His mouth closes over the tip and his tongue swirls over my slit. "I told you to be good."

I have to clench my abs and thigh muscles hard not to move as his hot mouth works over me at the same time as the vibration from the ring. "But… but… I am…"

A gentle nip almost does me in, and he lifts his head when I stay still. "I know. And you're going to *love* what's coming… besides us, I mean."

"There's more?" My eyes widen as the sting at my hips sizzles through me, putting me on that fine line between pain and pleasure. "Show me, daddy."

Teddy's eyes flash with the fire again, and I feel the air fill with his fog. It makes my dick weep and my struggle not to move even worse. He's definitely playing dirty, letting the incubus out to play as well, but that I'm used to by now. "Are you ready, baby? You sure you're ready? Daddy's gonna be rough."

Yes, please.

I nod, panting, as he digs into my hips a bit more. "I want it. Please."

My words make him lunge forward, grabbing the lube with a dark smile that promises I'm going to enjoy whatever he has planned. He lets go of me, rolling to the side as he opens the bottle. "Lift and spread."

Obeying automatically, I close my eyes and breathe deeply. His fingers probe my hole, pushing the lube he warmed in his palm in with a slow sawing motion. The stretch makes me moan and before I can beg him to give me more; he bites the inside of my thigh with sharp teeth. It makes my entire body tremble, and I look down at him pleadingly.

"Did it hurt, baby? Or did it feel good?" His voice is darker, more raspy and gravelly than normal.

"Good," I whimper. "But I need…"

"Oh, I know what you need, pup." His fingers slip out of me and he replaces them with the head of his cock, sinking into me inch by inch. "And you're going to get it."

"Can I move?" I have to give in and ask because I want nothing more than to pull him deeper inside of me. The vibration from the ring and the sharp stings and bites are going to make me lose my grip on the orgasm building in my balls.

His laugh is more of a bark and he thrusts forward, filling me completely. "I insist, actually. Wrap around me and move with me, Wolfie."

Winging my thanks to all the gods in the sky, I rock my hips into his hips as he thrusts in and out. His cock is thick and long, stretching me in the best of ways as the head bumps the sensitive spot over and over. His hands grasp my thighs again and that sting of pain comes back, making me shiver.

"I need… take it off… please…"

He keeps pumping into me, hips slapping against my ass as I writhe under him. "You're strangling my dick, baby. It's driving you crazy, isn't it? Being split in half while that vibrates and keeps you from coming too soon?"

"Yesssssssss," I hiss. "And your claws. I didn't know you could do that."

"I've never been with one of our kind. I've never felt comfortable letting the hound go with… except you and my *drugar.*"

"Fangs?"

His answer is a smile full of sharp points, and I throw my head back. "Daddy, please take the ring off. I want to come with you. I feel you getting close."

Leaning down, he slides the ring off slowly and puts his lips against my ear. "Good boy. Show me how pretty you are when you let your powers loose while you come with me."

Oh, shit. He wants me to….

Magic fills the air as I let the sparkling Fae loose, wings and all, looking up at him as he continues to slam into me. "Yes, daddy."

His eyes roam over me, glowing with the power of his hellhound and the incubus. "I know I claimed you, Wolfgang. I made my mark to protect you."

"I love it."

Our breaths are harsh as we move together and he leans down, putting his weight on his elbows. "I'm going to do something else. Something I've only done with our girl, but it seals the bond completely. Do you want that, baby?"

His question has more implication than it sounds like. He's really asking if I love him and I'm not surprised to realize that I do. We haven't had time to analyze any of this with all the chaos, but I think deep down, I knew. "Yes."

The snarl that escapes him precedes his hips, snapping harder and faster. I feel the emotions surrounding us increase, heading towards a crescendo that makes my heart thump like a bass drum. Suddenly, his cock pushes deeper and I feel it—his dick swells, pressing against my g-spot hard as it stretches me even more. Throwing his head back, he roars and fills me with hot come.

Was that a…

Just the thought of it makes my orgasm break free and I gasp as it rips through my body. My wings flutter against the sheets, throwing sparkles and dust into the air. I know it's going to make us loopy as fuck when we come down, but I can't help it. "Daddy…"

His voice is barely a whisper against the bite mark. "I love you, too."

That makes my ass clench, drawing a groan out of him, and I shudder as we come down. Fangs scrape over his mark just enough to create a trickle and I can feel his rough tongue lapping at the blood. My limbs are trembling and when his dick finally returns to normal, he slips out of me, gathering me into his arms. I wrap my arms around him, leaning my cheek against the top of his head as he suckles.

"Prez is gonna want to hear all about this," I murmur with a smile.

"Don't worry. He'll see. That ancient fucker has cameras everywhere in this weird ass museum," Teddy chuckles against my neck. "We can watch it together tonight. I'll enjoy his reaction. You might get spankings."

I groan softly. "You're assuming I'll be able to walk by then."

"If not, I'll carry you. Don't worry."

I could get used to that….

One Woman Army

Making the plan last night helped immensely. I didn't have the weird dreams about running through forests or odd magical gardens, so when I got up, I actually felt rested. That alone is a win, and it's helped me focus on getting a list together for travel. Packing my clothes and shit isn't hard; I moved around at the drop of a hat for years, but now I have companions and a bunch of other considerations.

Is this what people with kids feel like? If so, I know why they look tired all the damn time.

Jackson fought me a little when I presented the idea, but I expected that. I have some weirdo hiding in my bushes and a bunch of nasty bitches wasting their time trying to destroy me, so going out on my own sounds like an ill-advised plan. But since he and I are pulling enough strings to get my protectors allowed entry alongside me, it changes the landscape. With the wild cats, big dogs, python and giant eagle, I have enough distractions to allow me to run if necessary.

Not that I would.

I'm well trained in hand-to-hand combat and I'll be taking at least ten weapons to hide on my person. Whether he agrees or not, I'm not a damsel that needs saving. The fucking FBI trained me before they gave me the heave-ho, and I had plenty of experience with weapons and fight training in

Europe. Just because he remembers the pathetic girl curled up in her dorm room listening to Jewel doesn't mean it's who I am today.

Shaking my head, I poke my head out the back door and whistle for my crew. They come bounding up and I put my sunglasses on before checking to see if Eury is flying overhead. Once I confirm she's on board, I step outside and click the key fob to set the locks and alarm. We walk to the driveway, hopping into my car in a practiced order, and I peel out.

Time for yet another iffy journey into the belly of the beast that is this gossipy town.

"PEANUT!"

Oh, shit.

I turn towards the voice I'd know anywhere with a wide-eyed expression. Saoirse is waving her hands at me from across the store like a madwoman. I have seen little of my exiled family since I came home and I've been grateful that they are at least pretending to give me the space I demanded. I know I've felt Teddy's eyes at school occasionally, but he's stayed out of sight and kept his distance. Wolfie has made certain I don't see him at the farm. Even Doyle has behaved well enough that I haven't glimpsed his trademark fiery red hair.

But now Seer is here, and it's in public, so I have to be very cautious of how much information I give the wagging tongues about our rift. People will flock to get in the middle of the fight, especially if they think they can worm their way in between me and the guys. I'm not ready to decide like that yet and I don't need a herd of grasping debutantes making it even harder to work through.

So I walk down the main aisle of Atwater's with my head held high so the surreptitious glances don't see a chink in my armor. I know the animals are following me like a tribal leader and Isis gives me a fortifying squeeze from the inside of my jacket. I don't bring Eury inside of spaces like this, but I have the feeling she'd figure out how to get in if I needed her. Over the past few weeks, I realize my pets are purposefully surrounding me like a small army of fur, feathers, and scales to help me stay in balance as I process all the emotions rioting through me.

I'm grateful for it, to be honest.

I'd grown used to my found family during the short time we were assembled and without my companions, I am not sure I'd be doing as well as I am.

Once I get close enough to speak at a normal volume, I look at my bestie. She's as colorful as always, but there are dark circles under her eyes. Her face is pale and despite the makeup and accessories, she doesn't look as happy or full of sunshine as she normally does. I assume she's been staying with Julia and her men, which makes me wonder where the guys are. Some of them were in the middle of renovations to sell their places and for a tiny moment, I feel guilty.

That stops when a pang of betrayal echoes in my chest. I have a right to be angry with all of them and they are simply facing the consequences of their actions. With that thought, I give Seer a cool look. "Good morning, Saoirse. I didn't think I'd find many people here this early."

"I'm glad we ran into each other. Maybe we could grab a coffee at the diner and talk? I've been meaning to—"

"I'm very busy this morning. After I get what I need here, I need to drop it off and head out of town to the bigger stores for other things. I won't be able to do that, unfortunately." I give her a tight smile, hoping she understands I don't want to delve deeper into this conversation in this setting.

"But we need to talk, Peanut. It's been almost a month and—"

"Saoirse, I'm really glad we caught up," I say loudly enough for prying ears to hear. "We'll set something up later this week, okay?"

Her face falls, but she nods when she understands. I feel like a total bitch, but she should know this isn't the time or venue to discuss private things in the Hollow. There are too many people hoping to see me fail or looking to gather information to hurt me. Even something as innocuous as a fight with my best friend is fodder for their machinations and I don't have the spoons to deal with anymore bullshit right now.

"Looks like you're losing *all* of your allies, Jolene. Tsk, tsk."

My eyes get round as the grating tone of the woman who simply *cannot* stop digging her own grave hits my ears. I do not understand why Sherilynn Foster is incapable of understanding that I want nothing to do with her or this petty spat she keeps trying to propagate, but it's truly pathetic. Like Ursula in the *Little Mermaid* voice 'Pathetic'. I have set my boundaries over and over, both politely and in firm warnings, but she is so obsessed with making me her enemy that she refuses to let go.

It's going to ruin her reputation because I am only responding when she purposely provokes me. Her malevolent, toxic behavior will become obvious eventually and she will be the author of her own destruction.

I turn to look at the woman who has perfected an outward appearance of being a friendly, community focused citizen. It's no coincidence that she only personally attacks me in nearly empty grocery stores, closed door conferences, or the safety of her echo chamber at the restaurant. In public, she and her trolls send someone else like Antigone to do their dirty work. It's because they're all cowards and they want to maintain the 'welcoming committee' image they've crafted when others are watching.

Too bad I won't break like they want me to. Bigger monsters than them have tried and failed… even with sharper weapons.

"Sherilynn, I—" I'm cut off before I can finish my scathing retort by a flash of rainbow hair and colorful clothes.

Saoirse stands in front of the rail thin bobblehead, her expression full of fury. She's actually smaller than Sherilynn naturally, but the four-inch combat boots' heels bring her eye to eye with Princess Prada. They're like opposite ends of the spectrum: beige Burberry plaid and muted tones to a wild, punky rainbow raver. My bestie raises her hand and pokes the queen bee in the chest with one finger before she speaks.

"You, missus, need to Back. The Fuck. Off. Of. My Girl." Sherilynn looks like she's going to respond, but Seer stops her with another poke.

"I know your people, Foster. I've combed the files and I'm fully aware of what power you *think* you have and what you *actually* have. You may have gathered a cadre of low level hangers-on who are filling your head with delusions of grandeur, but that doesn't make their claims true. You are a self-centered, narcissistic, abusive bully that moves from target to target, pumping your undeserved ego for everything they can give you before you toss them aside for an alternative source. You don't have any power or skill of your own—you suck everyone around you dry, using them until they have nothing left to offer. That's why you have to take your frustrations from life out on others, even if they don't deserve it."

"You're crazy, O' Flanagan. You and that talentless hack you are friends with… you're both the bullies. You're telling everyone lies and making me and everyone who loves this town look bad by slandering us!" Sherilynn's head tilts as she makes that annoying smirk she thinks is cute. "Both of you need therapy and a life so quit being so awful to the people who make this place great."

I arch a brow as she continues to spout a bunch of nonsense full of psychiatric buzzwords and online catch phrases. *Does she think this makes her look more credible? Jesus Christ on melba toast, she sounds like some dipshit on social media waving their ass about shit they have no training in.* This will only make me look better if this devolves further than it already has. I mean, nothing on camera or in writing ever goes away. I guarantee Atwater's has cameras.

"Look, you fruitcake. Every time you approach Jolene like this, you show how incredibly unstable you are. One time, you got spanked by the Council. Since then, you've been coming at her like a stalker off their meds. I get that no one ever has ever called you out on your bullshit successfully because you dirty them up as much as possible so they can't fight back. That won't work this time. So take my advice and back off before one or both of us shows the world what lurks beneath the surface of that Facebook perfect facade. You won't like it when we do."

Something inside of me clicks and I let out a slow breath. It's not the right moment, but I think Seer just gave me an apology that triggered my forgiveness without even saying it out loud.

Damn it.

Movement behind Sherilynn catches my eyes and I see Benjy coming up behind her. I don't know if someone called him or this is fate, but he walks up to the group with a disapproving expression. "Ladies. This is not the place to have a street fight. It would mightily displease Nelia and the Council. I feel the tension in the air and just look at your animals, Jolene."

I blink, looking over my shoulder to see Jekyll, Hyde, Kali, and Hecate standing at the ready with pinned back ears and snarls. They're poised to fight if I give the okay and that would only get all of us in trouble. Sighing, I nod at Benjy and Seer. "He's right. This isn't fair to anyone here nor the Atwater's starting a brawl in their store. Seer, you and I will gather the rest of my stuff and leave. Sherilynn… I say this with the *utmost* disrespect. *Go. Fuck. Yourself.* If you don't stop coming at me, I *will* start caring about destroying you. I don't at the moment, but keep pushing me, and I will start caring."

Seer smirks at her. "You should see what happened to the last person she cared about destroying. It got us kicked out of Thailand. Several intelligence agencies had to cover our exit. It was epic in ways I *still* can't describe. You won't survive it; I guarantee. Your gremlins will flee, your support will vanish, and just like every other 'project' you've tried, you'll find yourself failed and alone."

Benjy gives her a look. "Enough." Turning to me, he pauses before he adds, "A friend as good as her isn't something to toss aside because of a disagreement. You should talk."

I give him a stern look and he shrugs, then takes Sherilynn's arm to lead her away as she complains loudly. That's the second time he's rescued me without asking for anything in return and I'm going to have to have a nice long talk with him, too, I think.

Christ, my life is complicated. I miss being footloose and fancy free.

No, I don't.

Fuck.

Scars to Your Beautiful

I should buy the bootlegger a bloody bottle.

Even with my heartfelt defense, I probably wouldn't have talked Peanut into hearing me out today. His intervention not only cleared that bint out of our airspace, but it forced my girl to allow me access to her as she shopped. Her animals are observing us, and I know they'd get in between us if I upset her. But that's not what I want.

What I want is to explain myself—not to excuse my behavior, but to help her understand my motivations.

"Look…" I pause as I gather my words. "I'm sorry for hurting you. I'm aware you have trust issues for a multitude of reasons from your past, and this cut you to the core. For that, I truly am regretful."

She looks at me with dark eyes, her face creased in a frown. "If you know all of that, it makes it worse, doesn't it?"

"Maybe?" I sigh as I pluck one item on the lists she's holding off the shelf and put it in my trolley. "I don't expect you to forgive my actions right now. I only want to explain what I can and hope we can build a new foundation together. Maybe you'll be able to forgive me later on and if so, we can repair the damage."

Jolene tosses another item into the basket. "You seem to believe that I'm incapable of understanding the explanation Julia gave me. I got it, but that doesn't mean I accept its premise. My best friend and lovers all know some huge secret about me I'm not allowed to know, and they developed relationships with me despite being aware of it. It poisons everything; I feel like everyone I've ever trusted is lying to me. The reason is irrelevant—you're all complicit."

"That's why I want to tell you what I *can* say so we can start… not fresh, but from a more honest place." I stop in front of the travel size display and my brows furrow. "Why are you buying this stuff? Are you going somewhere?"

"I don't believe it's any of your business at the moment," she sniffs. "If you have things to say, do it before we're done or don't do it at all."

Pinching the bridge of my nose, I try to wrangle words in a way that won't get me in trouble, but is also palatable for this public venue. The last thing I need is to get called in front of the damned Council. "We didn't meet by accident all those years ago. They sent me—for reasons you know I can't divulge—and that began the duration of my assignment. However, after spending time with you for a couple of weeks, I started thinking of you less as a project and more as my friend. That emotion grew quickly, and it didn't take long for me to be as devoted to you as my friend as I was to my work. I would have moved back to the States with you, but they ordered me not to."

She whirls around and glares at me. "You told me you had jobs lined up and would visit when you could—but you never did. Was that part of your 'orders', too?"

I nod. "Yes. There was a temporary person who watched when you came home. It's mostly for your safety and you're not the only person who has this type of… detail. I can't explain why or who commands it. But that person should have discouraged you from the path you chose and did not. No one knows why, but they've fallen off the grid since you got rejected and came here."

"What? The other person just disappeared?"

"Yes. There are people looking for them, but it's not been fruitful. That's part of why Julia and the guys traveled to Salem before Halloween. They asked me to join because I have specific skills that assist with tracking people who don't want to be found." Scratching the back of my neck, I ponder for a second and add, "We came back because a lead headed this way and it seemed to be dangerous. I don't know if that situation had anything to do with the fracas at the ball, I swear."

"Did they all know this? All of your shit? The reason for the trip?" Her expression turns unsure and my heart aches for my friend. She clearly loves those men dearly and after my weeks working on the mystery with them, I know they adore her.

"Some of it, not all. I made sure they knew when I'd be gone so they could help keep you safe while we were out of state. Each of them was aware of various amounts of the information based on their ties. We've been sharing more information now because everyone is worried about the creeper, the drugging, and a general unrest that seems to follow you."

Stomping her foot, she growls. "I'll just bet Teddy is neck fucking deep in all of this. His daddy is tied to everything in the fucking universe and the others are less encumbered by glorious purpose because of birth."

Oh, boy, is she wrong about that. Wait till she figures out my fellow fake Irishman.

"Edgar knows a lot. He's pretty ingrained in this shit because of heritage, but the others have their own purposes and duties. Jolene, you must understand that we *will* include you when the time is right. Right now, I honestly believe your lack of knowledge is safer than you realize. There's definitely someone or multiple someones putting pressure on you. Whether it's forcing you into the light or to harm is unclear, even to people who normally know everything. You *not* knowing yet is good—for now."

I walk closer, laying my hand on her arm. "We petitioned to give you more info once the guys started getting close to you, but they denied it. It's not the way things have been done and the people deciding do it for a much larger group than the amount of people living in the Hollow. The needs of the many and all that."

"Bullshit. I've been in many a hallowed hall of old money and influence. Those kinds of people decide based on what benefits *them* the most—never the masses." Jolene crosses her arms over her chest, glaring at me indignantly. "You know that as well as me. We were in those rooms and events *together.* We listened to the elites laugh about the 'little people' and 'peons' while they ate two thousand dollars an ounce of illegally imported caviar, Seer."

She's not wrong.

"I know, Peanut. Trust me, I know. And this... is not that. At least, not most of it. There are definitely *some* assholes like that involved, but the major players are fairly varied and more interested in protecting their people than making money or having influence. I can't explain how I know, but when we can show you, you will understand. I promise."

One cat lets out an irritated sound when she buries her face in her palms and moans in aggravation. When she raises her head, I can see how tired she is. I didn't notice before because I was focused on getting her to listen and then Sherilynn. But Jolene looks bloody exhausted, even if she's not acting like it. I lift my hand and pull back to give her some space. Her smile is grateful for a fleeting second, and it occurs to me she *must* be starting to absorb some of the guys' powers through the mating bonds.

That means pieces of them are in line with her own mysterious heritage.

"I'm being difficult because I'm hurt and I'm tired," she finally says. "I haven't been sleeping well. I don't know why; I slept fine on my own for years before those clowns came busting in."

Chuckling softly, I give her a knowing smile. "It's easy to get used to comfort and support, Peanut. But you need to sleep. Is anything else bothering you? Physically, I mean?"

My question is both out of concern and curiosity. If she's displaying physical quirks beyond what Prez knows about from the night Teddy mated with her, they need to know. A partially emerged, unaware shifter or supe is dangerous to themselves and others. I don't want some dickwad to send a hunting party after her out of spite.

"Yeah. I have weird fucking dreams—sometimes during the day—and I can only remember pieces of them. My body aches like my joints are on fire when I wake up and I've doubled the yoga trying to get it calmed down, but it's not working. I even added a shit ton of herbal stuff to my milkshakes and stuff to ward some of it off. But last night was the first night I slept well in weeks." She looks around for a moment, then pulls her sleeves up, showing me scratched up forearms. "I have this kind of shit everywhere. I'm thinking I'm scratching in my sleep. It must be the anxiety."

Uh, nope. She's shifting after she sleeps and the magic of the town, plus her binding, is keeping her from remembering everything.

"I think you need to visit Prez, Peanut. He might give you something to help you sleep. You can't run like that forever." I pause for a moment before I continue. "You could be… sleepwalking. That's dangerous. What if you fall down the stairs and no one's there? I mean, sure the animals, but by the time they found someone, you could die of a damn brain bleed."

Her skin pales and I know I made my point well. "Shit, Seer, I didn't think about that. I figured it was because of the stress and once I wrapped my head around everything, it would stop. It didn't seem like a big deal."

"It is," I say firmly. "See the doc. It's time you allowed the others to say their piece like I have—even if Benjy had to force it."

Her eyes narrow. "I'll consider it. Don't push me. We're not better yet just because we had this conversation, Saoirse. It's a start, but we still have work to do before I'm comfortable letting you tell me what to do."

I snort. "You're *never* comfortable with people telling you what to do."

That gets a soft laugh, and her expression softens. "Are they taking care of Wolfie and each other? Tell me they're okay."

She hates she feels like she has to ask, I can tell. But she wants to know.

"Yes, your darling boy is being looked after. Between the doc and the judge, he's being coddled to death. But like them, he misses you. They all do, even that assface Irishman."

"Good," she whispers. "I can't face them yet, but I don't want them to be alone."

"You're alone," I retort. "Why is that different?"

Her lips curve up. "Only sort of. I have the animals to keep me company and watch over me, plus other people have poked their heads in."

"Ah-ha. Besides Benjy, the white knight, I assume you've seen the history teacher and the prince, mm?"

Her eyes widen. "How did you know?"

I shrug. "I just do. Don't worry—that's not an issue. The guys won't be upset."

"Good goddess, Seer. How many dudes do they think I can handle? I am *not* adding any other people to my house. It's already a fucking zoo when everyone is in residence."

"Keep telling yourself that, Peanut. You've always been good at tragically lying to yourself." I smirk, then wink at her playfully. "I think you won't be given anything you can't handle—eventually."

Jolene takes in a deep breath and then grabs a few bottles out of the travel bins. "I am *not* caffeinated enough for this shit. Can we finish this list and grab some coffee on the way to my next errand? I'll let you come if you keep behaving."

The smile on my face is so big it feels like it might crack it. "Aye, Peanut. I'll come along for the ride. And coffee sounds like heaven in a cup."

"Let's go, guys," Jolene says as she jerks her head at the animals. "We've got shit to do."

EVERYTHING SUCKS

The errands and coffee turned into an all day adventure as I purchased the things I'd need for a month-long trip overseas. I was careful to omit items that might give away my intentions because I have at least a week before school is out. The things I want that would tip Seer off can be ordered online and until I feel comfortable with other people knowing where I'm headed, I'll sacrifice a convenience for secrecy.

Truth be told, having Seer spend the night while we talked and reminisced about our past helped a lot. I wasn't looking forward to wondering if I'd get a good night's rest when she left. Since she stayed, we might have been up late, but I didn't have confusing dreams or wake up aching. She helped me clean up our mess in the kitchen from cooking dinner and breakfast, then hugged me and left. It surprised me she didn't extend her stay more, but maybe she listened when I said I need time to work through all of my emotions.

I don't know that the guys will be as patient, especially once they find out I've spoken with Seer.

I pop my Airpods in and grab my mat. During the re-model, Teddy insisted we extend the back porch and build an enclosed living area with all the creature comforts for the winter. I thought it was silly and extravagant, but now that it's November and I can set my yoga stuff up outside but not in the cold, I may have changed my opinion. The damn thing even has an electric fireplace and I can let the morning light in by raising the shades.

It figures that asshole would design me the perfect space to meditate and by the time I figure it out, he's made me kick him out.

Jekyll and Hyde perch on the couch, standing at the ready as I turn on the fire and scents. Kali and Hecate hop onto the chairs while Isis and Eury find their own spots. My audience all waits for me to begin, and I chuckle. "I'm going to call Jackson and iron out the details. He was a little blasé when we spoke the other night. I need to make sure he's got everything settled."

"*Mrrp,*" Hyde responds. Barks echo her sentiment, so I know they'll all behave.

Positioning myself on the mat, I reach up and tap the earphone. "Call Jackson." Once the line rings, I forward fall, holding the stretch while I wait for my party loving friend to answer.

"*Hola!* Jackson's Party Line, how may I direct your call?"

Frowning as I wrap my arms around my legs, I snap, "Who is this? Jackson, if you're cheating on Eli, I'll chop your balls off and stuff them somewhere uncomfortable."

"Oooooooo! You *must* be the spicy Jo-Jo. I appreciate the sentiment, but alas, I *am* Eli, and I enjoy his balls where they are currently."

Christ on a unicycle.

I make my way to the floor, lying on the ground as I feel myself connect to my body and the earth. "That's comforting. Can I talk to Jackson, please?"

"You're breathing funny. Either you're exercising or doing something naughty while you're on this call, and I'm definitely hoping for the latter. I'll put this on speaker because Jackson is a little tied up."

"I can call back if you're—"

"Jo-Jo, he's being a shithead. I'm kneading bread dough, not tied up on a St. Andrew," my friend finally calls out.

He's... making bread? I'm much more inclined to believe the silver spoon-fed lawyer is on the aforementioned cross, honestly. "I'm weirded out by that, Jax. You burned water in college."

A deep, knowing sigh echoes over the line. "I will *never* live that down. Yes, Eli has me 'broadening my horizons', which I think is code for living like a normie. So today, we're making bread although we can order, buy, or jet plane to gourmet bread that is *pre-made* by five star chefs. It's quite the *experience*."

I release my foot and muffle my giggle at his ridiculous elitism. Jax isn't really as superficial as he pretends, but he's definitely not someone who's fully in touch with reality. "Eli, I commend your effort and patience. He's useless at everything that doesn't involve partying, shopping, the law, and sex."

"Truer words," the hacker replies. "So, for what do we owe the honor of your call this bright and early?"

"I spoke to him the other night about taking a month-long trip to Istanbul. He said he'd arrange for me to borrow one of the Thorn family jets so I can skirt the hassles at customs about my companions and weapons." I pause for a moment, rolling my eyes at myself. "I sound like some cheesy spy in a movie, but that is the reason."

"We settled that, Jo-Jo. You didn't need to call about it!" Jax yells. "Man, I'm giving my hands a hell of work out here. Poor Eli's sex life is gonna suffer when my fingers won't move for days."

I groan as I push up into a sea lion pose, stretching my lower back. "Gross, Jax. Don't be a perv. I wanted to make sure it would be okay if I maybe— not for sure—added a guest."

"Whiiiiich onnnnne?" he sing-songs. "One of those hunks found his way in the back door… maybe literally."

Eli snorts. "Only if he was lucky, I'm sure."

Hecate save me. I might kill them if they don't stop being so vomit-inducingly cute.

"No back door action here besides me coming out to the porch to do yoga and call you dipshits. But I started a dialogue with Seer and I haven't asked her because I don't want anyone to know, but—"

The snickers on the other end of the line confuse me. Is it funny that I might make up with my best friend? I can never figure out what the hell is going on in Jackson's mind since he and Eli became an item.

"What's so funny?"

"Oh, nothing, Jo-Jo. I'm sure one more person won't be a problem. The plane is pretty big, even with your furry cargo along. I'm sending the larger one because it gets used less. No one will notice it's gone."

Uh…

"Jackson, you *are* informing whoever the hell you need to that it's going to be in use, right?"

"Of course!" I hear a smack that says he's still working on the bread—probably not well. "But I'm going to have the accountants tuck that expense somewhere beneficial to me and I don't want people looking at its destinations too closely."

Great. Now I'm part of his tax scam. Good thing he's my lawyer.

"Okay. Are you working up an info packet with Eli? I'll need everything you can find on the cop, the embassy, and the area we're traveling in. I want to study it all on the long ass plane flight. I plan to be completely ready when I walk onto the tarmac." I lean over and fold my body in half, holding onto my feet. "The more prepared I am, the faster I can accomplish what I came to do. Then I can come home and you won't be worried."

"Fine! Eli will get it all ready and send along the files digitally and by courier in hard copy. But you promise you will not take chances while you're over there. Even if you bring those zoo refugees and your girl, I'm still not convinced it's safe."

"I promise, Jax. I'll stay in touch daily and I'll be careful. It's not my first time overseas or my first time in Constantinople."

"It's Istanbul, not Constantinople," he replies automatically.

I laugh at our nerdiness and reply, "Then I'll be waiting in Istanbul."

ONCE I FINISHED MY MORNING MEDITATION AND THE CONVERSATION WITH Jax, I showered and threw on my painting clothes. I had to be at my studio so Brittania and a few other older students could work on their projects. Since we didn't have school on the Wednesday before Thanksgiving, I volunteered to let them work on their shit while I started the cleanup for the winter break. I'd have to do this much more quickly at the school, but in my space, I can get the place ready for an extended absence.

Luckily for me, the teens were all way too focused on their pieces for exams to be jerks to me. I could get unused spaces straightened, the front gallery ready for another show in mid-January, and answer emails while they worked. When the last kid finally finished cleaning up their spot, I called the pack from the back and closed up. I'll have to do one more run-through before I leave and put a sign in the window, but the first two weeks of Winter Break in the Hollow usually consisted of the rich kids leaving to ski before Christmas and the not rich kids working.

I won't be missed.

The last thing on my list for the day is to file some paperwork with the mayor's office about the closure for the month and I'll be free to head home and veg. I'm thinking I should watch British comedies tonight, and if I order early enough, I can get DoorDash to deliver Chinese from one town over. I've earned a break from all the prep and chaos swirling around me as I go about my week, I think.

It's too cold to walk down to the office, so I load up my crew and drive the short distance to park in front of Town Hall. I buried Isis under my coat, sucking up all of my warmth, and the others are sporting matching sherpa lined fighter pilot jackets I ordered on the 'Zon. I'm sure Teddy has never outfitted his King Danes in anything but their spiky collars, but I refuse to let the wiry-haired guard dogs shiver as the weather gets colder. Plus, I kind of like the look of striding in with an army of leather jacket wearing protectors. It's *trés* West Side Story and if he doesn't like it, he can have a quarter to call someone who gives a fuck.

I walk into the main atrium, looking around for the odious toad who runs the desk. When he appears from behind a curtain, I damn near lose my shit. "Afternoon, Aldous. Were you getting ready to ask who dares approach the great and powerful Oz?"

His glare makes my heart sing. "You should know better than to insult the person who controls access to the building, Miss Whitley. I'll have you know that absolutely no one is available today and you've wasted your time."

Rolling my eyes, I unzip my jacket slightly to allow Isis to peek out. Her low hiss makes him jump, and he leans down to pick up two of the ugliest Sphynx cats I've ever seen. "Jesus Christ in pickle brine! Where did you catch two Gollums with tails?"

"Do *not* say such things about Poe and Parker! They have delicate sensibilities!"

Give me a break.

"I need to see the Mayor. I'm sure she has time for me. It will only take a moment, Aldous." I tilt my head and give him the patented, bitchily polite

Southern smile. "I doubt you want my overprotective gang of beasts around your precious…" I have to stop because my own unintentional pun cracks me up and I cover my mouth to keep from snorting.

"I never! You are the rudest little tra—"

A voice echoes in the wood paneled room, cutting him off. "Aldous, I hope to Hades you aren't going to finish that sentence the way I think you are."

My eyes widen and I look up at the staircase to the upper level to see Doyle smirking down at us.

Fuck, fuck, fuckitty, fuck, fuck.…

"I don't take orders from you, Haggerty. I'm only beholden to the May—"

Aldous' face turns red, and he chokes, his whole body shaking as he tries to breathe. The red-haired man descends the stairs slowly, his expression bland as he holds a hand to his ear. "I'm sorry, Longworth, I don't believe I can hear you. Do you need some water?"

The malevolent little Oompa Loompa glares at us and continues, trying to catch his breath. His cats hiss and jump from his arms, abandoning him to curl up in a bed near the curtain. When he turns purple, I look at the gleeful man I didn't intend to see today with concern.

"I hate this motherfucker, but maybe we should do the Heimlich. If he dies in front of me, I'll have to feel guilty."

"Oh, fine." Doyle sighs and walks over to the water pitcher on the sideboard.

The blockage seems to clear up immediately and Aldous takes the glass my lover offers with a murderous look in his eyes. "I'll get you for that, you nasty man."

Again, I'm reminded of the *Wizard of Oz* and I almost lose it. "Doyle, is Nelia up stairs? I need to speak with her."

"Aye, love. You go on up with your beasties and I'll stay here to help our struggling friend."

That doesn't sound sinister at all.

I decide I hate Aldous just enough to ignore my bad feeling. "Thanks. Come on, guys. We have to get this done before we can go home and relax."

Doyle waves as I turn on my heel and head upstairs, but I can feel his eyes on me the entire way.

Something tells me he will not stay away for much longer.

Love The Way You Lie

Doyle

The people in this town are infuriating, but my auntie won't allow me to deal with them in a manner befitting my bloodline. So I let that weasley little shite off with a warning that would have turned his hair white if it wasn't already. I've never liked his smarmy, entitled attitude, but I draw the fucking line at him calling my woman a tramp to her face.

It should have earned him a punishment equivalent to having his liver eaten daily only to regrow, but my hands are tied.

However, I sent Odie up to listen in at the Mayor's door while I took out the trash, and what he found out set me on the path I'm taking now. My raven is accustomed to sneaking around and staying out of sight—something that comes in very handy in this town. Most people don't even realize he's a companion, much less that he belongs to me. It's useful in more ways than I can count, as is the fact that he can show me what he sees when I send him out to spy.

Yes, yes. I'm aware some gits stole the old ways for a hit TV show. I'd like to smite Holly-wood, too, but again… auntie says 'no'.

I walk behind the column, waiting for Aldous to disappear into his cubby hole again and then disappear. I'm also not supposed to use portal jumps to travel here, but I can only follow so many rules before I want to test my immortality. It's bad enough that I'm stuck in Hicksville, USA, with these rich first and second gen supes who think money makes them untouchable, but limiting the use of my powers makes it so much worse.

Appearing on my front porch, I yank the door open and stalk inside. "Oh, LUCYYYYY, I'm HOOOMME!"

Wolfgang's head pops over the upper railing, and it occurs to me that Prez calls him that. He probably thought I meant for just him to come running, but I want these assholes to get down here. It's time for a family meeting.

"Oi! Boone, Hamilton! You, too. Family meeting or some shit," I yell as I walk into the lounging room. It's not a living room—all rooms are bloody living rooms if it's not a goddamned funeral home. I'll fight people on that because I'm old enough to remember when words weren't ridiculous. Pouring myself a Jameson, I realize I'll need to calm my ire before I set the alpha dog and his pups off with my bristly attitude.

When they finally file in, I plop onto one of the huge lounges, moving all the materials we've been using to research aside. "We need to talk."

"I gathered that, given your bellowing," Boone replies as he walks over and pours his bourbon. He looks at the other two and when they nod, he procures two more.

What a soft Dom that git is. He's taking care of them like he's claimed them both.

I pause my thoughts before they derail by shaking my head. It wouldn't be the first time I lost focus because I found something to poke at; I live for causing chaos and I haven't done nearly enough of it today. "Right before I left, our girl came in to talk to Nelia. I used Odie to listen in because I was busy taking care of an insect that needed to be squashed. But what he heard is important."

"What did he hear?" Wolfie asks as he accepts the drink from Edgar. The judge drops down next to him and he curls in between the two of them like a cat.

I'm feeling left out, and that irritates the shit out of me.

"I'm getting there. He showed me their conversation, and it sounds like she's planning to take off somewhere for the month you gits are off school. Shr didn't say *where* she's going, but it sounds like she intends to go without telling us."

Boone chuckles, looking at the vet with a smirk. "I know where she's going."

Prez and I both look at him in surprise. I run my hand through my hair and pace, trying not to take my frustration out on them. I hate not being in control. "Did a cat get your tongue or are you going to tell the rest of the class?"

"You just got home, Haggerty. Chill. I was going to call this meeting, too." Edgar stretches his legs out on the ottoman and stacks his hand behind his head. "Jackson called this morning. Tilly asked him to borrow one of his jets so she can go overseas with the pets."

"*Where* overseas?" Presley asks. He sips the bourbon calmly, but I can tell he's not happy.

"Istanbul," Wolfie supplies. "She's obviously going to look for that cop."

My temper flares and a burst of magic flares over me. "What?!"

"Calm down, Hades," Edgar says with a smirk. "Cool your godly bullshit. I took care of it."

"How?"

He grins at Presley and ruffles Wolfie's hair. "The same way I always do. With wit, charm, and a little pressure applied in the right places. Thorn will let us hop along over on his plane with her, but we have to go convince her to let us come."

Squinting, I look at the lounging alphahole like he's either simple or idiotic. "She barely spoke to me today. Exactly how do you plan on convincing her to allow us to escort her on a trip she's purposely kept secret from us?"

Boone just smirks and the other two look at one another before they say, "Wit, charm, and a little pressure applied in the right places."

"Gag me with a spoon, Doubledick Twins." I shake my head and let the magic coursing over recede. "That's not going to work."

"Care to place a wager on it, Haggerty?" The dark-haired judge is in his element now. Gambling is his third favorite vice, and he definitely knows how to play the odds.

But I know entropy like it's part of my DNA.

"Fine, I'll play along. But when she throws us out on our arses, you all have to post a video extolling your virtues on social media."

"Agreed," he grins. "But if you lose, deal with the animal clean-up for the entire trip."

I nod and jerk my head at the door. "Let's ride, fuckers. I can't wait to see Edgar discussing how magnificent my cock is on TikTok."

"You wish," is all he says as he struts towards the front door.

Huh. Maybe. We'll see Teddy bear.

WHEN WE ARRIVE AT MY TÍOGAIR'S HOUSE, I'M ABOUT AS HYPER AS I CAN BE without being destructive. It hurt a little to see her and have her look through me, but we all knew she was going to be angry. Normally, I would have stormed the gates and ignored the wishes of the person keeping me from what I want, but with Jolene… I don't want to fuck this up.

I've never felt like that before—not once in all the millennia I've been kicking around this spinning ball.

"I hope your fecking plan works," I grumble as we tumble out of the car. "Because I'm in no mood to get kicked to the curb."

"You need to calm down," Presley says quietly. "It's obvious that you're on the edge. That won't help anything. Take a couple of breaths and get it together."

My eyes narrow, but I nod sharply. He's not wrong and if it had been Boone who said it, I would have punched him. Luckily, the birdman and the Fae are the more placid of the four of us. "I'm trying. If I'd know we were going to do this, I might have burned some of this shit off, but you kept it to *yourself.*"

Edgar stops, rubbing the back of his neck. "Shit. I probably should have texted, but I didn't want to interrupt people since both of you had busy days. I wasn't actually hiding anything."

Again, Presley and I look at each other in shock.

Wolfie looks up at the judge and squeezes his hand. "That was good."

I'll be damned. The subbie is taming the big bad hellhound. Will wonders never cease?

"I appreciate that, Edgar, but personally, Jolene is always worth an interruption." The doc pushes up his glasses and looks at me. I nod in agreement and he continues. "Keep us all in the loop. Because if Doyle is right and there are more who will join, we will *have* to communicate."

"Bugger, don't remind me," I groan. "Four is hard enough at the bloody moment. Seven is going to be a feckin' nightmare."

"Uh, guys?" We look at Wolfie as he points at the front door. "We've been spotted."

I swear, it's like I hear the fucking death knell in my ears as we all trudge up the driveway to the porch.

"I don't recall extending an invite," my Tíogair says as we filter in and find seats among the various companions lounging on her furniture.

Looking around, I see she ordered Chinese and has been indulging in several flavors of milkshakes while she watched comfort movies. The scattered pillows and blankets tell me she's not sleeping in her room and, for a moment, guilt races through me. It's not an emotion I've felt often in my many years and I ponder the changes in me since I met the raven haired woman who's still grumbling at us. I didn't think it was possible to change beings as old and set in our ways as me, but here she is, barely a few decades old and dressing me down like a kid.

I'll be a two headed goat.

"Tilly," Edgar says, finally cutting off the flow of her irritable babbling. "We didn't come to make trouble, but there's no way in hell we can let you go overseas by yourself with all the shit that's happened."

Her eyes blaze and I grin as I see the hound he tries so hard to suppress flare up in our girl as easily as breathing. Jolene is going to be an absolutely stunning force of nature when her powers all emerge. She won't hesitate for a second to turn someone to ash if they make her angry—I can hardly wait. "*Let me?!!*"

I suck a slow breath in through my teeth and look at the docs with a smirk. The chaos is about to begin and it's making my blood hum. *This* is why I made the bet with dog breath; I knew he'd come on so strongly that our girl would lose her mind. Amping up the tempers in the room is *bound* to make for fun and games—something I didn't get nearly enough of today to feed my hunger.

None of them understands how much I thrive off of the energy that unpredictable mania gives off.

"I don't think he meant—" Wolfie starts, but her cutting glare cuts him off. He ducks his head, cheeks flushing as he shuts his mouth.

"It's not *safe*," Boone huffs as he looks at the three of us for support. "Hell, running around in other countries alone isn't safe for most humans, but definitely not for someone with a propensity for stumbling into trouble. Don't get me started on the stalker we haven't identified yet."

Presley pauses for a moment, then finds his spine. "It worries me, too, magpie."

She puts her hands on her hips, the fury in her aura swirling around her like a whirlwind. They can't see it, but I can, and it's magnificent. "Tíogair, no one is saying you can't take care of yourself, per se…"

Sue me, I'm fomenting the delicious dissent because I know where it's going.

"Per se???!!" she practically screeches. Her cats jump up, hair standing on end, and the snake on the floor slithers towards her like a homing missile.

Wolfie tries again, rising to his feet as he holds a hand out. "Sugarplum…"

"Don't. Patronize. Me. Wolfie."

I grin as that fire in her eyes flames up again, and the air thickens. Looking over at Edgar, I can see the ripples of his supe sides pushing at him. His jaw is set, fists are clenched, and his entire body is tense. A glance at Hamilton tells me he's having trouble as well. All is on schedule—the more Jolene's supernatural sides demand to be set loose, the more her mates and future mates will feel the burn to allow theirs to emerge as well. She might not remember a second of it tomorrow, but the effects of this will help us all move on.

Jolene walks away from the vet, striding over to our resident hellhound and bending to get in his face. I almost clap my hands in glee; this is perfect. "You four lost the right to have a say in where I go or what I do when you spent months *lying to me.*"

Edgar's hand shoots out, grabbing her shirt and hauling her onto his lap in a straddle. His other buries in her hair, wrapping it around his fist to pull her face back so he's looking up at her. "Not by *choice*. After our past, I would never do anything to hurt you again by *choice*. All I want to do now is protect what is *mine.*"

"I don't belong to anyone," Jolene spits back.

The scent of everyone's arousal fills the air, and I observe carefully. There will be a precise moment when I can allow my magic to spill, and that will be the tipping point. I have to do it at exactly the right moment, though, or it won't work.

Patience isn't my strong suit, so it's killing me.

"We all belong to someone, Sugarplum," Wolfie says as he approaches. He looks down at her as Boone holds her hair tightly, his expression serious. "There are three types of family: those you're born to, those you give birth to, and those you accept into your heart when you find them. The last one is us—you found all of us and now we're a family."

Her expression softens for a moment as she looks up at the Fae and I know the moment I'm waiting for is getting close. "Goddamnit, Wolfie…"

The growly hound she's perched on takes that opening, burying his face in her neck and nipping at it before he lifts his head again. "You're mine. He's mine. These idiots are mine."

There's the full on doggy, but I'm waiting for contestant number two.

The doc stands up, heading over to wrap his arms around Wolfgang as he looks down at our girl as well. "As poetic as that was, you're all mine, too. Don't you feel the same?"

She wants to keep fighting because her human side says there needs to be more words, more groveling, and more begging for forgiveness. But the truth is, forgiveness isn't supposed to be about demanding subjugation in exchange for approval. Sometimes, it's about accepting when people admit their mistakes and setting boundaries for the future. Maturity is knowing how to allow others grace when they fuck up without expecting people you love to prostrate themselves for failing.

I'm interested to see what my Tiogair chooses.

"I owe all of you an apology as well."

That garners a chorus of denials from the three men surrounding her, but I stay quiet. I want to hear what she has to say.

Jolene rolls her eyes up to look at the docs, then back down to Edgar, and over to me briefly. "I lashed out because it hurt me. My trauma from Trevor and the betrayal in the present collided to trigger the shit out of a wound I thought was long healed. I should have allowed you to explain, not sent you all packing without a word. It was unfair and I'm sorry for it."

Boone blinks, looking at Prez and Wolfie. They seem equally confused by the situation, and I sigh heavily. You'd think being one of the Greeks, I'd have the most dysfunctional family, but obviously, I don't. None of them know how to take someone taking accountability for their actions like a fucking adult.

"I accept your apology, Tíogair," I reply as I tilt my head. "I'm not ashamed that I could not be totally honest with you, but I am quite regretful that it hurt you. That I won't be able to give you everything you want despite this lovely conversation irks me as well. I'm displeased, but my hands are tied—not in a good way, either."

Someone had to address the elephant in the room.

"Don't be an ass, Haggerty," Edgar growls as he shifts under her. The movement pulls a groan from Jolene and his lips curve up. "Otherwise this won't end with nudity."

"Oh, I'm not worried about that." Our girl didn't protest at his remark and *this* is the opening I was waiting for. "Not when she's practically dripping for us over there."

Her head whips to the side to give me a dirty look, making Edgar's hold on her pulled harder. The sensation makes her gasp softly and the chain reaction starts. Presley hauls the vet against him and kisses him hard. The snarling judge tugs her back to kiss her roughly, and I stack my heads behind my head in satisfaction. All I have to do now is give the darker parts of my makeshift family a wee nudge and this will be grand.

"*Apeleftheróste ti nýchta mésa…*[1]"

As soon as the words leave my mouth, the darkness descends like a familiar blanket.

It's about to get very interesting in this house.

---

1. Unleash the night within…

I Wanna Be Your Slave

Jolene

There's no time to question what the hell Doyle just said because Teddy yanks me forward by the hair and kisses me like he's trying to swallow me whole. A jolt of energy sparks over my skin and it sets me on fire from head to toe. Wriggling my hips over the very noticeable erection I'm perched over, my mouth clashes violently with his as lips, teeth, and tongues battle for dominance. My fingers dig into his shoulders and my back arches, making the sting on my scalp intensify.

Holy Aphrodite in a brothel. I think I almost came just now.

Shivers run through me as I lament the impending death of the lingerie I'm wearing. There's no way any of it making it out intact, not with the sounds Teddy is making and the scent of my boys' arousal behind me. I vaguely hear tearing and zippers, then a dark moan of pleasure. Wolfie is definitely on his knees; I know what it sounds like when Prez is getting head and he's making those lovely little chirps and gasps. When Teddy tugs my head back, his eyes are almost black and his expression is hungrier than I've seen. It's like whatever the fuck Doyle muttered unleashed something in him and it's ready to feast.

His hands frame my hips, lifting me up to sit me on the couch facing the back of it. "Put your hands on the back and your ass in the air, *drugar*."

I don't always take orders, but fuck, he's hot right now.

I place my hands on the back cushions, holding on them as I position myself as instructed. Looking over my shoulder, I see Presley with his hands buried in Wolfie's hair, guiding his head as he sucks him off like a pro. That makes my pussy throb—the sight of them is always hot, but the adoration my little vet has gleaming in his eyes as he looks up at the doc is breathtaking. A sharp slap on my ass brings me back to focus, and I see Teddy standing behind me with that wicked look on his face.

"Good girls get to watch. You haven't earned it yet, Tilly. Turn around."

Fuck. Me.… please.

Shades of the first night I was home and he damn near destroyed me flash before my eyes, so I do as I'm told eagerly. Doyle suddenly appears in front of me, his cock out in his hand as he strokes it roughly. His smile is just as dark and delicious as my ex-bully's and I realize I'm about to have a *very* rough ride.

"Open those pretty lips, Tíogair. I'm going to watch him fuck you senseless while you suck me off. If you're good, we might even let Hamilton and the pup join in when they're done. Do you want that? Do you want to be completely filled?"

My eyes widen as another burst of energy pushes against my skin, making me even wetter. I don't know how they're doing this, but I'm gonna leave a spot on this couch for sure. "Yessss…"

"Then open your mouth, Tilly," Teddy says. He doesn't wait for me to respond. He simply reaches down and rips the crotch out of my silky PJ pants with one yank.

As if this couldn't get any fucking hotter.

I open my mouth, darting my tongue out to lick the moisture on the tip of Doyle's cock. He grunts and tugs on my hair roughly, making me wiggle my ass in the air. Being exposed while my cunt is dripping with arousal and the room is filled with lovely moans is making me clench inside. I need something and for now, this is what I'm getting, so I wrap my lips around him. Swallowing him down as far as I can immediately, I revel in the sound he makes as my tongue teases over the vein on the underside. I rub against it slowly, breathing in his scent as I slide back and bob over his dick.

"That's my girl," Teddy murmurs. "Keep taking him while I get you ready."

There's no mistaking what the means because I'm soaked, so he's definitely planning on fucking my ass. My lower body pulses again as I moan around Doyle. I'm not sure what's going to happen after tonight, but for the moment, all I can think or feel is this connection we all have. The desire is so thick that it's choking me almost as much as Lucky's cock, and I have no idea how I'm going to walk tomorrow.

Cool gel makes me gasp and I feel fingers working in and out of my ass slowly, scissoring as they stretch me. This is not my first time—thank fuck—but it's been a little while. I push back into his digits and Doyle thrust into my mouth at the same time. He brushes the back of my throat, but I breathe through it as tears fall from my eyes. When the fingers slip away, I look up at my Irish firebrand and for a second, I see a flash in his eyes I haven't seen before. He lets out a soft huff, pausing his thrusts as he stares at me.

"There she is," he whispers. His eyes tear away from mine to look behind me. "She's ready, Boone. Do it now and don't hold back. Take what you need."

Teddy's cock slams into me almost immediately and I cry out, the sound vibrating over Doyle's dick as it pushes further into my throat. It feels like I'm being split open as the dominant behind me stops when he's fully seated inside of me. His voice is raspy when he replies. "Hamilton, let the pup wiggle under her. I want to feel him push against me while we fuck our woman. He can keep sucking you once he's in position."

Oh. My. Goddess.

I close my eyes, letting them run the show completely. My teeth graze over Doyle when I feel Wolfie slide under me with more ease than I would have expected. Within seconds, the feel of his ladder sliding inside me damn near sends me over the edge. I've been holding on as the boys took control, but something about this room on this night is making me crazy. I'm going to come soon and I won't be able to stop it.

Another groan tells me my little Wolfie has Presley taken care of next to us. I run my teeth over Doyle's shaft lightly, loving how his hips buck in response. All of them surrounding makes my chest ache and I almost get teary-eyed for a very different reason. Humming softly, I push my hips down and back, reveling in the stretch. If Doyle wasn't fucking my mouth, I'd tell them how good this feels, but I can't, so instead, I let go of our problems to live in the moment.

"There we go, pup. Fuck, I love feeling you push me against while we do this. Suck on Presley's cock so daddy can watch." Another burst of arousal that makes me clench around them and suck hard on Doyle follows his words.

Shit. I was sure I didn't think the daddy thing was sexy, but day-yum when he says it to Wolfie....

Every inch of my body trembles at his words and the orgasm crashes into me before I know it. Squeezing both of them as the pleasure crawls over my skin, I have to consciously hold Doyle deep in my mouth as the muffled sounds escape me. Teddy's fingers dig into my hips hard, bruising my skin as he leans down and puts his nose next to my ear. I can vaguely hear some foreign words and then yet another orgasm slams into me. His lips land on a spot on my neck, and the oddest sensation takes over.

"Fuck, Boone, you might have triggered one…"

Doyle's voice sounds awfully far away for someone who has their dick in my mouth. The crawling under my skin gets more intense and I rock back into Teddy, then forward into Wolfie, spearing myself on them as I blindly work my mouth over the shaft in it. It feels like I'm chasing *their* climaxes now and though my vision is getting foggy,. I keep moving until I hear each of them make the telltale sound that signals the crest has hit them.

Pulling my head back, I swallow the evidence with a drowsy smile, squinting my eyes as I try to focus on the shadowy figure that is my fiery lover. "That wassss hottttt…"

It's all I can manage at the moment, but I feel the guys withdraw, and powerful arms lifting me up from the couch.

"You lose, Haggerty. Clean the fucking couch."

Even when we're not fucking, Teddy's an alpha asshole.

My eyes close and I let them take me wherever they want. I'm so lazy and buzzing with pleasurable sensations that I don't have it in me to fight. Just for tonight, I'm letting them be in charge while I rest for a bit…

MY EYES FEEL GRITTY WHEN I OPEN THEM AND I HAVE BLINK THEM SEVERAL times to see the room.

I try to move, and every single muscle in my body screams. It feels like someone tore me limb from limb and reassembled me—poorly. Tilting my head a little, I squint at the new view of the room, noting that it's completely trashed.

What the shit? I know they fucked the bitch out of me, but what fresh hell is this?

The fuzziness in my brain frustrates me and I loll my head to the other side, wincing as my neck protests. I know for sure I've never in my life had sex so gymnastic that I can't even turn my fucking head in the morning. These assholes have some explaining to do. Both me and my fucking living room are *destroyed,* and I can't seem to remember how it happened.

"Don't worry, sugarplum." His mumble comes from my left armpit and I carefully arrange myself so I can look down at Wolfie.

"Easy for you to say," I croak weakly.

A rumbling chuckle vibrates under my cheek and I realize Wolfie is curled up between Teddy and I. That means the body behind me is likely Doyle and Prez must be the one with his head on my stomach.

That's why it's hot as fuck in here. Too many bodies cocooning me.

"Gonna need air. You fuckers are roasting me." My eyes close and I smile a little, feeling better now that I can snipe at them a little.

Doyle leans over and presses a kiss to my temple. "Says the chit who *insisted* we make a nest on the floor to sleep on."

I did? Why the fuck wouldn't I want to go upstairs?

"Leave her be," Presley chides as he yawns against my skin. "She'll need to eat. We all do. Last night consumed a lot of energy."

"Thank you, Doctor McNuggies. Your clinical opinion is noted," I grumble. How do they know what happened and I'm drawing a fucking blank... as *always.*

"You haven't called me that in a while, magpie. I enjoy hearing your sass."

"You're gonna love when I let you dipshits have it for whatever the fuck went on in this room. All I can see is broken shit and torn up shit and it smells like a French cathouse in here. Ugh..."

They all laugh and I sigh deeply. Men will always preen at evidence of their sexual prowess, even if it gets them kicked in the balls. Which, to be honest, is looking like a distinct possibility if their smugness isn't dialed down a notch by the time I can move again.

"Pup, you and the other doc start breakfast. We have to feed this woman before she'll be capable of kicking our asses the way she wants to." Teddy rolls to the side and tugs me free of the pile. I glare at him because even that hurts like a bitch, but it's nothing compared to the sound I make when he bends down and hefts me up. Throwing me over his shoulder with my bare ass pointed at the group, he gives it a slap. "C'mon you lazy shits. Time to take care of our girl."

My mouth drops open and I protest, especially because now my ass is *cold*, but he rubs his hand over the spot soothingly and all the angry words disappear.

Fucking sex wizards, that's what they are.

"I'm not eating at the table naked!" I grumble against his back.

"Of course not. We're sitting at the counter," Doyle says cheerily.

"Find her robe, Haggerty. While you're at it, find us all pants. No one needs to eat naked unless they're at a hippie commune."

"Fine. But I already paid my debt!"

I raise my hand to pinch the bridge of my nose. If I had any idea what was going on, I'm sure I'd be much more irritated. As it is, I'm watching hot guys parade around my kitchen, flashing their biteable asses at me.

Maybe knowing what's going on is overrated.

TROUBLEMAKER

Lucy is a fantastic chef and I'm little more than his line cooks, but he whips up all of our girl's favorites with ease. Waffles, scrambled eggs, bacon, sausage links, and a pitcher of milkshakes that smell fruity and flowery at the same time grace the counter. Doyle found everything we needed to cover the important parts, though every time Magpie stops talking mid-sentence to watch one of our asses in the boxer briefs, I have to cover my mouth. She won't like the teasing, but I can tell she likes the view.

"More eggs, please," she says, wiping her mouth on the fancy napkins Lucy picked out of her drawers.

I grin, taking her plate and heaping more protein on it, including more bacon. Boone has her settled firmly on his lap and she's not moving anytime soon. He kept her hanging with her ass in the air until we sat down and no amount of wiggling deterred him. I know why, of course. Jolene can't see it because of the binding, but his eyes are still pitch black and he's still feeding off the sexual energy coming for her as she ogles us.

I wasn't the town doc when he emerged, but whoever was should be whacked over the head with a SMDM 2022.

No caladrius alive would have allowed him to emerge with two sides, but never learn to control one of them. That's not even addressing how he hid a *third side*, but I plan on having a talk with Andromeda Bane when she's back from her latest trip to Salem. I know the last doc here wasn't one of my kind

—he was a centaur because there wasn't an available caladrii when the doctor before him finally passed away. That doesn't excuse not keeping up with the yearly version of the *Supernatural & Magical Diagnostic Manual*. Taking care of emerging supes is our primary role in the enclaves, and that idiot clearly failed on multiple accounts.

"You can have as much as you want, magpie. We wore you out last night; it's probably still *draining your energy*," I say carefully. My eyes meet Edgar's and his face flushes a light pink. He'll never admit out loud that he's going to have to learn to control the incubus as well as he does the hound and the Quetzalcoatl. Though, I kind of wonder if he knows how to control the bird now, too.

Great. I've helped Lucy learn his mother's side and now I have to help Jolene and Edgar with their beasts.

"He's right, Tilly. We love watching you refill the tank after we… filled your tank." He smirks, but I see the glimmer of recognition in his eyes.

"Don't be gross, Teddy." Jolene leans back and rubs her nose on his jawline. "It's unbecoming."

"I'll be coming soon en—"

"No." Lucy points a piece of bacon at Doyle. "Bad."

Our girl giggles, and the sound makes my heart jump. I've missed her so much—we all have—and being here for the breakfast routine is familiar and comforting. "He's right. No jizz jokes at the table, please. We don't even have pineapple."

Doyle roars in laughter, rocking back on the legs of his chair. "Nice one, love. These idjits have no sense of humor. It'll be nice to be back with someone who does."

Her brow arches and she gives him a pointed look, then turns to pin each of us as well. "Last night, at least what I can remember of it, was amazing. I hurt, but it's a good ache and I'm enjoying breakfast. But you're not totally forgiven, and no one is coming home yet. I need to rebuild the trust we had before I can commit to that."

Edgar tightens his arms around her, frowning darkly. That's the hound, not the incubi, and I give him a warning look. "You're all mine."

"Yes, cave-Teddy, but I need—"

"No," he growls low. "No more separation."

Uh-oh. Lucy and Magpie got him to let the dark sides out and now he's even more of a possessive dickhole.

"Sugarplum, maybe we can sort this out after the trip." I grin as my peacemaker looks at the two of them with his patented, adorable smile. "Surely you can invite us to come along now? At least we'll know you're safe and it will make the sleuthing easier with more people."

Her brow furrows, and she thinks about it for a long moment. I watch Doyle and Edgar stare intently while Lucy just smiles prettily. At least one of us knows how to get our girl on his side. The frowning twins are going to piss her off—she's never going to let them tell her what to do when we're not in the bedroom. Personally, I like both of the facets of her personality, but then, I'm as much a switch as she is.

"Okay," she sighs. "You can all come. But you have to give me space when I need it. *And* you have to remember that they have trained me in weapons, combat, martial arts, and a slew of other things. I *can* take care of myself and did for years. Sure, I had Seer with me and I guess she was… watching me to help keep me safe or something? But even she would tell you I saved her ass just as much as she saved mine."

It looks like Boone is going to argue, so I jump in. "We understand. And I remember you hitting those damn cans from that distance in the backyard. Edgar wasn't here, but I don't know a lot of women who can hit all twenty-four targets with a Macmillan, like you did."

"I'm sorry, she what?"

Jolene's laugh is dark as she turns to look at him. "You, Teddy bear, haven't seen me shoot *or* fight. All you want to do is knuckle drag and beat your chest."

The change in the atmosphere is palpable, and I wink at Lucy. He did a good job of getting her to agree to us joining her, and I could calm the volatile judge down. So far, this morning is a win. If I can figure out how to get a message to Saoirse so she fills in the other 'candidates' in our supernatural bachelorette, we'll be on track.

"Haggerty, can you work on gathering paperwork for us to travel?"

Oh, that's a good question.

"I'm sure I can get us cleared. We'll all need physicals before we go, though, including you, Tíogair."

The Irishman looks at me, then darts his eyes to Jolene. I frown. *Why is he giving me that look?* Physicals aren't required by the Society or USCIS, so I have no idea why he's trying to act like it's necessary. "Uh, well. I'm sure I can fit everyone in tomorrow morning since the office is supposed to be closed over the holiday weekend…"

"Grand. It's settled then." He looks over at our girl, noting she's wolfed down her second portion and smile. "Boone, since you won, why don't you and our girl get showered while we clean up the kitchen?"

"Hey! I cooked and the rules are——"

I shake my head at Lucy. Doyle didn't lose a bet about house cleaning and he wouldn't take anything on willingly. He's got a reason for specifically asking the two of us to stay behind and I bet it is his 'physicals' charade. "It's okay, baby. Let Edgar take her up to get squeaky and when they come back, we can start ordering stuff for the trip."

His nose wrinkles, but I think he finally understands because he rises, pouring Jolene another milkshake. "Take this one to go, sugarplum."

"I swear this tastes like actual fucking spring, Wolfie. I don't know how you did it." His cheeks flush adorably and she laughs softly. "I love when you do that."

"It's the praise, you know," Doyle says with a smirk. "He responds to it. Tell him how good he is and you get a pink puddle of goo."

Edgar grins as he leans in and whispers something in Magpie's ear and suddenly, her cheeks turn pink as well. "Would you look at that? It works on Tilly, too."

Such a showoff, but you can't fault his methods.

"Go, you brute," I say, waving at him dismissively. "She needs a bath more than a shower. I can sense her aches and pains. Keep her company for a nice long soak and we'll deal with the downstairs."

"Are you su——-oooh, Teddy!"

The yelp of surprise as she's slung over his shoulder and hefted off yet again makes us all smile.

He's going to get his ass kicked one day.

ONCE THEY'RE GONE, WE CLEAR THE TABLE AND I WATCH DOYLE AS HE paces. Finally, I can't stand it anymore. "Doyle, why did you want to get us alone? Are you going to share with the class?"

"Buckle up, docs. I'm not sure if I'm right or what the feck all this means. Even for me, we're in uncharted waters. By Hephaestus' beard, I don't know if they have ever charted it."

Dramatic prat.

"Calm down and talk to us," Wolfie says as he stacks plates along his arm and takes them to the sink. "I assume it will not kill anyone or you wouldn't have sent them up to play in bubbles."

His lips curve up. "You know, I like it when you're a wee bit saucy, Fletcher. It's fun."

I roll my eyes and sigh. "Yes, it is. Now spill it for fuck's sake."

Doyle plops back into his chair and leans back precariously. "See, I've been curious. It seems like our girl is mating with all our bloody parts, which is rare enough. It requires some sort of... compatibility on her end with various things, as far as I know. And we don't have a ruddy clue what her lineage is."

"Uh-huh," I say, wiping the table while I think about it. "What significance are you attaching to that?"

"So far, you say she mated with the Fae and Boone's hound. I *know* she got the incubi last night and I'm damn sure she activated my mother's side before. Maybe that binding we're trying to investigate won't be released until *all* the mating's done. I mean, I don't know if her supe sides have to be reciprocated and emerged or if it's all of our shit, but it seems like every time one of us seals a mark, she seems to see a little bit more than she did the last time."

I frown. "And she gains shit she doesn't realize she has. Like the shifting after Edgar and the calling of animals near Wolfie, and..."

He smirks. "Oh, she definitely has serpentine eyes before she was out the first time last night and the *second* time, I think she was emitting as much buzz as the judge."

"That's dangerous as hell," Wolfie says. "I mean, she doesn't know any of this exists and she still can't see any of it happening. She has no idea she's wielding her companions like weapons or running through the woods at night."

We both whip our heads around and look at him in shock. He shrugs. "It's a rumor I heard. A new, big black dog in the woods at night with a pack. People haven't connected to Teddy or her or even come close enough to realize the pack isn't all dogs. I've been guiding people towards believing Kali or Hecate are out for a stretch."

Wiping my hands over my face, I groan. "Fuck, Lucy. We needed to know that. I mean, that's why she's not sleeping. If she's shifting and running all night and doesn't remember, no wonder she looked zombified this week."

He loads the dishes in the dishwasher and shrugs. "If I thought she was in trouble, I would have. We all know she's going to do better if she gets her subconscious used to this before she emerges. None of us were locked down or watched over so closely when I was pre-emergence."

"Love," I say softly. "Your mother… I mean, Aurelia was…"

"I know she was losing her marbles. I had to have her put in the home before I was sixteen. But I mean, even the other kids my age weren't monitored that closely. Supes need to find their way," he replies. "Shifting or playing with their magic on their own is part of that."

Fuck. That old doctor let these kids just run around figuring shit out on their own.

"That codger who worked here really did screw up three generations of hybrids before I got here. Didn't he?" I mutter.

Lucy laughs. "Hell, you should have seen how the hybrids, even five years older than Teddy and sugarplum, behaved. They were wild as shit and when they left, many rumors flew. Few ever came back."

"I can't imagine why," Doyle snorts. "Being allowed to free hand magic and shifting and fuck knows what else probably has them out doing ridiculously unethical shit in the real world. They weren't given boundaries and I suspect you'd find none of them even understand what they mean."

"Maybe." Wolfie takes the rest of the dishes we brought over off the counter. "Thorn is one of them."

Well, that explains a hell of a lot.

Human

It took some convincing, but I got the boys to go back to whence they came that night. I spent most of the day with them, including the invigorating soak in my tub, while Teddy read to me. But I just couldn't allow things to slip back into place completely yet. I'm not *angry*, but I'm not healed enough to jump in with both feet.

I met them at Prez's office the next morning and let him run a full court press on me and I let Wolfie cook us all a lovely yet non-traditional Thanksgiving dinner that evening. All I can do is give them as much as I'm comfortable with and, for the moment, that's my body and my time. My heart isn't there yet—not that I harbor any illusions about how I truly feel about all of them. I can't think about it yet, much less admit it out loud, and that's not fair to them. I want it to be solid when they come back to the home we're building.

Christ in a cartoon. Listen to me. This is why I can't let them stay in the house.

Monday came faster than I would have preferred, but it's also a few days closer to leaving for the trip. I filled Saturday and Sunday with trips to the Wally World in the next town, suitcases, and Wolfie mainlining caffeine as he worked to get us all organized and packed. I can do it myself, but despite his frenzied behavior, he seemed to enjoy himself.

Perhaps growing up with a mother whose mind was so disorderly made him crave order and stability outside of his home. It would explain the joy he feels when submitting, too. I sigh, feeling bad for whining about my disinterested parents when my guys have definitely had it worse. Teddy's mom is a nightmare and I'm sure his dad was heavy with the fists after a few bourbons. Wolfie and Doyle both have moms who don't care and mystery dads—even Wolfie's adoptive mom got sent to a mental health facility. Presley doesn't know his parents well because they sent him to boarding schools young.

I'm definitely not as fucked in the parents department as any of the guys.

I close up my classroom, checking that everything is off and all of my drawers are secured. Students won't rotate into my room again before Winter Break starts, and this is the last time I'll be here before I leave. When I'm sure I've got everything done, I pick up my bag and head out. I need to pick up the animals from the daytime companion area and head home. There are a few more touches I need to put on my things, especially regarding the pets, and I want to look over the lists I made for Niecy one more time.

Niecy and Gene will come over while we're away, making sure no one breaks in and the mail gets tucked away. I know she'll probably give herself some sort of cleaning project as well, so I made a mental note to buy them something nice while we're gone. Those two were always good to me when I was younger and they're still helping me now. I don't know what I would have done without seeing that first friendly face when I got home a few months ago.

Has it really only been a couple of months?

I shake my head, marveling at how much shit can go on in such a short time. So many small things have turned into bigger problems—like the weirdo in the bushes or fucking Sherilynn—and things I worried about earlier don't seem important. I'm not worried about Julia and her crew anymore; the conversation after I woke took care of that. Hell, I even asked her to monitor the place besides Niecy when she gets back from Salem. She's brusque and I need to get to know her better, but my initial knee-jerk reaction was fear of losing my only friend.

Little did I know my friend would almost do that to herself…

But Seer and I are on a good path right now and if she continues to be as honest with me as she can, we'll get back to where we were. I'm not going to hold what she did over her head like a sword of Damocles; that will only perpetuate the issue. We're starting fresh and I intend to do the same with the guys. I probably need to express it better out loud now that we're not crazy with lust and pent up sexual tension, but I believe we're going to get past this.

I'm so much healthier mentally than I was when I dated Trevor; I had no idea how co-dependent he kept me until now.

My life in Whistler's Hollow differs completely from what I imagined for myself when I was packing up in Richmond or even when I moved home from Europe. I'm not upset about that in the slightest. I wouldn't have expected to meet someone, much less several people, that I let into my heart, nor would I have thought I'd be happy teaching snooty rich kids and having small gallery shows. It's like I've found the key to why people come back to this ridiculous little town full of vipers and harpies... There's a sense of family and even comfort in the familiar and predictability of life.

Even when it's petty bullshit.

Shaking my head in astonishment, I put a few extra lingerie sets into the suitcase. They don't weigh a thing, but I'm pretty sure the boys will destroy every pair I put on. I'll still end up having to buy replacements—no, *they* will end up replacing them—but at least I have a good stash for the first week. A smile crosses my lips as I remember how shocked I was at the perfectly cleaned downstairs gleaming at me when I finally got out of the bath the other day. I'm sure Wolfie was the ringleader of that sideshow, but my house was put back together and I didn't have to lift a finger.

It was both sweet and an immense relief. The first thing I thought was 'I could get used to this', but I knew I couldn't say it out loud. At least, not until I'm ready for them to come home full time. It wouldn't be fair and if nothing else, I'm an extremely fair person. I accept my flaws and admit my mistakes readily; I only expect others to do the same. My standards don't always jibe with others'--especially raging narcissists like Antigone and Sher-ilynn—but I apply them just as rigorously to myself as I do everyone else.

That's why I admitted I jumped the gun by sending them away.

Looking over at the cats, I sigh. "Should I just let them come home, anyway? If I was wrong to send them away, keeping them away is bad, too, right?"

"*Mrrrp,*" Jekyll says before returning to cleaning himself.

"Some help you are," I mutter. "Hyde? Do you have an opinion? Isis?"

The python squeezes me tightly, and I have no idea what that means. Snakes are so much harder to judge than my expressive servals or Teddy's dogs. Hyde stands and stretches, moving each of her limbs before walking up to me. She looks up at me with huge eyes before tilting her head at the closet and letting out a mournful *'mow'*. "*That* wasn't subtle. I get it, girl. You miss Wolfie. He spoiled the hell out of you two, even if Jekyll pretends he doesn't give a shit."

What am I going to do?

Closing the suitcase, I jerk my head at my companions and head out the door of my bedroom. I haven't slept there since I got home from the hospital and that's getting old, too. I can't seem to get comfortable in some parts of the renovated house since then and it's contributing to my edginess. Everything is a bloody mess, and it's always lurking in the back of my mind. The night they stayed was the first one in weeks where I'm fairly certain I got proper sleep—not a lot, but enough to be noticeable.

"You need to decide, Jolene," I grumble to myself as I head down the staircase. "Do you need space or support? Can you stand by your own thoughts or will you let fear cost you something amazing?"

I've never been one to back down from hard work or a challenge. After Jackson found me that morning during my undergrad, I clawed my way back to normal with bloodied fingertips. I did the work in therapy that helped me focus on school and pursue my Masters. I took the position in the school in the city to pay off the loans and worked on my PhD online. When the environment became too toxic, I made the choice to leave, even though it broke my heart to know my students wouldn't have an art teacher anymore. And I made it on my own in Europe, building a reputation from the bottom up. I even let Saoirse in when we met, despite the bills I racked up in overseas calls to my shrink when I worried I'd be trapped in the same situation as high school.

None of that would have happened if I'd let fear rule me.

Descending the stairs to my bunker in the basement, I gather all the unpleasant emotions inside and let them flow through me. I open the cabinet with the smallest weapons, picking which ones I want to take along and methodically checking them as I think. Cleaning and maintaining my weapons is more of an automated process than anything else I've done today, and it allows me to really consider all of my options. By the time I get to the last pieces, I land on a solution that I can live with.

While we're away, the guys can stay with me in the small house I rented. We can live together like we did before the enormous blow up and if it's stable and comfortable, when we come home, so can they. I know it's not the same as being here, where there are innumerable pressures and expectations, but it will give me a foundation to build on again. I won't be dealing with a hundred other things and I won't be reminded of being hurt and humiliated in public in a foreign city, especially since I don't have any questionable experiences in Istanbul.

It might just be genius and I'm glad I worked this out the way I did. I needed to get my brain to split focus so I could see a bigger picture than my hurt was allowing me to see. They're supposed to stay home and pack wherever they're staying—goddess, I'm an ass because I didn't even ask *where* that was—so I can call and let them know what the housing arrangements will be when we get to our destination. That should cheer the boys up and it will make me feel like less of a fucking hypocrite.

Way to adult like a fucking boss, Jolene. You're killing it today.

Clicking the slide of the .44, I sigh in relief. It'll be great when I have people who can give me encouragement rather than talking to animals like they understand and giving myself cheesy ass 'girl queen pussy boss' speeches in my mind. I'd like to *not* feel like a giant tool when I'm trying to amp myself up for a while. I may have survived on my own while I was healing, but I'm not the bitch anymore.

I want it all, and I'm going to work my ass off to get it.

She's My Kinda Girl

Edgar

The pup convinced Tilly to let us come along and that alone earns him something special.

I'll have to ponder that a bit because fuck if I have any experience with this. Honestly, I don't have experience with *half* the shit I'm apparently into and all of it is a little overwhelming. I'm terrified I'll fuck something up—not that I haven't already—but Hamilton swears I'm doing fine. I have to take his word for it; it's not like I'm going to ask that hyperactive leprechaun *anything* and our girl is still figuring out her own emotions.

So I'm browsing websites I *never* thought I'd be looking at on my phone as I sit at the bar in the Speakeasy.

This town is fucking weird and everything that happens here boggles the mind.

"What are you glaring so intently at your phone—oh," my oldest friend says when he peeks over my shoulder. "I have to give you credit, man. You don't do anything by halves, even if people are going to give you shit about it."

I snort. "Not since high school, no. I'm lucky Jolene even speaks to me, much less…" I wink at him and shrug. "Because I find myself with the astoundingly good luck to have found a family that is light years better than the one I grew up in. I'm not willing to let judgmental fuckwits ruin it."

"That's why you're openly surfing gay bondage shops in the middle of my bar?"

"Yep." I raise my glass of bourbon in a mock salute. "Because I do not give a randy red fuck what anyone thinks about me or the people I care about."

Huh. I mean that. How… freeing.

Benjy claps me on the shoulder, grinning broadly. "Dude, that's fucking amazing. I know everyone thinks you thumb your nose at shit because of the bookie thing, but I know that's your business sense. The Senator sends more business your way than he does censure with that. Deciding to find happiness instead of doing that playboy fuck around shit… this is you breaking free."

I nod, tilting my head as I look at my old friend. "Leaving Sherilynn is your version of that, you know. You've been miserable since *high school,* man."

His face falls for a moment, but he finally rounds the bar, leaning over it as he replies. "Yeah, it was. I mean, sure, the whole 'finding a mate' thing helped me cut the cord, but you're right. I let both of our parents push us into a union that was never what I wanted. Hell, I don't even think it was what Sherilynn wanted. And we let them push us to adopt the kids—who my ex trained to hate me from the minute they arrived."

I wince. It couldn't have been easy to live in a house populated by people who treated you like a furnishing rather than a person for these years. "Yeah, I heard from another professor that they're all being twats about the divorce—loud ones, at that."

"Fuck, I know. Do you know how many times Bobbi Jo has called me about the shit they're saying at school? All I can tell her is Sherilynn has custody and I'm not able to help her. Then I get to hear the bullshit they're spouting and I have to defend myself to a principal. Some of it is outrageous—I haven't lived there since the papers were served."

"You need some time away from this garbage and I know just the fix. It might take a little finagling, but what's being a senator's kid for, if not occasionally recklessly abusing my connections?" I toss back the rest of my Blanton's and push to my feet. "Do you have coverage here if we take a brief trip?"

"I'm gonna say the same thing I used to say when you got that look when we were teens, Boone. If this gets me arrested, I'll dime you out for a pack of smokes."

Smothering my laugh with my hand, I tip my head at the door. "And I'll reply the same: you don't smoke and you'd do better offering your body for trade."

"Christ, that hits different now," he mutters as he grabs his coat. "But I'm in. Let's go on an adventure."

"Atta boy," I reply with a smirk.

WHEN WE PULL INTO TILLY'S DRIVEWAY, BENJY TURNS TO ME AND ARCHES A brow. "I thought you're all on the outs with her. What kind of adventure is this?"

I chuckle and shrug. "We're working it out. And luckily for me, the bird and the pup are *much* better at holding their tongues than I am. Hell, even fucking Doyle was even-tempered for the first part of the night."

"First part?"

Grinning, I shake my head. "You're not ready for that part yet, buddy. Suffice it to say that no one ever told me what happens when you let the monsters loose with your mate, but it's the hottest shit on earth."

He sucks in a slow breath, then looks out the window. "Didn't think I'd ever have the chance to know what that's like."

"I know, but you might now. You're not tainted by the betrayal thing because you weren't on the radar until Halloween. That gives you a chance to build shit as honestly as possible from the start. Let go of your regrets about your ex and get to know our girl for who she is now. I promise; you won't regret it."

Benjy turns back to me and shakes his head. "Who would have thought hound dog Boone would not only get mated to two people, but be giving *me* love advice? The world is topsy-turvy, I fucking swear."

"Shut up and get out of my car, Foster. We've got wheedling to do."

I'm definitely projecting a lot more confidence than I have in this situation, but I figure if I can get Benjy to buy in, we can do this. Tilly wasn't nearly as angry after the big growly fuck fest, and she was acquiescent when I took her upstairs for the bath. The rest of the weekend went well, even if we had to go home and come back the next day.

She's not going to blow her top when I show up without calling. Right?

"Once more into the breach," I mutter to myself.

"What?"

"Nothing." I wink at my friend and raise my hand to knock on the door. Before my fist strikes the wood, the door is flung wide and the sound of a hammer cocking fills the air.

I might have been wrong about that earlier statement.

"Teddy! What the unholy *fuck* are you doing sneaking around my house at night? I could have shot you in the face, you fool!"

Benjy looks between us and sighs. "Working on it, huh?"

The way she clears the chamber and latches the safety before tucking her bulldog into a pocket on the side of her yoga pants is hot as hell, but I wave my hand dismissively to calm my friend. "Yes. I don't know why my *drugar* is wielding a hand cannon like a maniac, but it's not because I'm unwelcome on the porch. Right, Tilly?"

My answer is an eye roll and a whistle that calls off the animals perched on the stairs behind her. I wait for her to speak and she huffs, "Yes. There were weird noises outside again, and I was out there trying to shoot that pervert in the ass. That's why I was prepared when I opened the door. The noises seemed to lead me back into the house and toward the front yard."

"You were crawling around outside trying to find the stalker?" Suddenly, the tactical yoga pants—who knew they made those—and the rest of her attire makes sense. She's got her hair pulled up high through a stocking cap and a long-sleeved black top on with them and some kind of low-profile shoes. I squint at her in disbelief, vainly hoping to control my temper before I explode.

"That seems a little dangerous, Jolene," Benjy says hesitantly. "Why didn't you call someone?"

Her gazes narrows as she looks at us. "I'm going to tell you apes *one more time*. I can defend myself without having to be rescued!"

"I'm not saying you aren't, *drugar*! But even law enforcement and feds don't go off without their partners except in movies!"

The porch goes silent for a moment and I'm certain we're getting tossed into the night or maybe even shot in the ass on our way out. But she thinks about my flip comment for a long moment and, miraculously, she nods. "Okay.

That makes sense. You're not saying I need to be rescued, only that I need someone watching my six."

Letting out a breath, I smile fondly as all my anger melts away. "Yes. That's exactly what I'm trying to say."

"Noted." The door opens further, and she holds a hand out. "Come in, gentleman. Now that we've sorted out our miscommunication, I'd be rude not to offer you a seat and a drink."

There's that Southern woman poking her head out.

"A Blanton's would be delightful, love," I murmur as we walk in and head for the living room.

"Benjy?" she calls over her shoulder as she pads towards the kitchen with her ponytail and her ass bouncing.

"Uh, bourbon's good."

"Back in a tick," Tilly says as she disappears into the other room.

My friend looks at me with a surprised expression. "Is she wearing yoga pants with a holster?"

"Apparently so." I shake my head, watching the doorway until she comes back with a tray full of glasses, ice, a bottle, and just like the first night, a small plate of charcuterie snacks. "And now she's serving us fancy meats. We really fucked up in high school, man."

"No shit," my girl says as she sits the tray down. "Good to hear you say it, though. Have a sip and tell me why you're at my door without an invitation late at night again, Edgar Boone."

The memory of her saying that the first time makes me smile and I pour Benjy and me a drink before I reply. "I'd like to request an amendment to our agreement from last week."

"Oooh. Procedural Teddy. This is the part of you that was raised by the Senator." She leans back in her chair and gives me a playful expression. "Present your amendment, Your Honor. Legislature is in session."

"Can I interject to say that it's weird how much flirting is going on when you're pretending to be lawmakers?" Benjy mutters.

"No," Tilly and I say in unison.

"Seems unfair, but okay."

"The chair recognizes the gentleman from Whistler's Hollow. Speak and be heard."

The gentleman thinks the chair enjoys being bent over this couch and that alone is going to get this amendment passed.

"Allow me to start at the beginning."

"Good thing I brought the bottle. You're going to be as full of hot air as your father." She looks at Benjy and winks. "Get comfy. We're going to be here a while."

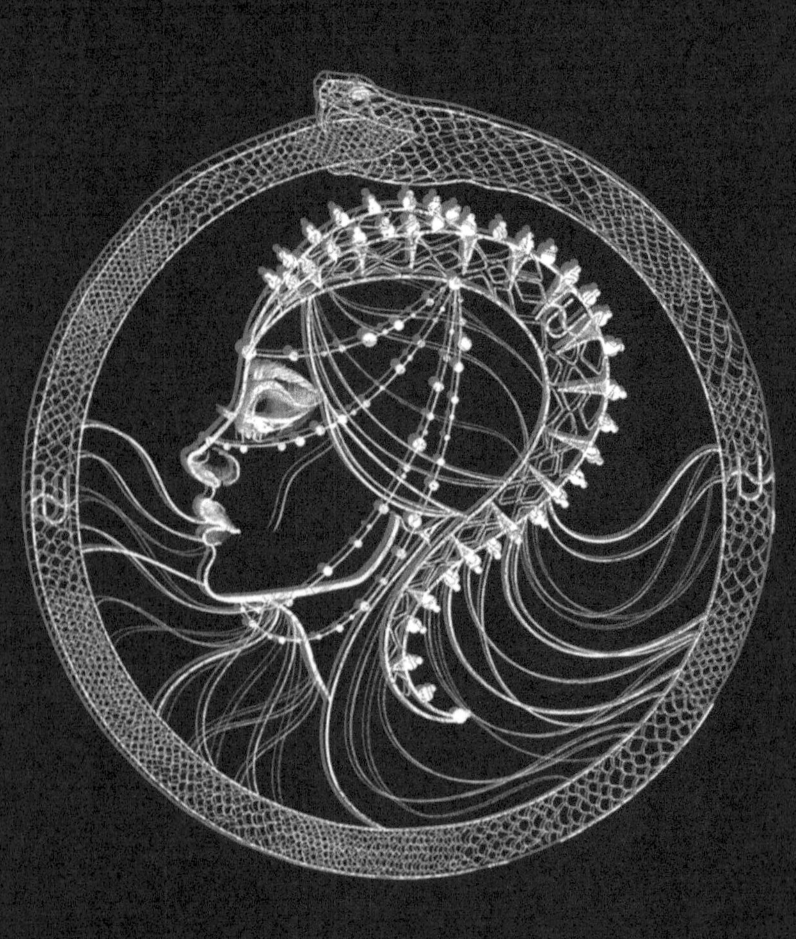

Freaks

*I*s being dick-drunk a real thing? Because I think I'm suffering from it.

Not only did I agree to allow Benjy to join us on the damn trip, but I let Doyle arrange for transportation to the airport. Much to my chagrin, that turned out to be an envoy of huge SUVs in a long ass motorcade that makes me feel like I'm riding along with a diplomat. Wolfie borrowed a cage for Eury from a friend who works at the zoo and she's currently hating life on one of the other cars. The rest of them can be free in the cabin, but he insisted my girl won't be able to stay comfortable unless she's in a nice, dark hold where he can go down and occasionally check on her.

I can't say I envy Presley and Wolfie their spot in that vehicle, but I'm also stuck with Teddy and Doyle sniping at one another. Benjy is riding with Seer and the luggage in the last car and if that doesn't make me feel like the Queen of Rich Assholes, nothing will. We could have done this a hundred less flashy ways, but they all seem determined to make me self-conscious.

Of course, I am the girl who called her friend to 'borrow' a plane, so I should probably shut up.

By the time we get to the tarmac, the boys have argued about sports, booze, cards, music, and the best way to collect on an unpaid debt. Spoiler alert: none of their methods are legal and I cannot believe that three months ago I was applying to the FBI and today I'm riding in a car with white-collar criminals to jet to a foreign country and hunt down a crooked cop. It's surreal, and I didn't even mention the whole 'cadre of boyfriends' part.

The guys hop out of the car, immediately helping the baggage handlers with Eury and the stowed luggage. It makes me feel a little better as I roll my small carry on towards the stairs with Jekyll and Hyde in tow. The dogs follow Teddy happily and for a second, I feel guilty that they were away from him for so long. Watching them renews my dedication to using this trip to repair the pieces that broke so everyone can come home. Not only do I want that, but our shared 'kids' want it, too.

When I step inside of the plane, I blink for a second. I shouldn't be surprised given how big Thorn Enterprises has gotten, but this is a swank ass plane. There's an open floor plan with a couch and chairs, a full bar, a hallway that I assume leads to a bedroom and bathroom, plus a workspace. The flight is over eleven hours and we'll have a brief stop at JFK for fueling; this setup will make that *much* easier. We left at the ass crack of dawn for a reason, of course. We should arrive in time to order dinner and collapse, then get up in the morning to go shopping for the shit we'll need while we're living in the villa.

I'd rather go straight to the embassy, but we couldn't get an appointment until two days after we arrived. Edgar said it was better that way because it gave us time to prepare and snoop around before we go through official channels. His reasoning was sound, so I didn't reach out to my contacts to push it. I'd rather be seen as clueless Americans than have the staff there on guard because someone influential requested special treatment. It would make it harder for the guys to sneak around.

"Not gonna lie, Jolene. This is baller," Benjy says as he comes in. "Thorn outdid himself."

I give him a gentle smile. Since he saved me twice on Halloween, I've noticed that he's a stark contrast to the rest of the guys. He's not completely gooey in the center like Wolfie, but he's also not as hard as Doyle or Teddy. Benjy falls into that mythical 'big guy with a heart of gold' archetype and I'm glad I let Teddy sweet talk me into allowing him to join us. His placid nature will help me balance out all the testosterone, I think.

"He did. I've not seen this one before, but I have been on ones like it with clients. This is like the one Seer and I took to—"

"Thailand!" My bestie comes bounding in with a broad grin. "Holy feck, that was a trip and a half. We barely got out of that country with our asses intact and I'd do it again in a heartbeat."

The rest of the guys filter in and arch their brows at me. I shake my head with a grin. "You have your high clearance secrets and I have mine. When you're able to tell me *everything*, I'll tell you about Thailand. Until then, you'll have to suffer."

"Doesn't seem fair," Teddy grumbles as he stalks in. Kali and Hecate make a beeline for the corner where my cats are curled up as he heads over to me, picks me up, and carries me to the couch in a fireman's hold. When he sits down, he positions me on his lap with a grin. "This will help, though."

I thump him in the chest hard. "You don't get to pick me up and move me, you big ape! Do it when we're not on a plane and I'll flip your ass on the ground."

"Uh, sugarplum?" Wolfie says as he comes over to join us. "I don't think that's much of a punishment."

Doyle nods. "I would have said you were threatening me with a good time, Tíogair."

Rubbing my hand over my face, I look at Benjy and Presley pleadingly. "Can you guys help me get these dipshits under control? I'll owe you."

That seems to get every male in the room to perk up.

"Wagers?" Doyle and Teddy say simultaneously.

"*No!*" I shout. "No bets on the plane. No fighting on the plane. No male bullshit on the plane."

"But there *is* a snake on the plan," Benjy points out.

That stops us all in our tracks, and we look at each other before bursting out laughing.

Okay, this might not be terrible.

"Can I get you gentleman anything?"

My eyes narrow as the flight attendant makes googly eyes at my men. She introduced herself as Coco before we took off and if that didn't indicate a problem, I would have figured it out after she primped once she saw the passengers. She's been in and out more often than is necessary and I wrote it off as nervousness at first. We have wild animals and odd shit going on, so I figured maybe she was just being overly cautious. But after the first six 'check-ins' during the hour and a half long flight to JFK, I wondered why Miss Messy Bun kept coming back here. Now that she's standing here with wide eyes and perfectly applied red lipstick, I'm certain I'm not imagining things.

Gross.

I doubt Jackson has any interest in her—he swings solidly towards men or gender fluid folks—but that doesn't mean the staff aren't hired with his clients in mind. And he's *definitely* the lawyer who would hire 'models' to work his various homes and luxury vehicles to keep his clientele happy. If this chick doesn't back off, I'll have to make it abundantly clear this isn't one of *those* trips or Jax will have to do an emergency replacement in NYC.

I won't be able to hold my temper for another nine plus hours to Istanbul; that's for sure.

Teddy doesn't pay attention to her. He's reading a research file from Eli with one hand and running his hand through both mine and Wolfie's hair. We're lying with our heads next to each but facing opposite directions as we work through our own documents. Presley looks up at her blankly from the far end of the couch, but he says nothing. Finally, Doyle spins around in his chair with a charming smile that means he's about to cause trouble.

"I'm sure the judge would love a bourbon, dear. Wouldn't you, Edgar?"

The man in question stops reading and looks up, realizing he's being rude, and turns on the Southern charm. "Why, sure, darlin'. I'd love one. Anyone else?"

Miss Fluttery Lashes simpers a little—I fucking swear she does—and puts a hand on her chest. "I'd be *delighted* to get your drink, Your Honor. We weren't told we'd have such *high-ranking* guests on this trip. I would have made sure everything was exactly how you needed it."

"Unlike us mere mortals who don't qualify for special treatment on a private jet?" I mutter under my breath. "Fucking spare me."

I can hear Wolfie snickering and I reach over my face to put my hand over his playfully. That little shit knows why I'm irritable and he's pretending it's funny. I bet if this was some eight packed dipshit with a white smile and bleached surfer hair, he wouldn't be so cavalier.

"Run along and bring the bourbon and a bottle of Irish whiskey, love. Don't forget the glasses and ice," Doyle says with a wink.

That motherfucker made his accent more noticeable on purpose; I know it.

"Oh, what a lovely Irish brogue!" Messy Bun says as she wiggles her way to the galley.

I repeat her words in a mocking, high-pitched voice as I continue reading my papers. This time, Presley snorts. Between him and Wolfie, I've got vengeance planned later on, but that will have to wait until the perfect moment. I'll teach them to make fun of my weirdly possessive feelings that I have no idea how to handle. Mark my words, I'll show them.

My spitefulness increases tenfold when I'm trying to figure out how to process emotions. It's a flaw and I know it.

"Something wrong, Tíogair?"

"Not at all." I don't look over, continuing to read as I ignore his bullshit.

The perky hostess comes back with a fancy cart and makes a big show of setting everything out on the small coffee table in front of the couch. She aims her ass at us as she pulls conveniently placed items on the bottom of it and then at the others as she pulls out more napkins and coasters. There's no way in hell that kind of drawn out shit is needed for two bottles of booze and ice, so my temper heads towards a boil.

"Tilly." I look up over my head at the reproving look Teddy's giving me. "There's no reason to get salty."

I snort and go back to my file. He sighs, but I can *feel* the smile on his handsome face. My idiotic jealousy is making these fools preen like peacocks and I can't stop myself. His fingers tip my chin up to look at me again, and I glare at him. His lips curl up and he chuckles softly as he looks down at me. Finally, he pushes my hair behind my ears and waves his hand at something, but I'm too busy looking into his eyes to pay much attention.

The clatter of the cart leaving the area breaks the stare and I look out at the rest of the room. Teddy taps my shoulder so I'll sit up, then he does the same to Wolfie. "*Drugar*, we're going to relax in the bedroom until we get to New York. I'll even read to you, so you get a little sleep."

"Uh, no, we're not. I doubt anyone here *isn't* a member of the Mile High club and it's too damn early for that shit." I cross my arms over my chest and he bursts out laughing.

"You look tired. If it will make you feel safer, I'll come," Benjy says softly. "I've been told I make a good pillow."

Blinking, I look over at Teddy, and he nods. My eyes skitter over the others, but they're all busy looking at their shit or drinking the booze that just arrived.

Well, shit. I guess Benjy's now considered part of the family.

Take Me to Church

Benjy

Edgar wasn't wrong.

We took turns reading to Jolene from some smutty book about a school full of horny shifter predators and she was out like a light. It cracked me up that she's reading about something that exists—exaggerated as that shit was—as fictional entertainment. The authors don't get everything right, of course. For one, teenage me would have *loved* if shit like that went on in school and professors may *not* fuck each other or students all over the place.

But our girl listened raptly, curled between the two of us as we passed her Kindle back and forth. Her eyes fluttered shut after a few chapters, but we kept reading to make sure she stayed asleep.

Not at all for research or anything.

After a while, I look over at my old friend. "Is this the shit you all get up when you go home?"

He chuckles and shrugs. "To be honest, I'd done a *lot* of shit before she came home and upended my life, but none of it is as wild as being part of her family. But I don't regret it for a second, dude. I figured out shit I didn't know about myself and changed things I realized didn't fit anymore. It's a rollercoaster of surprises and new things."

Running my hand over her hair gently, I look down at the girl I tried to save in high school. She's definitely become a woman worth fighting for and despite my divorce, it *will* be a fight once Sherilynn figures out I'm with them. "I get that. And I'm curious as hell, to tell the truth."

"You're worried about your ex-harpy escalating." It's not a question; Edgar knows she'll be a nightmare. He's the one who helped push my divorce through despite her asshole father hiring some big city lawyer who tried to tie it up in red tape. "Don't. Despite what I say, I know Tilly can take care of herself. She'll cut old Sheri to ribbons if she comes for someone she cares about."

I frown. "I don't think we have that kind of relationship yet, Boone."

His laugh is soft. "It doesn't matter. If you're part of the people she considers hers, she'll go to the mat for you. I guarantee it."

"Her friend has been sleeping like a corpse since she curled up in the big chair. That's kind of weird, right?"

"Yeah, Seer is odd. But those two are thick as thieves—or were before the incident—and now that they're back in sync, where Tilly goes, so does the rainbow wild child."

I consider that for a moment. Sherilynn had a clatch of women who followed her like adoring fans, but she never trusted any of them. She was always sure Ophelia or Reese or Jillian or Amy would betray her or try to wrest control of their various committees. They treated me with as much disdain as she did, even though we all hung out together as kids. I never understood it, but then I understood little about my ex-wife.

"It's so interesting how all of you seem to fit together, even though you're so different. And no one seems even a little concerned that I'm back here with the two of you." I rub my hand over my face and sigh. "It's completely unlike how the rest of the people in town act."

"Don't you want to be here?"

Jolene's voice startles me and Edgar laughs. "She can be a light sleeper when she's misbehaving."

"Shut up, Teddy," she grumbles. Shifting so she can look up at me, the dark-haired beauty slides a hand up my neck to my cheek. "You don't have to be here if you're not comfortable, Benjy. I won't get upset."

Damn, she's a kind person.

"No, I want to be here. On the plane and in here, I mean. I just don't want to contribute to you getting hurt again," I murmur.

My entire body seizes when she wriggles even closer to me, stroking a thumb over my jawbone. "That's good. Because I think I'd like you to kiss me."

Edgar leans down and murmurs something in her ear that makes her flush an adorable pink, but she slides a leg over mine. "Our girl wants you to kiss her, Foster. Don't keep her waiting or I'll be very cross."

I put my hands on either side of her face, pulling her closer until our lips meet. The minute the kiss deepens, electricity rockets through me and the animal inside of me wakes up for the first time in years. He's been quiet for so long I almost don't recognize it, but as I twirl my tongue around Jolene's, the dormant primal nature inside of me unfurls. When I pull back, a soft grunt escapes my lips and my eyes widen. I look over her head at my friend, concerned I won't have the slightest clue how to control myself.

And the fucker laughs. This must be what he means by wild.

"Excellent," Boone says before he turns her head and kisses her hard. Jolene arches her back, pushing back into him with a moan.

That's when my cock joins the fray, thickening in my sweats like I just flipped through my first *Playboy*. The leg resting on mine wraps around my hip tighter, urging me to scoot closer. I can't help myself; I press against her until the three of us are entwined. Her hips grind against me and I lean down to sink my teeth into her shoulder.

"Hot damn. I *knew* you didn't want to sleep," Jolene says when she breaks the kiss. "You boys are up to no good."

"Tilly, we have thirty-five minutes before we touch down in New York. I think we can make you come at *least* five times before then. What do you think, Benjy?"

I freeze for a moment. It's not the time to tell them I've never slept with anyone but my ex, but the needy look on Jolene's face tells me she won't care. Sliding my hand down her side, I pull down her yoga pants and cup the bare heat inside. "I think five is a good start."

"Well, boys. I'd say you need to get to work then," she breathes.

Arching a brow, I run my finger along her slit, teasing her. "As you wish, Princess."

She likes that because she bucks into my palm. Grinding it against her mound, I dip my head and suckle along the line of her neck. Edgar's hands move to the hem of her sweatshirt and when he pulls it up, I move back for a second so he can remove it. Almost at the same time, I discover Jolene has pretty jeweled nipples and a matching piercing down below. Making a strangled sound, I look at my friend and he grins broadly.

"Our girl is bejeweled and beautiful from head to toe. You'll love playing with them." His big hands cup her tits, holding them up for me to inspect.

I can't help myself, so I lean down, taking one into my mouth as I slip two fingers inside of her. The sound she makes almost undoes me. Flicking my tongue over her shield, I pump the digits in and out of her slowly. She's soaked and moving with me as I add another finger and place my thumb on her clit. A few soft brushes later and Jolene yanks my head up to look at me with fierce green eyes.

"I lied. I don't want you two to make me come five times."

"You don't?" Edgar murmurs as he bites a mark on her neck. The way she squeals tells me it must be his and I know that means she can't see it, but she can feel when he touches it. "Are you sure?"

I brush over her clit again and pump my fingers in and out slowly. "It feels like you do, baby."

"No, noooo…" Her head falls back onto Boone's shoulder when I flick her again. "I want you both to fuck me."

That gets my attention.

"*Drugar*, I didn't bring the bag in here because I thought you were going to sleep," Edgar whispers against her ear. "I don't have lube."

Her eyes are closed, but her smile is wicked. "We don't need lube. Stretch me together."

Holy. Fucking. Shit.

"I *like* it, Tilly. You're a bad girl this morning. Are you gonna scream loud enough to make everyone jealous?"

"Mmm. Fuck me right and I'm sure I will, big man."

They made these *two* for one another and I don't have a clue why I get to play along except that dark, growly feeling that's settled in my gut. It's the one that told me she was my mate and it's the one that wants me to jump into this shit with two feet.

"Get naked." The words surprise me when they come out of my mouth, but as soon as I remove my hand, she wriggles out of the pants like a contortionist. I nod at Edgar and he pulls back to deal with his clothes while I stare at our girl. "Take mine off now, Princess."

She gives me a minxy smile, hands slipping to my waistband and pulling my tee shirt up over my head. When it's tossed aside, she tugs my sweats down, freeing my cock. "Commando. That's my favorite kind of underwear."

"Which is to say none," Edgar says as he watches her finish ridding me of my sweats. "But we're agreed on that."

"Now for the fun part," Jolene says as she slides her thigh up onto my hip. "Benjy, you'll go first. Fuck me until I come hard. Then we'll take it further."

"Yes, ma'am." I reach down, positioning the head at her entrance before I grab her hips and slam my dick home inside of her. My eyes roll back when the tight, wet heat of her pussy grips me and the simian inside of me beats its chest. I feel it pushing me against my skin and I rock my hips, sliding in and out of the woman who's changed my life.

"Good job, *drugar*. Take his cock. Squeeze him. Feel how good it is when he fucks you. I want you to be so wet when we both slide in that it only takes a little before you coat us with come."

Who the hell knew Edgar has a mouth like that? It's making me *hot, for fuck's sake.*

"Teddy," she whines when her back arches and I trail my lips down her chest. "I want that. I need both of your dicks stretching me while you do that biting thing."

If I weren't being strangled by the sweetest cunt I've ever felt, I would question the 'biting' thing, but I feel these guys are letting their supe sides out with her. I slip my hand between us and pinch her clit to get her attention. "Princess, focus."

Jolene groans, her hips rocking up to meet my thrusts eagerly, and I keep stroking the spot that makes her clench around me until I feel her shiver. When her orgasm hits, I have to fight hard not to come at the same time. By the time she finishes riding it out, I'm getting my teeth.

That's when I feel Boone push inside along with me.

"Motherfucker," I snarl as my eyes fly wide.

He grins like a cat that got the cream. "Oh, not yet, but I'm not averse to filling our girl until she's got one of our babies in her."

"Absolutely not, you dickhead," Jolene pants. "Now shut up and fuck me before I kick you both out."

I chuckle softly, moving my hips in opposition to Edgar's. "Again, as you wish, Princess."

"Suck up."

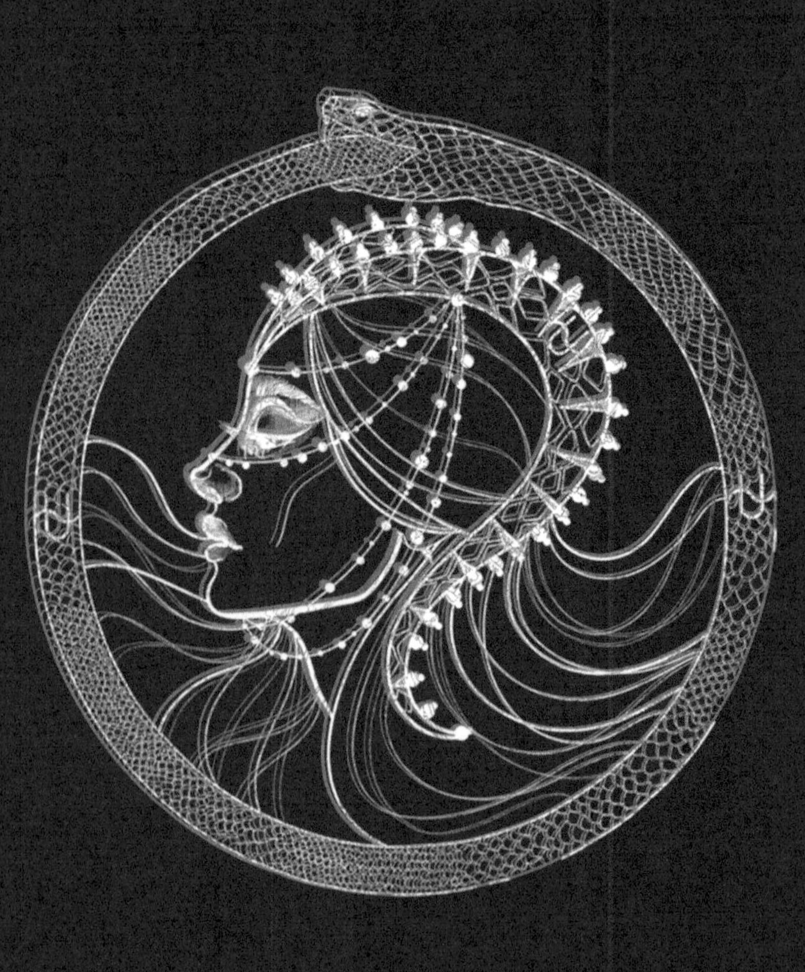

Woman on a Mission

When I wake up, I'm surrounded by the hottest pile of bodies in the Universe. Being cuddled in a puppy pile is an emotionally satisfying sensation, but the physical reality is feeling like you're wrapped in a hundred blankets at once. The lady bits find it sexy and my heart gets squishy, but my bladder says it's time to escape before we end up exploring a kink I'm not interested in.

I shift a little, wiggling out from under Benjy and Teddy's arms, only to discover I can't slide downward because Prez and Wolfie are firmly wrapped around my lower half. I assume Doyle is here somewhere, too, because there's no way he'd let himself be left out. Poor Seer must be snoozing in the cabin like an animal au pair.

My sympathy only lasts for a moment; I *really* gotta pee.

"You jokers need to move." I finally say.

"No." Teddy doesn't even open his eyes to deny my request.

Bastard.

"That wasn't a request."

"Princess, we're comfy. You slept through the pit stop, and we're probably over the Atlantic somewhere. If we sleep now, the jet lag won't be so bad."

He's not wrong, but that's not why I want them to let me up.

Wolfie rubs his cheek against my belly and mumbles, "He's right, sugarplum."

Oh, for crap's sake.

"Guys, I appreciate you reminding me of things I definitely know from years of international travel, but I need to pee. Unless you want to lie in a wet spot, y'all need to move."

They move like lightning, tripping over one another in their scramble to let me get up. My giggles don't stop until I close the bathroom door, leaving them bitching in my wake. Men are predictable and even in a group, they behave how you'd expect.

Once I finish my business, I step into the shower. True to form, there are already fancy schmancy toiletries waiting, so I take my time washing away the sweat and sex smell. I roll my eyes as I notice the bruises and hall-marks of the rowdy play that's characterized the return of my men to my bed.

Their fear of losing me seems to have manifested in some overly possessive cave dude shit, but nothing that's so annoying that I have to put my foot down. I finish washing the shampoo out of my hair, breathing the scent of lavender and rose hips in with a smile. At least I'll smell nice when I deplane, even if I'll desperately crave a change of clothes.

I dry off and hang the towels before standing in front of the mirror to put my hair back up in a ponytail. Something catches my eye and I squint at the mirror with a frown. My reflection looks normal, but it feels like what I'm seeing isn't right. Tilting my head back and forth, I turn around, looking at my body. I can't shake the niggling feeling, no matter how closely I look. Everything *appears* to be fine—piercings, tatts, a few little marks from sexy times, my frustrating softness in certain places—but my brain keeps telling me I'm missing things.

I haven't been this paranoid since Seer and I ate those magic cookies at the Beltane Fire Festival.

"Why does my reflection feel wrong?" I mutter. "How can it feel wrong?"

The lights flicker briefly, plunging me into darkness. I barely catch it, but a ring of fire flashes in my eyes, followed by a slit, then a sparkle, and suddenly, the lights come back on.

What in actual goddamned fuck *was that?!*

Wrapping myself in the last towel, I stride out into the bedroom, ready to demand they tell me if I ate some funky mushrooms or someone burned one while I was sleeping. The guys have exited the room and my clothes are laid out on the freshly made bed as if waiting for me. I tug them on quickly and stomp into the cabin, determined to find out why I'm hallucinating.

"Sugarplum!" Wolfie says with a bright smile. "I helped get breakfast ready. Now that you smell all flowery and sweet, you can have a seat and eat with us."

His enthusiasm deflates my irritation immediately and I accept the plate he hands me gratefully. "You are my favorite today, baby. Bacon and eggs and waffles always soothe the beast."

"Oi!" Doyle grumbles. "I made the mimosas."

"Thank you, grumpy pants." I wink at him as I pad over to sit on the couch next to Teddy. He's not asking for favor; no, he's smiling indulgently at our antics. "So who wants to tell me what weird shit went on that I'm having acid flashbacks this morning?"

Seer spins around in her chair, her mouth open. "Acid flashbacks? All of you idiots just got a *hell* of a lot cooler."

I roll my eyes. "Not the point, Seer."

"I think it is."

Benjy chuckles and takes the chair next to hers, pulling the tray up to sit his plate down. "No one did any party favors, Princess. All sex, no candy."

"Which *they* did not invite us to," Doyle grumbles as uses his foot to spin his chair in fast circles. "Party foul is more like it."

"There is no way we would have all fit in there for that," Presley counters. "We had to pile up like a football huddle to snooze together."

"Fine," the Irishman replies with a pout. "But I call dibs on the next round."

I pick up the knife from the table and point it at him. "First, he's right. Second, I am *not* ' shotgun' or a carnival ride. You act like you need a fucking Fast Pass to my pants again and I'm kicking you out of the damn theme park."

That makes everyone laugh, and I huff as I wolf down the waffle. When they finally stop snickering like teenagers, I take a sip of my mimosa and continue. "No drugs, then? Interesting."

"What did you see, Sugarplum? Was it bad?" Wolfie looks at me with concern as he walks over with the next two plates in his hand. He hands them to Prez and Teddy, then goes to get his before he takes the seat next to me.

"I don't *think* it was bad. I mean, I don't know. The lights in the bathroom went off for a minute and I was looking in the mirror. My eyes sort of changed—like I'd used a couple pairs of SFX contacts in rapid succession. And before they went off, I kept feeling like something was wrong with my reflection, but everything looked normal."

Teddy sits up straighter, his eyes darting to the others before he finally turns to face me. "What did your eyes look like in this weird little fever dream, Tilly?"

"Pretty cool, actually. There was a ring of fire, then sort of slit like a snake, and then this icy sparkly ring." I shrug and bite off a piece of bacon, chewing before I add, "They all looked good. I'll have to consider something like that for Halloween next year."

Doyle chokes on his drink, covering his mouth with a napkin as fast as he can. Prez whacks him on the back with an eye roll and Benjy howls with laughter. Only Teddy and Wolfie seem to be unamused. They're doing this 'conversation without talking' thing with their eyes and when I look at Seer, she's frowning.

Why is everyone being weird about this? Do they think I have a brain tumor or something?

"Uh, you guys don't think I had a stroke, right?"

Presley smiles, waving his hand. "Absolutely not. You probably had a drop in blood pressure that made your eyes play tricks on you. I'll monitor you to make sure, magpie, but nothing you said seems like we should worry."

"Then why is everyone being so fucking weird suddenly?"

"I don't know how you can tell," Seer mutters. "These nimrods are always weird."

"You're one to talk, O'Flanagan!" Teddy shoots back with a smirk.

Point well taken; we're all odd.

"Fine. I didn't have a stroke, and we're strange. Let's talk through the plans for when we land." I say as I finish my food. "As long as we're on course, we should hit Istanbul at four am because it's GMT plus three. We'll head straight to the rental and get our shit inside, feed the animals, and sleep for a couple of hours, right?"

"Right," Teddy says. He stands, taking both of our plates to the cart, and I cringe.

Coco will be here to collect that shit eventually and despite knowing my guys have shown where their loyalty lies, I'm not keen on seeing that chick again. I don't like feeling like I'm in competition with her because normally, I wouldn't even notice her bullshit. But the recent incidents with Trevor and Sherilynn have dealt my confidence a blow, so she's hit buttons I'm not proud of having. Most of the time, I could give a fuck less whether some woman was waving her ass around in front of me. Unfortunately, right now is not the time and I am not the one.

I'm far too volatile emotionally to handle a self-centered bint practically begging me to crush her like a grape.

Seer must see my frustration because she winks at me. "No worries, Peanut. That chippy has been dealt with."

This *is what genuine friends are for. Preventing you from strangling the people who are determined to bait you at every turn.*

"Thanks," I mumble. "That helps a lot."

The guys look at us both in confusion and my bestie shrugs. "It's a girl thing, gents. No ding dongs needed. Carry on."

"Christ, it makes me shrivel up when she talks about that," Teddy says as he returns to his seat. "Balls go right up into my fucking body, no lie."

"If you hurt my girl, I'll make sure that's never a problem again, doggy. Cross me heart and swear on a bottle of mead."

I give Seer a look and lean against the man cringing next to me. "He knows better now. We've had a chat about boundaries, haven't we, boys?"

"Yes, yes. Be good. Tell the truth. Don't hide shit if we can help it. All the Boy Scout stuff," Doyle says as he pours himself a whiskey. "Domesticated, the lot of us."

"Fuck, I hope not," I snort. "I like you all a little wild. Just cut out the bull-shit. Otherwise, I like you all for who you are, the way you are now."

That seems to brighten the mood, and Presley pulls out his tablet, waving it. "On that note, should we call Thorn before it gets too late?"

"Definitely. I want to know what he and Eli have to add before we set foot on foreign soil. They're supposed to be working on something we can download to help get access to the embassy files. That should unlock more info on our disappearing crooked cop."

Wolfie clears the rest of the plates while we all get comfy around the couch. Once he's done, Prez sets up the call as we peer into the screen like a bunch of Boomers trying to Skype their grandkids. It rings for a few moments and I frown. Damn, that party going fool. He's supposed to be waiting for this chat and it's not even two pm our time. He can't still be asleep from the night before.

"Hellloooo, weary travelers!" Jax says as he finally comes on screen. He looks a little worse for wear and I note Eli is lurking in the background rather than being front and center.

That's unusual; they seemed to be going pretty strong the last time we spoke. Fidelity isn't Jax's strong suit, but this time, I thought he might actually have landed a good one. "Jax, you look like shit. What's going on?"

His scowl darkens, and he looks over his shoulder briefly before coming back to us. "A little domestic dispute. *Someone* whose name I won't *mention* has a big, dumb, bearded ex who can't seem to understand that having a big dick doesn't mean you're not a fucking asshole."

"I *told* you he doesn't even know how to use it!" Eli shoots back.

"*That* is not comforting! You dated Nox for two years despite his rancid, two-dimensional personality and inability to fuck well. What does that say about your ability to ignore giant red flags in the people you date? What's wrong with me?"

I blink for a second, then grin, knowing exactly how to get Jackson to pull his head out of his perfectly shaped ass. "Jax, you're a spoiled, obscenely rich brat who spent a decade fucking around worldwide until your evil, abusive father died and left you with the keys to his kingdom. You have trouble with fidelity, addiction, elitism, and the attention span of gnat. However, despite those things, this adorable sweet dude seems to like you and is trying to make a go of it with you. Perhaps his ability to let go of people's flaws is actually a good thing?"

My words stop the pouting lawyer in his tracks. He squints into the camera, giving me a look I saw a *lot* after he found me holed up in grief in college.

"Jo-Jo, you know you're the only person in existence. I will allow to say that shit without looking up a hitman, right?"

"Yup," I reply. "But you'd do the same for me. Luckily, this time I figured it out on my own, so you don't have to use armchair Psych 101 on me."

He sighs. "Thank fuck. I only have so much repertoire in that arena before I have to make it up. Trust me, there are enough idiots out there listening to idiotic catch phrases from TikTok as if they're actual mental health advice. You don't need me to be one of them."

"I really don't." I chuckle softly and shake my head. "Can you imagine being that uneducated and condescending that you think telling someone to touch grass is a viable response? People that narcissistic *kill* me—they *never* see reality beyond their delusions of grandeur. And I say that as someone with degrees to back it up."

Doyle pushes into frame. "Not to break up your little Hallmark moment, but what did you and the hacker find, mate? I assume you didn't spend *all* of this time arguing about some roided out loser."

"Ah, yes. Thank you," Jax says. "Eli created a worm he's pushing to the devices we gave you for the college snooping trip. You should be able to sneak it into the Wi-Fi or through Bluetooth into some device in the building if you work in tandem. The second part of the scheme involves someone making a distraction and someone else using the other piece of software to disrupt their firewalls. Same phones, of course."

I frown. "So we'll have to split the party up in order to get some of us on our own and some of sucking up the attention of the staff and security?"

"Correct, Jo-Jo. You'll need to work as a team and stay in contact. I believe your bestie can procure some earwigs once you get to Turkey, right?"

"Aye, I can," Seer calls out. "I'll start hitting my contacts for a few things, and when we land, I'll peel off to go get them."

"Excellent. Then everyone, make sure you connect to Wi-Fi on those spare phones once you get on the ground, and let me know if you need help to get it all loaded up. Eli and I are going to have a chat, thanks to Jo-Jo."

I grin and wiggle my fingers at him. "Be good or be good at it, Jax."

"You, too, Jo-Jo. Over and out."

The feed clicks off and I look at the guys. "Okay, now it's time to talk brass tacks before we land."

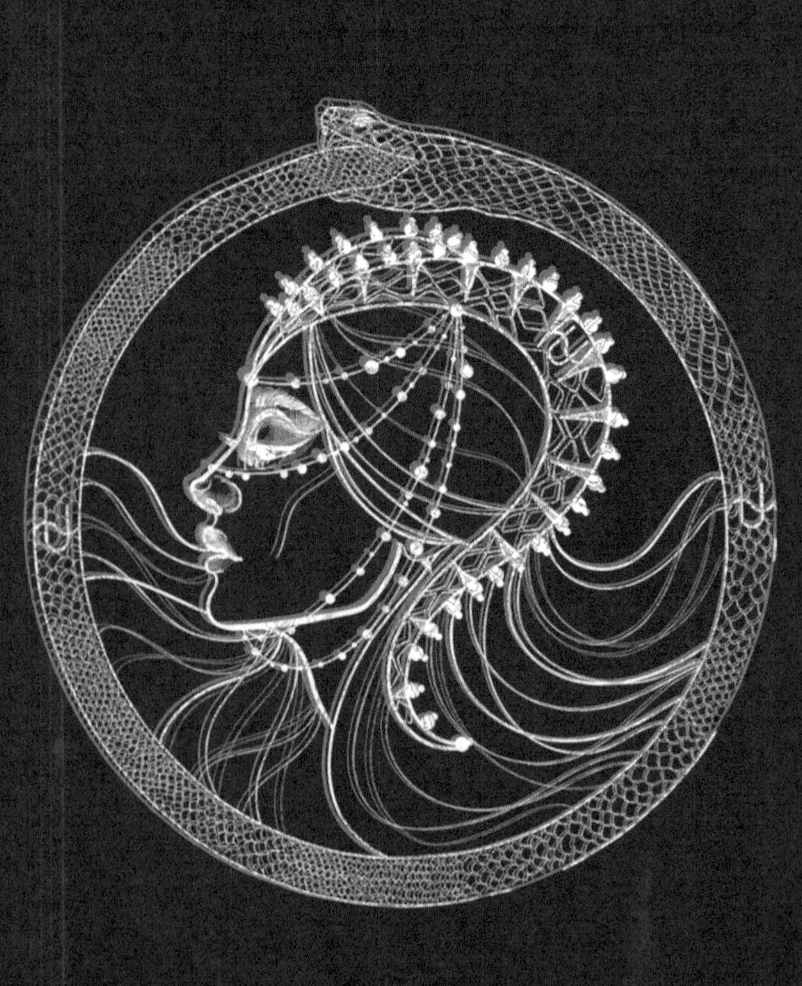

Fuqboi

Human travel methods are exhausting. They've done well in inventing faster shit over the years, but sitting in this rocket fuel propelled tin can for hours when we could have used hundreds of faster magical transports is killing me. I know supes like Boone and the others who are used to moving like they aren't what they don't notice, but being a demi-god with no ties, I hop portals more often than not. I'm sure Julia and her lot fly more often than they get in cars or planes for the same reason.

Until my Tíogair fully emerges, though, I'm stuck in the slow moving human vehicles when we move in groups.

The boredom is interminable, but I'm happy that she capitulated, so I'll suffer in silence.

"She's asleep again," Hamilton says. He's smiling as looks down at Jolene as she lays with her head in his lap and her feet in Boone's. "I bet she's slept more today than she has in a while. Especially given those rumors about the new dog in the woods."

"Stubborn as a mule, as always," Edgar adds ruefully. "She was so mad she didn't want to ask you about whatever symptoms she was having—whether they have to do with mating her emergence."

I think about that for a moment, concluding they're probably right. However, if she's been accessing any of her powers, it will have been noticed by more than the townspeople of Whistler's Hollow. Higher ups in the

Society or even some of our relatives have to know about it. For someone like Presley, it wouldn't matter if his mentor or people at the caladrius enclave found out. But for folks like me or Wolfgang? That could be extremely dangerous. We have far too many unknowns in our bloodlines and fucking with our mate might get our relatives' motors running.

"We haven't considered another potential issue," I interrupt. "While Boone and Foster's families or exes are basic, terrestrial threats that we can handle if need be… Wolfgang and I have a more complicated lineage. Our birth mothers enjoy torturing us and ignoring us, plus not knowing who our fathers are allowed for more chicanery. Many beings could decide to take an interest in us because of our raven haired unicorn."

"Son of a bitch," Edgar mutters as he runs a hand through his hair. "You're right. Most mate groups are 3 or less *at most* unless you count some of the pack animals. Even then, that's single species groups, not a mix of hybrids like us. As word gets around about Jolene, it will also spread that she's essentially powerless at the moment. It will paint a huge target on her back—and not just with our families."

Well, fuck. That's even worse than what I was imagining.

"Can we try to head some of it off? I'm sure Bane and Nelia will help with the Society," Presley says as he scratches his chin. "Seer and Julia can work on getting the Guardians to keep their eyes peeled for movements in the hunters, traffickers, and bad seeds."

"We can," Seer says with a nod. "And I might know a few ne'er-do-wells on the human side who owe me a favor. They can help put out a ban on humans being sent for her. I'm pretty sure I have the connections, but don't forget to ask Nelia. Some of her wildcards from the trial might have influence in other countries."

Closing my eyes, I press my hands together in a prayer pose against my lips as I think. This is good, but I think we need to be more proactive. I can slip home to the Mount and talk to my auntie anytime, but the actual question mark lies with our adorable submissive. He's not talking right now and I'm sure it's because he knows he can't control what his shitty mother does. We need him to steel his spine and help us protect our girl. "Wolfie, mate, I think you know what I'm going to say."

His eyes widen. "We can't."

"We can and we should," I counter.

He shakes his head and buries his face against the judge, who pulls him closer as he glares at me. "What the hell are you suggesting, Doyle?"

"I think we need to visit his mother—in person. Obviously, we'll have to stop by somewhere she feels comfortable after we handle our business in Turkey. But we should find the time to start negotiations after we land. I'm sure it will take a little time to get Tíogair to agree and longer to get his mother to do the same. But if we're in range of her lair, so to speak, we should see what she knows. If only to protect ourselves, we need to do it."

Wolfie lifts his head and gives me a pleading look. "You don't know what she's like, Doyle. She's so cunning and so calculating—if we take Sugarplum there, she'll spill the beans and everything will be fucked up."

"Oh, no she won't," I smirk. "If there's one thing I'm very good at, it's convincing people to do what I want without them knowing what my true goal is. I do it for amusement daily; she won't be able to resist when my intent is to trap her."

"Maybe. But she also knows how to hurt me. She'll spend the other half of her time hoping to drive a wedge in between us or picking at scabs until we have issues. I don't know why she's like this—it's not how her kind is supposed to be, but... I've always wondered if my father's absence made her lose it." The vet presses his face to Edgar again, and it's clear he will need an enormous amount of support to get through this.

But it's necessary. If his icy-hearted bio mother believes his birth drove the one person she cared about away, she'd be delighted to harm his lovers.

"Don't worry, pup. None of us will let her hurt you. Right?" Boone looks at all of us, waiting for us to respond.

"I've been waiting to smack some sense into that bitch for *years*."

I grin at the doc's vehemence and nod. "Absolutely. I'm not allowed to unleash on people very often in the Hollow. I could use some *real* fun—like having a super power fight with the winter witch. That sounds like a great time."

Benjy holds his hand up, giving us all a surprised look. "Uh, I know I'm not dialed all the way in but... Wolfie's mom is the Cailleach?"

"Ding ding, the gorilla's got it," I say as I put my finger on my nose. "And if you think that's impressive, someday I'll have a surprise for you."

"Fuck, I don't even want to *know* who they hell spawned you, Haggerty. The thought terrifies me," he replies. "But I'd be lying if I wasn't a little intimidated by what shit we may get up to on this seemingly innocuous trip Edgar invited me on."

His answer is just a shrug and a grin—classic Boone.

"I didn't think of adding destinations until now. But it occurred to me we agree that our woman is special—not just because we love her or she's unique, but because there's something hinky about her binding and mating. That won't escape people outside of our circle for much longer because she's attracting mates and companions like bees to honey." I sigh and pour myself another Jameson as I ponder it. "We have to figure out where the unknown dangers are before they come at us."

Seer folds herself into a pretzel in her big chair. "Mystery stalker is not unknown, but human surveillance and methods are failing. We should tap a magick user to see if the threat is supernatural. A couple of sigil traps around the house and yard should do it. I'll get Julia to start that process."

"That will help. I'll try to work a visit to my ridiculous relatives when it won't be noticed. My Auntie can be helpful when she's in the mood and I might visit a few others while I'm there. I don't know about my mother, though. That will require much more thought and some probing before I try to tackle her. She's… mercurial and cruel on good days, unlike her mythical reputation."

Edgar arches a brow at me. "Was that a clue? We should consider Greeks who aren't known for being mean by reputation?"

"You know I can't tell you," I sing-song. "But you're all clever; you'll get there, eventually."

"Greeks?"

Poor Foster—he really joined late, and he's been so sheltered in that town. His ball-busting wife kept him out of the Society meetings and he doesn't have a clue.

"Yes, Benjamin. Try to keep up," I say with a wink. "I'm forbidden from giving you many clues, so you'll have to work with a partner to catch up with the class."

"If we have to, we can arrange a visit with her," Wolfie finally whispers. "But everyone needs to understand that every word that comes out of your mouth can and will be used as a weapon. Even the negotiation about the meeting will be fodder for her to gather information she'll use later on to hurt you."

"You don't have to talk to her until we all do," Seer says firmly. "I can get word to her through my adoptive parents. They're big enough in that part of the world to make sure she shows up for a summoning."

"Perfect. So when we land, we'll split off to either get to the house or get equipment. Saoirse is in charge of the shit Jackson asked for and contacting Julia and her parents. Wolfgang and Hamilton can get the animals settled. I'll think you'll find a stowaway will magically appear in the cage with Euryale, but don't make a big deal of it."

"You cloaked Odie so he could run around and be your eyes, didn't you?"

I wink at Presley. "Aye. Secret weapons are never more useful than when they're actually secret."

"We've got our itinerary, then. Now everyone should shut up and make like Tilly. The time zones we've crossed are going to hit us and we need to be hyper aware since we have no idea if anyone is tracking us. Get some sleep —even I'm going to catch a few more z's."

I roll my eyes and give Boone a salute. If he wants to pretend to be in charge, I'll let him.

For now.

THE LANDING AND OUR TRIP TO THE HOUSE JOLENE RENTED WERE uneventful. With all of us working together, we wrangled the animals and the baggage with ease. Jackson's contacts came through—all the weapons and paper we didn't want examined were locked in diplomatic pouches and sealed boxes, so customs couldn't open them. It was the perfect plan and I'm surprised the git thought of it. I was worried I might have to do some difficult to explain magic to achieve our goals, but what do you know?

Sometimes even the squirreliest supes come through.

We pull into the gated community by the sea and I watch the scenery go by. Apparently, a British company started building this before that pesky virus ran rampant across the globe. It's near the Ottoman Palace and there's a five-star hotel, amenities, and a bunch of apartments and villas. I assume we're staying in a villa owned by one of Thorn's friends because I'm fairly certain nothing in this area goes for under three million. Boone could probably afford one and obviously I could, but our girl lives pretty normally. I doubt she's paying the premium that goes with this sort of place.

The car stops in a driveway and Jolene turns to look at us excitedly. "Isn't it beautiful?"

"Hell yes, it is," I grin as I look back at her. She's in the back seat with Boone again. He really is an overprotective pain in my ass. "Let's go look around."

She claps her hands, kisses him on the cheek, and throws her door open. Giving him a smirk, I follow suit, chasing her up the path to the multi-story villa with a lovely porch. We open the door with the code she gets off of her phone and walk inside to gape at the interior like rubes.

Inside, there are high ceilings with exposed wooden beams in the brick building. The first room is an open floor plan living and dining room furnished with huge spacious furniture and obsequious fixtures. I walk over to the mantle where there's an unnecessarily large television mounted on the wall, looking at the photos there. A snort escapes me before I can stop it and by the time my Tíogair comes back from looking at the kitchen, I'm dying of laughter.

"What's so funny, Doyle?"

"Yeah, what's got you going, Haggerty?" Presley asks as he guides the dogs and cats in first, lugging their supplies on his back.

I shake my head, trying to stop the amusement from making me howl. "Who did you rent this from?"

Jolene's nose wrinkles and she sighs. "The caretaker is an old friend of Jackson's."

That didn't answer my question, but I'll let it go for now.

"Well, we have located the most idiotic caretaker in all of Europe—that is, unless it's the owner. Walk around the lounging areas and have a look at these pictures."

She frowns, walking over to a set of frames on a low bookshelf, then gasps. "Holy shit. Does this guy have a douche-stache?"

"Yep," I say as I hold up an 8x10 of said guy pretending to whack off the statue of David in Rome. "And apparently, he's also about thirteen years old emotionally."

"He's like a walking, talking 'that's what she said' joke," Wolfie says when he holds up one of the olive skinned perv pretending to hump the lions outside of the Tower of London.

Tíogair shakes her head, looking at a few more of the ridiculous poses immortalized in the frames around the room. "I can't believe anyone wants to have anything to do with this moron. He looks like a graduate of one of those 'pickup artist' classes; only a shut-in with no experience in the real world would let a joker like this be in their bed. I wish Seer didn't have to go grab our equipment; she and I used to eat these morons for breakfast in clubs."

"You did, huh?" Edgar comes in and wraps his arms around her from behind, growling into her neck.

She rolls her eyes. "Yes, we did. There was a time when I was confident in myself and didn't worry about a bunch of judgmental fuckwits or creepy stalkers. I'd like to get back there as soon as possible, if you please."

Putting down the pictures, I walk over and take her hand, looking at her seriously. "We all promise that time is coming, Tíogair. Once we figure out what happened to your parents and why you were given the heave-ho, we can take trips like this anytime we want and not do detective work. Got it?"

Jolene's face lights up and she beams. "Got it."

"Good. Now let's finish getting settled so we can head out for the day."

Prince Charming

Jolene

"I'm sorry, madame. We simply cannot allow guests to visit the ambassador today."

Pulling off my sunglasses, I stare at the bespectacled man at the front desk. Both Jackson and I triple verified our appointment this afternoon and I have no idea why suddenly we're being denied entrance. "Look…" I peer at his name tag since whatever he said earlier made no impression on me. "…, Bennie. We've come a long way and I have confirmation that we had an appointment. What's the problem suddenly?"

He re-stacks his papers fussily, looking at me in annoyance. "I don't know what to say, ma'am. My instructions are to turn visitors away. You'll have to reschedule."

I'm ready to protest again when Teddy steps up. He gives the academic a charming smile, showing all of his impossibly white teeth. "My father is Senator Boone. He also assured me we could speak with His Excellency and tour the building while we're here on vacation. Perhaps there's someone you could call and check before I have to call him?"

The staffer rolls his eyes and sighs. "Fine. I'll call my superior and ask. But I doubt it will make a difference. We have children of legislators and statesmen all the time. It's not a special occasion."

Jesus, this guy is really full of himself for someone with the charisma of mashed potatoes.

I turn around as he picks up the desk phone and makes his call, irritated by the snooty tone he's taking as he talks to the person on the other end of the line. Wolfie walks over and takes my hand, giving me a smile that melts the ice forming in my veins slightly. His sunshine is always a good balm for the grumpy dominance of some of our group—including me.

"He's coming down to speak with you."

Doyle snorts and leans against the door frame. "How gracious of him. I suppose we'll wait in the entrance like idiots until *he* arrives, then?"

"That would be correct, sir." Bennie goes back to clicking away on his computer and I get the distinct feeling we've been dismissed as far as he's concerned.

I'd like to punch this little shit in the nose, but since we're guests, I suppose I should behave.

Teddy grins at me as I flex my free hand. "That won't help, Tilly. But it's sexy when you lose your shit, so I hate having to tell you not to do it."

His teasing helps a little, but I've noticed my temper simmers much closer to the surface than it used to. I don't know if it's because I was recently traumatized or because I'm getting comfortable in my new home and I feel like I can truly be me again. The behavior of the people in town has allowed me to cast off a lot of the polite, Southern exterior because I have every reason to be angry; when I first arrived, I didn't have the luxury. But when I think about it, I still feel like something in my gut is pushing me—it wants me to exact vengeance on people who wrong me or those I care about.

Am I losing my mind? Paired with the weird dreams and that flashback in the plane restroom, I'm not so sure.

"Excuse me!"

The voice pulls me out of my reverie and I turn back to face the desk where Bennie is smirking at us. Behind him, a tall, impeccably dressed muscle man is practically eye fucking my entire group. I arch a brow, giving the newcomer a bored expression when I respond. "Yes?"

"I'm Ozzie and I am the ambassador's executive assistant." His creepy grin widens and his eyes sweep over me in a way that makes my skin crawl. "Bennie called and asked me to dialogue with you."

This will not *end well; I can feel it in my bones.*

"Dialogue?" Doyle snorts derisively and rolls his eyes. "Mate, we have an appointment and we have confirmed it through multiple parties. Your door monkey here is refusing to allow us entry. Do your job and make it happen."

"Oh, sweetie, your accent is adorable, but I'm afraid that it won't change my answer. His Excellency is unavailable today." The blond angel faced pervert flashes his own pearly whites as he rakes his gaze over me and Wolfie. "I, however, am totally open to whatever this… is. I can give you my number."

Teddy pushes his way through the group with a snarl of anger, stepping in front of all of us before he speaks. "I suggest you allow us to keep our appointment and back off the cheesy player shit. Just because you work overseas doesn't mean my father and his friends won't pull your State Department clearance so fast your frosty tips will spin."

Fury fills my veins as the lampoon of a guy continues to lick his lips and stare at us. I have no idea how anyone finds this attractive, but I'm sure he'd get along with the douchecanoe who takes care of our villa. Is this normal behavior for guys over here or did we hit the asswipe lottery? Benjy pushes around me, joining Edgar in the barricade he's formed in front of us.

Great. Now the testosterone in this small waiting area is so thick I can't breathe.

"We may have to come back, magpie," Presley whispers in my ear. "The big guns are going to lose their tempers and we'll get booted for good."

I sigh, rubbing my temples as they continue to argue with the two-dimensional dipshit at the desk. Nothing I do is ever easy since that day when Agent Grant sent me packing—it's like there's a force actively fighting me and I'm so fucking tired of it.

"*Masa' alkhayr ya sayid.*[1]"

The deep, musical baritone is familiar and I turn around in surprise. Standing behind us with a cadre of employees is Dhameer. He's dressed in a sharp suit, but has a *kaffiyeh* and *agal* on. He didn't wear the headdress in the States, but that might have been because he didn't want everyone to recognize him. Today, he definitely wants these jokers to know who he is.

The question is, how did he get here and why the hell did he come?

But I can't ask that at the moment because the two men at the desk are frantically making hushed phone calls and the handsome horse-owning sheik is winking at me playfully. "Dhameer…"

He holds a hand up and shakes his head. "Later, *muharibi aleaziz*. We must negotiate with these gentlemen now."

"Your Highness, there is no negotiation with clowns," the suit-wearing woman next to him practically hisses. "Denial would be an affront to your family."

Ozzie goes pale, and he moves away from the counter to continue his whispered conversation with whomever he's informing about the Prince's arrival.

I squint at the small crowd of people behind the sheik and my eyes go wide when I realize Hugo is among them, just hiding under a *keffiyeh* with the rest of his staff. It makes me extremely suspicious and I turn a calculating gaze at the smiling prince as he patiently waits for the embassy staff to get their shit together.

When you have that much power, you don't have to do much beyond showing up to get people to bend the knee, I guess.

Finally, Ozzie and Bennie have a conversation and they come back to the group, all smiles. The perv isn't smirking anymore and his minion is quiet. "We are happy to receive you and your friends, Prince Dhameer Mirza Al Sharqi. The ambassador is, unfortunately, still detained, but I will take you on a tour personally. You honor us with your visit."

Dhameer gives the nasty fucker a brilliant smile. "Most excellent! Since we are many and you are few, we shall break up, don't you think? I should like a tour of the downstairs and the gardens first with my entourage and Miss Whitley. Perhaps your assistant could take the others upstairs to view the galleries and other architecture?"

"It's good to be the king," Teddy mutters.

"Shut up. He's getting us in *and* he gave you all a reason to be in the less trafficked areas. Do what Jax said and by the time we meet up, Eli will have a way into their system," I hiss softly.

"Can't look at a gift horse and all," Wolfie adds. "Besides, Sugarplum will have him and that extremely dangerous looking chick along to keep her safe."

"Agreed." Doyle looks at the prince with a grin. "We should get used to royal grandstanding, if you ask me."

What the fuck does that mean? I can not *with this many men surrounding me. I miss Seer already.*

"Fine, but I still don't like it. He's far too pleased with himself for saving our bacon. Maybe he set this up so he could save the day. He has the pull to do it," Teddy grumbles.

"No way, Edgar. That blond guy looked like he shit his pants when the prince arrived." Prez shakes his head. "I think someone else sent backup for us and we're lucky they did."

"Alright. But keep your eyes open and don't stray from his side, Tilly. We have no idea who we can trust except each other right now." Teddy leans down and kisses my forehead before he walks over to where the nervous-looking desk jockey is standing.

Truer words, Teddy bear. Truer words.

"How are your friends doing with their subterfuge?" Dhameer whispers as he leans in.

So far, we've gone through a slew of rooms that have some minor historical significance and a lot of artifacts that our reluctant guide clearly knows the bare minimum about. The contingent stays behind us, including Hugo, so I haven't been able to talk to him just yet.

"I don't know. They've got all the signals blocked in here so they can do what is needed, so I can't text. And Seer didn't make it back in time with the earwigs, so… I'm feeling blind, if I'm honest. That's not even mentioning that you showed up out of nowhere." I give him a pointed look after checking to make certain the prince's staff have Ozzie distracted for a moment.

He laughs softly, looking down at me with twinkling eyes. "Yes, I am well known for appearing when people need me. I daresay it's my trademark."

"I'm no damsel in distress you need to save, Dhameer."

His hands land on my shoulders, and his eyes delve into mine. "I am aware of that, *muharibi aleaziz*. However, I'd be lying if I said I am not enjoying being able to rescue you this one time."

I step out of the view of the babbling staffer, using his large body to block. Rubbing my temples, I sigh. "And I appreciate it. It must have been expensive and time-consuming to come here just in case we failed to get into the embassy."

"Oh, no, Jolene! I never rush into things without a backup plan. I am attending an auction tomorrow. I hope to add a few more studs to my stable; perhaps even one for Medhi one day. So all would not be lost had you not needed me."

My eyes widen, and I give him a shy smile. "A thoroughbred auction? Here?"

"Yes. Would you like to accompany me? It's quite an affair. The last time I attended one in Turkey was when I found your favorite horse and was convinced to let go of one I could not tame."

I ponder that for a moment, but I know the guys would rather I go horse shopping with the prince than skulking around the cop's house. I hate giving them the satisfaction, but I also really want to see the auction. I wrestle with it for a moment or two before I nod. "I would love to come. I think my companions have a task they want to deal with, and I'm sure I can get away to come with you."

"Excellent," he booms. The others look at us, pausing their conversations. Dhameer waves his hand and everyone goes back to doing what they were before he spoke. "I will send you everything you need to come along. MacAuley can help your men achieve whatever goal they have, and by the time they finish, we will return from the auction."

I smile shyly, taking the hand he offers me. "And here you are again, trying to make me soft on you. I see what you're doing, Your Highness."

His brow furrows, and he shakes his head. "No, *muharibi aleaziz.* You never need to address me in that way. You may call me Amiri—all of my most intimate relationships do."

That answers the question of why Doyle said they should all get used to having royalty about—the prince plans to stick around.

---

1. Good afternoon, gentleman.

Smooth Criminal

Hugo

I'll admit, I was a little intimidated when Mayor Nelia called me into her office a few days ago. She's been contacting me more since Jolene came to town and I have to be very careful what and how I answer when she does, lest I betray my first fealty to our temple. But this time, she wasn't alone. The prince who was training his horses at Cantwell's farm was there, smiling broadly when I arrived. It's a topic that's been whispered about in the break room at school and all over town, but few have actually encountered him.

He seemed almost normal, though the air of power around him was electric.

Nelia did not mention we would have company, and I knew by the look on her face that I was about to be conscripted for something. The Mayor is not subtle when she wants you to do her a favor and though I've been on the receiving end of that look more lately, I couldn't imagine why a Royal was involved until she revealed his secret…

"Hugo, I'm so glad you could make time for this meeting. I'd like you to meet Prince Dhameer, Mirza Al Sharqi." She gestured for me to have a seat and I did, though I was still puzzled.

"It is an honor to meet one of your kind, Mr. MacAuley, especially one as rare as yourself."

That made me panic. I'm not supposed to allow people knowledge of my purpose in town, nor am I to reveal what I am.

"Don't worry, Hugo. They gave me permission to share your secret with the prince and his with you. You are both needed to assist a mutual interest and the Society, as well as your patron, has granted us the ability to speak freely."

Nelia gives me a reassuring smile, but I am still nervous.
After all, knowledge of my existence has been strictly guarded. I am not the only one of my kind by far, but I am an anomaly by gender.

"I knew one of your kind many, many years ago. She is of very high importance in your temple now, thanks to my intervention all those centuries ago. But back then, crossover between species was taboo and now we work together to help protect all supes through the Society. It is not a system without flaws, but it is an improvement, to be certain."

I blinked at the prince. There could not be many who realized such a public figure was not human. Was that true of most of his family or only him? I didn't sense his presence when he arrived in town, but perhaps if he was as old as he said, he mastered cloaking himself.

"Nelia, I must admit to being confused. What conceivable use could you have for me that involves a prince?"

She laughed and shook her head. "It is not solely about Amiri. You are both required to ensure someone else can find what they need and you are both uniquely qualified for the task."

That surprised me. "What task involves two such vastly different people?"

"You are asking the wrong question, young MacAuley. The one you should ask is who are we uniquely qualified to assist and why." The prince grins again, holding up his hand before I answer. "I am obviously not the image I project—I am one of you. And like you, I have recently come upon something I did not expect to find in my thousands of years on this planet: a mate."

What? I don't have a—oh.

"Much like you, Hugo, there are few of Amiri's kind left. That is because they have strictly monitored their breeding over millennia because of their immense powers and capability to change the course of history, much like your people." Nelia pauses and considers

for a moment before continuing. "But we all know someone special has arrived and, with her, possibilities that have never been imagined."

Jolene. She was talking about Jolene and mates.

"Jolene has mates already and—"

"Her pack, so to speak, is not complete until we join, Hugo. I have seen it in the whispers of smoke and they are never wrong. You must have had visions," the prince says as he studies me. "Things that are clouding your thoughts unlike any others before."

How did he know that?

"Smoke?" I reply carefully. "What does that mean?"

"I perform at Howl when I am in town. She was there the first night I arrived in the area and I had a feeling she was significant. I called her up from the audience to grant her a boon—something I am not supposed to do without contracts, but I enjoy doing occasionally to help troubled souls." He shrugs, his eyes dancing. "I am ancient enough that no one can stop me, not even the Society, so they look the other way when I step out of line."

Granted, her a boon. Was he a—

"A djinn, yes. As the Mayor said, we are very slim in numbers and highly monitored. I have survived by playing by the rules—mostly—and providing those I am asked to with favors. It is not a sordid arrangement, for I have the freedom to decline should the smoke tell me something is not the will of the universe. But your Fates and I are not on good terms, as you can imagine."

I would have thought not. Those women were infinitely more terrifying than my patron, and they answered to no one.

"Over the long years, they periodically attempt to redirect my booms or use someone to remove me from the board, but we are evenly matched strategy-wise. I've escaped their machinations more times than I can count—the most recent time led me to the horse that brought me to your town. I am still unsure of the motives behind that incident, but it gave me my greatest desire: a mate."

The Mayor shook her head. "I doubt finding a mate is a trick of the Fates to eliminate you, Amiri."

She clearly didn't know them like the two of us. They were absolutely devious enough to have wrapped a weapon as a gift.

"Regardless, I am here and we are needed. Nelia has asked me to transport us to Istanbul to follow our future family and ensure their current mission is successful." The prince's expression turned troubled as he added, "There seems to be unknown forces gathering in many places and their intent is unclear—that you know after your bout with the witches. Our mate may be the nexus of the unrest given her special circumstances."

I didn't know how to take any of this. It was all too much.

But after a long conversation, they convinced me to come with the prince as part of his entourage. In the end, they were right; Jolene needed us at the embassy. Now, I've been sent to help Edgar and the rest of her family with locating a cop who they believed to be part of a cover-up surrounding her parents' death. I'm not completely sure how that will help Jolene, other than give her closure, but I'm willing to be part of anything that helps her find peace.

"MacAuley? Hey, MacAuley!"

The shout gets my attention and I leave the questions in my head as Presley approaches with Wolfgang. "Yes?"

"Let's get moving. Eli just texted the coordinates, and the guys were waiting in the SUV. We have to get this done before magpie gets back from the horse show with the sheik. None of us want her anywhere near a potential killer," he says as he jerks his head at the doors to the lobby of the hotel I'm staying in.

"Got it." I roll to my feet, sitting the paper I was holding on the table. I didn't get to read much; only that some rockstar went missing briefly after a bar fight in Paris and was found intact. Humans have so little care about their mortality that it's shocking, but I guess rich humans are as bad as rich supes.

I say as I climb into a hundred thousand dollar armored SUV provided by the ancient prince I'm staying with.

The irony isn't lost on me,

○

"This place is as swank as the one we're staying," Benjy remarks. "How in the hell does an ex-rookie cop who works low-level security for an embassy afford a place like this?"

"Exactly," Edgar replies. "This is a gated community in the capital city, near the seaside. When I looked up what the villa we're renting goes for on purchase, it *started* at two point two mil. Jolene has friends in high places, like Thorn, so it doesn't shock me we're in such a nice home. This guy, however, should live downtown in a walkup."

I'm about to reply when it hits me like a piano dropped from the top of a building. My eyes go completely white and my body tenses as the vision rockets through me like a jolt of lightning. There are a lot of unclear images and symbols I can't place, but when I finally come out of it, they're all looking at me in fear. It's not unusual for people who haven't witnessed the onslaught that is a hallmark of my gift; it resembles a seizure, so it scares people.

"Sorry," I pant. "I didn't feel it coming. I couldn't warn you."

"Are they… Are they always like that?" Wolfie says softly. "If so, I'm sorry. It must have been terrifying when they first manifested."

I shrug. "Sometimes. Occasionally, it's worse and for much longer. I've lost days before. Luckily for me, I grew up in a place where it's commonplace and my gift was expected. They prepared me when I came of age."

Edgar arches a brow. "I'll bite. What age is that for… whatever kind of seer you are?"

"Five." I give him a tight smile, ignoring the looks of horror on their faces. "Again, everyone in my original home has them. We, much like Hamilton's people, know what our powers will look like and are trained from the moment we can walk and talk to prepare for them."

Benjy is the only one brave enough to speak. "That's a rough childhood, man. You're a strong dude for surviving it without losing your marbles."

"Not really," the Irishman says as he smirks at me. I knew he'd toss in his opinion soon enough; he's from the same side of the world as me and he definitely knows exactly what I am because of his own relatives. "Hugo is one of hundreds of his kind and they all accept their visions young. It's not a shock, and it doesn't hurt him in the slightest. It merely *looks* painful and jarring. I'm well acquainted with his people."

I nod, giving them all a reassuring look. "He's right. It's dramatic on the surface, but it doesn't cause me pain. It is frustrating to sort out what I'm allowed to share and what I must guard the knowledge for fear of altering the threads of the tapestry, but otherwise, I am fine."

Presley leans in, touching my neck to feel my pulse briefly. When he pulls away, he sighs. "He's telling the truth. His heart rate isn't even elevated."

"So what can you tell us?" Edgar asks, as he points to the house behind the iron bars. "I assume your visions come when they are needed."

"Yes, they do." I look at the house and think for a moment. "Someone will need to bend the bars. We must go inside. It is imperative that we learn what this place is hiding. We will need to be in true forms to go in; it may be dangerous. That's all I can say."

Doyle claps his hands in glee. "Everyone has to get naked! I *love* it!"

"Naked?" Benjy says, his expression confused. "We're breaking into a house without clothes?"

Edgar claps his hand on his shoulder, laughing softly. "No, dude. We all have to shift before we go in. Naked as in… let the ape escape, buddy."

My eyes widen. I didn't realize how little I knew about these guys until it became clear I was going to see supe sides I didn't know about.. Of course, I'd seen Wolfgang's gorgeous Fae wings and Hamilton's feathered caladrius at the trial, but the others didn't show me anything. I'm a loner most of the time and I don't go to things where supes might let it all hang loose. The night of the Halloween ball, I went along with Saoirse, Bane, and her friends. That was the most uncloaked supe shit I'd seen in town since I got here, even with the trial.

Now I'm going to be part of their secrets, just like Amiri.

"Let's get it done, boys," Doyle says as he flings his door open.

The others follow and I watch in wonder as Judge Edgar Boone shifts into a giant hellhound. It has to be his dominant form because he does it within the blink of an eye and without so much as a growl of pain. Presley unfurls his beautiful white wings, choosing only a half-shift, and Wolfie's shimmering skin and Fae features appear in a shower of glitter. I'm not sure what his wing dust does, but I'm not getting near enough to find out. A loud grunt catches my attention and when I look over, a gorilla four times the size of a normal one is looking at me through the sunglasses belonging to Benjy.

His grin makes me think of that comic book villain, Grodd, and I walk over to look up at him.

"Goddamn, you and Boone are huge when you shift," I mutter.

"Just wait," Presley says with a chuckle. "I'm pretty sure that Irish fucker is waiting to enter like the drama queen he is."

I turn, and a burst of radiant energy flashes in front of my eyes, blinding me. When they finally adjust, an eight foot tall version of our companion is smirking at me through the telltale haze that surrounds a demi-god when they ditch their human form. The surrounding aura is golden, which tells me he's got Greek lineage, but the swirls of black and emerald surprise me. It can mean several things, and I'm fairly certain no one has ever shared those with him. If he knew what his aura said about him, I believe he'd be twice as obnoxious as he is now.

"Behold my true form, MacAuley," he preens.

Spare me, dude. I've seen plenty of full-blooded gods and even more of their mixed-race children.

"I'm not impressed. Quit swinging your magical dick around so we can figure out what's in this damn house."

Hound Edgar makes a sound of approval and, I swear, his giant fangs form a canine grin. With a brief howl, he takes off towards the back edge of the property with flames in his wake. I look at the rest of them and we all follow behind, stepping around the fires he left in his wake as he ran. When we catch up, he's sniffing around a tree several yards from a back gate. His eyes swing to Benjy, who immediately climbs the tall oak and drops over the wall with ease. A few moments later, the sound of breaking metal fills the air and the gate swings open.

"I could have done that without breaking shit," Doyle grumbles.

"Why didn't you?" I ask with a grin. He doesn't answer and I follow the winged docs as they enter the yard behind the huge flaming dog.

The son of an uncaring goddess doesn't like being questioned, I suppose.

Doyle snorts at me as he makes the locked French doors in front of us disappear by looking at them. "I save my parlor tricks for when they're more striking."

Of course he does.

The smell hits me as soon as we walk in—the copper tang of blood and the unmistakable scent of bodily gasses that escape during decomposition. Edgar rears back, letting out a howl of indignance and I don't blame him. Dogs, even hellhounds, have noses a hundred million times more sensitive than humans, even those of us with supernatural powers. If this is killing me, it has to be making him sick.

"Boone is going to struggle with this because of his canine instincts. I'm used to the smell because of my training, and so is Wolfie. We can leave the rest of you out here," Presley says.

A growl of disagreement echoes in the kitchen, and I shake my head. "As bad as it may be, I believe we all should stay together, and clearly Edgar does as well."

Benjy grunts his approval and Doyle shrugs at me. "I've been on many a battlefield over the years. My uncle's realm doesn't bother me. Let's go figure out what the hell happened here."

"I'm suddenly thrilled your royal friend invited Sugarplum to the horse show," Wolfie says softly.

I nod as we head through the dining room to another room, and the smell gets worse. "Agreed."

The sight that greets us there is one straight out of a crime TV show. There's blood everywhere—and the body of a middle-aged guy that appears to have been tortured for information via having his skin peeled off. It's disgusting, barbarous, and still not the worst thing I've ever seen—live or in a vision.

A shimmer catches the corner of my eye and I look to see Boone back in his humanoid form. He has fiery eyes, black hands and claws and sulfur is coming off him in waves, but the dog is no more.

"Motherfucker. This guy has a wife and kids," he says as he walks closer to examine the mess. "Haggerty, you check upstairs with Hamilton. I suspect there's nothing good up there, either."

"How do you know, Teddy?" Wolfie asks. I'm wondering as well, so I nod.

"You were all focused on the smell of death, but I smelled rotten food as we walked through the dining room. There was breakfast on the table for five people that had blood on it," he sighs with a sigh. "That's not a good sign."

Holy Hades. He thinks they're going to find dead kids upstairs. That's why he sent those two.

"I'm going to call the Mayor, Edgar. She wanted to know what we found and I think this qualifies as something that will require a clean-up team before humans find it." He nods and I walk back out through the dining room, noting he was right about the food.

Something tells me we've stumbled onto more than they bargained for with this trip.

But how does it relate to Jolene?

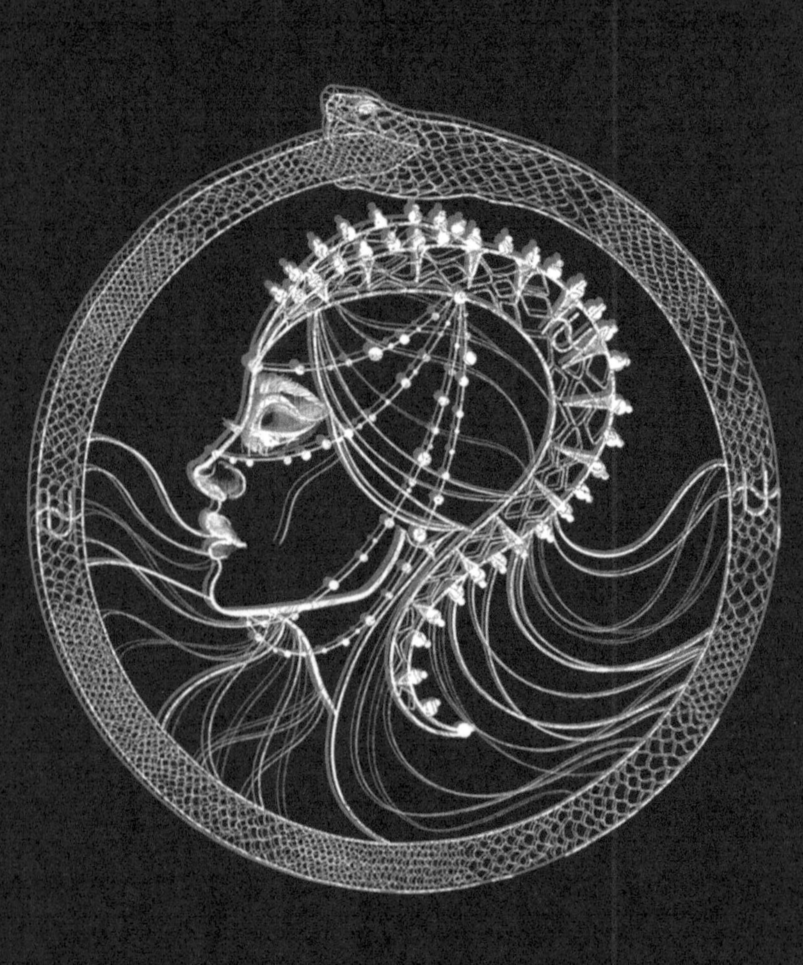

Rich Girl

The box that was delivered to our house this morning contained every single item of clothing I'm wearing. I'm not certain how he managed to get all of this on short notice and perfectly my size, but I suppose being a freaking prince has its benefits.

Adjusting my special shades, I look around the sales arena curiously. It's fairly small for *Arqana* and the event is late in the season. I wipe my hands on the understated couture jeans, noting the amount of expensive clothing and accessories on the people who are filing in. The black blouse and natty black straw fedora Amiri sent are sleek and sophisticated while kickass, block-heeled lambskin boots mold over my calves until they hit my knees. It makes me look like I fit right in with this crowd—outside of my non-surgically altered curves. He has my arm tucked in his, and despite wearing more casual attire, the kaffiyeh tells everyone he's someone to be deferred to.

I've had more people bow their heads to me today than ever before in my life.

"Amiri, people are staring holes in my back. Is this what it's like to be you all the time?" I whisper when we pause to look at an animal.

His smile is genuine as he nods. "If I identify myself. It's why I don't wear the traditional garb when I am not representing the family—or at least, when I am expected to by virtue of where I am."

I shake my head as I wrap my arms around myself. "It's creepy as hell. I can feel the emotions zipping around me; it's everything from jealousy to fear to hatred. I've been in the spotlight plenty of times, but *this* is a whole different level of weirdness."

"Very true, *muharibi aleaziz*. I suppose over the years I have grown accustomed to it and it no longer bothers me. But for someone who has not experienced it as part of their everyday life, it would be very jarring," he muses. His hand comes up to tuck a hair behind my ear and he looks at me seriously. "If it is too much, I can have Isra lay my bids and we will leave."

"No, no. I've wanted to come to one of these for a long time. I won't let the same kind of people who whisper about me at home drive me away here, too. Even if these people make those people look like paupers." I wink at him and he lets out a bellowing laugh. There are a few flashes around the room and I sigh. Those pictures are either going in a paparazzi rag or online; I can feel it.

Dhameer leans forward and whispers near my ear. "Don't worry. Isra will take care of the amateur journalists. She is *very* convincing and we will not appear anywhere we do not wish to."

Sounds a little scary, but I suppose it comes with the territory.

"And how does your fierce protectoress feel about me?" I ask curiously.

"Ah, well. Isra does not like new people. It took her many years to get used to Fazal. But she will come around eventually. Her level of suspicion is part of what keeps me alive, so I allow her to run my security as she sees fit. However, she does not get a vote when it comes to people I choose to care about."

My cheeks flush and I grab his hand, tugging him away from the fence to walk towards another horse. I knew he wouldn't be bidding on the one we were next to, but we can't speak freely when we're moving in a crowd. There are far too many people looking to get dirt on the prince. "Don't be mushy."

"Ah, but I enjoy the response, *muharibi aleaziz*. You are very strong and capable, but when you soften, it is a thing of beauty."

"Don't be cheesy," I say as we stop at the next stall. The horse is a beautiful thoroughbred with a long neck and powerful hindquarters—this one could be a possibility. Dhameer picks up one of the cards, perusing the information quietly. When he's done, he holds it up and Isra appears out of nowhere to take it from him with a nod.

He sees my surprised expression and shrugs. "She is always watching and her training allows her to move with stealth and speed. It is very unusual to look for her and not find her within seconds."

"Isn't that a bit weird? I mean, it doesn't leave a lot of room for private moments."

"Would you like to have a private moment? I believe Isra will be occupied for another three to five minutes, though if I called that would change," he teases.

I roll my eyes at him as we head to another animal's stall. "That's not what I meant and you know it."

The prince gasps softly and I whirl around, looking for what caused him to sound alarmed. "*Reine Panthère*[1]..."

Frowning, I follow his gaze to a tall, redhead dressed in black from head to toe. Her leather pants and boots are even more expensive than mine and she's wearing a slinky silk top that clings to every one of her curves. Her long red curls hit her thighs as she stalks in front of the horse we were about to look at. Large old Hollywood-style sunglasses cover her eyes and there's something very familiar about her that I can't place. She definitely has the show stopping charisma down pat, though.

"Who is that?" I ask. When my companion doesn't answer, I shake his shoulder. "Amiri, who is that woman?"

His face is pale as he turns to me. "That is the Panther Queen. She is well known among a certain element of people, though she's a fairly new addition to her employer's stable. I know this because I had Isra do extensive research on her after she decided to strike a bargain with me rather than kill me at a show like last year."

"I'm sorry...what?" I blink at him, feeling panic rise in my chest. A hot sensation starts in my chest and crawls through my veins as I look over at the woman who might be a threat.

He shakes his head. "Do not get upset, Jolene. She wasn't here for me and I was able to bargain with her for an animal I was already contemplating selling. It was very amicable at the end, though, at first I was not certain it would end well."

His ability to shrug this off, despite the obvious physical reaction he's exhibiting, makes me think there's more to the story, but I don't think I'll get it out of him now.

"Your Highness!"

Oh, shit.

The redhead practically oozes her way over to us with an excited wave. I have to rub my eyes when she approaches because I'm certain she's being followed by a tiger with a cola black ferret riding on its back. But that can't be right, can it? We're not in the Hollow; no one would allow a woman to be walking through a horse show with a goddamned white tiger, right?

"Jolene, it is my turn to ask if *you* are okay?" Dhameer murmurs before he holds his hands out to the woman. She darts in and does the air kiss thing with him, but he doesn't say a word about the wild animal.

Maybe I am losing my fucking mind. Maybe I have a tumor.

"Who is this lovely creature you've brought along?" she says with a smile that is half beautiful and half feral.

"Pardon me, *Reine Panthère*. This is my date, Miss Jolene Athena Whitley of Kentucky," the prince says formally.

"Oh my," she says. Her hand goes up to her glasses and she takes them off, studying me with sapphire eyes that seem to see right through me. A delicate sniff of the air makes her lips curve up slowly. "She is a special find, Your Highness. Quite fitting for you, I think. I am glad we were able to come to terms last year. Something about your date tells me I won't regret it."

My eyes narrow as she talks about me as if I'm not even here. "It's nice to meet you as well, Panther Queen. Have you ever been to the States? Something about you feels very familiar…"

"I bet it does, darling." Her wink is playful and I swear to shit, she looks over at the tiger I'm certain no one but me can see with a smirk. "However, I don't think today is the day we will discuss that. I'm on a deadline, you see. I have a job and I'm not quick about it, I won't make it home before my husband. He's such a bear when we're late to dinner with our spouses. It's a total bloodbath."

Dhameer arches a brow, but I ignore it. This woman doesn't feel like a threat but I can't seem to get my body to stop sending fight or flight signals to my brain. I'm flushed and I can't figure out why, nor can I understand why I'm having a hallucination involving jungle cats at a horse show.

"It was delightful to see you again, *Reine Panthère*," the prince says as he lifts her hand to kiss it. "Please reach out to my staff should you want to contact me about your horse."

Her grin is absolutely wicked as she flips her hair over her shoulder. "Oh, that won't be necessary. Hippolyta is doing very well in my stable. She terrorizes the staff and my family, but we are perfectly matched as horse and rider."

"Excellent," he says. I can see the surprise on his features, and it makes the woman laugh more.

Her eyes flash at me as she nods and for a moment, the memory of the airplane bathroom and my weird vision of my eyes changing in the mirror. "Enjoy the show, Jolene. I'm certain we will see one another again."

I wave as she turns to go, unsure of what to say to that. Our meeting today was by chance and despite the intense sensation of familiarity, I highly doubt our paths will cross again as she suggested. A tap on my arm brings me out of my thoughts and I give the prince a sheepish look. "I'm sorry. I just… I have the oddest feeling that I know her and I can't place where we might have met. It could have been in a million places during my time with Seer, so it's going to drive me crazy."

"Perhaps it will come to you when you are not so focused on it. Come, let's go find the refreshments area. You're flushed and I would be remiss if I didn't get you some water." Dhameer takes my arms and tucks it in his again, guiding me away from the viewing stables.

"You know, for a prince, you're very approachable," I say as we stroll through the arena towards the door. "I know the people here are all in your sphere, but I saw you with Jamie at the farm. You like him and you don't act like he's your staff. Even at the embassy yesterday, you threw your weight out with those assholes, but you didn't act like my… boyfriends… were any less important than you."

"I have learned that wealth and fame do not make a person good. In fact, many times, it's the opposite. The constant fulfillment of your desires with little effort tends to make good people turn demanding and shrill. Even those who are not obscenely wealthy or successful are misled by the siren's call of their egos. It can ruin friendships, destroy marriages, and decimate the people around them when they start believing the pretty words whispered in their ears."

Sighing, I think about his words for a moment. Whistler's Hollow has families with a great deal of generational inheritances and it definitely causes a divide in those who and those who have not. The children of the founding families are afforded a status and grace others are not, further pushing the gap between the two sides apart. It's why shrews like Sherilynn and Amy and their ilk felt perfectly fine humiliating someone at an event where most of the town was in attendance. They believe that because they have an elevated status in our community, they can get away with anything. Unfortunately, history has proven them correct over and over again, so the cycle repeats *ad nauseum*.

"I agree. At home, I'm struggling against a group of women who haven't taken the time to reflect on what behaving the same way they did in high school says about them." I stop and he follows suit. His hand comes up to cup my face as I continue. "It took a long time for me to heal from the scars of my youth and when I came home, I would have been happy to be quietly civil instead of reliving the past. But from the second I arrived, these women picked up their campaign of terror like I'd never left. It's disheartening to see the good people around us sit back and watch."

His thumb brushes over my cheek bone and he leans in to brush a light kiss on my lips before pulling back. "I'm sure you know this, *muharibi aleaziz*, but we are all victims of our past. All of the bad and good that happens helps to forge the core within us and teach us how to navigate the world more successfully. The women you speak of may be finding joy in trying to hurt you again, but where they have not evolved, you have. Your strength was fired in the flames of their abuse, so whereas they are still the bullies they have been, you grew into a smart, funny, capable woman."

I lean into his hand and give him a rueful smile. "Are you getting ready to tell me they're just jealous of me? They want to shine as brightly as me, so they work to dim my light? Because it's sweet, but I'm definitely too old to fall for that old chestnut."

"Ah, Jolene. I do not know enough about them or their lives to make that assumption. What I do know is that you have traveled the world, met with princes and CEOs, been a teacher, interviewed to be a profiler... and even when you were kicked in the teeth, you moved home and picked up your pieces without missing a beat. That kind of resilience and confidence in yourself is enviable to those who secretly doubt themselves."

Put that way, I could see how my presence, especially after the guys attached themselves to me, might be a threat to their self-assigned queen bee status.

"They're afraid this time around, I could take their crowns?" I squint up at him, trying to wrap my head around that seemingly impossible theory.

"Yes," he says. "They know they have limited appeal and if you are given the opportunity, you will eclipse them without trying. Your Edgar and Benjamin are walking, talking proof of your ability to win without even playing their games. Their fear is not unwarranted; I wholeheartedly believe once the larger populace sees who you really are, there won't be a comparison. Their power will be gone in the blink of an eye."

"Thank you," I whisper. "I don't know if I believe you, but thank you for being honest about your feelings. The guys defend me and I know it's because they care, but I'm not sure they understand why I can't seem to ignore the pokes and prodding."

Dhameer steps back, offering me his arm again. "It is because you are a born warrior, Jolene Whitley. One day, you will show everyone the ferocity I see in you and when that happens, there will no longer be doubt."

Be still my fucking heart, Prince Charming.

---

1. Panther Queen

Outsider

Benjy

It's terrifying how matter-of-factly the rest of the guys are going about searching a murder scene. Sure, MacAuley peaced out to call Nelia, but once he was gone, Presley and Doyle trooped upstairs like Edgar commanded. Wolfgang surprised me by walking around the room snapping pictures without being told and my oldest friend made a beeline for body, crouching next to it with his own phone.

"Uh, what… What should I do?" I ask, rubbing my hand over the back of my head as I watch the surreal scene in front of me.

"Check the doors. Well, the ones Doyle didn't fucking disappear so he could show off. See if they show signs of forced entry," Edgar says distractedly.

Does he expect me to have CSI experience or…?

"Teddy, you know he didn't do the training. He wasn't shipped off because he's not active."

I frown at the vet, watching him continue to snap photos as he makes his way around the room. "Training? What training?"

"Shit. Those morons sent his idiot ex to that. She fell in a kiddie pool full of sewage and stormed off. I remember now." Edgar rises to his full height, giving me a sheepish look. "Sorry, man. Your ex really cut you out of everything and left you running the store—literally."

"She did? Like what?" I cross my arms over my chest, feeling angry at myself all over again for staying married to a woman I didn't love for as long as I did.

"Society stuff, man. She was the rep from your family so she went to all of the meetings, trainings, and active agent shit. If it makes you feel better, she sucked ass at almost all of it and some of the places we went refused to allow her to stay after the first day." My friend tilts his head. "Where the hell did she tell you she was going when we did all of the out of town jaunts?"

My head falls back on my shoulders and I look up at the ceiling, closing my eyes. "Spa getaways with the girls. Goddamn it. That woman controlled every damn thing in our lives so tightly that I missed everything."

"You're free now," Wolfie says as he turns to look at me. His expression is sympathetic yet hopeful and I arch a brow at Boone.

"Yes, he's always this way," the judge says with a smirk. "It's both infuriating and endearing at the same time. And completely impossible to say no to."

The fae blushes under his blue tinted skin. "Stop it, Teddy. We don't have time and it's gross in here. And I'm not being sunshiny—I really mean it, Benjy. You're free now and you can do whatever you want. Sugarplum will support you and so will we."

"That's true. We all went to the stupid shit you missed, so we'll teach you as we go along. Tilly would love to work with you on martial arts or shooting. Just ask her." Edgar chuckles and shrugs. "For now, go check out the locks on the front door. Look for scratches like someone tried to pick it or splinters in the frame like a crowbar opened it."

This is not what I imagined when Edgar told me I should come on a trip overseas with them, but when in Turkey, I suppose.

"Got it," I say with a lot more confidence than I feel. I'd Google a video, but the guy with the cell net device is upstairs doing…things I don't want to imagine. At least they didn't ask me to go hunt down tiny bodies.

And that is a sentence I just said in my head—great.

"You know, I think she's warming back up to us," Wolfie says randomly. "Look at how easily we all fit into the house. She didn't even complain about everyone piling in on the plane until she had to pee."

"There's still distance emotionally, though. I don't like it," Boone growls. "I want it gone."

Kneeling by the door to do as they asked, I call over my shoulder. "Have you actually addressed the past with her? Like besides just telling her how she became the Catastrophe? You may have been honest as much as possible about our secrets, but have you truly worked through what you did *before* that?"

"Shit."

That would be a 'no'.

"Do you really think she needs to hear me lay out how badly I felt afterward? After all of these years?" He comes up behind me, his brow creased in concern.

"Uh, yeah, dude. I think she does. I can come with you if you think you're going to fuck it up as usual."

He nods, then points at the loose strike plate. "Definitely forced entry, but they knew what they were doing. I wouldn't have caught it if we weren't looking closely. This wasn't random; I think someone took this guy out."

Footsteps sound on the stairs and I see a much paler Hamilton and Doyle descending them with solemn expressions. They shake their heads when we look at them and I swallow hard. That means they found the rest of the family and by the look of them, it wasn't pretty.

"Jesus fuck," I mutter. "What the fuck did this asshole do that got his kids slaughtered?"

"I don't know," Edgar says tiredly. "What I do know is that we *cannot* tell Tilly what we found. We have to say he was gone. This is part of the necessary lies until she's ready to defend herself."

Wolfie walks over and wraps around Presley. The taller doc relaxes immediately, his wings coming around them both.

Doyle looks over at us with mischief in his eyes. "No one wants to comfort the deli-god, eh? I see how you all are. Speaking of Greeks, where's the spook?"

"Spook?" I ask in confusion.

"MacAuley. Is he still listening to our fine Mayoress chew him out for breaking into a crime scene?"

"I think so. I don't envy him that, though you and Hamilton got the short end of the stick," I add with a shudder.

The red haired supe looks at his hands and shrugs. "It's not the first time I've seen shit like that and likely won't be the last. Humans are constantly coming up with better ways and flimsier reasons to kill one another. I gave up trying to understand it centuries ago."

Ouch. It's easy to forget how old he is until he says shit like that.

"Are we done here?" Presley asks from under his wings. "I'd like to get the hell away from this massacre and have a few dozen drinks to forget."

"We are," Edgar replies as he looks around. "When we get back to the house, we'll check on the animals and wait for my *drugar* to get home. Benjy and I are going to take her out tonight. If I can be honest about high school, maybe we can get her to open up about the Trevor shit."

"And what the hell are we supposed to do while you two wine and dine our woman?" Doyle asks indignantly.

Wolfie sighs and comes out from under the doc's wing shelter. "We can get Seer to help us do a summoning for my mother. We should get it over with before anything else terrible happens. If we do it while they're out, I can avoid her seeing Sugarplum."

"Good thinking, pup," Edgar says as he pulls him close and drops a kiss on his head. "I'm proud of you."

The Fae blushes so hard his blue skin almost looks purple and I chuckle.

Yeah, it's hard not hard to get why everyone is soft on the vet.

"Let's get the hell out of here," I grumble as I turn to walk to the front door. "We're all going to smell like death if we stay here and the lover boy over there has a date with our woman tonight."

Wolfie smiles patiently. "When I texted Saoirse, she asked me to look up a place where we could get supplies for the bullshit with my mom. It seemed unlikely that the joker who watches our rental would have what we needed in the house."

I roll my eyes as I think about the pictures of him dressed in frat boy style costumes and making prepubescent Insta shots in public places that are strewn about the house like badges of honor. "Yeah, that makes sense. That dude seems like the guys we were in the frat with in college—emotionally stunted, insecure, and dying for attention for all the wrong shit. Sadly, much like him, those dudes are probably *still* doing that well into their thirties despite being lawyers, doctors, stock brokers, and military men. His name is probably Vann or Chad or something."

Edgar laughs as he whips the SUV into a tight spot on the street like a pro. "Do you remember that one dark haired guy with the angel wing tattoo on his back? His dad was from that big metal band and he acted like he was related to the king of Hell? His lineage got him in, but he stuck out like a sore thumb even in a frat full of rich assholes like us. What was his name… Slade? No, Razor. No… shit, Benjy."

"Mage. The dude called himself Mage, man. He really leaned into the whole 'my dad says he's Satanic' thing. It was comical in a place so strait laced and preppy as State U. He was from Bay City, I think. Supes are *weird* out west." I laugh as I think about him running around being broody and alternative, thinking that would attract the elite women who attended our college. "I guarantee he didn't get laid once all four years. He was about as dark as a mocha latte."

Presley's eyes widen and he snaps his fingers. "That guy is an archivist up in Salem. I only recognize it because I requested all those files from other enclaves when our girl came to town. I was trying to find out where she'd been left as a baby before the Whitleys adopted her and his response email was in a four beat iambic verse like a Poe poem. I laughed so hard I spit my salad out."

"I remember that!" Wolfie chimes in. "We made fun of it for days."

"Yeah, he was a complete tool," Edgar says. "Some of the founding in other enclaves make ours look *way* less wacky."

"Now that we strolled down memory lane, we should get this crap and get home," Doyle says, his voice full of boredom. "Some of us didn't join fake Greek party clubs for social cache."

"It's not our fault you're older than most developed nations, Haggerty," my old friend says. "It probably chaps your ass that one of your relatives is the god everyone worships at parties."

He opens his door, grinning. "I'm rather fond of the old drunk, actually. He's a shitty poker player and I kick his ass in the deity tourney every decade." We all look at him, trying to imagine playing in a poker tournament full of various gods and demi-gods. He shrugs and exits the car. "Let's go, dickwads."

That gets everyone moving and we follow suit, walking to the small, cramped entryway of the store. The sign says '*Destiny*' and it's slicker than the surrounding shops. The walls are shelves bursting with magical books, items, and various spells ingredients. I sniff the air, trying to identify the scent wafting around us.

"It's a mixture of jasmine, vetiver, clove, and patchouli," the Irishman says under his breath. "It's supposed to attract money, which I suppose makes sense in a store. But it means the owner isn't completely full of shit. Maybe."

"Maybe is right. There's stuff that feels real and things that are complete tourist traps," Wolfie remarks as he holds up a Tarot deck featuring characters from a TV show. "This kind of stuff is to get sales from tourists. I have a feeling we need to go deeper to get to the things we'll want."

"How do you know?" I arch a brow at him, curious since he doesn't seem like the type.

"Aurelia and my father were both agents up until…everything changed. He was Fae—Daybreak Court—and she was a witch with the gift. I grew up with all the ceremonies and knowledge they could give me. Now I wonder if it's because they knew my real mother would find me one day and they wanted me to be prepared."

Edgar looks over his shoulder as he leads us through the winding rows and shelves. "She won't hurt you, pup. You can do this and you'll have plenty of people to keep her in line tonight."

"I trust you all. But we have to find the true stock—the things supes use for their magical working or my mother won't respond. She's a snob as well as a sociopath."

"What a combo," I mutter and the others nod.

As we make our way deep into the seemingly never ending store, we find a spiral staircase that leads downward. The vet nods his approval, letting us know this is where we want to go. Before any of us can start our descent, a loud, baritone voice echoes out of the stairway.

"Nothing you have here is powerful enough for a witch such as me. I am one with nature, a child of the forest, and people seek out my brews from all over the world!"

"Uh-oh," Wolfie groans. "That doesn't sound good. Should we come back?"

"Negative," Boone says. "We don't have time to double back before Tilly is due home. We'll have to navigate around this nutter, get what we need, and get out."

Great. I cannot wait to meet the person behind that self-important ranting.

One by one we trudge down the narrow staircase, spilling into the huge underground warehouse. This time, I can actually *feel* the buzz of power coming from every direction. Scents mix and float by on gentle breezes as if to draw me in the direction of the emotions they evoke.

Candles and dim lamps are randomly scattered throughout the room, placed to highlight small signs that mark the locations of different items and ingredients. A tall case behind the counter gives off a scary vibe and I'd bet Cantwell's farm that nothing in there is fake tourist crap. I don't even want to know what is kept in there, honestly,

"Do you see the men with me? They are powerful allies who recognize my dark power. You need to heed my words, shopkeeper, or you will regret it!"

Our group approaches the counter carefully, letting Wolfgang take the lead. The woman who is shouting like a lunatic is short and angry looking, but nothing like I would have imagined based on her claims. She's got several dudes with her, but they seem to be standing off to the side while she throws her hissy fit. By the looks on their faces, they're used to it and choose not to get involved. I don't blame them; I wouldn't want to be part of this nonsense, either.

"Excuse me? Can you point me toward the fresh herbs?" The vet charges in with more confidence than I would have expected, but then, this is a world he's comfortable with. Maybe chicks like this haunt occult shops acting like fools everywhere. I sure as hell wouldn't know.

The shopkeeper comes out of the shadows where she'd been quietly allowing the other customer to wear herself out. When she's visible, Edgar turns to look at the rest of the group in shock, cutting his eyes at her point-edly. I frown, not sure what he's getting at. She's tall and powerful looking, dressed in some sort of metal armor like get up that feels more fitting for a geek con than a magic shop. An enormous black wolf is standing by her side glaring at us.

"Oh, shit," Wolfie mutters. "It's the wildcard woman."

Her laugh is deep and rich as she nods at him, completely ignoring the other customer as she continues to stomp around in her yoga pants and combat boots bitching. "It is me, young Fletcher. This is my shop and it is always there for those who are in need. Hand me your list and *Destiny* will find what you need."

This is weird as hell and I'm a gorilla shifter who lives in a town full of supernaturals who hide in plain sight.

"Thank you," he says simply. "But the list was sent digitally. Do you have a pen and paper?"

She nods, producing a piece of parchment, a peacock feather, and an ink well. "Write it down and it will appear. I will charge it to my sister."

"Your… what?" I sputter.

The woman smiles and I can see the magic of whatever she is in her eyes. "My sister. She's much older, of course, but we discovered one another when she arrived in your town to take over. Nelia and I share the same biological mother. That's why she came to Whistler's Hollow in the first place—to find me."

We all gape at one another, unable to figure out what to say. This woman is intimidating as hell and according to her, she's related to our Mayor and from our hometown. Silence falls over us as we try to process all of that information.

"This seems like a lovely reunion, but I was here first." Heads swivel to look at the shrewish witch as she glares at both us and the shopkeeper. "Since I am the more well known magic wielder, I demand you pay attention to me and offer the respect I deserve!"

Even I know that was a mistake.

A flash of black fur, blue eyes, and sharp white teeth leaps over the counter in a blur of motion. The wolf is standing on the chest of the obnoxious twat, snapping its jaws in her face menacingly. She shrieks in fear, looking at the people standing behind her, but they don't move. The shopkeeper drifts out from behind the counter gracefully, looking down at the prone witch with a feral smile.

"You've angered Argus and most beings that do so do not survive to tell the tale. Your hubris will be your undoing; I can feel it in your aura, witch. The Fates have conspired to continually toss the apple in your path and you will forever pick it up. It is your curse and why you act in this way." Her head tilts as she waves her hand over the woman's face briefly. "However, since I find your squawking pathetic and beneath me, I will ask him to let you live if you simply take your minions and never return. You will cease your prattling about things you have no concept of."

The woman nods, looking as though she might have just pissed her waffle printed pants. Argus steps off of her, tosses his head and howls into the air. That signals the men and they grab the witch, dragging her towards the stairs without another word. Our hostess smiles wickedly as she watches, then turns back to us.

"Now, allow me to help you collect what you need to summon the Cailleach, young Fae."

Okay, now this woman is even scarier.

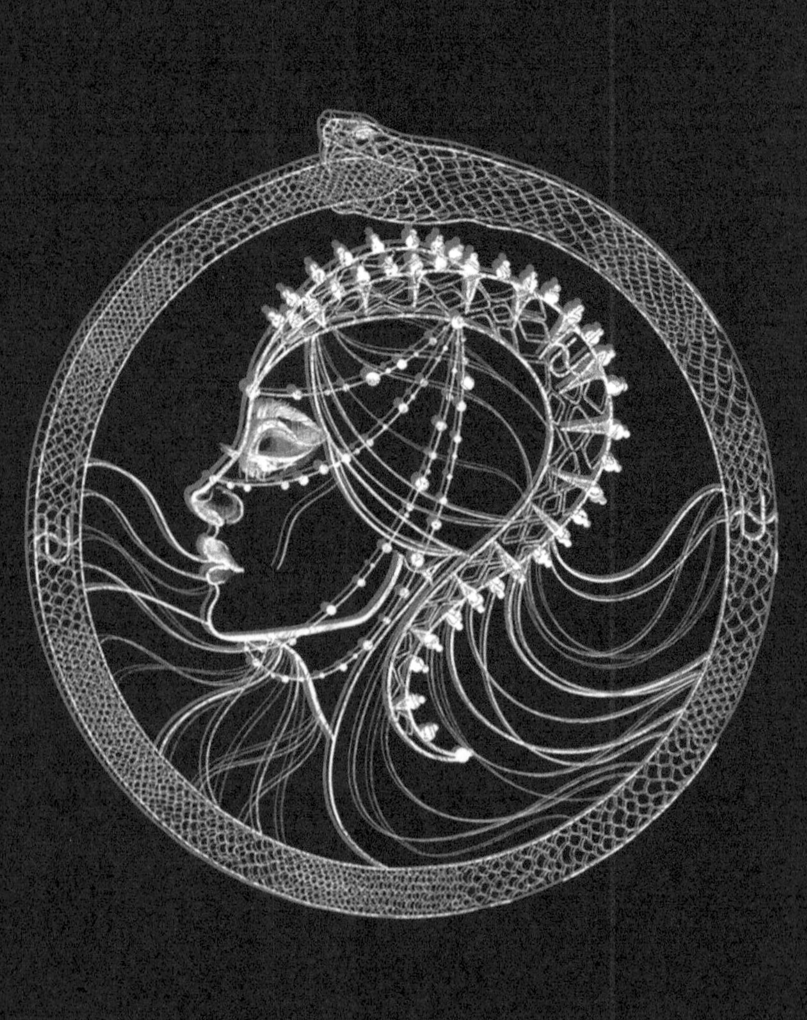

Sorry Not Sorry

Jolene

When we pull up to the villa, Dhameer insists on escorting me to the door and saying hello to the guys. His 'ye olde' gentleman stuff is cute, so I let him get away with it. It's hard to imagine the rest of the guys behaving so formally and not cracking me up, but with him, I find it more endearing than silly. I punch the code in, leading the prince into the foyer with a smile. He looks around, his expression approving as he takes in the decor. The sound of laughter is coming from the sitting room, so I take his hand and drag him towards the noise.

"I'm home, you reprobates!" I call. "Say hello to the prince."

A chorus of muttered greetings are the response and I roll my eyes when I figure out they're all piled on the couches playing Mario Kart on the big screen. They've got beers and snacks littering the formerly pristine table, making the room look more like a frat house than an elegant villa.

"Clearly, I've been missed."

Dhameer grins and holds up my hand, kissing it. "Obviously. However, since Hugo is not here, I assume he is awaiting me at my suite. We have some business to attend to this evening, so I will leave you in the capable hands of your entourage."

I roll my eyes. "That, Amiri, is very subjective."

"Oi!" Doyle shouts. "I'm extremely capable. In fact, I'm capable of kicking Boone's ass and I'm doing it *right now.*"

All it takes are sports or video games and every single man in existence becomes a teenager again, I fucking swear.

The prince leaves and I walk over, flopping down on the couch beside Presley. He tugs me to his side and looks at me. "Did you have a good time, magpie?"

"I did, actually. What did you guys find when you went to the address Eli gave us?"

Teddy snorts as he works the controller with expert precision. "The guy was gone. We couldn't question him or his family. Did a sweep of the place, but didn't find any useful information, but we sent all the pics and shit to be analyzed. We might have missed something; who knows?"

I sigh, frustrated that every lead seems to dead end in nothing. "What else can we do? Now I feel like we came here for nothing."

"For tonight, Edgar and I are going to take you to dinner, Princess. You looked happy when you came in and I think the distraction did you good." Benjy looks at me over his shoulder quickly, then looks back at the race where he's trying to maneuver his Donkey Kong around Doyle's Waluigi.

"Just us?" I echo. "Are the rest of you okay with that?"

The last thing I need is a bunch of macho internal jealousy stuff flaring up.

"Of course we are, sugarplum," Wolfie says quickly. "We had to do a lot of shit to search that place from stem to stern and I'm perfectly fine with lounging at home with take out. Besides, we have all month away from home; we can all take you on dates if we want."

Presley nods in agreement. "What he said."

"Doyle?"

"Peace in the Middle East, Tíogair. Except for in this feckin' game, of course." His eyes tear away from the screen and he gives me a playful wink before he turns back.

Did they all get high or something? This is weird as hell.

"Oooookay. Well, if that's how you all feel, I'm going to go upstairs, shower, and relax while I get ready. It was fairly hot and dusty at the arena, so I need to freshen up before we go anywhere nice." A scent catches my nose and I frown when I recognize it—but that can't be, so I shake my head. "Someone here should hit one of the other bathrooms, too, especially if you're going out with me. It smells like decomp in here for some reason."

Silence is the response so I shrug and head upstairs.

Men are so goddamned bizarre.

THE BATH WAS LUXURIOUS AND EXACTLY WHAT I NEEDED.

I read while I soaked, got everything squeaky and soft, and finally got a text from my errant best friend. I tried not to worry about her when she didn't make it to the house in time to go to the embassy and when she didn't show up last night, I struggled not to set off alarm bells. But long before she landed in my hometown, Seer would disappear for days and I never felt the need to track her down. The paranoia from the bullying and the weirdo watching me have made me act like a schoolmarm and I have to let my friend and lovers do shit without panicking when they're out of touch.

Don't be a controlling asswad, Jolene. Saoirse can definitely take care of herself and whatever she got caught up in with this contact is probably important. She's not abandoning you and she's not tied up in some creep's basement.

But now I have to put myself together for a night out on the town with Teddy and Benjy without my personal 'girly shit' coordinator. I wrinkle my nose, plodding over to the closet where Wolfie insisted on hanging my clothes. I swiped a few of the expensive designer things in my mother's closet to bring in case we had to attend something a little dressier just in case. Thank fuck my compulsive packing gene made me do it or I'd have to wear jeans to a nice restaurant.

Studying the three outfits, I finally pick the *Balenciaga* cocktail dress. The brilliant emerald cocktail dress has a strapless sweetheart neckline that dips almost to the bottom of my ribs and a skirt that sits just above my knees. The real showstopper is the back—it stops right above my ass and there's a deep slit in the skirt. Normally, I wouldn't wear something that clings this tightly, but…

I refuse to worry about what anyone thinks of me anymore. There are people who care about me who don't give a shit if I'm not airbrush perfect head to toe, so fuck the expectations of small minded idiots.

Twisting my lips, I pace back forth around the room as I think. The real question is: am I brave enough to back that sentiment up? I don't mind wearing a strapless bra, but I'd like to enjoy dinner. I won't if I squeeze myself in shapewear to make smooth lines in that dress. Waffling over it for a moment, I wiggle into the wizardry that is my bra and panties.

You know what? Fuck it. I'm not doing it. Let them stare.

With that decided, I leave the dress on the bed and walk to the bathroom to start the hair and make up thing. I'm not going to ask Wolfie to help—though he'd probably love to—because I'm going to go as Jolene (mostly) Au naturel. If the boys don't like it, they can find someone else to play with. Feeling free, I set my phone to play a 'going out' playlist and sing along as I wait for the curling iron to heat up.

A few minutes later, I'm dancing around as I squeeze and release the fat curls when a voice startles me.

"Sugarplum? Is everything okay up here?"

I almost drop the hot iron as I shriek. "Hecate in a handbasket, Wolfie, you scared the *shit* out of me!"

His expression is sheepish as he walks in, barefoot and rumpled. "Sorry about that. You were just… uh. It sounded like…"

"Like someone strangled a cat, right? And Jekyll and Hyde are downstairs with the others, so you thought maybe I was being attacked?" I give him a wry smile as I flick the last curl out of the iron's grip.

"Maybe?"

"I can't sing. Everyone thinks I don't know, so they pretend they don't notice. But I'm not deaf or profoundly stupid—I realize I sound like dying water buffalo, but I love doing it. So I do it anyway and people seem to play along." The significance of that philosophy hits me and I cover my mouth.

Wolfie smirks. "Did you figure something out just now?"

"Shut up, smarty pants. Christ, if my therapist could hear this. That woman barely finished our time together with all her hair on her head and *now* I figure this shit out." Stomping over to the sink, I slip the soft headband up my neck to gingerly push the untouched curls back so I can do my face.

"And what is it?" he asks as he walks over and starts picking through the neatly packed pouches of various shit Seer thought I might need.

"I should have been—should *be*—living life with the same philosophy as I take with my shitty singing voice. It's not perfect and occasionally really bad, but I do it anyway no matter how many people think I suck. Because it's for me, not them, and they can suck a giraffe dick if they don't like it."

"Bingo!" he says, bopping me on the nose with a big powder brush. "Give the lady a kewpie doll."

"Alright, alright," I grumble. "No need to be sarcastic."

"Since you had such a momentous discovery, I think I can reward you by helping you with this." He gestures at the makeup on the sink with a knowing look.

"Aren't I supposed to be the one rewarding you?"

"Po-tay-to, Po-tah-to," he shrugs. "You probably just didn't want to admit you needed help anyway, right?"

My answer is a glare and he winks at me. If this was anyone but Wolfie, I'd give them an elbow to the sternum, but he truly isn't making fun of me. "Fine. Do something pretty but no fancy stuff. I decided I'm going sort of natural tonight. No lashes, no contouring, no Spanx.. Just me."

"Good for you, sugarplum. I don't know why you've even bothered. None of us even want you to wear underwear, much less that boned shit." He pauses as he picks up a sponge. "Okay, Teddy loves to rip the fancy lace, but I think it's more like an ingrained dominant thing more than a fetish."

"Wolfie, have I told you how much I missed you?" I open my eyes and reach up to ruffle his hair. "Out of everyone, your feet are so firmly planted on the ground. You take care of all of us without being asked and you have this eerie sixth sense for when people need you. It's really lovely."

His cheeks flush and he wrinkles his nose. "I'm supposed to put blush on you, Sugarplum. You've got everything backwards today."

"Mmmm, well, I'm happy to be backwards with you. Hell, I'd be happy to be upside down with you again, but that will have to wait until later." I bob my brows at him and he laughs as he picks up a shadow palette.

"Yes, it will. Now, hold still so I can finish you up so the boys downstairs don't get too squirrely. I think Teddy and Benjy are a wee bit excited, so I don't want to keep them waiting because we were flirting."

"Oh, that wasn't flirting. It has been a while since we've played if you think that was flirting, darling boy."

"You can teach me a lesson later." He bops me with a powder puff. "Now, hold still."

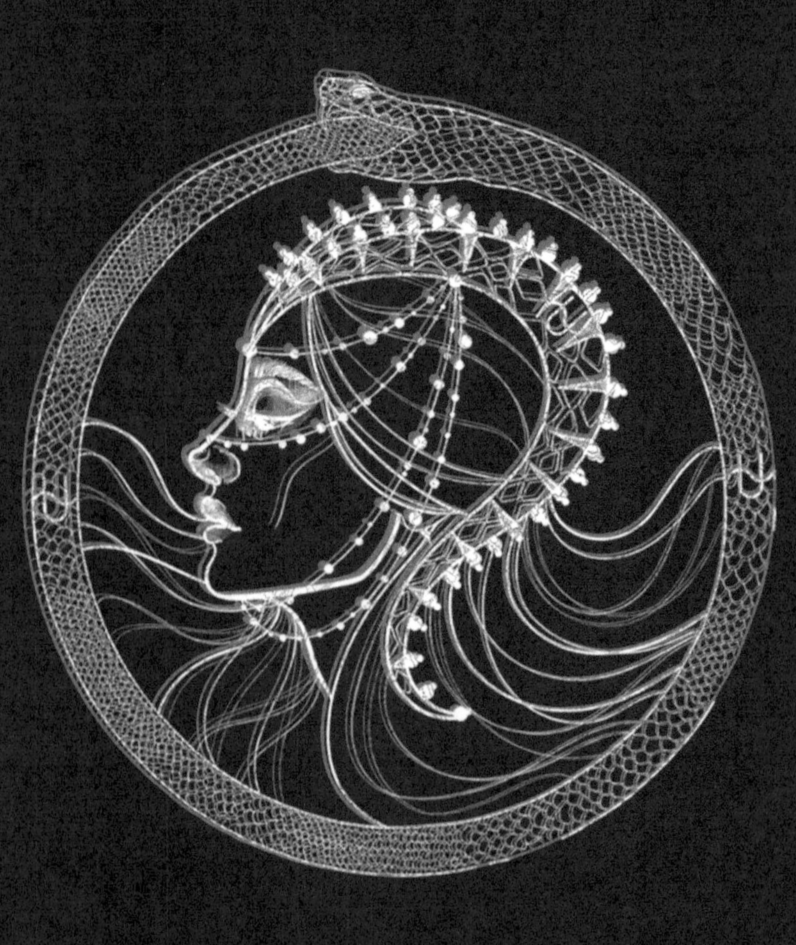

Season of the Witch

Wolfgang

"I hope they have a good time," I say as we hustle to the door of the innocuous building located in a back alley.

Doyle knocks on the door rapidly in a familiar rhythmic pattern and a hole opens in the center eye of the carving on the heavy wood. They don't say a word, simply staring at us with monocular suspicion. The Irishman sighs and places his finger on the fingerprint scanner panel that opens on the right side of the door, then says, "*Diatírisi, prostasía, yperáspisi… o kýklos den teleiónei.*[1]"

The voice behind the door is raspy as it replies, "*I epivíosi enós eínai aioniótita gia ólous*[2]."

"Are we done with the ridiculous cloak and dagger shite?" He pushes on the door. "It's hot as hell here even in the evening."

An affronted sniff is his answer, but the door opens slowly. We follow him inside and I peer around in curiosity. I'm sure Doyle and Presley have been in plenty of Society safe houses in other countries, but I know I haven't. The atrium is a dark, cherry wood paneled room that looks a lot like one of the waiting rooms in our Society meeting hall and I wonder if they design them all as similarly as possible to make people feel comfortable. There's a bar full of crystal glasses and decanters, big leather chairs, and a large stand like a hostess would stand it in the front of a restaurant.

"What is your purpose?" A short, gnarled woman steps out from behind the lectern, eyeing us with the same glare that was visible in the peephole.

Holy shit, it's a Muma Pădurii!

I look at her with wide eyes, knowing what her kind are famous for. It seems odd the Society would place one of her kind in a safe house, but I suppose they place the children in enclaves and adults come to the safe houses. There wouldn't be temptation if her food source never comes through the doors.

Prez whispers in my ear, "Why do you look terrified?"

The old witch cackles and points at him. "It's rude to whisper, young man. Your friend is scared of me because I am a supernatural legend from which many fairy tales sprang. They're all nonsense, of course. Not *all* fairy tales— those are usually based on a supe who has achieved legendary status in the human world and therefore, immortality—but the ones about *my people* aren't true. Humans fear what is different and that sometimes passes on to supes in less… educated areas of the world."

"*Hansel and Gretel* is about your kind," I grumble. "I figured it was one of the real ones."

A newspaper flies off one of the tables, rolls itself up, and bops me on the head. "You aren't very bright for a Dark Fae, boy. Only trolls eat children."

In a flash, Doyle is standing in front of the woman with absolutely no regard for whatever other powers she might have. "Do. Not. Strike. Him. Old Woman."

The shiver that runs through me is ill-timed, but I can't help that possessive Dom shit is hot, even when it's this asshole.

She lets out another crazy laugh, slapping her thigh as she looks at us in amusement. "Oh, to be young and stupid again. Imagine thinking it's a good idea to threaten a thousand year old magic weaver. Such grandiose gestures men make when they are full of baby juice and bravado."

"Ew," Presley says.

Agreed.

"How do you know what we are, crone?" Doyle finally breaks the standoff. "These places are supposed to be magic-free unless members use specific rooms for rituals or casting."

"Do not question my methods, son of…" She pauses again and I roll my eyes. "…oh, you don't know! Far be it for me to spoil the surprise, exiled demi-god. To answer your rude statement, I am the keeper of this house and it's my job to identify, catalog, and record the supernaturals who come through my doors. Do you not have a keeper in your Society hall?"

I frown and shake my head. "Not to my knowledge. Do we have one, Doyle?"

"Yes, we have one, but ours hides in plain sight and doesn't sass the members." He gives the woman an assessing look as if he's considering how he can shake the name of his father out of her before we leave.

Fuck, I hope someone dispels that plan so we don't get turned into fucking newts or something.

I look at him in shock. "We do?"

"All the halls have keepers. You idiots in the Hollow don't travel anywhere, do you?" The demi-god gives us a disgusted look. "Ours is Zareb. His eyes see all and because he has a special relationship with Nelia and her mates, they are able to use what he sees and smells to form our records. Prior to Nelia's arrival, it was a gargoyle, but that guy is retired in the Carpathians by now."

"See? There are beings with my position everywhere and we keep our homes safe in different ways. I'll bet that lion wouldn't hesitate to eat one of you fools if you stepped out of line." The Muma totters over to her lectern again, opening a large book and waving her finger at the quill next to it. "Now, let's see here… it's December second, year two thousand and twenty-two at nineteen hundred hours local time. I am Irina, keeper of the safe house and I make these entries of my own free will."

Glitter fills the air as the notations from her guest book appear in front of us as if to verify what she's recording.

The following supernaturals have been granted entry:

Wolfgang Lucien Fletcher- dark Fae, son of Cailleach, father unknown, hybrid
Presley Hemingway Hamilton- caladrius of Whistler's Hollow
*Doyle Aloysius Haggerty- demi-god, son of *** goddess and *** god, hybrid deity*
*Hugo MacAuley- oracle of *** goddess*
Dhameer Mirza Al Sharqi- djinn

"What? MacAuley and the prince are here?" Prez looks around as he scratches his head. "Where did they come from?"

The men in question step out from behind the partition that blocks the rest of the hall looking equally frustrated. The Muma must have driven them as crazy as she is us and they elected to wait until she finished her rant to poke their heads out.

"I feel like we're focused on the wrong thing," my lover rumbles. "Anyone else notice this nutter made sure to bleep out information we aren't allowed to have even in her magic book?"

"Of course I did! I've been doing this longer than *most* of you have been alive. I never betray the gods when they make rules. I cannot reveal what is not known to you anymore than your friends can, healer." Irina looks affronted again, and she slams the book shut.

We're never getting out of here if someone doesn't calm her down.

"Ma'am, no one is saying you are not an excellent keeper. We're eager to get to the summoning room so we can finish an unpleasant task. I'm afraid it has put all of us on edge."

She cackles and points at me. "Your mother will not be pleased to be called to a group chat, young Fae. Be wary of her words and mind what any of you reveal."

Is this woman a fortune teller, too?

"Mumas can hear thoughts," Hugo says. "You're all broadcasting every-thing she's pretending to reveal."

"Stay out of my head, witch." Doyle's skin starts to glow and I move back, hoping he's not going to lose his shit with this irascible old biddy.

"Come, friends. Irina will allow you entry and cease being rude since you have been recorded. Isn't that right, keeper?" The prince gives the witch a look that practically dares her to argue and for once, she shrinks back.

She's not more powerful than a djinn—good to know.

"Go, go. I prefer the quiet when my waiting room isn't clogged with horny men anyway."

"Ugh, gross," I mutter as we all walk behind the royal supe and into the main hallway. "Why does she keep talking about sex?"

Hugo looks over his shoulder, grinning smugly. "Mumas are extremely blunt and highly oversexed. Legends get so much wrong when the people telling them have an agenda. They don't eat children, you see. They turn boys into men."

That gets a resounding groan of disgust from the entire group and we all stay quiet as we make our way to the summoning chambers.

There's nothing any of us can say to make that less offensive.

"*NOCHDADH, MATHAIR, CAILLEACH, BANA-BHUIDSEACH A' GHEAMHRAIDH...*[3]"

Presley looks at me nervously, his hand squeezing mine tightly. This isn't the first time he's met my biological mother and he knows what contacting her costs me. Every single word, every expression, and every tiny twitch is cataloged by her sharp gaze and stored for future use against me. When Aurelia first started to lose it, I thought maybe my real mother was involved because it would amuse her to take something else away from me.

But it wasn't true; something else made my adoptive mother have a break with reality, and it could have to do with Jolene's parents' death.

"Who dares to...ah, my son!"

I swallow hard as I look up at the crown of antlers on her head first, then at her icy visage. She changes her looks with her moods, but today she appears to be not much older than me. Her hair is violet, hanging in a long braid over one shoulder, and she's wearing ice blue and white adorned with snowflakes and ivy. Her rosy lips curve into what she believes to be a friendly smile, but it's easy to see the malevolence behind it.

"Good evening, mother."

Her brow arches as she looks over the group, studying each of them before she speaks again. "You've brought friends. How lovely! I was certain you would never have any beyond your lowly healer."

The hand in mine squeezes and I can feel Prez's temper sparking. My natural empathy makes it easy for me to read a room and the tension in this one is building slowly. I can only hope everyone manages to stay calm—you cannot negotiate with an emotional terrorist like my mother. She will find every one of our fears and spit them back at us just because she can.

"Veiled One, we have come to parlay!"

Blinking, I look over at Doyle. Quoting movie lines at her rather than actually talking is… an interesting plan, I suppose.

My mother's porcelain features pinch for a moment, but they relax into that suspicious smile again quickly. "I accept your request, demi-god. What knowledge do you seek and what do you offer in trade?"

Oh, no. Trading her information is never a good idea.

"We seek an audience with you in person to discuss our terms. Such delicate negotiation cannot be done through astral channels. Far too many supernaturals have the ability to access the planes," Dhameer interjects.

My eyes widen and I shake my head. That's even worse. If we visit her in person, I won't be able to avoid my sugarplum coming with us.

"*Have you all lost your minds?*" I hiss.

"Wolfgang, darling. Don't be so dramatic. Your new friends wish to pay me tribute in person. I've not met a djinn in person before and the rest of them —even your poor, not fated boyfriend— interest me as well."

This time, I squeeze Presley's hand, knowing the barb about our mating hit him square in the heart. She doesn't know what's happened since last we spoke and she's clearly too distracted to use her power to pick at my shields. "Mother, I don't think we can—"

"Nonsense. Djinn, I accept your invitation. You will meet me at *Tiagh na Bodach* in four days hence. Do not be late; the Cailleach waits for no man… even her son."

A loud clap echoes in the room and she disappears in a cloud of snow.

"So… that was my mother," I say as I rub my hand over the back of my head.

"She's a peach," Prez drawls as he pulls me into a tight hug. "Don't let her bullshit get to you."

Dhameer clears his throat. "I understand you may not see the wisdom in meeting her in person, but trust me. I was able to read her face like a book. She would not have given us any information that someone could trace back to her with magic. The astral realm is as traceable as the internet if you find the right…hacker, so to speak."

Doyle frowns, responding before I can protest. "Which means the bitch knows something good and doesn't want it to splash back on her if it gets out."

"Exactly." The prince looks over at Hugo, tilting his head. "We have done our part for this evening. If we are lucky, perhaps this will jar out seer's visions. I will contact you if it does."

"Okay, but you don't have—"

Prez's words are cut by both Hugo and Dhameer disappearing in a puff of purple sparkling smoke, leaving all of us gaping.

"Could people *stop* fucking beaming out like Scotty?" I throw my hands up in the air in frustration, finally losing my patience. "I've seen more spooky shit today than a fucking Winchester."

"And I suspect there's more to come." Doyle grimaces at us as he stares at the spot where my mother was. "Especially once we're in Scotland."

"Who's going to tell Magpie?"

The chorus of 'not it' echoes in the chamber and we all look at one another. Finally, Doyle grins like a loon and says, "Boone can do it. After all, I'm on shit duty because of him."

This should be interesting…

----

1. Conservation, protection, défense…the circle does not end.
2. To survive, we must protect the young.
3. Appear mother, crone, witch of winter…

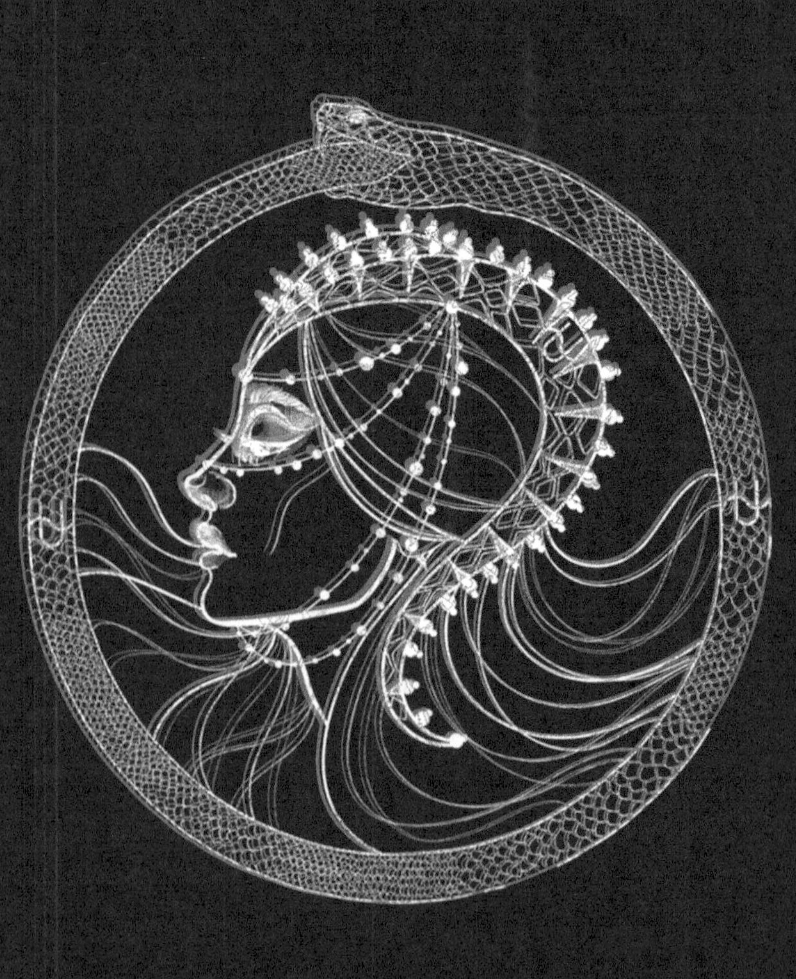

MONSTERS

Tilly looked radiant when the pup sent her down.

I don't often regret things, but our past will haunt me until the day I die.

Benjy and I took her to a five star restaurant in one of the fancier hotels in town. Together, we drank and tried way more food than we could ever eat. My *drugar* was in high spirits—I don't know what he said to her while they were upstairs, but she smiled in a way I haven't seen since we were kids. It's how she smiled… before.

But as the meal ended and we were all full to the brim with good food and company, I knew the time was coming to have the talk we brought her out to have. I hated to wipe that look off of her face, but I also know that in order for us to keep moving forward, we have to knock this out of the equation.

So now we're walking along the sea in the community where the villa is located, surrounded by the gentle noise of the waves and the light of stars. Benjy keeps looking at me, waiting for me to start the dialogue, but I haven't been able to get my tongue unstuck. As beautiful as she looked at the restaurant, she's even more gorgeous walking with bare feet on the sand, her hair unbound, and her heels slung over her shoulder. The moonlight highlights her curves and the twinkle in her eyes as she kicks the water with her toes.

"She walks in beauty, like the night, of cloudless climes and starry skies, and all the best of dark and bright, meet in her aspect and her eyes.¹"

Jolene turns and looks over her shoulder at me with a crooked smile. "Edgar Olivier Boone! Who knew you paid attention in senior English?"

Benjy snorts and shakes his head. "He didn't. Dylan tutored him at my house on the weekends."

"Ah, that makes sense. Sherilynn's nerdy book-loving younger brother kept you eligible for football seasons," she says with a soft chuckle.

"Hey!" I frown. "Dylan only helped me with the boring shit. I was smart enough to pass the bar on my own and make law review, Missy. He wasn't there to hold my hand then."

"Boring shit is awful snarky for a guy who just quoted Byron off the cuff," she sing-songs.

My friend walks up to our girl and picks her up by the waist, stopping her in her tracks. "You're a smarty pants, Princess."

Tilly pretends to kick and fight a little, but she puts her hands on his shoulders to balance as he lifts her higher. "Benjy! If you drop me, I'm going to gut you like a Cumberland bass!"

He looks over at me and I rake my hand through my hair. "Okay, put her down, B."

"My hero!" she says when her feet hit the ground. Tilly throws her arms around me when I get close enough, holding on tightly.

"Maybe not for long," I say as I lift her arms from around my neck. "I want to talk about high school."

Her brows furrow and she steps back, looking from Benjy to me in confusion. "High school? Why? I mean, we talked on Halloween for a bit."

Dropping onto the sand, I wait for her and Benjy to join me before I reply. "I'm worried that if we don't settle the old scores now while we're building the foundation, it might come back to bite us in the ass later."

"We screwed up, Princess. I mean, less me than that jackass, but we were total douches even before the Cotillion."

Jolene gives him a wry look. "Duh. Everything changed the minute we all stepped into the building at WHFS from the Formative School. It was like some sort of magical spell blanketed the building and the gulf between the cool and not cool opened up like a chasm."

"More like we all got the same 'representing the family name' speech from our parents the night before," Teddy sighs. "I know the Senator and old Mags weren't in the least bit subtle with mine."

Benjy nods. "Vlad and Flan were pretty specific, too. They made sure I knew I was supposed to follow Edgar's lead and I was expected to date one of the girls. Sherilynn was mentioned by name; hell, for all I know they arranged it with Zelda and Oscar from birth."

"Oh!"

I arch my brow and look at Tilly as she holds her finger up, her face screwed into an angry expression. "What is *that*?"

"You will never believe what I found out while you guys were in exile. My parents… well, probably my mother more than my dad… tried to arrange a marriage for me and Jamie!" Her indignation shines through the declaration and she stomps her foot on the sand.

What in the actual hell? First Benjy, now Tilly? Were all the parents playing some sort of Victorian matchmaker when we were kids?

"Cantwell is like… four years older than you." My friend looks perturbed by that, but Jolene just snorts at him.

"Benjamin Foster, age is a human construct. Don't be a dick."

I lean in and whisper dramatically, "She says that because she's more than a decade older than the pup."

A hard smack is my thanks. "Shut it, Boone. You're the same age as me, last I recall. We can rob the cradles together."

Tilting my head, I study her with adoring eyes. I would have never expected to be where I am, with who I am, before she came storming back to our town. I owe all of the happiness I've felt since then to her. "You realize that in kindergarten I asked you to marry me, right?"

Benjy's eyes fly wide and I wink at him.

"Teddy, you'd better not even *think* about it!" Jolene scolds.

I laugh, enjoying both of their reactions immensely. "I'm not. I'm just telling you I was smarter at five than I was at eighteen and I'm smarter now than either of those dummies. I want you to know I'm in this for the long haul and I can admit when I was a super douche."

"Fucking hell, Teddy," she grumbles as she holds her hand to her chest. "Don't scare me like that again. We've been dating for like a couple months and three weeks of that, I kicked all of you out. You're *still* living with… someone. I refuse to explain to people that I not only slept with you the first night I was home without making you apologize, but then I found out you all lied to and I accepted a proposal! It's too ridiculous for fiction, even."

I grin and shrug. "Oh, I'd ask you if I thought you were ready to admit how much you can't live without me."

"How exactly would that work, even? I mean, with her and the vet…and the fake Irishman and me and the doc and now…a prince and a teacher?" Benjy scratches his head as if trying to fit Legos together in his mind.

"The Council will have ways. We would not be the only polyamorous group in town, remember. The others aren't very public, but they exist," I say as I look at our girl.

"Stop it! I can't hear you! La la la la la la la…" Her fingers are in her ears as she sings to herself in a key I swear I can only hear because of the canine part of me.

"Tilly?"

She stops and looks at me. "What?"

"Shut up and kiss me."

-----

1. Lord Byron

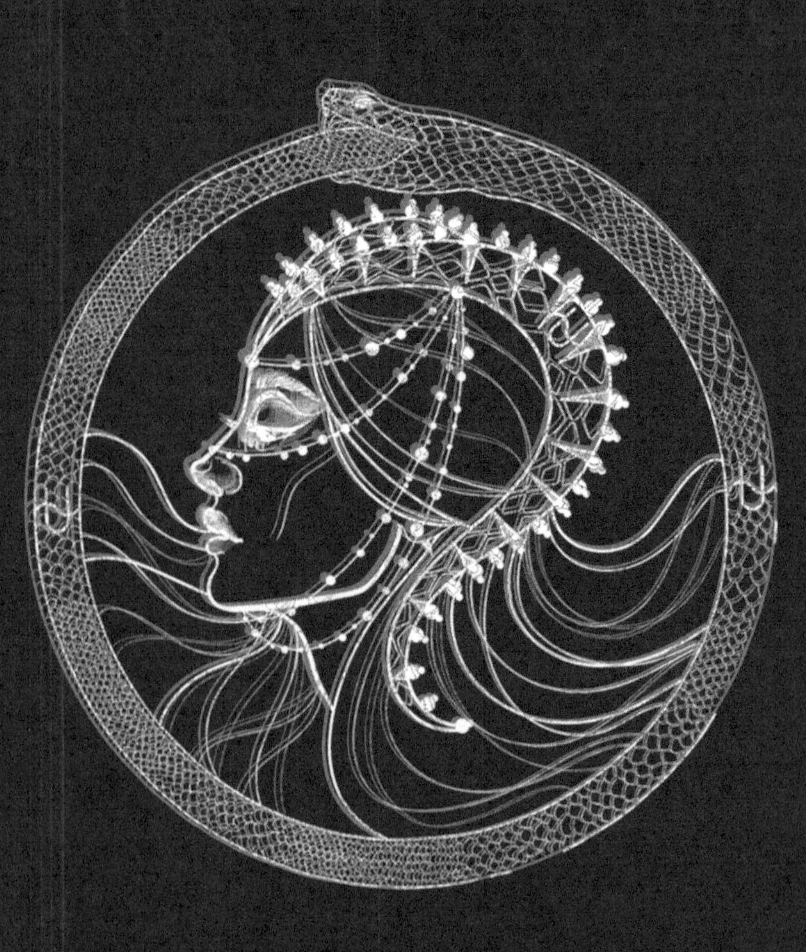

Bad Dreams

Jolene

"She still has shown no signs of emerging, Andrew."

I peeked through the crack in the doorway, hoping to understand why my mother was so mad when I got home. She'd been gone for two weeks and I came home excited to see if she brought me something from her work trip. Instead, she slammed around the kitchen during dinner and sent me to my room as soon as I asked how recruiting went for the college. I know most girls my age fight with their mothers all the time, but I tried hard to please mine.

After all, I know she's disappointed that I don't look as glamorous as the other girls in my class. She's never said it to me, of course, but when we go shopping for school clothes or dresses for the debutante balls, I've seen her gazing wistfully at the girls who could pick armfuls of gowns off the racks. Every time we've found something for me, she has to take it home and ask Niecy to take it in because we bought sizes from the plus size department so the dress would fit.

Without Niecy's skills, I would have been left to ill-fitting things or having my gowns handmade.

So I tried not to do anything else to let her down. My grades have always been perfect, and I worked hard at dance, so I'd shine in the deb classes. My art got selected for several shows at the college and in galleries in the city. But nothing ever made her happy.

Today, I didn't even have time to say 'hello' before she fell into one of her snits.

"Eloise, give it time. We don't know what she is and you know different species emerge at varying intervals."

My mother scoffed, slamming a glass on the counter. The smell of gin was never a good sign in our house. She's not an alcoholic—I looked it up—but she wasn't a friendly drinker, either. "Don't lecture me on biology you will never understand. You're not one of us."

"Why do you always throw that in my face, Eloise? It never mattered until Jolene came into our lives."

"It matters because they gave us a defective one! It's humiliating—everyone is smirking at me, I know it," my mother complained in a bitter voice. "Especially the wealthy members. They know I've got a dud and I can see it in their eyes when I have to stand in front of them and give reports on my missions."

My dad sighs and I imagined him taking off his glasses to pinch the bridge of his nose. "You're her mother. I'm her dad. We're supposed to love her no matter what."

"What if I don't agree with that? They promised me a ticket out of mediocrity when we took her in and I'm not getting a return on my investment. I have a right to be angry." Her heels clicked on the floor as she walked across the room, and I scrambled into the shadows of the hallway. "If she doesn't come through, Andrew, we're cutting her loose after high school. She can make it on her own."

I wake up in a pool of sweat, looking around the room in confusion. The dream was so vivid, but that scene wasn't familiar. I don't know if my mind is filling in gaps to make me think I'm remembering more of my childhood or if that really happened. If it did, what in the hell was my mom talking about? It seemed like she was saying I wasn't their biological child. But nothing I've ever found in their house or documents after they passed indicated I was adopted.

My brain has to be mush from all the sex; that's it. Teddy and Benjy fucked me so well that my brain isn't making up fantasies—it's creating nightmares instead.

That makes little sense, even in my groggy state, but I shake my head and rub my hand over my face. All this tells me is that I definitely have to find out where the hell that cop went and Eli needs to dive deeper into my parents' lives. If I was adopted, there's a paper trail somewhere, no matter how hard anyone tried to bury it. And I'd be lying if I didn't admit to myself that it would explain a lot about my childhood and teen years—especially the distance my parents kept from me after I graduated.

"Sugarplum, are you awake?"

I look up to see Wolfie peering down at me. He's holding his hand out and I take it, letting him help me up from the low bed. "I am now. Do I smell breakfast?"

He beams and nods. "You do. I was coming to get you, honestly. Everyone is downstairs waiting."

"Everyone?" I run a hand through my tangled waves, wondering if it's just my guys or if we have extras in the house.

"Well, Doyle and Teddy and Prez and Benjy and me. Teddy said we needed to make sure you eat well because they wore you out last night."

Blushing, I grumble, "I hope they didn't brag like idiots."

He blinks. "Of course not. But they told us all about your outing."

"That doesn't bother you?" I ask curiously.

"Not at all, sugarplum. We all care about you and want to see you happy. Our family only works if we can share like adults—even our grumpy, alpha dogs know that. They might bluster and snarl, but they wouldn't begrudge you a date or time alone with any of us."

I smile in relief. "Good. I'd hate to be hurting anyone's feelings."

"Nope. I spent time with Prez, which was wonderful, and we even hung out with Doyle before we went to bed. Not a bruised ego in sight, sugarplum."

Wolfie leads me down the hall and down to the kitchen. The others are waiting with smiles on their faces and an enormous plate of food that smells like heaven. I inhale as I sit down, and my stomach makes a rumbling noise. That makes Teddy snort and reach over to tug a strand of hair.

"Eat, Tilly. We've got something to run by you, and I'm very familiar with what happens when we don't feed the beast before we pose questions."

My eyes narrow and I point my fork at him menacingly. "You get stabbed, is what happens."

"Exactly," Prez says as he passes me another mimosa. "So fill your belly and then we'll talk."

If I wasn't so damned hungry. I'd take issue with that.

"So this dude at the table next to us was *RIDICULOUS*," I say as I stuff another bite of eggs in.

Teddy groans and puts his hand over his eyes. "Fuck, I'd almost forgotten about that."

"*How?*" I ask once I swallow. "I mean, even listening to him degrade that guy in public was embarrassing. It was like the male version of a Karen."

"He was definitely a grade-A dipshit." Benjy reaches for the fruit bowl and heaps some on his plate. "I'm not very experienced in that… arena… but I could tell he was pretending to know what he was talking about."

"Christ on a trampoline, he was talking to his sub like a bad porno!" I giggle as I puff my chest up and do an impression of the self-important douche. "*If you're a good boy, you'll get my dick when we get home. Don't speak when you're not spoken to, boy. Daddy wants to reward you, but you're being so baddddd.*"

The whole table snickers, and Teddy shakes his head. "It was painful, pup. I almost had to get up and ask the waiter to move us. The poor guy he was 'disciplining' was trying hard to comply with all his bizarre directions, but it kept getting closer and closer to infantilization and you could tell it wasn't comfortable."

Benjy peels his banana and wags it at us. "Supposedly, his dick would taste better than any dessert on the menu."

I choke on my drink, almost spitting it out. "I'm going with no fucking way on that. Their tiramisu was to die for. None of you have dicks that sweet— don't even ask."

My declaration gets another round of laughter, and finally Presley looks at me seriously. "I know this is off-topic, but we can come back to how our dicks taste after we talk about where we go next."

"Like… as couples?"

"No, Tilly. I think I made *that* very clear last night," Teddy says with a wink.

Scooting to the edge of my chair, I stretch my leg until I can kick him hard in the shin. "Enough of that. It's too early for that shit."

"Oooh, tell us," Doyle says as he leans forward on his forearms. "I want to know."

That motherfucker just wants to cause chaos, and he's not getting it right now.

"Stow it, Haggerty," Presley says as he pushes his glasses up. "Magpie, we think we need to go to Scotland. Saoirse has been in contact and she's working something pretty hush-hush, but she said we need to meet her there."

I frown, irritated that my bestie is contacting them and hasn't said much to me at all since she yeeted herself off the face of the earth. "What kind of contact?"

"We don't know," Teddy says, his gaze cutting over to the others. "It could be dangerous, but since the trail is cold here and we have plenty of time, I messaged Thorn about gassing up the plane."

"This isn't a discussion; it's a foregone conclusion," I reply coolly. "You're telling me we need to get packed."

"Well…"

"Don't well me, Presley. I know a con when I see one." Tossing back the last of my drink, I push my plate away. "When do we leave for Scotland?"

"In three hours," Wolfie says softly. "If you get your stuff ready, I'll get the guys to help me clean up and get the animals together."

I blink, groaning under my breath. "We *just* got Eury to quit shitting everywhere because she was mad about the cargo hold!"

Doyle gives me a sour look. "Don't remind, Tíogair."

"That's what happens when you lose bets." Teddy gives him a smug look and I roll my eyes.

I'm not even going there.

"Fine. I'll go pack up and you guys do all of this… stuff." I pause for a moment, frowning. "Are Hugo and Amiri following along?"

"We've contacted MacAuley. He says the prince is finishing up some business here and they'll join us when they can."

I smile at Prez, appreciating his thoughtfulness. He's a good organizer, even if Wolfie does the more physical parts of that job. "Good. I wouldn't want anyone to think we left them out, since it seems like I have to travel with an entire entourage now."

"How long is the flight again?" Doyle asks as he clears the table.

"A little under four and a half hours to Inverness for the flight, but we'll have a long car ride to the Highlands after."

I look at them both. "We're going to the Highlands? By car? With a fuck ton of animals?"

Teddy chuckles softly. "We'll let Eury fly during the car ride and the others will be fine if we give them space to lie down."

"You'd better add some time to whatever calculation you made for pit stops. I'm not riding for hours in a car with yowling dogs and cats who have to pee," I grumble. "And if we run into ghosts, I'm skinning all of you. A stalker is bad enough."

They look at one another and then at me. Benjy finally takes the hit when he asks, "You believe in ghosts?"

"I believe in anything I haven't seen proven false. And some places Seer and I went had eerie fucking vibes. Leave me alone."

"Don't worry, Tilly," Teddy says with a smile. "I ain't afraid of no ghost."

I rise to my feet, smacking him in the back of the head, and make my exit on that high note.

At least they didn't ask me if I believe in vampires, too.

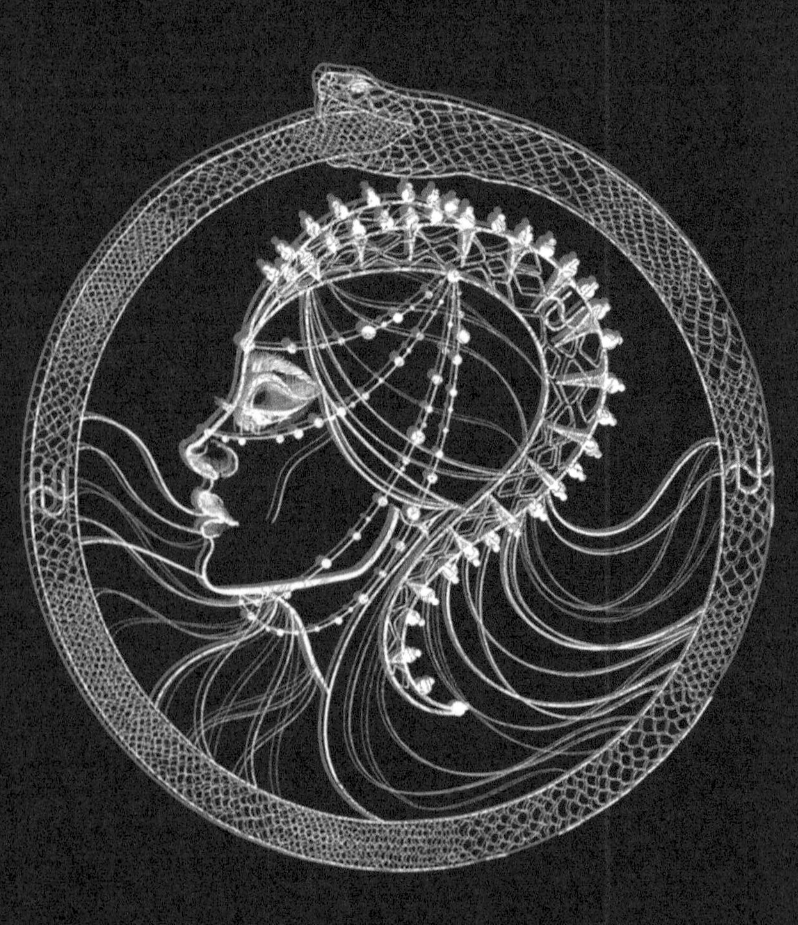

High

We got everything closed up and went to the airport on time—which was a miracle. Between the traffic in town and the locals on the tarmac getting wigged out over the animals, it was a fairly close call. But now that we're in the air, everyone is engrossed in their own shit, and it leaves me to fret over the details.

For instance, taking magpie to meet Lucy's mother.

I know I told him not to worry; that's my job. But knowing his mother like I do and seeing how she behaved when we summoned her, I'm worried that she'll break the rules just to hurt him. The Cailleach certainly knows she cannot reveal the existence of our world to a non-emerged supe, but she can be less than subtle and point our girl in a direction she might not have headed on her own. If she snoops before it's time, all hell will break loose. Her *not* knowing is protecting her right now, even from pests as small as Sherilynn's crew.

There's also the fact that Lucy has mated with Edgar and your bond isn't fully completed. She's going to figure it out.

I sigh and lean my head back against the pillows on the bed. Taking my glasses off so I can rest my eyes, I consider what kind of manipulation his mother could achieve with that knowledge. It's neither of our faults that Reiki is being stubborn—my caladrius simply refuses to do his part until the moment is right. What the fuck *that* is, I can't imagine. He's just resistant to doing it before he's ready.

"What's wrong, love?"

Squinting at the doorway, I roll to my side. I know it's Lucy, but I can't see a damned thing. I should have gotten LASIK or an oculus spell years ago, but I was too stubborn to admit I needed it. Now I'm regretting that prideful decision. I hate wondering if I'll miss something because I need specs when I hop out of bed. At least I don't have that problem when I'm fully shifted, but I do that so rarely it almost doesn't count.

"I'm worried about so many things." He walks over and sits next to me, pulling my head into his lap and combing his fingers through my hair. "Your mother, of course. I know we can handle her, but I don't want her scarring you more. And I know magpie can hold her own, but I also don't want her finding out about our world through some bullshit trickery."

"All valid concerns and things we've discussed. What else?" he murmurs as his fingers travel over my scalp soothingly.

"Your dad. Obviously the Muma had an idea and we're so close to that part of the world. There will be a gate near your mother's chosen spot." I lift my head and look up at his fuzzy visage. "I think we should go into it and see if we can get intel on your dad."

The shift in the room is immediate, and I know he's holding his breath. When he lets it out, Lucy's voice is soft. "Why?"

"Because it bothers you, and perhaps he didn't abandon you. We both know your mother would relish hiding you from him and telling you he didn't want you. It would hurt everyone involved and she'd get her rocks off on manipulating people. Doyle's mother seems exactly the same."

"How in the hell will we manage getting sugarplum in and out of the Faerie without giving up the ghost?" He chuckles softly. "Fae are the most gossipy of all the fair folk."

"True. But maybe Seer can find us something to help keep her from seeing anything for what it is. I mean, the binding alone will cloud her vision. She won't see any of it for what it really is," I muse. "Have you seen any signs that it's loosening?"

Lucy thinks about it for a moment. "Outside of the hound and the dreams, no. As far as I know, she's blissfully unaware."

"Good. Then I think we might swing this." I smile up at him, even though I can't see him clearly. "I think it's important for you to try while we're here."

"I can't wait to hear what Teddy's going to say," he says wryly. "I have a feeling it'll be colorful."

"That's a future Lucy/Presley problem. Why don't you come lie down and we'll figure that out after a nap?"

"Sounds like a perfect plan."

THE BED DIPS AND I OPEN MY EYES, LETTING THEM ADJUST TO THE DARKNESS slowly.

"Shh. I don't want to wake Wolfie up," Magpie says in a low whisper.

The body next to me shifts and I feel his face run over my chest. "Too late, sugarplum."

She crawls up and wiggles her way into our embrace. The feel of her snuggled in with Lucy and me makes me smile broadly. I love that she's comfortable coming in to be with us and that it feels like she's meant to be there. Her hair spills over my bicep as she presses her warm skin to mine and I feel Lucy move again. Before I can ask what he's doing, his warm mouth is trailing down my stomach, pressing kisses as he goes.

"Oooh! Someone's being naughty," Jolene sing-songs. I can almost *feel* her grin as she leans down and bites my arm.

Shit.

Her teeth combined with his mouth wake my dick up and I have to move to relieve some pressure. "I'd say more than one person is being naughty."

"Perhaps," she murmurs as she nips her way up my arm to my shoulder. When she reaches the juncture of my neck, the air in the room gets thicker and heat flares over her skin.

Uh-oh. I think one of her sides is waking up and I'm not sure how that's going to go in an airplane bedroom.

"Lucy, you may need to cool our girl down a little," I whisper.

She shakes her head, biting a little more firmly. Before she licks the spot. "No, I like it hot."

Unable to argue with that, I bury my fingers in her hair as her mouth moves over my neck and my darling boy pulls down my sweats. His mouth is warm when he takes my dick into it, but not as hot as Jolene is getting. My eyes close as Lucy suckles the tip, his tongue flicking over the sensitive underside while his hand cups my balls. The fiery woman in my arms bites me again, and this time, I feel the skin break. She laps at the trickles coming out of the wound as he does the same to the pre-cum and I moan. Both of them following one another is almost too much... and not enough at the same time.

For the first time, I feel the bird inside of me stretch out and allow his power to fill my veins when I'm not healing a patient. The faint echo of a screech in my mind makes me shudder. I'm not sure what is going to happen, but I know I don't want it to be when I'm not inside of the people I love.

"Stop," I murmur softly.

"But you taste good," Lucy mumbles.

"Agreed." Jolene's voice is dark and growly—a hallmark of the hound inside of her that seems to break free a bit more day by day. "Tassssssty."

Was that a hiss?

I blink as my mind whirls, trying to figure out what creature she might be manifest that hisses, but the insistent push of Reiki inside of me destroys my focus. "I want... I want to fuck someone. Now. I need to."

"Maybe we'll make *you* wait this time."

Lucy chuckles against my skin, and my hips buck with the vibration. "Can we?"

"No!" I reach down and yank Magpie up, smashing my lips against hers. The kiss is violent, a battle of tongues and teeth, and when she breaks away, I know I can't wait. "Not now. Magpie, get on my dick and Lucy, I want you in my mouth."

"Well, if you insist," she says. Her hands land on my shoulders and she slithers up my body, her skin like fire against mine. Her thighs bracket mine when she sits up and within seconds, she sinks down onto me, hard and fast.

Her moan is like music to my ears.

Lucy rises to his knees, scooting up to the top of the bed. His cock is hard, and the steel is cool when I tug him closer and swallow him down. He groans and holds onto my head, pulling me closer and shoving his dick farther into my throat. He knows I have very little gag reflex, so his hips rock and push deeper with every thrust.

"Prez, I'm going to ride you until we all collapse."

I can't answer, but I hum around my boy and he fucks my mouth. The intensity only increases when Magpie lifts and drops, moving her hips in patterns on top of me as her inner muscles squeeze me hard. The heat coming from her is making the air more and more oppressive as she rocks over me. Every muscle in my body is tense when Reiki pushes more magic out; the sensation is incredible and I rake my teeth over Lucy. His shiver makes me do it again, but this time, I feel the delicate skin break.

The second the blood hits my tongue, combined with his fluids, I know we're in trouble. My skin prickles with the feathers as they poke through slowly—not how I usually shift at all. I pull back, popping Lucy out of my mouth so I can speak. He'll have to use his magic to keep Jolene from seeing what's about to happen.

"Dust, baby. We need the dust. Reiki's coming."

"Holy fuck," he whispers.

Magpie rakes her fingers over my chest as she pants. "Who's Reiki?"

"Now," I growl at Lucy.

As soon as he lets the Fae out, everything goes sideways. I knew when I asked that he wouldn't be able to control it in this small space and it would hit me, too. We've been together long enough that it doesn't affect me like it will Jolene, but it definitely still packs a punch. "There we go."

"Woooo! Who spiked the punch?" Magpie says as she keeps riding me. "I feel like I'm back in Germany, but better. Damn, I love a good dick and a double-stack."

I blink for a second, then laugh as I look over at my boy. "Well, you made her high and apparently, that makes her horny, so that's a win."

"Less talk, more fucking!" she calls out.

Lucy shrugs, moving back into place, and I hum in satisfaction as his dick slips between my lips again. "Whatever my sugarplum wants, she gets."

Satisfied that I've covered for what I assume is going to happen, I work my lips and teeth over Lucy as I buck my hips up to meet her movements. The circle of pleasure is complete as we all pant and grind and rock together until my wings pop free. Closing my eyes, I let go of everything as my caladrius finally decides to completely take over.

"Prez, I'm going to—"

"Meeee tooooo."

I reach up and tug Jolene down, giving her access to the spot on my neck she bit before. The moment I feel fangs sink in, I let go of my orgasm. My cock kicks inside of her, spilling my seed as she suckles at my neck and I swallow Lucy's come. Her walls clench hard, strangling me as her climax ripples through her and claws sink into my chest.

A vision flashes behind my eyes, showing me spirals of magic and fire and glitter twining together like vines climbing up into the air. Wings like mine sparkle at the bottom of the swirls, then catch on fire, flexing as they burn.

I have no idea what it means, but it's definitely important.

Jolene finally stops moving, her cheek resting on me as she shudders and pants her way through the aftershocks. Lucy pulls back, taking himself out of my mouth before rearranging himself to press against my side. Hot and cold bodies surround me as we come back to earth together. I slide my hand up Jolene's hip to her back and she whimpers. I frown, using my other hand to do the same to Lucy. His answer is a groan of pain.

Something tells me I'm going to be in trouble when we all get up.

Oh, Reiki, what have you done?

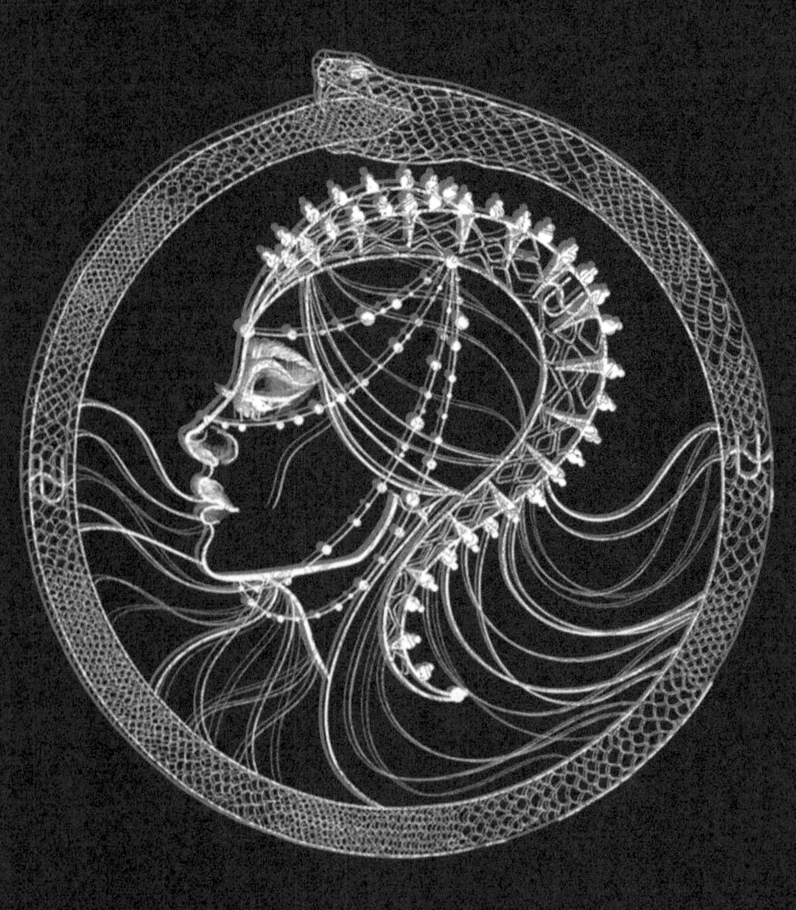

Witchy Woman

Jolene

I was strangely sore when Teddy came to wake me up because the plane was landing. Prez and Wolfie were already up and about, gathering their stuff, so I freshened up in the bathroom. I had another one of those weird flashes, but this time, I didn't tell anyone. It occurred to me it's been years since I traveled across time zones and stayed up late every night getting railed until I passed out, so maybe the passage of time has simply caught up with me.

Who wants to admit that in front of their Energizer bunny boyfriends? Not me, that's for sure.

So I stumbled down the stairs to the SUV blearily and curled up next to Teddy in the back seat with a yawn. Hyde joined us this time because Presley wanted one of my cats to come with us and the other to stay with Doyle and Wolfie in the second car. Since Seer isn't here and Eury is flying above us happily, we are crammed into two instead of three. We have to hoof it back to the airport to fly out anyway and that meant we could leave the big ass cage, so it worked out well enough.

"Are you doing okay, Magpie?" Presley asks as we turn onto the road behind the other car.

I frown, stretching a little and tilting my head. "You've asked me that ten times since I came out of the bathroom, Prez. Do I look that bad?"

He grumbles under his breath as the other seems to speed up quickly once we're on the highway, then shakes his head at me. "Not at all."

"I think you've been tired more often than usual and he's just checking in. Right, Hamilton?" Teddy runs his fingers through my hair as I lean against him and I sigh in pleasure.

I also love being stroked like a lazy kitten, apparently. I'm learning new shit about myself every day.

"Probably the time changes and all the bustling around," I mumble. If I parrot my own thoughts back at them, it makes them true, right? I fucking hope so because I have enough problems with the stupid ass blackouts. I don't need another health issue to randomly crop up and make even my small town life impossible.

"I'm sure the sexy times aren't helping," Presley says as he smirks into the rearview mirror. "You're definitely keeping us all on our toes."

My face turns bright red and I give in to the urge to bury it against Teddy's arm. I'm not shy about how much I enjoy getting laid, but these guys make me act like such a girl. I think I love it and I hate it at the same time. "Shut up. Wolfie started it last night."

"Ah, love, but you most certainly helped finish it."

A rumble of laughter vibrates in Teddy's chest, and I thump his abs. "Don't laugh, buster. You and Benjy haven't been any less frisky. If y'all keep this pace up, I'll be walking funny for the rest of life."

"That seems like a worthy goal," the judge says as he notes me peeping up at him. "I'll put it on my planner."

My eyes widen comically. "Don't you dare! Other people see your fucking calendar, Teddy."

Shrugging, he pulls his phone out and starts flicking through the screens. "I think the phrase is 'let's give them something to talk about', isn't it?"

Presley snickers and I sit up, grabbing for the phone. Teddy keeps moving it, his powerful hands keeping a tight grip as he clicks over the screen. His grin is wicked when he finally stops to click the screen off. I growl low, eyes narrowed as I look at him.

"What did you do?"

"I put a daily reminder to make your thighs wobble until you can't walk—with no end date."

By the horns of Hel, I'm going to murder this asshole.

"Teddy, everyone in the goddamned courthouse can look at your schedule!"

"Yep. It occurred to me that people at home are going to talk whether or not we want them to; I might as well amuse myself if they're going to poke their noses into our business. I'll think of more fun stuff to horrify them as we travel."

Rubbing my palm over my face, I imagine the stares we'll get when we get home. Sherilynn and her cronies have enough ammunition—this will only give them another thing to crow about. "You know this is going to cause problems."

"Ah, but it's *my* shot across the bow. The more we push back at their judgmental fuckery, the less effective their barbs are, Tilly. I'm not ashamed of you or the rest of our family. Letting them know that's not a pressure point actually takes weapons away."

I blink, thinking about that for a second. He's right. If they want to come at me by trying to humiliate me in public, telling them my life is nothing to be ashamed of will take all the starch out of their bloomers. "That's an excellent strategy, actually. Throw their barely concealed jealousy in their faces."

"Exactly." His chest puffs out, and I put my hand on it as I look at him.

"Thank you. I needed that, baby." Stretching up, I kiss his cheek.

"Aw! Innit that cute." Presley teases from the front and I make a face.

"The only reason I'm not smacking you is because you're driving. Don't think I'm not keeping count, though."

Teddy rubs his cheek against my head. "That's my girl. Keep him on his toes."

◯

"Presley?"

"Yes, magpie?"

I look out the window at the craggy glen, studying the mostly barren hills curiously. "This is really far out to be meeting a contact. I've only seen a couple of structures as we passed by. Who are we meeting again?"

The silence is heavy in the car for a moment before he sighs. "We're going to see Lucy's real mother. She's... not one for civilization. She lives a bit like a hermit, and this is the only place she would meet us."

Blinking, I feel my chest tighten and my entire body freeze. I don't have the best luck with meeting the mothers of men I've dated. Teddy's mother was a nightmare of Lucille Bluth proportions and the last matriarch I met before that was *many* years ago. To say the relationship was strained would be severely underestimating it—Trevor's mom looked at me like I was sent by Satan and raised by wolves. She wasn't any wealthier than my parents— unlike the Boones—but she had airs to climb the ladder.

Marrying me would not get her there, and she made sure I knew what she thought of all my 'faults' as often as possible.

Seeing Trevor with Antigone at the ball was a shock for many reasons, one of which was that her family's status was only marginally better than this. I can't imagine how she got his snooty mother to allow them to tie the knot, but I assume it was through treachery and sneaky shit. That seems to be the oeuvre she picked for herself.

"What's... What's his real mother like?" I ask. My hands fold together and I squeeze them, trying vainly to control the anxiety rising within me.

"Relax, Tilly. She's not like Mags, though she's definitely not one to trifle with. At least, that's what I hear. Right, Prez?"

It's quiet again as the doc turns onto a dirt road and the terrain gets bumpier. "Well, she's not without her challenges. She won't dislike you because of shit like money or a family name. She'll analyze every word out of your mouth for a weakness so she can find a place to stick a knife. But it's not about you—her goal is to hurt or upset Lucy."

I feel anger well up inside of me, touching that place that seems to be a hair trigger for me lately. "Why? Why is she actively looking to hurt her son? Wasn't giving him up to strangers enough for her?"

"Nothing is enough for her. She feeds on emotions and she enjoys strife more than joy. I'd prefer he have no contact with her at all, but once she found him as a kid, that became impossible. Her reach is too vast and battling her isn't worth the struggle. He keeps her at arm's length by occa- sionally speaking with her, but it definitely wears on him. You need to be very cautious about what you share with her—even if it's only about you."

The warmth of Teddy's body helps me center as bit as he tugs me closer and wraps me up in his embrace. "I'll do everything I can to protect both of you, *drugar*. We don't know what information she has, but since she seems to think we will bargain with her for it, we had to come."

"Okay. So treat her as if she's made of C-4 and I'm walking across a tightrope in a room full of gas and matches. Got it." I exhale slowly as the fire inside of me calms to a cool, detached sensation full of suspicion. "I can do that. I assume she'll be more interested in striking out at you and I, Prez, because Wolfie won't have mentioned Teddy."

"That's true. He plays his hand very close to the vest to keep from piquing her interest. The less she knows, the more likely she is to stay away and not meddle."

"Good. That gives me an edge. I can honestly say I know things she does not, which will make her defensive and possibly throw off her game." I tap my fingers against my lips, imagining the possibilities in a three-dimensional strategy. Since this woman is not part of my rocky past, it's much easier to separate myself from the emotion of the situation and start plotting moves. It's a skill I was paid highly for at one time and now I need to use it to protect the people I care about.

I'm not gullible enough to believe she won't aim for the jugular with Doctor McNuggies, too.

Women like that play dirty because they play to win. Luckily for my boys, so do I. I'll stay back for as long as I can so I can assess her just as she's studying us and when the time to strike presents itself, I'll circle back for the kill. I want her information—assuming it's useful—but I also refuse to allow one more self-centered bitch to manipulate us.

"What's her name?"

That seems to give Prez pause. "Uh…"

"Obviously, it's not Mrs. Fletcher; that's Aurelia."

"The pup told me she likes to play games. We'll have to see what she tells us when she arrives. He warned me she could show up looking like anything from an old woman to a forest goddess to a socialite. What she wants to be called will depend on what 'skin' she wears, I think."

I think about that for a moment, nodding slowly at Teddy. "She likes to throw him and anyone who comes with him for a loop by subverting expectations. Interesting. It sounds like the only reason she wants him to stay in contact at all is to keep him dancing to her tune. She doesn't actually give a shit what he's doing… or whom."

"That's it on the nose, Magpie."

The car stops by the side of the road. Eury swoops down and perches on the luggage rack on the front car as Wolfie unloads the dogs and Jekyll. He looks worried and I hate seeing him without his usual sunshine demeanor. It makes me angry, but I channel the fury into the cold, calculating part of me that is eager to have a fight with someone I can actually lash out at without getting in trouble.

At least, I think I can.

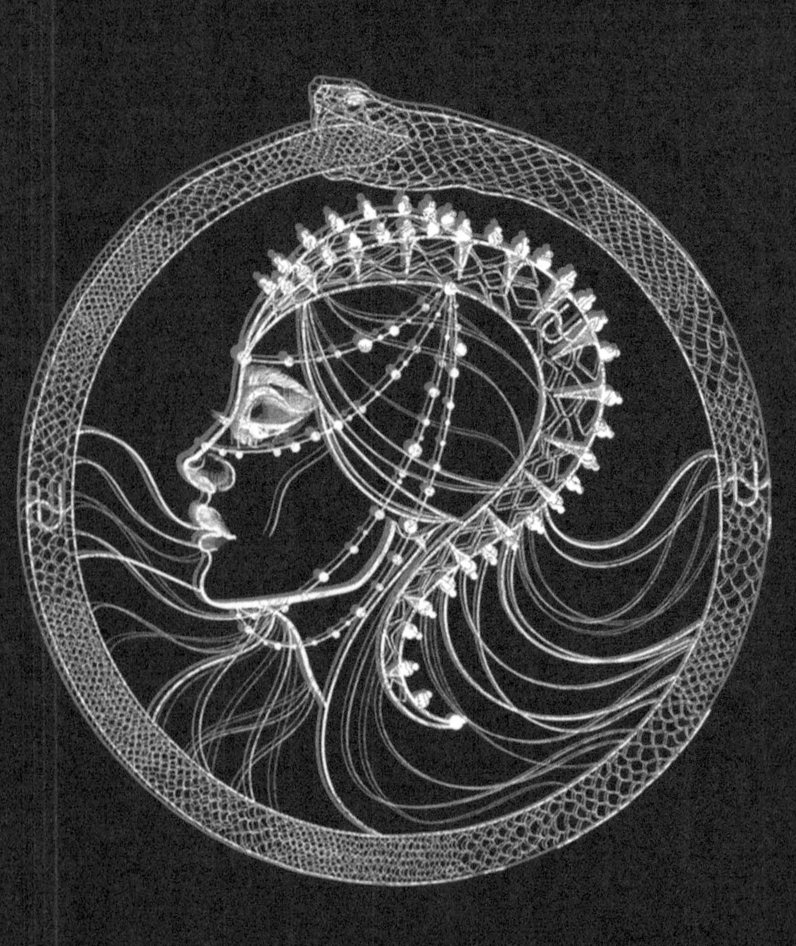

Madness

SAOIRSE

I've avoided contacting Peanut more than necessary because when I stopped by the Society safe house that morning in Istanbul, I received a message from Julia. She and her men have been trying to quell the bad coven problem in Salem since before Halloween, but every time they think they have a handle on it, a new group of bad seeds takes root. I had to meet with a couple of high-ranking officials on the Guardian allocation team, and that wasn't even something I could share with her men. The training and allocation of Guardians, especially ones that have not been assigned lost ones to mind, is highly secretive. The representatives of the major magic lines were called in to discuss the problem and whenever you get a high-ranking witch, mage, wizard, and warlock in the same room, it's chaos. Unfortunately, my big wigs needed to find out why those eejits weren't minding their stores, so to speak.

It's uncommon for the non-creature based magic wielders to have need of Guardians—they dislike mixing of the species even more than deities and rare species. I believe it's the humans in their lines because it seems like a bloody good idea to mix a Fae with a witch or a mage with a dragon if my goal is to get more power within the community. But bias against those who are different is a blight even among supe types.

Could be the reason no one's fought a territory war on a global scale since the 1940s, though, so maybe it has a purpose more positive than I know.

I snored my way through all their pompous meetings—of course, my ruddy parents were there—and finally, I got free. Since I was stuck in the building with only that psycho Muma for company, I slipped into one of the offices and did a little insider recon on the Society's records. I could get into Whistler's Hollow's server and even into some of the agent profiles and reports, but I ran into a wall when I got to the timeframe when Jolene's parents died. There were so many password protected files and firewalls that I knew I was going to get caught if I even attempted it.

By the time I closed everything up, it was time for the meeting to be over, so I checked in with my bosses and got the hell out of there before I got held up again. I thought I'd be able to go back to the villa and meet up with the group, but my phone rang the second I got into the cab.

You don't screen calls from Andromeda Bane, but I wish I had.

The favor she asked of me led me to Greece, and that meant I definitely would not make it back in time to go to Scotland with Peanut. So while she's gearing up to meet Wolfgang's mother, I'm running around Athens gathering items for an equally tenuous appointment. I would have declined this shit-tastic mission outright if it hadn't been Andromeda asking. Dealing with the women I'm visiting is well above my paygrade and it's not even to help someone I care about.

No, it's to get a clearer view on another lost one's path because Bane says there's trouble brewing across the country in Bay City. Some unassigned Guardians are about to get tangled in a big way, and she wants to see if we can head it off at the pass. Their future charges are supposedly *very important* —though where that info came from, I haven't the foggiest clue.

But everyone knows asking the sodding Fates for a favor is ill-advised.

Apparently, if you don't have an appointment in their books, you have to show up with special tributes for each of them. Mind, appointments are made *centuries* ahead, so you can imagine their constantly getting emergency tributes to hear questions. And they rarely answer of the damn questions, so this is doubly stupid. The Society board would be better off getting a fucking Ouija board than trying to pry info of these women.

But here I am anyway, running around Athens in search of their freaking presents.

I look at the market, trying to figure out if a section of it might have the necessary items. I found Clotho's favorite candy; I have a fancy Ring light for Lachesis, and now I have to find this list of shit for Atropos. I don't know what the hell she wants with these herbs, but I'm tiring of running errands for people who have their own staff. A sign down the street a little more has a symbol on it that makes me think it's a shop for practitioners, so I rush down it.

The faster I get this shit, the faster I can get this meeting over with before I stick my fat foot in my mouth and end up as a newt.

THE UBER DROPS ME OFF AT A FANCY VILLA ON THE CHI-CHI SIDE OF Athens. I sort of expected a long ride out of town to a weird cave in the mountains, but I guess the weavers of destiny have gone Insta friendly. They demanded a ring light as a tribute, after all.

"Alright, Saoirse. You can walk up here, give them your shit, and ask *without* losing your temper if they act like shitehawks. If you do all that bloody yoga breathing Julia has been teaching you, the valkyrie side will chill out so you don't get woven into an earthquake or something."

My little pep talk with myself is a necessary evil. I'm almost physically allergic to snotty women and Peanut would testify that I'll jump into a fight I can't win to teach someone a lesson. My powers aren't anything to waggle your finger at, but they aren't on par with immortal demi-goddesses who hold the strands of destiny in their fingers.

Though, they weren't strong enough to take on that fucking ice elemental/yeti hybrid in Moscow, but I dove in headfirst, regardless.

This is why Peanut and I made such a good team for all those years. We're good at being triggered by different things and even though she doesn't know my big secret, she's always helped me stay on the straight and narrow ——-mostly.

Putting my curiosity about how she's doing aside, I heft my bags of bribes and head up to the immense door. There's a large knocker on it in the shape of an infinity symbol and I pick it up, giving the oak a good whack. The sound echoes around me, but nothing moves. Not a sound from inside and no sign of anyone coming to allow me entrance. My eyes narrow as I lift the shiny knocker and give the door another few hard knocks. It's annoying as hell to wait like this. Andromeda assured me they were expecting me during this time span.

After a few minutes of waiting with no answer, I give up on the knocker and try the handle. It opens and I blink. *Okay, then.* When I step inside, I realize the damn thing is yet *another* Mary Poppins portal—that must be a favorite trick of the Greeks. The inside of the house is a massive cave with only low burning torches placed every couple of feet, so I can't see much beyond what is right in front of me.

Freya, save me from dramatic ass supes who want everyone to see how great their damn power is.

I heft the bags of gifts and make my way down the tunnel, looking at the walls, floor, and ceiling suspiciously. I wouldn't put it past the Fates to have booby traps or puzzles embedded to keep people from getting in if they aren't 'worthy.' When I get to another smaller door with a peephole, I sigh. If a crazy old coot asks me what my name and my quest are, I'm out of here. Bane can deal with these nutters herself.

Lifting my hand, I give the door a rap with my knuckles, praying this is the end of this nonsense. The entire building rumbles around me and my eyes fly wide as the wall in front of me moves, revealing an open cavern with stairs leading deep down below the level I'm on. It takes every ounce of control I have not to scream, but I head down into the blackness carefully. The trip takes me so far below the house I wonder if this is heading towards the center of the earth, but finally, I reach the end.

Three women are standing in front of a cauldron, watching it simmer. The room illuminates as I step towards them and I look up to see a tapestry covering the cave walls from the bottom to the top of the stairs. It covers every inch of the stone for three hundred and sixty degrees and the details work on it is so tiny that I cannot make things out from this distance.

This is a history of the world and the key to the future is hanging like a poster in a college kid's dorm room.

"Greetings, Saoirse Viola O'Flanagan, daughter of Odin and a keeper of lakes."

I do an awkward curtsy, unsure of what else I'm supposed to do otherwise. "Hello, great and powerful Fates,"

That gets a chorus of laughter and the tallest one steps away from the cauldron. "Do you have the tributes? The boil is almost ready and I need my ingredients."

Guess that's Atropos.

"I do," I say as I walk forward and sit the three bags on the ground next to their pot and back away carefully.

"Sisters, someone has been spreading rumors again. Look how scared she is of us! This is a Guardian, one whose ferocity they hone to protect the young, and she shrinks from us as if we're going to put her in our pot for dinner!" The short, round woman shakes her head and walks over to pick up the bag with the candy with a bright smile. "Excellent, young Guardian!"

"Well, Attie did that weird, mysterious greeting thing again. I keep telling you it wigs people out," the final Fate shakes her head, sending crazy red curls flying. She's definitely Lachesis; I can tell by how fancy her makeup is. She's the one who asked for a new Ring light.

"Thank you?" I reply to the sentiment from Clotho, giving them a tight smile. I don't care how down to earth they seem; it seems prudent to be cautious, anyway.

"Our requests seem ridiculous, I know. But we have to do this to test people —otherwise we have schedules full of cancellations and it's a giant waste of time. We have plenty, of course, but no one likes to feel as though they've been taken advantage of. So even though we want for nothing, we find various things to require so we know people who come for 'emergencies' are serious."

Actually, that's pretty reasonable.

"And my light *just* broke and I have a *Live* performance tonight. I can't read cards for my fans if I don't have proper lighting. I'd look ghastly," Lachesis says with a shrug. "Andromeda's call came at the perfect time. Plus, Attie's been wanting to try this new mask recipe and her requests were the things we were short on."

"Oh, well, I'm glad I could help." I wait for them to flit around with their bounty for a moment before I ask, "Are you ready for the question, or should I wait?"

Clotho snorts as she waddles around the simmering iron pot. "We know what your question is. We are the Fates, dear."

I squint at her. "You know it before I ask?"

"Oh, the field right before the door has a spell in it, dear. We know what question you are supposed to ask for the grumpy banshee, as well as what question you would like to ask for your friend. Nothing can be hidden from the threads of Fate once you walk through them," Atropos says as she stirs her mixture. "They hang over the doorway like a spider's web."

I knew there were feckin' booby traps!

"That's very clever." I pretend to think about it for a moment as I look around suspiciously. "What should I tell Andromeda about the problems in Bay City?"

The sisters gather around the cauldron, standing behind the steam, and an eyeball appears in the air in front of them, spinning and shining like it's the Snitch in the wizard movies. They speak as one creepily monotone voice when they answer. "Tell the banshee there is one there who will rise to the top. She will be the one who is in the center of the chaos and from her rise, there will be both blood, vengeance, and eventually peace. The turmoil in the home of the Trials will also fall when another comes to light."

"Cryptic," I mutter.

"Our answers are not meant to be horoscopes, shield maiden. They require interpretation, and every thread contributes to the ultimate solution. We cannot tell you what the picture will look like until the strands form pictures." Lachesis tilts her head at the tapestries with a shrug. "We are keepers of destiny and we follow what the universe weaves."

"However," Clotho adds. "We *can* tell you that you are not meant to join your friends in Scotland. You must travel to Prague. Answers you have been seeking are there—a powerful woman, a new face, and a shadow from a time long past will help guide you."

Making travel plans based on the Greek equivalent of a fortune cookie doesn't make me happy, but what voice do I have?

"Thank you. I will head there at once."

"Be cautious. You may find more enemies than friends as you search for the answers you seek. Your charge is not safe, even in places she should be. We cannot see what forces are seeking her as she seeks her truth."

I nod at Atropos, and the eyeball stops spinning, disappearing in a trail of sparkles. I think that means they're done with me. "Enjoy your tributes, ladies. I will take my leave."

"Do not trust the ones who look alike!" they call out as I turn to go.

Twins? Is that what they mean?

Jaysus, I hate riddles. Bane owes me a hell of a lot more than a favor for this bullshit.

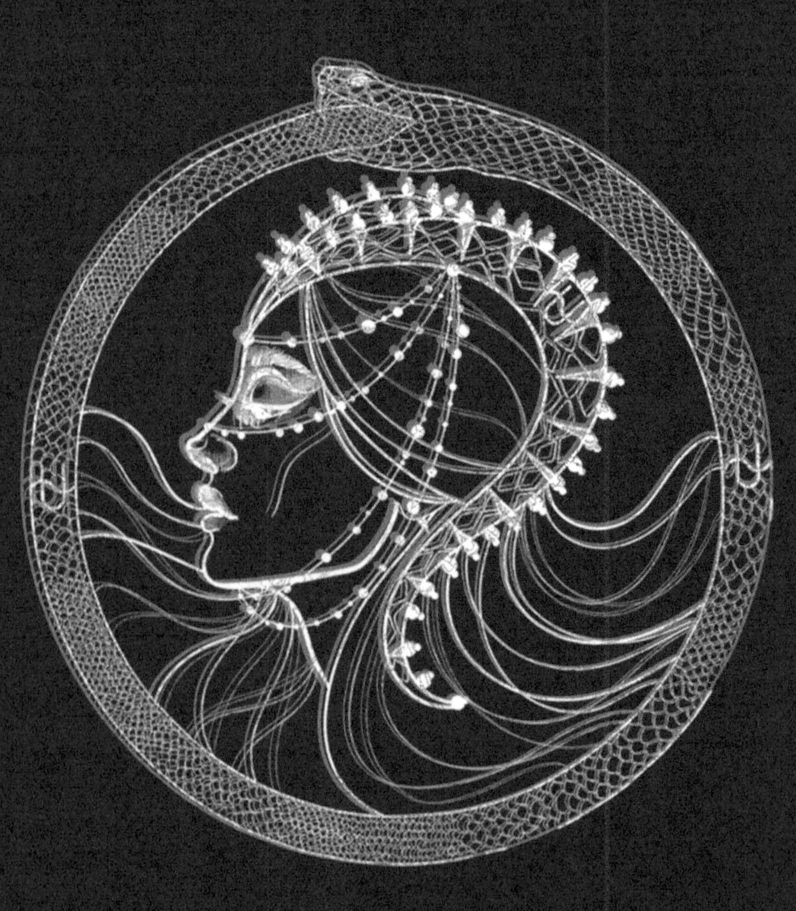

Dark Lady

Jolene

The guys lead me to a weird-looking pile of rocks shaped like a fireplace. There are piles of rocks around the small structure with random items on them. Everything from bowls of fruit to bouquets of flowers to vials of liquid is sitting around it like they've been purposely left. The last time I saw stuff like this was when Seer and I visited Stonehenge on a pagan holiday. The locals must use this for offerings, but to whom, I don't have a clue.

Wolfie comes up to me, lacing our fingers together and lifting my hand to his lips. "I have to keep my distance from you while we talk to her. Don't be upset."

I smile softly, stopping to respond. "I won't be, but thank you for telling me. Teddy and Prez made it very clear what kind of woman your bio mom is. I'll be careful."

Doyle approaches, arching a brow. "Whatever they told you, multiply it by a million. She's a right bint."

"What he said," Wolfie nods.

Super bitch—got it.

"I can handle it, even if she attacks us." The cold, slithering sensation in my gut comes back, spreading through my limbs like ice. "I know what to do."

"Come on, guys. Let's get this over with," Presley says as he walks past with the animals at his heels. "I don't want to be here any longer than we have to."

Teddy and Benjy catch up with us, each of them carrying a bag. Wolfie looks relieved, so I arch a brow at them, but they only shrug.

Fine, keep your secrets, jackasses.

I walk over to a big flat rock, sitting down with Jekyll and Hyde on either side of me. "When is she going to get here?"

"When the sun sets," Presley says as he drops onto another stone. "So, now, we wait."

AFTER A FEW HOURS, I GET UP, STRETCHING MY LEGS AND BACK. I'M NOT sure what the hell the guys expect, but I'm tired of sitting on my ass. Wolfie's mom is inconsiderate and I don't care if she shows up while I'm taking a walk. I was on a plane getting my guts rearranged, then riding in a car, and now plopped in a field like I'm waiting for a UFO to beam us up. My ass is sore, my muscles are cramped and I'm getting hungry, to be honest.

If her goal was to piss us off, it's working.

"This shit better be good or I'm going to—"

"You're going to what, my dear?"

Whipping around, I drop into a defensive pose as the voice comes from nowhere. "Who are you? Fuck that. *Where* are you?"

A woman walks out of a mist like she's straight off the pages of a Victorian ghost story. She has long raven hair in loose waves, pale skin, and bright red lips. Her dress is made of lacy white material and she appears to be about forty—only a few years older than me. The smile on her face is cunning and her gaze is sharp as she looks at me.

"I'm pretty sure I spoke English. Who are you?" I repeat. My fists are up and the icy knot in my gut crawls farther up into my chest, spreading through me slowly like it's unfurling.

Her laugh is like breaking glass—cutting, hard, and pointed. "I am Wolfgang's mother, of course. You may call me... Callie."

I don't move; I simply look over my shoulder and call out. "She's here!"

That causes a minor commotion as Teddy, the dogs, and the rest of my crew come over to the small copse of trees I'm standing beneath. Once they all spread out in a semicircle, I finally drop out of position. The heavy aura of distrust in the air makes my skin crawl, but I refuse to let this woman know she's creeping me out. I step back, letting the cats and dogs surround me.

"Your bird is quite magnificent," she says as she looks up. "You have quite a few companions."

I nod. "I do."

"So unusual. But I admire your dedication to your animals. My son has always been an animal lover."

Wolfie sighs loudly and walks up to her. "I have, but you don't actually know that. You didn't show until well after I was in middle school. This charade is silly."

Callie pouts, tapping matching red nails against her chin. "There's no need to take such a tone. I'm merely pointing out that you've always been soft-hearted with… strays."

Presley makes a disgusted sound and joins him, his body full of tension. He's never this irritable; Wolfie's mother gets under his laid-back exterior in a way I haven't witnessed yet. "You agreed to negotiate. What do you want for your information?"

That gets her attention and the glee that flashes over her features isn't lost on me. Her jab was aimed at Presley, though I can't figure out why. He doesn't have a pedigree like Teddy or Benjy, but he's a doctor. I don't think her problem is with him being male, so it's not bigotry. But the idea of forcing us to give her something she wants is more important, so she lets go of her need to poke at the doctor.

"I have very useful things I could tell you. Things about the past, things about your home, even things about this fiery woman you brought along despite her ignorance. What are you willing to pay for my knowledge, I wonder? Will the price be too high?" She holds her hand up, and a crow appears out of nowhere, landing on her finger and cawing loudly.

"Jesus Christ," Teddy says as he folds his arms over his chest. "Is this a Bond movie? Tell us what you want. We all know you have something specific in mind and nothing else will do. So give it up or we can climb in the car and leave."

Wolfie's mother glides over to him, sniffing delicately before her face breaks into a smirk. "Oh, how delightful! Darling, you didn't tell me you'd landed another one. And *this one* is so much more… powerful."

The tension around us ratchets up immediately, and I put my hand on Kali's head so she stays in place. "I believe he said you need to put up or shut up, Callie."

That got her attention.

"Yes, he did. This one truly believes he's in charge, but despite whatever silly bedroom games you all play, it isn't the case." Her gaze falls on me and that evil grin comes back. "The one with all the power here is you, my dear. Everyone from the monkey in the middle to the fatherless Irishman gravitates to your every word. They are so concerned with keeping you from the truth that they gave away the game long before I arrived."

Playing on our weaknesses, just like Prez warned.

"I don't see how our dynamic is any of your business." I cross my arms over my chest, fixing my expression into one of boredom. "I think you're just enjoying stringing your son along. You know nothing, and we're wasting our time."

She laughs softly. "Taunting me won't work, child."

"Baiting me won't, either."

Callie arches her brow as the animals around me let out unhappy sounds and she shrugs. "No, I suppose it won't. You are stronger than Wolfgang's previous lover—the good doctor is much easier to read. There's some-thing… reptilian about the manner you're handling this. It's as if you have something deep inside of you, lending its strengths to the weaknesses of other parts of you."

I frown, but before I can respond, Teddy stomps over to her. "You tread very close to the line, witch. There will be consequences, even for you, if you continue on this path."

"He's right, mother," Wolfie adds softly. "Before you do something you cannot take back, tell us what you know and we will pay a reasonable price for it."

"Reasonable," Benjy echoes. "That's the key here."

Sliding my gaze to Doyle, I marvel at how quiet he is. His temper is as fiery as his heritage, and I'm surprised he's not the one threatening this awful woman. "What do you know, and what do you want for it?"

"Since I'm growing bored with this game, I will accept a truth from all of you… a deep, dark one that you do not want anyone to know. And of course, you will be honor bound to keep my involvement in this affair a secret. I do not have a reputation for being helpful, especially at such a small cost." Her eyes sparkle with excitement and she tilts her head. "Go on. One of you begins before I change my mind."

"I never loved my ex-wife, and they pushed me into marrying her." My eyes widen as I look at Benjy, but he's clearly ashamed of his admission.

"Perfect," Callie says, clapping her hands.

Teddy sighs. "I had a crush on Jolene in elementary school and my parents found out. They forbid me to interact with her because she wasn't suitable and that's why I couldn't intervene when the girls started going after her. Hell, based on my mother's bullshit, it may be *why* the girls went after her."

Yet another reason to despise old Mags.

"You treat your son like garbage and it pisses me off. My family was hands off, but they don't purposefully ditch their children because they broke rules and don't want to be held accountable." Presley's voice is harder than I've ever heard it, and I can tell he didn't want to tell Callie this, but he had to.

"Finally!" she cries as she looks at Wolfie. "Your lover grew a pair. I wondered how good your sex life could be when he didn't have the balls to confront me."

"Gross," I mutter.

Her gaze whips to me. "Criticism is reserved for those who have the courage to face their truth, Miss Whitley."

That odd feeling of something crawling through me, unwrapping itself from the bottom of my gut and working its way through my body returns, but this time, I let it have free rein. Blinking, I peer over at the nasty woman staring at me, so self-satisfied in her faux wisdom. She can't force me to fear or respect her—it's driving her crazy. I roll my neck on my shoulders, letting the liquid sensation in my bones calm me. "I will take my turn when I am ready."

"You claim to know about my father, much like you do about his," Doyle points at Wolfie with a grimace. "Your games mirror those of my own mother and I'd like to show you what little power you truly have, but I cannot. The rules of engagement are set and I cannot subvert them."

That makes Callie happy again because she walks up to him, whispering something in his ear that makes his face go red. It looks like he might hit her, but a deep breath and a muttered response I can't hear seems to keep him from doing so. She turns back, looking at Wolfie and I. "One or the other. I'm owed two more payments."

Wolfie lifts his gaze from the ground, pinning her with his eyes. "I only stay in contact with you to prevent you from meddling in the lives of those I care about in retribution. I feel nothing for you, and even the hope that you might reveal the identity of my father isn't enough to force me to visit you anymore."

"Ouch," she purrs. "I've trained you well, son. Your arrow was quite sharp."

"Leave him alone." I step forward, putting Wolfie behind me as shadows cloud my visions. I have to do this before I have one of my episodes—though I didn't feel this one coming until now. "I'll give you my truth. You give us ours, and we're done here."

"Agreed."

I wait until Teddy and the other guys come closer. I'll need them to catch me when I go down. Once they do, I close my eyes and gather every bit of strength I have inside of me. "I can't have children because of a procedure done when I was in my early teens. It's not genetic and people thought I had an appendectomy. My parents thought it was an appendectomy—I've been told. Some quack doctor in the city fixed the odd female problems I was having by doing an illegal and non-consensual surgery that resulted in sterility. I've never told anyone before—not Trevor, not Seer, and not any of you —because the therapist I saw afterward said that I had to move on and not reopen the wound every time the subject came up."

Every single person in the glen is silent, even the venomous bully we came to see. When she finally speaks, it's almost as if there's sadness in her voice. "I accept your payment."

"Then give us what we came for."

"The answers you seek are in the place the doctor has considered visiting. If you can navigate your way through that place without breaking any rules—

theirs or the larger set—you may discover things about yourself you never knew. That is not just about you, Jolene, but your Irishman, my son, and even some who are not here to pay their prices."

Is she fucking kidding me? That wasn't worth one *of our secrets and* definitely *not mine.*

"You owe me more than that, Callie. But since I'm tired of your games, I'll accept it for now." I turn to the guys. "We're leaving. On the way back to the airport, I want to hear about this place we need to go. Wolfie and Prez, you're in my car this time."

"Good luck." Callie's tone is insincere, and she walks away from us into the night.

Why is everyone we meet so goddamned evil?

Secrets

HUGO

The prince has been off doing whatever he does for his family for days. I don't mind being at the hotel; I've gotten all my exams graded and gone out to explore the city a couple of times. But I wish he'd sent me with Jolene and the rest of the crew when they left for Scotland. Something felt off about it from the moment it was decided and I haven't been able to figure it out. I've tried meditating, projecting, and every other method I know to find the tiny thread of worry that's hanging on, but nothing seems to force a vision.

That is, until now.

The sensations that occasionally preface the onset of a premonition started while I was eating breakfast in a cafe nearby and now I'm trying like Hades to get back to the hotel before it hits. I don't have minders like the prince, and there's no one around to catch me if I go careening into a busy street. That's the drawback of my gifts and though I've been able to keep myself safe for a long time, I know the possibility of an accident is always there.

Especially when the symptoms are as strong as they are right this second.

Cutting into an alley, I put my back against the stone and close my eyes. I won't make it to my destination in time, so I need to pause and allow the vision to take over while I'm in a semi-safe place. But the shrinking field of sight doesn't come as I wait; instead, the pull of something completely different grabs me. In a blink, I know I've been summoned home—to my actual home.

My patron demands my presence.

I LOOK AROUND THE FAMILIAR TEMPLE, SCRATCHING MY HEAD AS I WAIT TO be received. It's incredibly unusual for one of us to be called to the stand before our patron and even *more* uncommon for it not to be the High Priestess. I've only been in the goddess' presence a few times over the years and it was never alone.

What does she want with me?

"Hugo." The voice echoes in the room before she appears. Her faithful companion owl is with her, giving me a look as I'm filthy and should get smited.

Dropping to my knees, I lower my gaze as she approaches. "It is an honor to be summoned."

"Oh, please, rise and speak with me like a normal person. I tire of groveling." Her tone is full of amusement as she watches me roll to my feet.

"Yes, Wise One." She may have given me permission to stand, but she definitely did not tell me I could address her familiarly.

Her sigh is full of frustration. "You are attempting to be respectful, and I appreciate that. But this conversation will take much longer than necessary if you continue being so formal. I called you here because I need to speak with you about several things, including my nephew. It will be simpler if you call me Thea."

I don't even know how to respond to that.

"Yes, ma'am," I reply as I try to digest her words. "I will do everything I can to assist you."

"Good. I must be careful what things I tell you directly because there are many delicately woven strands being watched by the Fates. In fact, your Guardian friend has been to visit them recently, and it's why I called you here. She didn't go to them for information about the situation you are involved in, but they took a shine to her and revealed more than they should have. It's a constant, yet completely unmanageable problem for all of my family, even my blustering brothers."

I blink. It's well known that even Zeus cannot control the crones, but I've not been party to one deity trying to play catch up because they made a mess. "What can I do?"

The goddess sits back in her lounge chair, tapping her fingers against her lips. "Your friends and my errant nephew are about to embark on a trip to a dangerous land because of someone's big mouth. The Guardian is traveling to search for a shadowy figure that does not want to be found. The first group will cross to another realm, so I do not want you to join them. You and your ancient companion should seek the Guardian instead."

Frowning, I tilt my head. "But, my lady, wouldn't another realm be *more* dangerous, especially with a lost one who is not yet emerged?"

"It would if my nephew was not joining them. However, his power outweighs or is equivalent to most of the beings in this land. But your Guardian is looking for someone whose power is ancient and so immense that she needs help from you and the djinn, or something terrible could happen."

"This… being… is a threat?" I ask.

"No, but the ones protecting the secret are. And while I believe the secret will come out when the time is right, the one your Guardian seeks has spent millennia keeping themself hidden to wait for the prophecy to be fulfilled. You must convince her to stand down," the goddess says.

I have to stop Saoirse? My powers aren't offensive, so that must be why she wants me to get Dhameer to come along.

"You don't expect me to… harm Jolene's friend, right?"

Her laugh is musical. "Oh, merciful Olympus, no. I simply want you to impede her progress a bit and keep her from finding someone who does not wish to be found until the Fates have declared it so. Why they would contradict their own weaving, I don't know, but they get bored easily."

I nod, thinking about what she's said. "Is this person going to hurt my friends? Is that their primary goal?"

"No. That is not the destiny of your newfound family, Hugo. I cannot tell you what the threads hold, but I can assure you I am not sending you on a mission that will hurt them."

"Then tell me where we need to go and I will talk to the prince. If I can keep something bad from happening to any of my friends, I'll do it."

"You need to go to Prague…"

WHEN I REAPPEAR IN THE ALLEYWAY, I HAVE ENOUGH INFORMATION TO convince the prince to come to Prague with me. I don't know *why* the mystery person is there or why they're important, but my patron made sure I had enough to fend off the mouthy assistant and his guard. They weigh in far more than I would expect, but I suppose when you've been around as long as Dhameer has, you learn to keep loyal employees despite their glaring flaws.

At least then you don't have a revolving door of incompetence and disappointment.

I make my way back to the hotel, plotting out how I'm going to approach our abrupt about face. We'd planned to join the others in Scotland once the prince finished up with his bankers, but now we have to head in another direction. And I have to convince him *without* relaying that I got zapped to Olympus for a secret meeting with a goddess.

That shouldn't be hard at all.

Rise

The guys have been watching me like hawks since we got back from our trip to visit Wolfie's mother. I think they expect me to break down, but I let go of my emotional attachment to that part of the past a long time ago. It's something that happened and by the time I knew about it, there was nothing that could be done. That was my first time in therapy and I worked on it for a year before. I didn't get upset in the feminine aisle at the store. But after that, I had to accept reality and grieve.

You cannot undo what is permanent and there comes a time when you have to accept your fate.

That was a hard lesson to learn as a preteen and sessions with Andromeda helped. She picked up where the therapist left off and guided me through that and my mother's growing disappointment in me. Eventually, I had other things to worry about—like the popular kids' wrath.

"The more I learn about the world I grew up in, the less surprising it is that my brain has blacked out most of it," I murmur to Teddy.

"You struggled a lot more than anyone knew," he replies. "I don't know how you got such good grades and did all the shit you did without once letting anyone know what was going on."

I snort. "Oh, hell, Teddy. There are people who go through much worse than I did and keep it under wraps. No one beat me or starved me—I just had a lot of emotional garbage that fucked up my head enough to make my brain misfire all the time. And overcoming that is something people do every day."

"Tilly, that secret you shared is assault. It should have been prosecuted. You were harassed and bullied so badly in senior year that you had to go to home school. That should have been pursued. Your fiancé was a tool, and your parents were probably murdered. No one is asking you to compare your hardships to people with even worse issues. Trauma doesn't need to be qualified for it to affect you deeply."

"Someone's been reading my old textbooks," I say with a smile. "That's Psych 101, Teddy bear."

He tugs me onto his lap and squeezes me close. "I have to, Tilly. You've got a degree and none of us stands a chance with all of this adult shit, especially when you manage to constantly amaze us with your strength."

"Teddy, if you don't quit doing all of this shit to make yourself look good, I'm going to think I conked myself on the head four months ago and ended up in a coma fever dream full of romance novel dudes."

"Fuck, no, magpie. Who would dream up an asshat like Haggerty on purpose?" Presley comes into our hotel room with Wolfie and carryout in tow. "Now, Lucy and I, on the other hand…"

"Oh, don't start this shit again," I say as I accept the bag with my food. "I am *not* ranking any of you—not by stamina, length, annoyance, muscles, smarts, humor… That is a hard 'no' from me. You're all different and I like that. There's… balance in your differences that I find comforting."

"Well said, Princess." Benjy grabs his food and flops on the couch. "Both diplomatic and honest."

"It would be more impressive if every time this shit came up, you fuckers didn't point at me as the sore thumb," Doyle bitches. "Because I allow all of you to live without doing something I would *not* regret, I'm the most amusing git in the room. Plus, I'm the least concerned with consequences."

Presley ponders for a moment. "He's right. If we had to send someone flying into a dangerous situation, I'd nominate him first."

Teddy's chest rumbles with laughter, and I bury my face against his shoulder. Their bickering doesn't bother me; in fact, it feels like the shit a family does. The sense of camaraderie between my guys makes it easier to accept that we all really can live together and be happy. When I stop snickering, I give Doyle a fond smile. "You can be the kamikaze psycho if it makes you happy. But I know you're more than that and so do they."

"Whatever," he grumbles and dives onto the other couch.

Uh-huh.

I open the container of delicious smelling, meaty stew and inhale before I look over at them. "So who's going to tell me where we're going and why no one told me you were considering adding a stop to our trip?"

"Once more into the breach," Doyle mutters before he looks at me. "The doc thought we should try to find the pup's dad in his hometown. We hadn't decided if it made sense to go, but since the bitch said we need to talk to people there…"

That story is full of holes, but they all seem to think I'm going to buy it.

"I don't even know where to start with this. Why are we trusting that woman? How does Wolfie know what town we need to visit? And how am I supposed to accept all of this wacky shit like that woman staging her entrance and exit with some sort of fog machine and weird effects, like she's a ghost on the moors?"

For a few long minutes, the room is completely quiet. They all look at me curiously, as if they're waiting for something to happen that doesn't.

"Hell, I told you she was crazy, magpie. She must have hired a crew or something. Callie is rich, evil, and bored, so nothing she does surprises me. You heard what she said to all of us." Prez shrugs and gives me a sad look when my gaze cuts over to Wolfie.

"Fine. She's insane and willing to go to great lengths to fuck with Wolfie. How does that translate to following her leads?" I say as I pinch the bridge of my nose. I must be hungry because my head is hurting. While I wait for them to answer, I take a bite of the stew, groaning happily as the heat slides down into my stomach.

"We picked the right thing," Wolfie says as he grins at Prez. "I can tell by her sexy food sound."

"I do not have a 'sexy food sound'; take it back!"

They all look at one another and say in unison, "Yes, you do."

"Traitors," I hiss under my breath as I take another bite. "When I get finished, I'm going to punish all of you."

Teddy shakes his head. "No, you're going to eat and then take a nap, Tilly. We've been running since we got up yesterday morning. You slept a little on the plane after you played around with the docs, but since then you haven't gotten a wink."

He's not wrong. The headache might be a lack of sleep.

"Fine. I'll eat and take a nap. But when I wake, someone better have a better reason for us to go running off to Ireland because some mean old witch said to."

That doesn't get an answer, either, so I let them chew on it while I eat.

If they think I'm joking, they'll find out soon enough that I'm not.

I'M SURROUNDED BY GLITTERING TREES AND PLACID WATERS. THE AIR IS HEAVY with the scent of flowers and something sweet I can't identify, but I know I should follow it. Sniffing, I pad through the forest, watching carefully for threats. I'm not sure why I think I need to watch for things I can't see, but when I look up at the starry sky, laughter echoes off the hills.

Nothing about this place is familiar, yet I feel like I know where I'm going.

Coming to the edge of the dense copse of trees, I look out into the clearing in wonder. Crystalline waterfalls spill into an oasis surrounded by vibrant plants, and there's a small table set with a tea service.

That's the smell… It's an herbal tea steeping in the pot.

I rise from all fours, though my mind can't process why I would be crawling. My body aches for a moment as I stare at the set-up, waiting for the reason I've been drawn here to become clear.

A hooded figure emerges from behind the rocks of the waterfall, gliding through the water. It seems to allow the person to move through it without soaking them and I know I have to be dreaming again. But this dream isn't like the ones where I feel animalistic or the waking dreams I believe are memories. No, this dream feels as though I'm in a world apart from the one I live in and I'm here because they have summoned me.

One hand appears from under the robes and gestures for me to come closer and I do, despite the anxiety warring within me.

"I'm so happy you accepted my invitation," the person says. The voice isn't immediately identifiable as male or female, but the tone makes me believe it must be a woman. Men simply don't speak that way.

I tilt my head as I take the seat she's gesturing at. "I don't believe I had a choice."

"True. You would have heeded my call whether you wanted to or not, but you made a choice to follow the scent."

Looking down at myself, I note that I'm wearing the clothes I fell asleep in, but I'm covered in dirt and brush, just like I am when I wake up from the weird animal nightmares. "Why am I here?"

"So much like me," she murmurs. "You are not carbon copies, but you all possess the grit you need for the future. I am proud to see the world has not withered your thorns."

I give her a suspicious look. "That wasn't an answer."

"Also true! There are things I, too, cannot relay to you, Jolene, but I am not your enemy. I brought you here because you are about to undertake an important journey and it will require you to trust those around you implicitly. Like me, they are trapped by rules put in place many centuries ago to protect our kind. You are not yet at the place where you will understand, but it is imperative that you follow their lead."

"I swear to Christ, that weird drug from the club must have fucked up my brain somehow. All this bullshit with bizarre dreams and odd physical ailments cannot be normal."

"Your life was never meant to be ordinary, Jolene. However, it will take time for you to see the truth. What is important now is that you listen to what I tell you and follow my instructions exactly. Deviation could cause terrible consequences." She lifts the pot, pouring me a cup of tea before she continues. "That sounds rather distressing, but I must get you to understand."

I will not touch this crazy woman's drinks; I saw Alice in Wonderland and the Princess Bride. Who the hell knows what she put in it?

Instead, I give her a curious look. "What are your instructions? I can't agree to something if I don't know what it is. That's like signing a contract you don't read."

"Excellent! That suspicion will serve you well on your trip. Remember those words any time someone asks you a question, Jolene. The people you meet are very tricksy and they seek to trap people with their words."

"Again, you're dodging my question and I'm getting irritated. I'd much rather be dreaming about getting laid than solving riddles," I say with a sigh.

That earns me a throaty laugh. "Ah, yet again, the apple and the tree. Yes, I believe you would enjoy that more. But alas, this is urgent and you'll have to put off your spicy sexcapades until we are through."

This time, I don't even reply. I just look at her in annoyance.

"Fine, fine. I'll get to the point. Your family is taking you to a place to seek clues. There is a quirk of fate which deems that both a place they should not be taking you at this time, but it is also your destiny to go there. You are not ready for this, though the binding is loosening every day, so I must intervene to help them." She reaches into the pocket of her robes and pulls out a pair of rainbow cat eyed glasses. "These do not have a prescription, per se, but they will help your vision and your headaches. You must wear them anytime you open your eyes while you are there. If not, the consequences for your men could be dire."

Something inside of me pushes my hand out and I take them. When I put them on, the beautiful world around me turns into a grungy pub. We're not the only ones here, but everyone else seems to ignore our presence like we're ghosts.

"What the fuck?" I whisper.

"Indeed," she says solemnly. "An ancient friend who married someone he wasn't supposed to gave these to me. I have no need for them now because I have many pairs and I can spare one for you in order to keep you safe."

"Why would you do that?"

"Why does anyone do anything, Jolene? It is in my best interest to keep you safe and happily, I also want to do so. So I am here, breaking more laws than I can count, providing you with a tool to prevent you from making mistakes that will alter important events." She pauses, and it's eerie how empty the hood seems when she's not talking. "Do you agree with my terms?"

"This will help keep the people I love from getting hurt?"

"Nothing is fool-proof and your men have free will, but this will help keep you from being threatened by forces I have yet to identify while you are on this quest. That is as much as I can tell you now. There are no guarantees in life, and I would be lying if I gave you one."

"Okay. I'll do it."

"When you wake, they will be in your pocket. Keep them close and do not ask too many questions when your family explains where you are going. They will be clumsy and inept with their excuses because they do not want to lie, but also cannot tell the truth."

"Great. More lies."

"Only of necessity, Jolene. Now close your eyes and when you wake, remember only my words and your agreement."

"But I—"

I jerk awake when the alarm goes off on the bedside table. The guys are all draped in various places around the room because the bed was too small to fit everyone. They must have given me the bed, so I'd sleep rather than wiggle around until we got frisky.

"Sugarplum?" Wolfie says sleepily. "Was that the alarm?"

I nod, feeling oddly rested and groggy at the same time. When I roll over to turn the obnoxious noise off, something pokes me in the hip. I reach into the pocket of my yoga pants and pull out a pair of rainbow glasses, frowning at them for a moment, until I hear a voice in my mind.

"You must wear them anytime you open your eyes while you are there. If not, the consequences for your men could be dire."

I rub my hand over my face, trying to remember if we'd been drinking before I went to sleep. But if we had, these damn glasses wouldn't be in my pocket, would they? Someone has to be playing a prank on me—maybe it was Doyle. I turn to see if he's smirking, but he's still dead to the world in the big armchair.

Why is my life a cosmic joke? Dream glasses? I definitely have a tumor.

"It's not a tumor," Presley mumbles, and I realize I said that out loud. "The internet is ruining medicine."

My lips curve up and I wait for the others to slowly awaken as Wolfie gets up and starts packing things. There isn't much left besides the animals and a set of clothes for each of us, so I know he had everyone get ready while I was taking my weirdly prophetic nap. "Where are we going again?"

"Ireland," Doyle says. "To find the pup's da."

I frown, squinting at him suspiciously. "Wolfie's not Irish."

"Keep them close and do not ask too many questions when your family explains where you are going."

The voice in my head makes me want to cry in frustration, but I heed its words when Teddy comes over and kisses my forehead. "It's where his mother said to go, *drugar*."

"We think we'll find… clues… that will help us identify him. In… Dublin," Prez adds.

Benjy elbows him in the side and he grunts, turning to lean in and whisper something to him that makes them both laugh.

Nodding quietly, I pretend I'm going along with their charade.

After all, I don't think they meant for me to hear Presley say, "It's not like I can tell her we're going to the Faerie."

I'm pretty sure they did not mean me to hear that.

REVIEWS, PRINT, AND MERCHANDISE

If you have enjoyed this book, please leave reviews! It helps other readers
find my work,
which helps me as an indie author.

Thank you!

Reviews are appreciated on the following platforms:

Amazon
Goodreads
Bookbub
StoryGraph
TikTok
Instagram
Facebook

To purchase print copies or merchandise, go to The Worlds of Cassandra
Featherstone

SNEAK PEEK: VEILED FLAME

LOSER

Kat

The little blue icon on my app has been glaring at me all day, but I'm too damn nervous to open it. Everyone at Woodlawn High has been buzzing all day with their notifications and the squeals of joy and moans of despair were too much for me to take. My anxiety is through the roof—this is the moment I've been waiting for since middle school, but I can't seem to force myself to bite the billet and check.

Maybe it's because I don't have the support system most of my classmates have?

That's probably true, given I've always been a loner and I don't fit into any specific 'caste' here. It's hard to make friends when you get shuffled from foster home to foster home over the years. I've rarely stayed anywhere long enough to make a friend, much less a group of them.

I'm not delinquent or anything—the families I've been placed with just return me like a pair of pants that doesn't fit after a year or so. The case-workers click their tongues sympathetically and hunt down a new place-ment, but I've never been given a reason *why* people don't want me around. One lady said I must be born under a bad sign and hell if I knew what that meant other than I'm not good enough to keep around.

It would be different, almost understandable, if I misbehaved or got bad grades. But I don't—I'm always in the top five percent of my class and I do everything I'm asked. I don't even lord my smarts over the other kids or adults. Being presentable and unassuming was something I adapted long ago to improve my probability of staying in a home long term.

Unfortunately, it never worked and though I should be a shoo-in for scholar-ships and acceptances galore, I can't bring myself to be rejected yet again.

So I wait for the last bell of the day, slinging my bag over my shoulder and trudging home to the latest in my temporary housing. I can't even contem-plate looking at the possible heartache waiting for me in the college applica-tion system WHS insisted we use. The fear is too great and despite knowing I'll be on my own for good at the end of this year, I'm unable to risk the pain.

I hate being this way.

My court mandated therapist says it's some sort of attachment disorder that's common in foster kids, but I think that's bullshit. The problem isn't *me* not forming attachments; it's asshole adults not forming one to me. Being left at a safe haven in a fucking basket as a baby wasn't because *I* did anything wrong—again, fucking adults couldn't handle their commitments.

As usual, I arrive home to an empty house. There are two other kids who live here—Bryce and Blake—but they're at football practice. Of course, the Jamesons *love* them; they get to strut around at games because their strays are the stars of the team. I'm not mistreated, but I'm definitely an afterthought. Both of my 'parents' are still at work, so I drop my bag on the couch and head for the kitchen to get a snack:

Don't get me wrong. I *could* have been placed in far worse homes than any of the seven I've been in since elementary school. None of the ex-fosters starved, beat, molested, or abused me. They were all decent folks with jobs and houses that weren't hellholes, but they never liked me.

I have no idea why. I tried to be everything they wanted.

But when the end of each school year came, I was handed in like a textbook and off I went to some group home until the next contestant stepped up. It baffled everyone, not just me, but that's what happened every single time.

Sighing, I pull some fruit out of the fridge and grab a soda. I have homework to do and if I want to have time to work on my stories, I'll need to get it done before the house is full of people at dinner time. Bryce and Blake will have gotten messages about their applications, too, and I'd bet my pinkie toe those idiots got into some big sports school. Brett and Allison will be oozing happiness for them and I don't know if I'll be able to keep food down if I have to admit my failure when they ask.

Being eighteen sucks ass.

After I grab my books and tablet, I head down to the den. I have to give my current parents credit; they set up a very nice workspace for us to study in the converted basement. By the time they took me in, the Jamesons created a cozy room down here where the three of us could relax and do our work for school without being interrupted. It might have been more for the boys than me, but I appreciated it all the same. Desks, a couch, big chairs, and bookshelves fill the space, making it almost seem like our mini-library. They even put a small fridge for drinks and snacks in case we had to be up late to cram.

It's my favorite place in the entire house and I spend most of my time here.

I sink into the huge armchair, putting my drink and snack on the side table. It only takes a few minutes to arrange myself in the soft cushions and I pause to tug my headphones out of my pocket. Music always soothes my jagged edges and I need it to stay focused on the bullshit AP Calculus I need to keep my average up in. My course load is heavy, but I applied to tough colleges. I wouldn't have a chance to get in, especially on a scholarship, if I wasn't taking equally challenging classes in comparison to all the prep school kids.

As always, the sounds of Vivaldi carry me away as I scrawl equations on my screen and before long, thoughts of the blue notification completely fade away.

○

"Kat!"

The shouts barely register as I continue working on the problem set, gnawing on my lower lip in concentration.

"Jesus fuck, where is she? I could eat a hippo!"

"Kat!"

Thumping followed by what could pass for a stampede of elephants jerks me out of my math filled trance when Bryce and Blake come down the stairs. They smell as bad as the aforementioned pachyderm's cage, so they must have rushed home right after practice. The blond twins glare at me as if I'm the offending element despite being sweaty and covered in dirt and grass stains.

This doesn't bode well.

Usually, they're tired and hungry after practices so I'm used to cranky ass boys, but tonight, there's a light to their faces. That had to mean they've gotten their letters and dinner will be a gush fest in honor of their perfection. I'm going to need all of my strength to fake smile and nod as Brett and Allison fawn over them.

I don't begrudge them their success—not really. They work hard and play even harder on the field. It's not their fault they're the American dream teens and I'm the nerdy basement troll no one wants. But it's awfully hard living in the shadow of their bright light, especially when I'm no less intelligent or talented.

"I'm finishing the AP Calc, guys. What do you want?"

They roll their eyes at me before Blake scoffs. "It's not due until Monday. You're so hyper."

Duh. I take anxiety meds, douchebag; of course I'm 'hyper.'

"I can only be who I am, Blake." That earns me a snort from Bryce and I know it's because he thinks that's the problem. "Is dinner ready?"

"Almost. Get upstairs and set the table so we can shower—Brett's orders."
Blake grins smugly.

The two of them seem to always arrange it so chores get passed to me for
some half-assed reason and this is no exception. Sighing, I put my stuff
aside, fully intending to hide down here after the dinner mess is cleaned up.
Likely by me, but like I said, I could definitely live in worse foster homes so I
let it go. Doing some chores isn't worth risking the group home for the last
few months of my high school career.

They take off running up the stairs and I wait for them to disappear before I
follow suit. My phone is tucked in my pocket and I feel like it's a stone of
shame I have to bear. I know once the adults make over the twins' success,
they will remember me, and I'll be forced to find out what disappointment
lies in wait for me. The dread weighs on me, but I head into the sunny
kitchen and pick up the pre-prepared pile of plates, silverware, and napkins
on the counter.

Allison looks up from the stove and gives me a half-smile, nodding as I take
the dishes into the dining room. Like I said, no one is mean or horrid, they
just seem…obligated. After a while, it makes it hard to waste time trying to
be bright and sunny. Being reserved makes it a hell of a lot easier not to feel
rebuffed when they don't pay attention to you regardless.

"Make sure you include champagne glasses for your dad and I!" she calls
from the other room.

*The twins definitely got acceptance somewhere big. Brett must have gotten the bubbly on
the way home.*

Once I set the table, I return to help Allison bring out the roast and sides.
I'm a little amazed at her efficiency when it comes to getting the housework
done while working full time, but I suppose it's something people with real
parents get taught as they grow up. My home life has been so fractured that
I haven't learned how to cook more than very basic shit from YouTube
videos. That may be a problem after graduation, but I've never felt comfortable enough to ask Allison if she'd teach me. I'm sure she would try, but it
doesn't feel right.

"How was school, Kat?"

I look over my shoulder, seeing Brett in the entry to the dining room. He's
already changed from work and smiling, but I see the distraction in his eyes.

He's waiting for the boys to come down. "It was fine. I've got a Calc test at the end of the week. I'll be studying a lot to get ready."

"Good, good. No matter what happens with applications, keeping your grades up will ensure no one pulls any offers," he says.

Those words aren't for me. They are for the two wet haired boys who just appeared behind him.

"Kat's too much of a geek to ever let her grades slip, Dad," Blake says as he pushes past his brother and drops into his usual chair at the table. "Grab me a Powerade since you're in the kitchen, mouse!"

Both Brett and Bryce stare at me and I turn around, heading to the fridge despite the fact that I was *not* closer than the other twin. Out of habit, I take two of the drinks and a soda for myself. I've been here long enough to know Bryce will send me back to get him one as well. It would feel like typical sibling stuff, but for some reason, I just *know* they do it to fuck with me. I have no idea why I feel that way, but trusting my gut has been the one thing that helped me get through all the upheaval in my life over the years. It's a good gauge for knowing when I'll get booted or if people are being earnest in their reactions.

The therapist says that's some sort of trauma induced early trigger warning shit, by the way.

After I hand out the drinks, I sit down on my side of the table and we wait for Allison to come out. Brett is at his seat at the far end of the table and the twins are punching each other as they look at something on their phones. I know where this is all going but I drop my gaze to the table, swallowing the coppery taste of fear as it courses through my body.

I'm going to be exposed and there's nothing I can do to stop it.

Read the first three episodes free on Kindle Vella: https://www.amazon.com/kindle-vella/story/B0BSTMB1X3

Sneak Peek: Bloodthirsty

Queen Bee

Remy

The lights are dimmed in the club, and the spots click on as the curtain starts to slide open.

It's a full house tonight in the little burlesque club off the Rue Pierre Montaine. *Chez Arc En Ciel* is not well known in comparison to the *Moulin*

Rouge or *Le Lido*, but the wealthy from both sides of the Seine gather here for shows four nights a week. If you pass the various layers of security checks to even be permitted to book a reservation, you also have to be able to afford the two thousand euro per guest cover charge. That's if you don't eat or drink anything the entire time, and that behavior would get you blacklisted before you even hit the doors to get escorted out.

Intro music starts to pump through the speakers and I stand on my mark in the opening position. My cane is resting on the wooden boards of the stage by my front foot as I pretend to lean on it. Roars of applause echo through the room as our troupe of dancers catch the lights, sequins sparkling like diamonds when the stage lights rise. We're dressed in pinstriped black pant suits and fedoras to match the big band style opening to the song. As soon as the horn-filled intro finishes, the dance begins.

I follow the routine with precision, snapping and popping my hips to the beat as we spread out across the stage. My eyes are scanning the crowd, but you'd never know by the huge fake smile on my face. Two fan kicks later, I've rotated past the proscenium, and I think I've found my mark. Twirling, I stop exactly in the place I need to be for the bridge, singing along with the pop song as if my life depends on it. It might, to be honest, because I need to sell my cover tonight so no one notices me.

The Guillotine moves in the shadows, but tonight, she's in the spotlight.

My ass shakes as I dance my way through the song, swinging the prop cane I'd replaced with one of my own design. You'd never know the difference by looking at it, but it's not the painted balsa wood the other dancers have for a very specific reason. I need it to complete the mission that forced me to spend two months in Paris working my way into this job at *Chez Arc En Ciel*. If I can't strike tonight, the surveillance, counter intelligence, and time spent building this cover will be wasted because my mark is leaving for Asia tomorrow.

Tonight, the Cobra dies for his sins.

As the break of the song slows the music, all of the dancers pour into the crowd to wiggle around the rich assholes. It's choreographed, but it's also to advertise each girl for private dances in the lounges upstairs. We're not strip-pers—not that there's a damned thing wrong with a woman using her body to support herself—but we do bare more skin in the closed rooms. The typical *laissez-faire* attitude of the owners is that as long as we kick thirty percent of the fees customers pay for those dances, they don't care what any of the girls do in the rooms. I'd find it sleazy, but the girls who work here are highly skilled performers who choose to make thousands of dollars a night rather than peanuts in some ballet troupe or chorus line.

By the time I've flirted and schmoozed my way to the VIP tables, the Cobra is staring intently at all of us. Spotlights pin each one of us on the floor at the bass hits, and I swivel my hips as my free hand slides down to the secret spot on my jacket. In unison, we tear the jackets off to reveal rhinestone studded bras with straps crisscrossing our waists like shibari ropes. A lift of the fedora and pop of my hip along with the beat draws the fierce looking brawler's eyes directly to me. I pout prettily and stalk towards his table with the swagger of a tiny dicked asshole that owns a monster truck.

His thin lips pull back over the famed curving fangs he had implanted. Dark glittering eyes follow every move I make as I approach, and I pretend to whip my hair side to side as I check for his guards. They're here some-where, but I need for them to be far enough away that I can beat my escape before they notice. When I get within inches, I tap his leg with my cane and spin around to shake my ass in his face. The grunt of approval makes me want to heave, but I turn, holding onto the prop with both hands. My feet click on the floor in a softshoe step as I make 'fuck me' eyes at the dirty bastard. He leans back, his pants tented as he gestures towards his lap.

Fucking gross.

I don't necessarily care about his weapons trade or what happens when people get the shit he moves. My job is to take him out, and I haven't the slightest clue why. The reason he's been sentenced to death isn't part of my contract, and I'm nothing if not a dispassionate observer of the darkest parts of human desires. Twelve years at *l'Academie* ensured I care very little about anything that isn't directly related to my ability to complete my jobs.

Sighing, I dance closer and drop onto his rather unimpressive erection and wiggle. There's plenty of cloth between us to prevent him from doing anything I'd make a scene over, so I focus on the task at hand. I slip the cane behind his head, resting the wood against his neck as I tug him forward. The move reads as playfully bringing his face to my breasts, but at the last second, I click the release built into the custom weapon. One end slides open to reveal the razor sharp garotte and before he can say a word, I yank it through.

Faint gurgling is the only noise besides the end of the song, and I carefully slide the sides of the cane together. Climbing off the nasty fucker, I put my hands on his cheeks so I can pretend to flirt with him while I arrange the head so it looks as if he's leaning back in the booth. It has to look realistic enough to allow me to get back on stage with the others and the next number to begin. When I have it settled, I back away from the booth blowing fake kisses as I walk backwards through the crowd. I almost collide with a dark haired guy with his collar pulled high as I head for the stage, and I roll my eyes. Whatever celeb that is trying to keep their face away from the paps is doing a shitty job of it.

My heels click on the wood as the entire troupe takes a few bows and shuffles off stage left to the wings. The next group enters on the opposite side, and I let out a slow breath of relief. I haven't heard shouting yet, so I don't think the Cobra's men realize he's down. All I have to do now is take this emetic pill, have an episode in the dressing room, and I'll be sent home without another thought.

That's when Arabella Montaigne the burlesque dancer will cease to exist, and Remy Arsine Benoit will re-emerge.

I smile to myself as I chew on the tablet that will have me wretching my guts out in a few moments. This is a more complex extermination than I usually prefer, and I can't leave my normal calling card behind. The Cobra's head had to remain in the booth to provide cover rather than be delivered to his home in a basket.

Such a shame, that. I quite enjoy the reactions my little gifts engender when they're discovered.

Walking into the dressing room, I carefully begin to strip my costume off, putting all the pieces in my bag. Every item in the locker room that belongs to gets placed in the duffel carefully as I wait for the effects to hit me. It won't do to leave loose ends even if my prints have never touched a single surface in this place. My gut starts to roil and I turn, facing one of the other dancers as the vomit finally comes. Gracelia screams like she's being skinned when I hurl on her and it's everything I can do NOT to smirk through the chunks.

"*C'est la merde!*" she shouts, running for the showers as if she's on fire.

It takes less than a minute for the owner to come in and send me home for the night with a concerned look. I walk out the back door of the building with everything in my bag just as the sirens start to scream in the distance.

Perfect timing, as always.

I jump into the first cab I can hail, directing him to the *Hotel de Crillion.* Their suites are the ritziest in Paris, and it's my go-to hideout when I'm here. I used to exclusively stay in the Bernstein Suite, but some rich fuckwad purchased it six months ago. If I could track them down and beat the hell out of them, I would, but my schedule is booked until late 2025. Assassins with my skill set and accuracy are getting harder to find. The digital age has forced many of the old guard into retirement because they refuse to adapt. Too many cameras, crime labs, and hackers running about to be able to do everything Cold War style.

The future of murder for hire is millenial, people. We're old enough to be stable but young enough to be agile with new technology and methodologies. Plus most of them are broke AF from crooked ass student loans.

It's not an issue I have, obviously, but I've been in the business since I hit double digits. You don't survive *l'Academie des Invisibles* if you haven't killed someone before the end of primary school. It's unheard of.

I was eight the first time I used the weapon that would become my signature.

Shivering, I tap on the window of the cab and bitch the driver out. He's taking a longer route than necessary to raise my fare, and I'll have his guts for garters if he doesn't knock it the fuck off. A string of curses in French erupt from him when I voice the accusation, and I slam my palm on the window with enough force to crack the plexiglass barrier. He almost drives into another car, but when he regains control, he makes the requested adjustments to our route.

After a few more arguments and a traffic jam around the *Champs*, we finally arrive at the front entrance to the *Crillion*. I throw the euros at him in disgust, memorizing the medallion number for later. He's not worth my time in terms of a mark, but I have quite a few contacts who might be interested in blackmailing a cabbie in town. Getaway cars are cliche in the crime world now. Most ne'er do-wells like myself find greater comfort in anonymous taxis or ride-share accounts hacked through the deep web accessed on burner phones. If your ride doesn't know you're a villain, there's no one to flip if law enforcement comes looking.

Of course, it helps that I never look the same for any job—not ever.

Arabella Montaigne will not be used as a cover in the future, and once I move to the location of my next job, I'll ensure that she meets with a terrible fate. It's a lot more work to slowly kill off my alters once I've used them, but it's also why I've never even come close to being caught. The dancer with long wavy red hair, freckles, and big green eyes will never grace the streets of Paris again after I hop a plane. She will, however, get a small story in the paper and an obituary when I decide how she tragically dies.

And like a phoenix, The Guillotine will rise from her ashes to be born again.

Get Bloodthirsty now!

Sneak Peek: Come Out & Prey

Just A Girl

Delores

Sighing, I look around my bedroom at the posters and decorations covering my walls. My obsession with pop music, musical theater, and high school rom-coms sickens my parents. They would prefer me to be into heavy metal and horror movies like the other kids my age.

Being the only child in a family as prominent as mine is difficult when you don't fit the mold. My parents—like their parents and all my friends' parents —are apex predators. Preds rule our world, and the division between us and prey is so severe that we regulate them to a completely different echelon of society. Prey shifters are weak and beneath our lofty abilities. The ruling class of elite predator families stretches back generations, and they've evolved into a bunch of assholes who only care about succession and greed.

My animal has not manifested yet, but it will soon enough. Luckily for me, none of my friends have manifested their inner animals, either. I'm part of the in-crowd at school, and my boyfriend, Todd, is the most popular guy in my class. While he and I aren't officially engaged yet, we've talked about it enough that I know it's only a matter of time before he puts a ring on my finger. I should be on top of the world, but I can't help but feel like my life just doesn't fit me the way it's supposed to.

Every teenager wishes their life was different, but I dream of becoming an entirely different person. Not inside, mind, because I'm pretty comfortable with who I am. I don't want to be part of this legacy, this society, or even this family. They are all focused on competing to be the richest, the deadliest, or the most powerful, and I want no part of it.

I walked over to my closet and pulled out the outfit that I had chosen for my tour of Apex Academy. My mother hired her personal designers to create a custom school uniform for today and expects me to present the 'appropriate' image of the sole heir to a Council seat.

I hate having to pretend to be like them because I'm nothing like them.

Regardless, I pull on the short, pink pleated skirt, three quarter length sleeve blouse, knee socks, and Mary Janes that comprise the uniform for my exclusive private high school. Since I'm using a 'college visit' day to tour the Academy, I'm expected to represent Shifter Secondary as well.

Shifter Secondary is the most exclusive high school for unmanifested shifter teens on the East Coast. Unfortunately for me, it was not my parents' first choice for my education. They hoped I'd follow in their footsteps by choosing to force my animal to emerge early. If I had done that, I could have attended *Apex Academy Lower School*.

I didn't have the stomach to use my body in that manner at fourteen.

Their heirs followed my lead, which made my mother and father furious and their hoity-toity council colleagues angry. My closest friends, the

Heathers, also refused to force their animals to emerge, as did Todd and his friends. That was the first time the adults in our circle decided I was a bad influence. After that, I had to toe the line at every turn, ensuring that I followed all the strict rules and regulations that govern the heirs to council seats.

Everywhere I went, I had to dress in a manner befitting the next Drew to sit at the table. They forced me to take dance lessons, piano lessons, diction lessons, and other more humiliating tutorials to prepare for the day that I became a true predator. In our society, teenagers have no say in how we prepare for our animals to emerge.

Your parents make all the decisions, choose your friends, choose your mates, and decide every detail of your life down to what you eat every single day. At least, that's how it is in my family, because my mother is from the old world.

She came over from Slovenia when she was incredibly young and met my father on the society fundraiser circuit. Her idea of preparing her daughter for the future involves lessons in makeup, clothing, jewelry, and on how to keep your mate satisfied. Lucille is completely unconcerned about whether I end up happy, only that I attend to my council seat and my husband's *needs*.

Once I get dressed, I grab my vintage Vuitton bag and peek at the mirror for a last check before I head downstairs. I tuck my perfectly highlighted blonde tresses behind my ears, and the smokey eye and winged liner are on point with this year's fashion trends. I apply a quick swipe of cherry red lip gloss and open my mouth, inspecting my teeth to make sure they are pearly white. Even though once I develop threatening incisors or sharp fangs, something will inevitably cover them in blood, my parents want my smile to look like a toothpaste commercial.

It's all such utter bullshit.

I take a deep breath and turn on my heel, heading for the door. I can already hear my parents yelling in a Scotch and vodka induced rage in the drawing room. It's only eleven thirty in the morning, for Hera's sake.

Lucille and Bruno don't fuck around with cocktail hour. They are nicely sauced by ten a.m. every day, without exception. I can't remember a time when my parents didn't get drunk off their asses at an event or party, much less in our 'home'. They liquor up and fight until they part for the day, and then start again once they arrive home from their daily commitments.

I brace for the barrage of criticism my mother will subject me to when I cross the threshold. Closing my eyes, I whisper words of encouragement to myself via lyrics to some of my favorite songs, desperately trying to hype myself up before she can tear me down.

"Delores! I hear you breathing at the top of the stairs, darling. Come down this instant and let your father and I inspect your presentation."

My mother's purr *sounds* friendly, but believe me, it's not. I roll my eyes as I make my way down the stairs, knowing my mother won't hesitate to send one of the staff if I don't acquiesce to her command. Most of their staff would gleefully jizz themselves with being chosen to drag me downstairs for inspection.

At this time of day, the only servant in the drawing room will be Matilda —my ex-nanny turned personal assistant—and that request would test her loyalties. As the only person in my household who has my back, I don't want to put her in that position, so I answer. "Yes, Lucille. I'm on my way."

I'm not allowed to refer to her as 'mother' because it makes her feel old. 'Lucille' is always what I've called the woman who supposedly gave birth to me. I'd be tempted to disbelieve we shared any DNA at all if it weren't for our similar bone structure. She's about as nurturing as a rattlesnake, and if it weren't for Matilda, I might have died as a child. If the kitchen staff whispers are accurate, I have to accept that my mother neglected to feed me much of the time.

"You coddle her far too much, Lucille," my father growls. "As the heir to our family seat, Delores will come without being instructed to do so. We will not tolerate her insolence after her animal emerges. She will behave as I command or suffer the consequences."

The last of Bruno's rant echoes off the marble walls of the foyer as I step onto the hideously expensive, endangered teak floor. Schooling my features into the mask of indifference I wear whenever I have to deal with them, I enter their den of drunken fights with my spine steeled for an emotional assault.

"I apologize for my tardiness, Father. I only wished to perfect the image I will present during my tour of Apex Academy. I realize it is imperative I impress the Headmistress and her staff."

The humanoid features of his face shift seamlessly, and the hungry crocodile inside of him gives me a toothy smirk. "You will impress them, daughter, or so help me… I'll send you to Bloodstone Isle."

My stomach drops like a stone as I barely suppress a shiver.

Bloodstone Isle is a reformatory school. It's surrounded by spells and enchantments to prevent students from escaping—a feat that has only happened once in its one thousand years of existence. The most feared cat group in the shifter world—the Khan ambush—runs the school, and they're rumored to consume errant students when the Council allows it.

It's the threat both rich and poor shifter parents used to keep their children in line. Wealthy parents like mine use it as a method of controlling any heirs that refuse to conform to the rigid structure of our society. Predators don't value the lives of those who are weak, and they label heirs who refuse to take their rightful place at the top of the food chain weak. Everyone knows Bloodstone is full of criminals, miscreants, and psychos, and even they don't seem to survive.

Bloodstone is a death sentence—pure and simple.

"Y-yes, Father. I understand," I croak out. As if the pressure of touring my new school isn't enough, now I worry the Dean will relay something to my parents that gets me shipped off to Death Island.

"Bruno, darling, if you scare her, she'll frown. That causes wrinkles. Delores, chin up and smile for us."

Swallowing the lump in my throat, I flash my mother my brightest smile. Her blood-red lips curve, and her leopard fangs burst free as she all but purrs. "I will not have you sullying the family name, Delores. It's bad enough that your education gave you ideas about your value beyond breeding stock. You will take the seat on the Council when it is time, but the husband we select will control the business—as nature intended. Do you hear me?"

My eyes narrow briefly, and for what is possibly the millionth time this week alone, I nod at my mother to appease her temper. "Yes, Lucille."

"Excellent!" The leopard fades as she claps her hands. "Matilda!"

The tiny woman steps up, her eyes wide behind her glasses. She's a pred, but the smaller size of hawk shifters puts her in the servant class. I believe she genuinely lives in fear of one or both of my parents deciding to eat her. "Yes, madam?"

"Fetch Bruiser. He will accompany Delores to the academy for her tour. Tell him to take the Escalade—it won't do for her to arrive in a tiny car—it will draw attention to her extra weight. We must make an impression."

Matilda nods, and I feel the fear radiating from her, and I don't blame her. Bruiser is one of my parents' bodyguards and our frequent chauffeur. He's a Komodo dragon shifter and the house staff are terrified of him. It's hard not to be, given that he prefers to play with his food, then eat it after it's dead. The kitchen crew believes he 'handled' the gardener that looked too long at my mother when I was ten. He disappeared without a trace.

Once Matilda scurries away, I watch my parents drink and bicker about their plans for the day. Bruno is going golfing with a congressman, and Lucille is going to the spa. We all know that both outings will include stops at the homes of their current pieces of ass for a quickie, but no one talks about it. The appearance of the loving couple has to be maintained, although neither of them has slept in the same room since I was a baby.

They don't give a damn about fidelity; I learned that at an early age. Children often discover things they shouldn't because of adults discount their ability to understand the conversations happening around them.

I stopped keeping track of who they're boning long ago, because I'd need an assistant to keep the affairs straight.

While my parents' marriage is a sham, I remind myself that my boyfriend, Todd, isn't like them. Yes, his parents only own half the live entertainment industry, but my father allows me to see Todd. The other parents will force the Heathers to accept an arranged betrothal, and I'm grateful I'm lucky enough to have found the perfect match on my own as my high school sweetheart.

"Delores, Bruiser is ready to escort you to Apex. He's pulling the car around now," the hawk shifter says softly.

Snapping out of my reverie, I smile at the trembling woman. Bruiser must have scared the living hell out of her. For no other reason than it amused him, I'm sure. He's as much a brute as his name implies, and I don't look forward to riding alone to the academy with him.

Something about that shifter gives me the creeps…

Sneak Peek: Children of the Moon

PROLOGUE

Twenty-one years ago…

A powerful wave of apprehension hits me as we approach Claridon's house. Pausing at the edge of the forest, I wait until we can see what awaits us. The silence is deafening as we take in the wreckage of what was once the home of our dear friends.

They splintered the heavy cabin door in pieces littered around their yard like an explosion sent the shards flying. When the wind shifts, the foul stench of death and rot slams into us, making my wife gag. Lights are flickering ominously in the shattered windows and another scent—burnt food—catches the breeze as we approach.

"Cast protection before we reach the porch," I murmur.

"*Ego invoco deus ab mihi. Protego mihi ab hostili et malum.*[1]"

I nod solemnly, repeating her words to invoke our Goddess' watchful eyes on me as well. The scene in front of the house does not inspire confidence about what we will find inside.

The air is thick as we step onto the porch and another smell wafts towards us—blood. Its metallic tang invades our senses almost to the point of tasting copper on my tongue. Climbing over the debris, I look at the once cozy living area. Shredded cushions, torn drapes, stuffing, and other destroyed furnishings lie scattered around the room. When I bend to examine the destruction, I find coarse animal hairs embedded in the remnants. I pick some up to sense the aura of the creature it came from, but all I feel is death.

The bloody hoof prints puzzle me—I do not recognize them as belonging to any creature I'm familiar with. Whatever came to this house was not a normal shifter, nor was it a common magic user. The level of malice and lack of emotion concerns me. Its aura is like that of a necromancer or one of their creations.

I follow a set of heavy prints to the hallway leading to the dining area and kitchen. Swallowing hard, I prepare myself for the carnage I know will appear. The rotten food and decomposition scents are so bad I have to raise my shirt to cover my nose before I vomit.

It is certain our friends are dead; no one can lose the amount of blood that coats the surfaces and walls while staying alive.

"What made those claw marks? I've never seen such deep furrows," my wife whispers.

I shake my head, holding a finger to my lips to keep her quiet. I've never seen that type of mark, either, but we don't know if there's anyone still here. We must stay silent while we explore. The food on the stovetop is burned and has flies on it—that's the rotting smell. Wood is barely burning in the oven, just a few embers remaining, but it tells me our friends were caught unaware.

It means the malevolent being that attacked the wolves did it within the past few hours.

My heart stops when I remember their baby girl. Feray had to be here when it happened; it's the New Moon and both of her parents stay home during the start of the new lunar cycle.

"Freya, forgive me. I almost forgot the baby," I hiss at my wife.

Her eyes widen and her hand flies to her mouth. I see the tears forming as she thinks about what the condition of this place means for a defenseless infant. Together, we leave the kitchen, intent on heading back through the outer room to the stairs.

Just beyond the landing, we stumble over the body of Claridon. His corpse is mutilated, but I recognize those battered hands anywhere. He clearly put up a hell of a fight to keep the intruder from making it past him. Despite that, it ripped his chest open and his intestines are hanging out. Blood spatter decorates the once lovingly decorated walls, painting them vermillion and signaling his desperation to protect his family.

Swallowing again as I look at Imogen, I tilt my head at the trail of bloody hoof prints that lead to the nursery. We were here when they found out they were expecting, when they assembled the room, and even after Feray was born. Now the beauty of that memory has been sullied by the scene before us.

We have to be strong…

Once we're both ready, we follow the prints to the door of the baby wolf's room. The sight that greets us is horrific: it splayed Lyra out as if nailed to a cross and impaled her head on a post of the baby's crib. Blood is dripping down the whitewashed wood, making its way to the pink carpet. Dead eyes stare sightlessly at us as we hold our breath and enter. The injuries to our friend are a testament to how hard she fought to protect her child, though in the end, she also failed.

I don't want to see what this monster did to the baby we considered a sister to our child. Forcing myself to approach, I stare at the empty crib in astonishment. There's no sign of Feray, nor that it harmed her in this room. I whip my head around to look at my wife in shock.

Was this a kidnapping? Why would they kill everyone so brutally instead of simply sneaking in to snatch the baby?

My eyes dart around the room until I reach the closet. I stalk over, throwing the door wide. There's a pile of dirty linens and blankets in the bottom, which is unlike Lyra. She always kept everything tidy, so much so that we all teased her about it. Tossing the clothes over my shoulder, I dig down until I reach the floor. I call for light and my magic brightens the dark space enough for me to see a tiny seam at the baseboard.

Claridon was always paranoid, and I never understood why. We both lived simple lives in a small town of magic users and shifters, well outside the dangers of the big city. He was a master craftsman and Lyra ran a bakery; there was nothing to worry about. Humans were far away from our little town and the stench of corruption from the gangs and Councils doesn't exist in Silver Falls.

But I recognize a bolt hole when I see one, so I search frantically until I find the lever that will spring the door open. It takes several tries to successfully open the door—Claridon was top-notch at his trade—but when it swings out, I gasp.

There, wrapped in her father's shirt and Lyra's clothing, is Feray. She has the warding amulet Imogen made for her on her chest, and I realize that even while scared for their lives, Lyra and Claridon ensured the beast wouldn't find their child. Between the magic of our amulet and their scent swaddling her, the baby is hungry and tired, but safe.

I lift the tiny infant out of the hole gently, my eyes filling with tears. Her baby scent makes my heart hurt for my fallen friends and I clutch her to me tightly. It's our responsibility to take care of her now; I know that. Imogen nods when I look at her with a sad expression, then walks over to the dresser, opening a drawer. When she hands me the baby sling, I know she feels the same.

Once I secure Feray to my body, we make our way back to the stairs and head out of the house. It will need to be burned to keep that creature or anyone else from following the scent trail to our home. We don't want anyone to know Feray is alive; she will be safe with us as long as we continue to have her wear the amulet that suppresses her wolf.

Raising her with our daughter, in a new town, is the only way to keep her alive.

I didn't wake up this morning knowing I'd have to abandon my entire life and our home, but I know as surely as the sun will rise tomorrow what we must do to protect this baby. Looking down at her curiously, I ponder the situation again. A magical beast used as an assassin seems like overkill if their target was the infant. Slaughtering her family was also unnecessary—that thing could have slipped into her room and killed her before anyone knew it was there.

Lifting the magic on her amulet for a moment, I wait until Feray opens her eyes. That's when I realize why my friends put it on her. My wife walks up beside me and runs a finger over her cheek. Her red hair looks very much like mine and as long as we keep the magic refreshed for the spell, she will look as though she is our natural daughter.

"We must pack up and move immediately," Imogen says as we walk out. "The capital city is vast, and no one knows us there. That will allow us to raise her as our own—a sister to Fiadh."

"Yes," I murmur. "I will send a message to the local council to inform them we are moving. The death of our friends and their daughter are too much for us to bear here. You simply need to keep her secret in our home until we leave."

She nods. "What about the monster who did this? Who would send it to kill a baby, and why?"

"Someone who scared Claridon enough to make a secret bolt hole in the nursery and forced Lyra to ask us for that amulet. I don't know what they were up to, but obviously, it was much bigger than our tiny town."

Imogen frowns. "We made three amulets, love. Why weren't Lyra and Claridon wearing theirs?"

"I don't know, Gen. Whatever the reason was, they took theirs off and someone powerful hunted down their daughter. Nothing is what it seems here, but we must protect Feray. We will keep her wolf suppressed for as long as possible—up to her Ascension if we can. She'll grow up and if she's destined for something bigger, she'll be able to assume that mantle when she's ready."

Taking this baby on and keeping her secret violates our coven laws; we both know it. Hiding her means we will always be on the run—we need completely new identities when we flee to the capital. It's a lifetime commitment, but the look on my wife's face tells me she's certain this is the right thing to do.

I know without a doubt that being was pure evil, and it came with one purpose: *assassination.*

Tomorrow, we begin our lives on the lam with two babies—there is no other option .

Get it now: **https://books2read.com/newmoonrisingCOM1**

---

1. I call on the gods. I protect myself from enemies and evil

About Cassandra Featherstone

Cassandra Featherstone has channeled her lifelong passion for writing into a flourishing career, a journey that started when she first grasped a pencil as a gifted child with ADHD.

Her debut novel, born during the solitude of COVID lockdown in March 2020, draws on a tapestry of personal encounters and insights that resonate deeply with her readers.

An international bestseller, Cassandra has topped Amazon charts in categories such as LGBT Anthologies, LGBTQ+ Mystery, and Bisexual Romance, among others. Her works navigate the complexities of bullying, PTSD, body dysmorphia, mental health struggles, personal reinvention, and the empowerment of claiming one's own space. Importantly, Cassandra offers a thoughtful and respectful portrayal of LGBTQIA+ relationships, subtly reflecting her own connection with the community through her narratives.

Her literary repertoire spans sci-fi fantasy, urban fantasy, paranormal, and comedic genres in academy whychoose settings, with a strong commitment to portraying consensual, safe, and accurately depicted BDSM and kink lifestyles. Her books are an invitation to explore transformative stories that are both inclusive and engaging.

Often affectionately called 'The Muppet' for her wacky theater kid personality, she resides in the Midwest with her tech-savvy husband, their creatively inclined college student, a literary-minded dog, and four scheming cats.

READ MORE AT CASSANDRA'S WEBSITE OR HER FACEBOOK PAGE. SIGN UP FOR EXCLUSIVE CONTENT AND UPDATES HERE.

Join her Master List for promo and ARC opportunities by scanning the QR below:

ALSO BY CASSANDRA FEATHERSTONE

THE MISFIT PROTECTION PROGRAM SERIES

Road to the Hollow

Return to the Hollow

Home to the Hollow

Rejected in the Hollow

Revealed in the Hollow

Healing in the Hollow

Revenge in the Hollow

AUDIO OF THE MISFIT PROTECTION PROGRAM SERIES

Road to the Hollow

APEX ACADEMY CAPERS

Come Out and Prey

Let Us Prey

In Prey We Trust

Oh Holy Spite (3.5 novella)

Eat. Prey. Love.

Prey It By Ear

AUDIO OF THE APEX ACADEMY CAPERS SERIES

Come Out & Prey

Let Us Prey

In Prey We Trust

TRANSLATIONS OF THE APEX ACADEMY CAPERS SERIES

Come Out & Prey (German)

Let Us Prey (German)

In Prey Trust (German)

DISCORDIA UNIVERSITY

Veiled Flame (Book One)

Quiet Burn (Book Two)

Zero Spark (Book Three)

SECRETS OF STATE U

Blood on the Ice (Book One)

Suspicions on the Stage (Book Two)

FAETAL ATTRACTION

Hell on Wheels (Book One)

Jammer in the Box (Book Two)

F.E.A.R. ACADEMY

Failed State (Book One)

Title TBA (Book Two)

VILLAINS & VIXENS

Bloodthirsty (Book One)

Ruthless (Book Two)

Wicked (Book Three)

AUDIO OF THE VILLAINS & VIXENS SERIES

Bloodthirsty

Ruthless

TRIANGLES & TRIBULATIONS

Hoist the Flag (PQ)

Yo-Ho Holes (Book One)

CHILDREN OF THE MOON- WITH SERENITY RAYNE

New Moon Rising (Book One)

Waxing Crescent (Book Two)

Waxing Gibbous (Book Three)

Samhain Secrets (Novella 3.5)

Full Moon (Book Four)

Waning Gibbous (Book Five)

Waning Crescent (Book Six)

RISE OF THE RESISTANCE

Ream Exclusive Prequels

Hooked on a Feline (Book One)

Peacock Me Like A Hurricane

Love The Way You Lion (Book Three)

REAM SERIALS

Secrets of State U

Discordia University

Denizens of the Dark

Faetal Attraction

Agents of the Ouroboros

Rise of the Resistance

F.E.A.R. Academy

ANTHOLOGIES

Unwritten

Shifters Unleashed

Jingle My Balls

Love is in the Air

Silent Night

Snowed In

All Hallows Eve

9 781737 410089